BLOOD IN THE DUST

A HUNTER BUCHANON BLACK HILLS WESTERN

BLOOD IN THE DUST

WILLIAM W. JOHNSTONE
AND J. A. JOHNSTONE

WHEELER PUBLISHING
A part of Gale, a Cengage Company

Wheeler Publishing Large Print Softcover Western.
The text of this Large Print edition is unabridged.
Other aspects of the book may vary from the original edition.
Set in 16 pt. Plantin.

**LIBRARY OF CONGRESS CIP DATA ON FILE.
CATALOGUING IN PUBLICATION FOR THIS BOOK
IS AVAILABLE FROM THE LIBRARY OF CONGRESS.**

ISBN-13: 978-1-4328-9015-5 (softcover alk. paper)

Published in 2021 by arrangement with Pinnacle books, an imprint of Kensington Publishing Corp.

Printed in Mexico
Print Number: 01   Print Year: 2021

BLOOD IN THE DUST

CHAPTER 1

"That coyote makes me nervous," said shotgun messenger Charley Anders.

"You mean Bobby Lee?" asked Hunter Buchanon as he handled the reins of the rocking and clattering Cheyenne & Black Hills Stage, sitting on the hard, wooden seat to Anders's left.

He spoke through the neckerchief he'd drawn up over his nose and mouth to keep out at least some of the infernal dust kicked up by the six-horse hitch.

"Yeah, yeah — Bobby Lee. He's the only coyote aboard this heap and that there is a thing I never thought I'd hear myself utter if I lived to be a hundred years old!"

Anders slapped his thigh and roared through his own pulled-up neckerchief.

"No need to be nervous, Charley," Hunter said. "Bobby Lee ain't dangerous. In fact, he's right polite." Buchanon leaned close to the old shotgun messenger beside him and

7

said with feigned menace, "As long as you're polite to Bobby Lee, that is."

He grinned and nudged the shotgun man with his elbow.

"If you mean by 'polite' give him a chunk of jerky every time he demands one, he can go to hell!" Anders glanced uneasily over his left shoulder at Bobby Lee sitting on the coach roof just above and between him and Buchanon. "Hell, he demands jerky all the damn time! If you don't give him some, he shows you his teeth!"

As if the fawn-gray coyote had understood the conversation, Bobby Lee lowered his head and pressed his cold snout to Anders's left ear, nudging up the man's cream sombrero.

"See there?" Anders cried. Leaning forward in his seat and regarding the coyote dubiously, the shotgun messenger said, "I ain't givin' you no more jerky, Bobby Lee, an' that's that! If I give you any more jerky, I won't have none left for my ownself an' we still got another half hour's ride into Tigerville! I gotta keep somethin' in my stomach or I get the fantods!"

Hunter chuckled as he glanced over his right shoulder at Bobby Lee pointing his long snout in the general direction of the shirt pocket in which he knew Anders kept

8

his jerky. The coyote's triangle ears were pricked straight up.

Hunter gave the coyote a quick pat on the head. "Bobby Lee understands — don't you, Bobby Lee? He thinks you're bein' right selfish — not to mention womanish about your *fantods* — but he understands."

Hunter chuckled and turned his head forward to gaze out over the horses' bobbing heads.

As he did, Bobby Lee subtly raised his bristling lips to show the ends of his fine, white teeth to Anders.

"See there? He just did it again!" Charley cried, pointing at Bobby Lee.

When Hunter turned to the coyote he'd raised from a pup, after the little tyke's mother had been killed by hunters, Bobby Lee quickly closed his lips over his teeth. He turned to his master and fashioned a cock-headed, doe-eyed look of innocence, as though he had no idea why this corkheaded fool was slandering him so unjustly.

"Ah, hell, you're imagining things, Charley," Hunter scolded the man. "You an' your fantods an' makin' things up. You should be ashamed of yourself!"

"He did — I swear!"

A woman's sonorous, somewhat sarcastic voice cut through Anders's complaint.

"Excuse me, gentlemen! Excuse me! Do you mind if I interrupt your eminently important and impressively articulate conversation?"

The plea had come from below and on Buchanon's side of the stage. He glanced over his left shoulder to see one of his and Anders's two passengers poking her head out of the coach's left-side window. Blinking against the billowing dust, Miss Laura Meyers gazed beseechingly up toward the driver's box. "I'd like to request a nature stop if you would, please?"

Hunter and Charley Anders shared a weary look. Miss Meyers, who'd boarded the stage in Cheyenne a few days ago, was from the East by way of Denver. Now, Hunter had known plenty of Eastern folks who were not royal pains in the backside. Miss Meyers was not one of them.

She was grossly ill-prepared for travel in the West. She'd not only not realized that the trip between Cheyenne and Tigerville in the Dakota Territory took a few days, she'd not realized that stagecoach travel was a far cry from the more comfortable-style coach and buggy and train travel to which she'd become accustomed back east of the Mississippi.

Here there was dust. And heat. The stench

10

of male sweat and said male's "infernal and ubiquitous tobacco use." (Hunter didn't know what "ubiquitous" meant but he'd been able to tell by the woman's tone that it wasn't complimentary. At least, not in the way she had used it.)

Also, the trail up from Cheyenne into the Black Hills was not as comfortable as, say, a ride in an open chaise across a grassy Eastern meadow on a balmy Sunday afternoon in May. Out here, there were steep hills, narrow canyons, perilous river crossings, the heavy alkali mire along Indian Creek, and, once you were in the Hills themselves, twisting, winding trails with enough chuck holes and washouts to keep the Concord rocking on its leather thoroughbraces until you thought you must have eaten flying fish for breakfast.

Several times over the past two days, Miss Meyers had heralded the need for Hunter to stop the coach so she could bound out of it in a swirl of skirts and petticoats and hurl herself into the bushes to air her paunch.

So far, they hadn't been accosted by owlhoots. They'd even made it through the dangerous country around the Robbers' Roost Relay Station without having a single bullet hurled at them from one of the many haystack bluffs in that area. Nor an arrow,

11

for that matter.

Indians — primarily Red Cloud's Sioux, understandably miffed by the treaty the government had broken to allow gold-seeking settlers into the Black Hills — had been a problem on nearly every run Hunter had been on in the past year. He'd started driving for the stage company after his family's ranch had been burned by a rival rancher and the man's business partner, his two brothers murdered, his father, old Angus, seriously wounded.

He wanted to say as much to the lady — a pretty one, at that — staring up at him now from the coach's left-side window, but he knew she'd have none of it. She was a fish out of water here, and in dire straits. He could see it in her eyes. She was not only road-weary but world-weary, as well.

Though they'd left the Ten Mile Ranch Station only twenty minutes ago, after a fifteen-minute break, and would arrive in Tigerville after only another ten miles, she needed to stop.

"Hold on, ma'am — I'll pull these cayuses to a stop at the bottom of the next hill!"

She blinked in disgust and pulled her head back into the coach.

"Thank you, Mister Buchanon!" Charley Anders called with an ironic mix of mockery

12

and chiding.

"Now, Charley," Hunter admonished his partner as the six horses pulled the coach up and over a low pass and then started down the other side, sun-dappled lodgepole pines jutting close along both sides of the trail. "She's new to these parts. I reckon you'd have a helluva time back East your ownself. Hell, even in the newly citified Denver!"

"Yeah, well, I wouldn't go back East. Not after seein' the kind of haughty folks they make back thataway!" Charley drew his neckerchief down, turned to Hunter, and grinned, showing a more-or-less complete set of tobacco-rimmed teeth ensconced in a grizzled, gray-brown beard damp with sweat. "She's hard to listen to, but she is easy on the eyes, ain't she?"

They'd gained the bottom of the hill now, and Hunter was hauling back on the ribbons. "I wouldn't know, Charley. I only look at one woman. You know that."

"Pshaw! You can't tell me you ain't admired how that purty eastern princess fills out her natty travelin' frocks! You wouldn't be a man if you didn't!"

"I got eyes for only one woman, Charley," Hunter insisted. Now that the mules had stopped, the dust swirling over them as it

13

caught up to the coach from behind, Hunter set the brake. "You know that."

"Yeah, well, sounds to me like it's time for you to start lookin' around for another gal. Sounds to me like you an' Annabelle Ludlow are kaput. Through. End-of-story." Charley narrowed one eye in cold castigation at his younger friend. "And you got only one man to blame for that — yourself!"

Gritting his teeth, Charley removed his dusty sombrero and smacked it several times across Hunter's stout right shoulder. "Gall-blamed, lame-brained, cork-headed fool! How could you let her get away?"

Hunter had asked himself that question many times over the past few months, but he didn't want to think about it now. Thinking about Annabelle made him feel frustrated as all get-out, and he had to keep his head clear. You didn't drive a six-horse hitch through rugged terrain haunted by desperadoes and Sioux warriors with a brain gummed up by lovelorn goo.

He climbed down from the driver's boot and saw that Miss Meyers was trying to open the Concord's left-side door from inside. She was grunting with the effort, her fine jaws set hard beneath the brim of her stylish but somewhat outlandish eastern-style velvet picture hat trimmed with faux

14

flowers and berries.

"I'll help you there, ma'am."

She looked at him through the window in the door — a despondent look if he had ever seen one. She was, however, a looker. He couldn't deny that even if he had denied noticing to Charley. He felt a sharp pang of guilt every time he looked at this woman and felt . . . well, like a man shouldn't feel when he was in love with another gal.

"It's stuck," she said, her voice toneless with exhaustion.

"I apologize." Hunter plucked a small pine stick from the crack between the door and the stagecoach wall. "A twig got stuck in it somehow, fouled the latch. I do apologize, ma'am. How you doing? Not so well, I reckon . . ."

As Hunter opened the door, she made a face and waved her gloved hand at the billowing dust and tobacco smoke. "The smoke and dust are absolutely atrocious. Not to mention the wretched smell of my unwashed fellow traveler and his who-hit-John, as he so colorfully calls the poison he consumes as though it were water!"

Hunter helped the woman out. He glanced into the carriage to see the grinning countenance of his only other passenger — the Chicago farm implement drummer, Wilfred

15

Farley. The diminutive, craggy-faced man with one broken front tooth and clad in a cheap checked suit — which seemed the requisite uniform of all raggedy-heeled traveling salesmen everywhere — raised an unlabeled, flat, clear bottle half-filled with a milky brown liquid in salute to his de-staging fellow passenger's derriere, and took a pull.

Hunter gave the man a reproving look, then turned to the woman, removing his hat and holding it over his broad chest. "Ma'am, let me apolo—"

"Will you please stop apologizing, Mister Buchanon? I'm sorry to say your apologies are beginning to ring a little hollow at this late date. My God, what a torturous con-traption!" She looked at the coach's rear wheel and for a second, Hunter thought she was going to give it a kick with one of her delicate, gold-buckled, high-heeled ankle boots.

She thought about it for a couple of seconds, then satisfied herself with a chor-tling wail of raw anger and tipped her head back to stare up at the tall, blond-haired, blue-eyed jehu hulking before her. "And must you continue to call me ma'am?"

"Uh . . . uh . . ."

"How old are you?"

16

"Twenty-seven, ma'a . . . er, I mean, Miss Meyers." At least, he hoped that was the moniker she'd been looking for. If not, he might end up with a swift kick to one of his shins, and in her state of mind, even being such a light albeit curvy little thing, he didn't doubt she could do some damage.

"Now, see — I'm younger than you are. Not by much, maybe, but I am young enough that you can feel free to call me Miss. *Miss Meyers.* Not ma'am. For God's sake, don't add insult to injury, Mister Buchanon!"

"I'm sorry, Miss Meyers, it's just that you seemed older . . . somehow." *Wrong thing to say, you cork-headed fool!* Backing water frantically, Hunter said, "I just meant you *acted* older! You know — more mature! I didn't mean you *looked* older!"

He'd said those wheedling words to her slender back as, fists tightly balled at her sides, she went stomping off into the brush and rocks that littered the base of the ridge wall on the west side of the stage road.

"Don't wander too far, ma'am . . . I mean, Miss Meyers!" he called. "It's easy to get turned around out here!"

But she was already gone.

17

CHAPTER 2

Hunter stared after the pretty, angry woman.

Something nudged his right arm. He looked down to see Wilfred Farley offering his bottle to him, and grinning, his thin, chapped upper lip peeled back from that crooked, broken tooth.

"No, thanks. If that's the stuff you bought at the Robbers' Roost Station, it'll blind both of us."

"Pshaw!" Farley took another deep pull. "Damn good stuff, and I see just fine."

"That's how Hoyle Gullickson lost his top knot." Charley Anders was climbing heavily down from the driver's boot, his sawed-off, double-barrel shotgun hanging from a lanyard down his back.

"What?" Farley asked. "Drinkin' his own skull pop?"

"No — brewin' it." Anders stepped off the front wheel and turned to face Hunter and the pie-eyed Chicago drummer. "He sold it to the Sioux. Several went blind, and the others came back and scalped him."

Farley looked at the bottle in his hand as though it had suddenly transformed into a rattlesnake. "You don't say . . . ?"

Hunter snorted softly. He knew the story wasn't true. Hoyle Gullickson had lost his top knot when he'd been out cutting wood one winter and was set upon by four braves who'd wanted whiskey.

Gullickson had refused to sell to them because he'd already done time in the federal pen for selling his rotgut to Indians, and he wasn't about to risk returning to that wretched place. Incensed, the braves scalped him, so now he wore the awful knotted scars in a broad, grisly swath over the top of his head, making any and all around him wince whenever he removed his hat, which he loved to do just to gauge the reactions and turn stomachs.

Charley Anders, however, preferred his tall-tale version, which he related often and usually at night around some stage station's potbellied stove to wide-eyed pilgrims in his and Hunter's charge.

Hunter glared at the drummer. "I thought I told you not to smoke around that woman, Farley. And to stay halfways sober."

19

"Kills the time," Farley said with a shrug, raising a loosely rolled, wheat-paper quirley to his mouth and leveling a defiant stare at Buchanon. "I offered to share my panther juice with her, but she turned her nose up. That offended me. So I got the makings out and rolled a smoke."

He pointed his bottle toward where the woman had disappeared in the rocks and brush. "That pretty little bitch can go straight to hell."

"He's got a point, pard," Charley said, reaching through the stage window. "Give me a pull off that, Farley. I could use a little somethin' to cut the dust."

"I thought you said it'd blind a fella!" Farley objected sarcastically.

Anders jerked the bottle out of the drummer's hand and swiped the lip across his grimy hickory shirt. "I been drinkin' the rotgut so long I'm immune to blindness by now." He stepped back and started to take a pull from the bottle. As he did, a rabbit poked its head out from between two shrubs roughly ten feet off the trail.

Hunter, who'd been looking around cautiously, wary of a holdup and also starting to get a little worried about the woman, had just seen the gray cottontail pull its head back into the shrubs. Bobby Lee gave a mewling yip of coyote excitement, leaped from the roof of the coach onto Charley Anders's right shoulder to the ground.

Charley jerked back with a startled grunt, dropping the bottle.

Bobby Lee plunged into the shrubs between two boulders, then shot up the ridge, hot on the heels of the streaking rabbit, the rabbit and the coyote darting around the columnar pines.

"Damn that vermin!" Charley wailed, clutching his right shoulder with his left hand. "He like to have dislocated my arm! What gall — using me as his damn stepping stool! Has he no respect?"

Hunter snorted a laugh. "That's what you get for being so tight with your jerky, Charley."

"The bottle! The bottle!" wailed Wilfred Farley, pointing at the bottle lying on the ground between Anders and Buchanon. "Good Lord, you're spillin' good whiskey!"

Hunter crouched to pick up the bottle. There was still an inch or two of rotgut remaining. Not for long.

Grinning at Farley, Hunter turned the bottle upside down. The whiskey dribbled out of the mouth to which dirt and pine needles clung. The liquid plopped hollowly onto the ground.

Farley was flabbergasted. "Good lord, man! Are you *mad*?"

"Jehu's rules, Farley." Hunter tossed the bottle high over the coach and into the trees and rocks on the other side. "No drinkin' aboard the coach."

"You're sweet on that gal!" Farley shook his head in disbelief. "You must like a gal who runs you into the ground with every look and word. Me — I got some self-respect. No purty skirt's gonna push Wilfred Farley around!"

"Speakin' of purty skirts," Anders said, staring off toward where the woman had disappeared. "What in the hell's she doin' out there — knittin' an afghan?"

Hunter glanced around, making sure no would-be highwaymen were near. He didn't like standing still here on the trail like this, making easy targets. It was always best to keep moving between relay stations, as a moving target was always harder to attack than one standing still in the middle of the trail with good cover all around for would-be attackers.

Hunter stepped forward and called, "Miss Meyers? You all right?"

No response.

"We'd best get movin', Miss Meyers!"

Hunter took another couple of steps

forward, then stopped again, concern growing in him. "Miss Meyers?"

He didn't want to call too loudly and risk alerting anyone in the area to their position. He and Anders were carrying only two passengers, but aboard the stage they had ten thousand dollars in payroll money, which they were hauling to one of the many mines above Tigerville.

Hunter glanced back at Anders, scowling his frustration. Anders shrugged and shook his head.

"I best look for her," Hunter said. "Charley, stay with the stage. Keep a sharp eye out. I don't like sitting out here like a Thanksgiving turkey on the dining room table."

"You an' me both, pard," Charley said behind Buchanon, as Hunter stepped off the trail and walked into the rocks and brush littering the base of the western ridge.

Hunter pushed through the brush, wended his way around rocks. "Miss Meyers? Time to hit the road, Miss Meyers!"

He saw a deer path carved through the brush. It rose up a low shoulder of the ridge. Hunter followed it, frowning down at the ground, noting the sharp indentations of the heels of a lady's ankle boots.

As the path turned around a large fir tree,

the indentations of the lady's heels became scuffed and scraped. Amidst the scuff marks was a faint print of a man's boot.

Instantly, Buchanon's hand closed around the pearl grips of the silver-chased LeMat secured high on his right hip in a gray buckskin holster worn to the texture of doeskin. He clicked the hammer of the main, .44-caliber barrel back and, his heartbeat increasing, the skin under his shirt collar prickling, he continued following the scuffed trail.

The prints led up and over the rise then down the other side, through tree shadows and sunlight. Somewhere ahead and to Hunter's right, a squirrel was chittering angrily. That was the only sound.

Hunter continued forward for another fifty feet before he stopped suddenly.

Ahead, a man crouched between two aspens. He seemed to be moving in place, making jerking movements. He was also talking in a heated but hushed tone.

Hunter could see a second man — or part of a second man — on his knees on the other side of one of the aspens. Hunter could see only the man's boot soles and the thick forward curve of his back clad in a blue wool shirt. This man, too, was making quick jerking movements.

He seemed to be holding something down.

Hunter stepped to his right, putting the left-most aspen between himself and the crouching man. He moved slowly forward, both aspens concealing his approach from both men before him. As he moved closer to their position, muffled cries blazed into the air around him.

Muffled female cries.

Hunter stepped behind a tree. He peered around its left side. From here, he had a clearer view of the two men and of Miss Meyers on the ground between them, partly obscured by tree roots humping up out of the forest duff.

The man on the right knelt by the woman's head, leaning down, holding her head against the ground with both of his hands pressed across her mouth. Miss Meyers was kicking her legs out wildly and flailing helplessly with her arms, making her skirts flop and exposing her pantaloon- and stocking-clad legs.

Thumping sounds rose as did the crackle of pine needles and dead leaves as she thrashed so desperately, her cries muffled by one of her assailant's hands. The kneeling man laughed through his teeth as he held the woman down, his brown-mustached face swollen and red.

The other man, tall and skinny with long black sideburns and a bushy black mustache, had pulled his pants down around his boots and was opening the fly of his longhandles, grinning down at the struggling woman.

"Hold her still, Bill. Hold her still. I'll be hanged if she ain't as fine a piece o' female flesh as I —"

Leaning forward, exposing the evidence of his craven lust, he grabbed Miss Meyers's ankles and thrust them down against the ground. Leaning farther forward, he slid his hands up her legs from inside her dress, a lusty grin blooming broadly across his long, ugly face with close-set, dark eyes set deep beneath shaggy, black brows.

The man clamped her legs down with his own and reached for her swinging arms, grabbing them, stopping them as he lowered his hips toward the woman's. He stopped abruptly, turning his head sharply to see Buchanon striding toward him.

The man's eyes widened in shock. "What the . . . *hey*!"

Hunter had returned the big LeMat to its holster and picked up a stout aspen branch roughly five feet long and about as big around as one of his muscular forearms — as broad as a cedar fencepost.

It made a solid thumping, cracking sound as he smashed it with all the force in his big hands and arms against the black-haired man's forehead. The branch broke roughly a foot and a half from the end. As the would-be rapist's head snapped sharply back, his eyes rolling up in their sockets, the end of the branch dropped with the man into the deep, narrow ravine behind him.

The other man cursed and leaped to his feet, his amber eyes as round as saucers and bright with fear.

"No!" he cried as he saw the stout branch swing toward him.

He tipped his head to one side, raising his arms as if to shield his face. Buchanon grunted as he thrust the branch down through the man's open hands to slam it against the man's left ear, blood instantly spewing from the smashed appendage.

"Ohhh!" the man cried as he hit the ground.

Buchanon stepped forward, raising the club again, rage a wild stallion inside him. Only the lowest of the lowest gut wagon dog did such a thing to a woman. This man would pay dearly — and he did as Hunter, straddling the man's flailing legs, smashed the club again and again against the man's head. After the third or fourth blow from the powerful arms and shoulders of the big, blond, blue-eyed man standing over him, the man's cries faded and his flailing arms and legs lay still upon the ground.

Hunter raised the club for one more blow but stopped when the crackle of guns rose from the direction of the stagecoach. His heart shuddered. He hammered the second rapist's head once more, then kicked the still body, the dead eyes staring up at Hunter in silent castigation, into the ravine.

It landed with a thump near the other carcass.

Hunter whipped around, crouching and drawing the LeMat from its holster, facing in the direction from which guns blasted angrily and men shouted.

Another man screamed.

Yet another man bellowed, "Ah, ya low-down dirty devils . . . !"

Hunter recognized the bellowing voice. It was followed by the twin blasts of Charley Anders's sawed-off shotgun and one more scream.

Charley's scream.

CHAPTER 3

Hunter turned to Miss Meyers.

She was sitting up, dirt and leaves in her mussed hair, which had fallen from the roll she'd had it pinned into atop her head. Her hat was gone. Her dress was torn. So were her petticoat and pantaloons.

Her hands seemed to be idly trying to close the flesh-revealing tears in her clothes as she stared up in shock at the jehu, her face pale, her eyes round and glassy. She had a bruise high on her right cheek. In a few hours, that eye would likely be black. The lace-edged bodice of her spruce green traveling dress had been ripped wide open, exposing the bodice beneath it, which was also torn, revealing a good portion of one bosom and part of another.

The shooting continued, men shouting, hooves thudding.

"Stay here!"

Hunter bounded off through the forest,

sprinting back in the direction of the stage road. He climbed the rise along the mountain's shoulder, ran down the other side. Beyond the shrubs and rocks, he saw men milling around the stage on horseback, dust rising.

"Where the hell's the payroll money?" yelled one of the horseback riders. He was kneeling atop the coach. To his left sat the steel-banded strongbox, its lid open, bullet-torn padlock hanging askew. Envelopes of all shapes and sizes were strewn around the box; they were tugged this way and that by the breeze.

The highwaymen had blown the strongbox and had discovered that the mine payroll was not inside.

"It's not in the box?" asked one of the men on horseback.

"No, it is not!"

The man on horseback — tall, bearded, and wearing a black hat — cursed and looked around wildly. "Where's Buchanon?"

"Who's Buchanon?" asked one of the others.

"The jehu!" returned the man in the black hat.

"Buchanon's right here!" Hunter said as he stepped onto the trail from between two rocks and a twisted cedar.

He'd seen Charley Anders and Wilfred Farley lying in bloody heaps on the ground beside the coach, so he was in no mood for discussion. He tripped the latch to engage the LeMat's stout, twelve-gauge shotgun barrel and blew a fist-size hole in the cheek of the man in the black hat before the man could level the carbine that he was holding barrel up from his right thigh.

The man gave a loud yip as the buckshot punched him back off the tail of his horse.

There were four or five others milling in a ragged circle around the Concord.

Hunter flicked the lever back to engage the LeMat's main, .44-caliber barrel and shot the man on the coach next, then shot a rat-faced man with long red hair off the hip of his skitter-hopping cream. The redhead managed to trigger one shot, which spanged loudly off a boulder to Hunter's left, before his head slammed against the iron-shod rear wheel of the coach with a resounding thud.

He bounced off the wheel to the ground where he lay unmoving, his cracked skull leaking brains.

The sudden commotion had spooked the six-horse hitch, and now the team, whinnying shrilly and pitching, lunged forward, dragging the locked front wheel until the wood brake broke with a bark and fell to the ground. The team tore off up the trail, pulling the coach along behind it, dust blooming in its wake.

The coach didn't get far before it fishtailed suddenly. One of the front wheels must have hit a boulder or a tree leaning over the trail, for the contraption's front end lurched upward sharply. The coach crashed loudly onto its side. The terrified horses neighed shrilly and kept running, tearing free of the rigging and running, all six still harnessed together, on down the trail.

Hunter was only partly aware of the fate of the coach, for he watched now as another killer booted his big American horse through the coach's still-billowing dust toward him, leveling a Sharps carbine. Hunter calmly aimed and fired, but the man's large-caliber round burned across the nub of Hunter's left cheek, making him pull his own shot slightly wide.

Hunter's bullet plunged into the Sharps-wielding man's right arm clad in red and black calico.

The man dropped the rifle, grabbed the wounded limb with his gloved left hand, and shouted, "Pull out! Pull out!" He'd lost his hat.

His bullet-shaped head was pink and bald as a baby's behind while a big walrus mustache mantled his mouth. He loosed a string of shrill curses as, neck-reining his horse around sharply, he cast a fiery glare over his right shoulder at Hunter. "You ain't seen the last of us, Buchanon!"

The three other surviving highwaymen swung their horses around to follow the other man, whom Buchanon had recognized as Ike Talon, head of a notorious bunch of thieving killers who'd been haunting the Black Hills in eastern Wyoming and western Dakota Territory for the past year. Hunter didn't know where the gang was from — he'd heard Utah — but when they'd arrived in the Black Hills, the route between Deadwood and Cheyenne had become fraught with even more peril than before — and that was saying something.

Hunter fired two more shots at the other three killers, but they triggered a fusillade from horseback at him as they fled, and he had to drop down behind the rocks to keep from getting his head blown off. As they galloped off up the trail to the south, Hunter ran out onto the trail and fired his last round at the trio — a wasted shot, for they were now out of short gun range.

Hunter lowered the smoking LeMat and turned toward where Charley Anders and Wilfred Farley lay in the dirt beside the

33

coach's fresh wheel ruts.

Rage coursed through the big, blond-headed, blue-eyed rancher-turned-jehu, like poison in his veins. He dropped to a knee beside his old friend, a man he'd known for half of his life. Hunter's father, Old Angus, and Charley had been drinking buddies up in Tigerville, which was the town closest to the Buchanon Ranch.

When they'd had the ranch, that was. Now it was gone, burned to a crisp, Hunter's two brothers dead — courtesy of rival rancher and Confederate-hating Yankee, Graham Ludlow and his savage business partner, Max Chaney, not to mention the crooked county sheriff, Frank Stillwell. Chaney and Stillwell had died bloody for their sins, but Graham Ludlow was still alive, though a heart stroke had turned him into a shell of his former self. Now Hunter and his aging father, an ex-Confederate soldier who'd lost an arm in the War of Northern Aggression, lived in relative squalor in a seedy rooming house in Tigerville.

"Ah, Charley."

Hunter patted the dead man's shoulder. Charley and Old Angus had known each other during the war. Hunter had fought in the war, too, but not with his father. His hunting prowess, including his stealth and

knife-fighting skills, had earned him a position in a small, elite group of guerrilla warriors who'd worked mostly at night, killing
Union officers and blowing up trains and
munitions dumps behind enemy lines.

Charley Anders had been shot three times
— twice in the chest, once in his upper left
thigh. He was a bloody mess. He'd lost his
hat in the ambush, and his thin, gray-brown
hair slid around his liver-spotted scalp in
the breeze. His washed-out blue eyes glinted
in the sunlight dancing down through the
pines from a faultless sky as blue as fresh
snowmelt.

"Crazy damn time to die. Such a nice
day . . ."

Hunter looked at the drummer, Farley.
The man lay belly-up, arms and legs spread
as if offering himself, body and soul, to the
gods above. The coat of his cheap checked
suit was spread to each side, like the wings
of some shabby angel.

A bullet had torn a hole in the drummer's
shoulder. Another bullet had carved a
puckered blue hole just above his right eye.
Both eyes stared skyward, bright with
reflected sunlight, opaque in death.

A soft yip sounded.

Hunter gave a start, reaching for the bowie
knife sheathed over his left hip as he turned

his head to look over his shoulder. He silently berated himself for not having reloaded the LeMat.

He knew a moment's relief as Bobby Lee moved out of the brush with the dead cottontail hanging limp in his jaws. The coyote dropped the half-eaten rabbit with a plop in the dirt and looked around, sniffing the air and narrowing his eyes. He walked tentatively up to Hunter.

"We lost a good friend, Bobby Lee."

The coyote walked slowly, mewling softly, over to Charley Anders. Bobby sniffed the man's left ear, turned to Hunter as though in question. The coyote lifted his long, clean snout and gave a mournful wail.

"My God."

The woman's voice had come from behind Hunter. He swung around to see her standing at the edge of the trail, looking as though she'd been dragged and rolled. She'd managed to arrange her torn dress some, so the rips and tears weren't quite so revealing, but only a little. Dirt and needles still clung to her hair and in the lace along her low-cut bodice.

That bruise under her eye was growing darker, swelling.

She studied the two dead men in shock, then slid her gaze to Hunter. He pulled the

LeMat from its holster, broke it open, and turned the wheel slowly as he shook out the five spent .44-caliber cartridges.

They plunked into the dirt at his feet, clinking together.

When he'd reloaded the five main chambers, he plucked a twelve-gauge wad from the back of his cartridge belt, replaced the spent wad with the new one, and snapped the frame closed.

The singular LeMat was as fine a piece of shooting equipment as Hunter had ever used. It was hand-engraved with tiny oak leaves and a breach lever in the shape of a miniature saber. His own initials, HB, had been carved into each side of the long, sleek main barrel by the man who'd gifted him with the gun after Hunter had saved the man's life from a sharpshooter's bullet.

That man had been none other than the Confederate General Pierre Gustave Toutant-Beauregard, or "Little Creole" as he'd been known though there'd been nothing little about G. T. Beauregard's fighting spirit.

The LeMat had been the general's own, designed by himself and fashioned on commission by a French gunsmith in New Orleans. After Hunter had saved the general from a sharpshooter's bullet at Shiloh, taking the bullet himself, Beauregard had ordered the crafty gunmaker to change the monogram. He then gifted the handsome piece to the young Georgia Rebel who'd saved his life and whose own fighting spirit had already made Hunter Buchanon something of a legend, his name spoken nightly in admiring tones around Confederate cook fires.

G. T. Beauregard, a dusky skinned little man with dark eyes and a dark mustache, had handed the weapon over to the starry-eyed young warrior late one night in a hospital tent on one condition — that Hunter recover from his leg wound and continue killing the venal Yankees.

Hunter had vowed he would.

And he'd done just that.

Now he returned the handsome smoke wagon to its holster and turned to see Bobby Lee lifting his leg over the man who'd been wearing the black hat when Hunter had blown him off his horse. The coyote sent a fine yellow drizzle into the man's beleaguered-looking face and half-open eyes.

As he inspected the other three dead killers, Hunter saw that one wasn't dead but only wounded, albeit gravely. This man, the one Hunter had shot off the stage, lay off the trail's far side, grunting and groaning softly as he reached for an ivory-gripped Bisley revolver lying just beyond his outstretched fingers.

Hunter glanced at the woman, who also stared at the surviving killer, her mouth opening, eyes widening in renewed fear.

"Turn away," Hunter told her as he slid the LeMat from its holster.

The woman looked at him, frowning as though not quite understanding.

"Turn away," Hunter repeated a little louder.

She looked at the big pistol in Hunter's right hand, and turned away, lowering her head slightly and closing her hands over her ears.

Hunter walked over to the wounded killer, who turned his head to gaze up at Hunter standing over him, the man's eyes turning wary. His ruddy, bluntly chiseled face was a mask of sweat and misery. Long, greasy, auburn hair hung in tangles down his back. An angry grimace curled his lips back, showing two silver front teeth.

"Why'd you attack the stage?" Hunter asked the man in a cold, even voice, staring down the LeMat's main barrel at the man's sweating face.

"Payroll, ya damn fool," the man wheezed

out, gritting his teeth in dread and fury. He slid his gaze to Laura and added with a faint, lewd smile, "An' the woman."

"You weren't supposed to know about the payroll."

The man gave a taut smile.

"How did you know about the money?" Hunter asked him.

"Go to hell!" the man spat out, glaring.

The LeMat barked, flames and smoke lapping from the barrel.

Bobby Lee hurried over to anoint the dead man.

"Couldn't have done it better myself, Bobby Lee."

CHAPTER 4

Buchanon plucked out the spent shell and replaced it with fresh. He spun the cylinder and dropped the LeMat back into its holster.

He turned to the woman.

She still had her back to him. She still had her hands over her ears. She was shaking, head bobbing. Sobbing.

He looked around for the dead killers' horses. He didn't see a single one. They'd likely fled with the other men and mounts.

Now in the aftermath of the attack, Hunter realized the direness of his and the woman's situation. Ike Talon would likely be back. Not only had Hunter identified him and his men, but Talon wanted the payroll money. He and his men hadn't had time, thanks to Hunter, to give the coach a thorough going-over.

They'd return to do just that, and to kill the witnesses to the murders. Two of his

41

men, apparently having gone rogue, had attacked the woman. The gang had likely been closing on the stage from the wooded ridges to either side, and the two men Hunter had killed and thrown into the ravine had gotten distracted when they saw Laura leave the trail alone.

Somehow, they'd lost track of Buchanon himself.

Hunter considered himself damned lucky they had, or both he and the girl would have gone the way of Charley and the drummer.

Hunter glanced along the trail to the south. Seeing no sign of Talon and the three others, he strode quickly down the trail to the north. The coach lay on its side only fifty feet away, in the middle of the trail.

Hunter leaped up onto the coach's right side, which was now the top, opened the door, and dropped inside. He hoisted himself up and out through the same door less than a minute later. He crawled up to the driver's boot and grabbed his canteen, which he'd tied by its lanyard from the wood seat's steel frame. He slung the canteen's woven lanyard over his head and left shoulder, and leaped back down to the trail.

He slung the saddlebags he'd found inside the coach over his left shoulder and walked over to the woman who had turned to watch him with a strange mix of fear and curiosity.

"Where did those come from?" she asked.

"Under the seat."

"You mean Mister Farley and I were sitting on the payroll money?"

"That's right."

It had been Buchanon's idea to hollow out the seat and carry inside what most owlhoots would look for in the strongbox. Why flaunt valuable cargo by carrying it up top in a strongbox that anyone could see from half a mile away, and that anyone could open with a single pistol shot?

He grabbed the canteen and unscrewed the cap. "Water?"

She shook her head.

Buchanon swirled the canteen. About half-full. Good enough for now. He took a sip, returned the cap, and slid the canteen out of the way behind him.

"Come on. We can't stay here." Hunter grabbed the woman's arm and pulled her along behind him as he headed along the trail to the north.

"What do you mean?" The woman pulled back on her arm. "Why don't I stay here while you go for help? How far are we from Tigerville?"

Hunter held fast to her arm despite her resistance. "Fifteen miles. I wouldn't make it on foot before dark. Besides, those killers will be back. Likely, soon."

"Why?"

"They know the money's on the coach. Don't ask me how they know. Nobody was supposed to know besides the mine superintendent, the bank in Cheyenne, and me and Charley. They must have inside help. Which means they'll be back for it, all right." Hunter turned to her sharply. "Why the hell are you resisting me, lady? Do you want to die out here?"

She pulled her arm free of Buchanon's hand, brought both hands to her face, and sobbed. "I'm injured. I'm tired. I'm scared . . . and . . . and I *just want to go home!*"

She dropped to her knees in the trail and leaned forward, lowering her head to the dirt. "I just want to go home!"

Hooves thudded in the south. The thuds grew louder, kicking up a wicked rataplan on the hard-packed trail.

Talon . . .

"Come on, dammit!" Buchanon reached down and pulled the woman brusquely to her feet. He gazed up trail again, seeing three hatted heads jostling into view near

44

the crest of the first hill to the south. "They're back!"

Bobby Lee snarled and yipped, then ran into the brush.

Hunter pulled the woman off the trail's right side and into the forest. He pulled her up the slope. She no longer resisted, but she couldn't run as fast as he could, so he half-dragged her at times.

When they came to snags of blowdown, he wrapped his arm around her waist and carried her over obstructions before setting her down, grabbing her wrist again, and pulling her along behind him.

Halfway up the ridge, she dropped to her knees. "No!" She lowered her head, gasping for breath. "I can't! I can't! My feet . . . my boots . . . !"

Buchanon gazed back down the ridge. He could see bits of the trail through the trees. He couldn't see the riders. He didn't know if they'd seen him and the girl before Hunter had pulled her off the trail.

But he couldn't see them yet. A good sign. Still, they had to keep moving.

"Here." Buchanon dropped to a knee, picked up her left foot.

"What are you doing?"

"What's it look like?"

He quickly unbuttoned the shoe, removed

it from her foot, and tossed it over his shoulder. It thumped onto the ground.

"No!" she cried. "It's my only pair of . . ."

Hunter held up the other one. "You want to die for these boots? You can't run in them and, lady, you need to run!"

He tossed the other shoe back over his shoulder. It struck the soft forest duff and rolled several feet down the decline.

Hoof thuds sounded from below.

Hunter gazed down the slope. Four riders were just then swinging off the trail and into the trees, climbing, batting their heels against their horses' flanks. Hunter heard the squawk of tack and the raking sounds of the horses' straining lungs.

He cursed, pulled the woman to her feet, headed straight up the hill, and ran, grabbing at the ground with his booted feet, pulling the woman with his right hand.

He glanced behind and below.

There were quite a few trees between him and his pursuers, offering some cover. He couldn't tell if the riders had spotted him yet. They'd likely seen where his and the woman's tracks had left the trail, but if they'd laid eyeballs on him, they gave no indication.

Ahead, at the top of the ridge, lay a cap of mottled gray rock with strewn boulders offering cover.

He ran harder. The woman dropped to her knees with a groan. He dragged her into a niche in the wall of caprock. The niche, partly concealed by a wagon-size boulder, was like a closet that angled back slightly from the door, maybe six feet deep. Hunter shoved the woman in ahead of him.

She slumped against the wall, head down, breathing hard. She was as limp as a rag, long hair hiding her face.

Hunter slid the LeMat from its holster, clicked the hammer back, and held the revolver barrel up in front of his chest. He doffed his tan Stetson and leaned his head to one side, edging a look out over the slope.

The four riders rode abreast, roughly fifteen feet apart. They were coming hard, their horses lurching off their hind feet, the killers jouncing in their saddles, flapping their elbows.

Hunter saw that the second rider from the left was Ike Talon — a big, bald-headed, dark-eyed, dark-faced man riding low in his saddle, letting his wounded right arm hang straight down his side. Talon's walrus-mustached upper lip was stretched back from his picket-fence teeth in the agony of his wound.

Hooves thudded resoundingly, crunching

dead leaves and pine needles.

As the four approached the caprock, they reined up and looked around, the sun angling through the pine crowns dappling them with gold. The brims of their hats half-shaded their hard, unshaven faces.

Hunter slid his head back into the niche, his heart beating in his ears. The killers were close enough that Hunter could smell the sour stink of their sweaty bodies mixing with the musk of their blowing horses.

The killers didn't say anything, but Buchanon could hear one of them wheezing loudly. That would be Talon sucking breaths in and out through his gritted teeth. Hunter could sense not only the pain in the man — his bullet had probably shattered the bone in his right arm — but the fury.

To his mind, he'd been outfoxed. In reality, Buchanon had gotten lucky. If two of the man's goatish renegades hadn't tried to rape the woman, all likely would have been lost. But since they had, thus luring Hunter away from the coach, Buchanon and the woman were still alive.

And Hunter had the saddlebags containing the mine payroll draped over his left shoulder.

So far so good.

So far . . .

Just keep riding, Buchanon silently urged the four men spread out before him now, looking around and listening intently for the slightest sound that would betray their quarry's position.

Just keep riding. Nothing to see here. They're gone. You've lost 'em. Go back to your snakepit. Tomorrow's another day . . .

Buchanon heard the squawk of saddle leather and a faint grunt as one of the men must have gestured to the others. Hooves thumped and bridles clanked against toothy jaws as the riders put the spurs to their mounts. He could tell from the thuds that the group was dispersing as it continued on up the slope, to each side of the caprock.

The sounds dwindled quickly.

Hunter canted his head to the left, sliding that eye around the niche's covering wall to stare out over the forested slope again. He saw only the arched tail of one horse to the far left as one of the killers continued on up the slope to the south of the caprock.

Buchanon exhaled a breath he hadn't realized he'd held.

He turned to the woman. She sagged low against the wall on his right.

"They're gone."

She didn't look at him.

He touched her arm. "We have to keep

49

moving."

Keeping her chin down, she shook her head. "Leave me."

"No."

She lifted her chin, weakly shook her hair back from her face. "I'm too tired. I'm too exhausted. Leave me. I'll stay here. Come back for me . . . later."

That wouldn't work. He may not get back to her before morning. On her own, she'd be fair game for any predator in the area, and he knew there were more than a few — wildcats and grizzlies included.

And then there were the human kind, the most dangerous predators of all.

He couldn't leave her. He didn't much care for her. Too prissy and bossy. But he couldn't leave her.

"We're going together." Hunter tugged on her arm. "Come on — let's go."

She pulled her hand out of his and glared up at him, hardening her jaws. "I told you to leave me here! I don't care how" — she looked him up and down, critically, and with more than a little revulsion, as well — "large and brutish you are! You can't make me come with you when I've told you I want to stay here! You can't force me to do something against my will! Doing so would make you little better than them!"

She tossed her head to indicate their pursuers.

"All right." Buchanon nodded. "Have it your way. I'll try to make it back. I don't know when, but I have a feelin' you're gonna have a long night out here."

"I don't care. I'll be fine."

"All right." Buchanon stepped out of the niche. He turned back as if in afterthought. "Oh, if that wildcat returns before I do, just bang two rocks together. That *might* frighten him off."

He turned away again. She grabbed his arm.

"What wildcat?" she asked skeptically, anger glinting in her pretty hazel eyes contrasting the tangled chestnut hair hanging down both sides of her face and across her shoulders.

"The one that holed up in here last night."

"How do you know a wildcat *holed up in here* last night?"

Hunter pointed at the finely ground gravel and dirt on the floor of the niche. "Wildcat scat."

It was rabbit scat, but he didn't think she'd know that.

She looked down, frowning. "That's not wildcat scat! You're a bald-faced liar!"

"All right."

Still holding the LeMat barrel up in his right hand, he looked around and then began striding along the base of the caprock and the strewn boulders, heading toward the northern end, intending to work his way around the stony crest of the ridge.

"Wait for me!"

Hunter turned to see the woman step out of the niche and, holding her skirts above her bare, dirty feet, followed him along the base of the caprock. She glared up at him from beneath her brows and wrinkled a nostril in disgust.

Hunter snorted and continued walking, looking around cautiously. She moaned and groaned behind him, and he, as tired of her as she was of him, tossed a glare at her from over his shoulder. "Keep it down!"

She gave him another cold-eyed glare. "You try walking barefoot over sharp rocks!"

"You'll soon be toe-down if you don't shut up."

Behind him, she made a soft, guttural cry of rage.

Hunter approached the north end of the caprock. He stopped and looked around the side of the rock humping up darkly from its pediment-like base of gravel and small boulders. Spying no movement in the forest to his left or ahead, he continued walking, setting his boots down quietly.

"Ouch!" the woman cried.

Hunter looked behind him again, glaring. She returned his glare, hardening her jaws again. "That one really hurt!"

Hunter cursed. He holstered the LeMat, swung around, crouched, and drew the woman up over his left shoulder.

She gave a deep grunt of surprise and exasperation.

"Be quiet!"

"Put me down!"

"I said be quiet or I'm gonna put you down and shoot you!"

It was no idle threat. He was ready to do it.

CHAPTER 5

Carrying the angrily chuffing and grunting woman like a sack of feed grain over his left shoulder, Hunter hurried forward along the side of the caprock, peering down the slope ahead and to his left.

The branches on the columnar pines didn't start until roughly twenty feet up from the ground, so he had a good view through the forest around him. He spied no sign of his pursuers.

He considered returning to the trail, where the walking would be easier for his barefoot charge, but quickly nixed the idea. Talon and the others would sooner or later swing back to the trail and run him and the woman down.

Dead Horse Canyon was only a half a mile or so to the east, straight ahead of him. The canyon ran more or less north and south, so following that canyon, giving him better cover than the trail offered, would eventually bring him near the southeastern out-skirts of Tigerville.

The canyon was a badland maze of rock, timber, and chalky buttes carved long ago by Dead Horse Creek, which was usually only a slow-moving stream now in the mid-summer. Plenty of cover down there. And water. They'd need water.

"Put me down, damn you!" the woman berated him under her breath.

"Be quiet."

"Put me down this instant!" She slammed the heel of her fist against his lower back.

"Be quiet."

"Damn you!"

"As soon as we reach the bottom of the next slope, I'll set you down. But for now, we can't be lollygaggin'."

"I wasn't lollygaggin'!" she said tightly, mocking his Southern accent.

He stopped at the rear of the caprock and looked around again. The ridge dropped away before him, through more pines and scattered aspen. Green, sunlit leaves glinted in the warm, humid breeze. Spying no movement either to his left or down the slope ahead, or behind the caprock to his right, he started forward, negotiating the declivity carefully.

He'd taken only three strides when his

right boot came down in a fresh pile of horse apples, which he didn't see until that boot slipped out from beneath him. The slope was steep — nearly forty-five degrees — and the trees widely spaced. He fell awkwardly and struck the ground hard on his right hip and shoulder, the girl tumbling off his other shoulder, and rolled.

So did the girl, groaning shrilly, skirts and hair flying wildly around her.

"Damn!" Hunter heard himself exclaim as the ground hammered him.

He bounced as he rolled, sharp twigs, branches, and pine needles gouging his skin through his shirt, the ground ruthlessly shoving dirt and needles between his lips. The woman rolled against him — hard.

She cried out and continued rolling, Hunter's body slamming down on hers, his broad chest smashing against her lumpy one, making her cry out again, more loudly. Then she inadvertently kicked him across his left temple as they continued rolling, limbs entangled, down the steep decline.

At least, he thought the kick was inadvertent. As mad as she was, she might have kicked him on purpose. He couldn't really blame her. Damn foolish move, thinking he could carry even something as light as she down the steep ridge.

Finally they both piled up a few feet away from each other at the base of the ridge.

Hunter quickly took stock as he lay on his back, facing skyward. He didn't think anything was broken. He hurt like hell, but he'd broken bones before, even dislocated a couple back during the Fight for Southern Independence, but he didn't hurt that bad.

He turned to where the woman lay beside him, also on her back.

"You all right?"

She didn't say anything. Was she passed out?

Maybe dead?

He sat up to get a better look at her. She wasn't dead. She was crying. Quietly crying, her body quivering, her face scrunched up, eyes squeezed shut.

She lifted her head and cast another fierce look through her tears. "I would have been safer with that wildcat!"

Hunter spied movement to the east, straight out away from him. A horse and rider were galloping toward him. One of the killers had a rifle raised, his right cheek pressed up against the stock.

Hunter flung himself onto the woman beside him.

She screamed as, rolling onto his right shoulder, he picked her up and hurled her over him, to his left, behind a tree. As he rolled toward her, a bullet thudded into the ground where she'd been lying a moment before, blowing up a gout of dirt and grass.

The thud of the bullet was followed by the whip-crack of the rifle of the fast approaching rider, the rataplan of the scissoring hooves now reaching Hunter's ears, as well.

Hunter threw himself behind the tree as yet another bullet ripped into the ground behind him, followed by the rifle's crashing report. The girl sat up, looking around wildly, sobbing fearfully.

"Stay down!" Hunter told her.

As she hunkered low, Hunter looked around the right side of the tree. The rider was within fifty yards and angling straight toward him, raising the rifle to his cheek again.

Hunter removed his hat, waved it out to the right of the tree, and dropped it. He'd no sooner dropped it than a bullet buzzed through the air to skin off the tree's right side, flinging bark and bits of wood in all directions.

Hunter unholstered his LeMat and aimed it around the tree's left side, lining up the sights on the rider plunging toward him.

He fired once, twice, three times.

The man had jerked back after the first shot. As the other two bullets hammered into him, he sagged even farther back in his saddle, pulling the reins back sharply. His cream gelding whinnied fiercely as its head went up, snout aimed nearly skyward.

The horse dropped its rear and skidded forward on its belly. The rider plunged down the horse's left hip and the cream tumbled onto him.

The man screamed.

He screamed again as the cream gained its feet, trampling its wounded rider, kicking him. The man wailed. "Oh . . . oh . . . oh Christ!"

"Wait here!" Hunter told the woman and ran forward.

The cream shook itself as though to clear the cobwebs. Its saddle hung down its left side.

"Whoa boy, whoa boy," Hunter said, approaching the mount, holding both hands up, palms out, trying to calm the beast. The horse might be his and the woman's only chance to make it to Tigerville alive.

He continued forward too quickly.

The horse wanted nothing to do with him. As it turned sharply, Hunter dove for the reins. He got one ribbon in his right hand, but the horse, wheeling sharply a hundred and eighty degrees, tugged the leather free before Hunter could make a fist around it.

Loosing another angry neigh, it lunged off its rear hooves and galloped back the way in which it and its rider had come. It ran as though it were running a Fourth of July race with tin cans tied to its tail.

Hunter punched the ground and cursed.

The thuds of the fleeing cream's hooves dwindled. They were replaced by the growing rataplan of at least two more horses.

"Oh God!" the woman sobbed, staring toward the north.

Hunter looked beyond her. Sure enough, two more of the stage-robbing gang members were heading toward him and the woman, coming hard and fast.

Hunter scrambled to his feet. He glanced at the cream's rider, who lay still now in the grass and sage, his body twisted and broken, his chest a bib of fresh blood.

Dead.

Good. One down, three to go . . .

Hunter rose and ran back to where the woman sat on her knees, head down, bawling. The two killers were two hundred yards away and closing, whipping their horses with their rein ends. They rode straight toward Hunter and the woman from the north, between the base of the ridge on

Hunter's left and a long sweep of pine forest on his right.

Hunter looked around for the saddlebags. He'd dropped them in his tumble down the ridge.

He ran up the ridge, suppressing the aches and pains incurred in the plunge. Fortunately, he found the bags not far away, piled up against the base of a large cedar. He slung the bags over his right shoulder, ran the fifty feet back down the slope, knelt beside the bawling Miss Meyers, and palmed the LeMat.

That's all it took to cause both riders to rein their horses in suddenly. They'd been privy to Hunter's work with the LeMat earlier, and they weren't about to make themselves such easy targets again. The black horse of the rider on the right whinnied and reared. The man on the right, riding a steeldust, curveted his own horse, swung down from his saddle, and sheathed what appeared a Winchester carbine. He dropped his horse's reins and took a knee.

The other man dismounted, as well, throwing down his own reins, hefting the rifle he was holding, and stood near where his horse casually lowered its head to tug at the shin-high yellow wheat grass.

"Turn over the money and the woman,

and we'll let you go, Buchanon!" The standing man was sixty yards away; Hunter could see the line of his teeth as he grinned.

The woman moaned.

"All right." It was Hunter's turn to grin. "Come an' get her!"

"Oh God! Oh God!" the woman cried into her hands.

"Don't worry! This ain't my first rodeo, sweetheart!"

"Oh God! Oh God!" the woman cried again.

Still grinning, Hunter extended the LeMat, and fired. The standing man flinched and slapped his hand over the left side of his neck. The kneeling man returned fire. The bullet plunked into the sod three feet in front of Hunter.

Buchanon slid the LeMat toward the kneeling man and fired. Just as he did, the standing man yelled to the other one, "Take cover, Emory, fer Christ-damn-sakes!" and bolted to his feet.

Hunter's bullet blew up dirt and grass just beyond him.

Both of the killers' horses had run off when Hunter fired the first shot, so the kneeling man, cursing loudly, ran back north and to Hunter's right, the flaps of his broadcloth coat winging out around him.

The other man joined him, also cursing, as they lumbered, spurs ringing like sleigh bells at Christmas, for the cover of the trees. Hunter aimed but didn't shoot. He didn't want to waste another bullet. Neither man was running fast, but they were just out of the LeMat's accurate shooting range.

Hunter wished he had his Henry repeater, which had belonged to his older, now-deceased brother, Shep, but he rarely packed the handsome sixteen-shooter on stage runs. When you had your hands full of leather ribbons leading out to a six-horse hitch, you couldn't handle much more than a hogleg. In the past, his LeMat and Charley's twelve-gauge shotgun had been more than sufficient for holding off some of the gnarliest owlhoots in the territory.

Charley . . .

In his mind's eye, Hunter saw Charley lying piled up on the trail beside the drummer, and his rage renewed itself, a fist of fire opening around his heart.

He pulled the LeMat down, glared off toward where the two killers were just then approaching the trees, and muttered, "Till we meet again, you sons of Satan . . ."

He holstered the LeMat, grabbed Miss Meyers's arm, and pulled her to her feet. "Come on!"

"Oh God, no — I can't!"

"Yes, you can!"

"No!"

"If you think those two will treat you any better than I have, I'll leave you. That what you want?" He was running hard, pulling the unwilling woman along behind him.

"No, but . . . oh, go to hell!"

The killers shouted angrily behind Hunter. He could no longer see them, because he and the woman were running through the trees now themselves. But he knew they were fetching their horses.

They'd resume the chase soon. They had no choice. They had to kill Buchanon, because he could identify them as killers, and they wanted the money and the woman. It was anyone's guess which they wanted more, but glancing behind him at Miss Meyers and the torn dress that could just barely contain her assets, he had a pretty good idea.

Money was one thing. The satisfaction of male lust was another.

There weren't many women who looked like Laura Meyers anywhere in the territory. She'd be a hell of a prize though she probably wouldn't live through the celebration following her acquisition.

"You're welcome, lady," Hunter said,

chuckling drolly as he ran, leaping deadfalls, pulling, sometimes carrying, her along behind him.

Finally, Dead Horse Canyon opened ahead of him. The dark gash grew wider as he and the woman approached.

As the forest drew back behind him, he pushed through thirty feet of brush and wended his way around small boulders until he stood on the lip of the canyon. The woman dropped to her knees behind him, too exhausted now to even cry.

The canyon was roughly two hundred yards wide at this point, its shelving walls of salmon and pink sandstone and limestone dropping two hundred feet to the canyon floor. Dead Horse Creek, roughly twenty feet wide, was a glinting black snake curving between banks of high, green grass, green shrubs, and towering pines and Douglas firs. Water-carved caverns with gently arching portals, and of all sizes, lined the base of both cliffs.

Hunter knew the layout of the canyon, because he and his brothers had often hunted and fished along the meandering chasm, which was a font of game including deer, elk, and wild turkeys. Here, he and the woman had the advantage. It wouldn't be a hard descent, because the walls shelved relatively gently, offering good footing and plenty of handholds.

Men on horseback, however, wouldn't make it. At least, not here. They'd have to find an easier way down.

Hearing hoof thuds in the forest behind him, Hunter grabbed the woman's hand again. "Come on. We're almost there."

She shook her bowed head. "Where?"

"To the bottom of this canyon."

She looked up wearily, her pale features slack. When she saw the canyon dropping before her, her eyes widened and sharpened again in horror. "Oh God, no!"

Chapter 6

The thumping of the oncoming horses was growing louder.

Hunter pulled Laura to her feet. He sandwiched her face in his big hands and gazed into her pretty hazel eyes, forcing her to look back at him. "You're gonna follow me down. It's steep but it's easy. Lots of places for your hands and feet. Now, take a deep breath and follow me!"

She gazed back at him, and gradually, the terror left her gaze.

She drew a breath, released it, and nodded.

Hunter stepped over the lip of the canyon, setting his boots down on the small shelves of rock jutting out from the side of the ridge.

"Hurry, now," he said. "Don't look down. Just look at your hands and feet."

She stepped over the lip and started her descent, slow at first, but when she saw that there were plenty of hand- and footholds, she seemed to grow more confident and hurried her pace. Occasionally, she looked down at Hunter crawling down the wall directly below her, where he could catch her if she fell.

Seeing him near seemed to calm her, encourage her, and she continued crabbing down the wall just above him.

The sounds of approaching riders along with the shouts of their pursuers ebbed down into the canyon, echoing faintly. A few rocks rained down from above, bouncing off the wall several feet to Hunter's right.

He stopped and looked up just as one of the killers angled his head over the lip for a look into the canyon. He was above Hunter and the woman and a little to their right. The man pointed, shouting, "There they are!"

Hunter stepped to the right and said, "Keep coming, Miss Meyers!"

"Oh God," she gasped, looking up.

Hunter unsheathed the LeMat. "Don't look up! Keep going down!"

The other killer poked his head over the canyon's lip, the breeze bending the brown brim of his high-crowned Stetson. Both men raised their rifles to their shoulders and angled the barrels down at their prey.

Hunter had already raised the LeMat and

was aiming down the barrel. He squeezed the trigger. The LeMat roared, and the man to his left on the canyon's rim stumbled back away from the wall without firing his weapon. The other man triggered his own rifle, but Hunter's shot made him fire wide — into the wall only a few feet below Buchanon.

Hunter fired at that man, too, driving him back away from the rim.

Laura cried out as her bare feet slipped off the narrow ledge she was on. She dropped straight down.

As she shot past Hunter on his left, Hunter reached out with his left hand and grabbed her right arm. The force of her fall made him lose his own precarious footing, made even more precarious by the fact that he was no longer holding on to anything with his hands, his left one holding her arm, his right one clutching the LeMat.

An acidic dread churned in his belly as he dropped straight down the wall, involuntarily releasing Miss Meyers's arm as well as the LeMat and raking all ten fingers along the rock wall sliding up past him in a gray-brown blur.

Madly, he tightened his jaws and clawed for purchase.

The woman gave a clipped scream.

Vaguely, he heard a thump close on his left. A half an eye blink later, his boots slammed onto a strangely yielding surface and then he fell on his back, ears ringing, vision swimming.

He lifted his head. The girl lay beside him, writhing on the wiry green bushes they'd both fallen onto, cushioning the drop. God had reached out his hand in the form of evergreen shrubs growing up from an outward bulge in the ridge wall to catch them before they could fall the last fifty feet to their deaths.

Hunter still had the saddlebags, to boot. They were hanging over his left arm. He'd fallen on the canteen. He winced at the ache in his lower left back as he reached around to slide the canteen out to his side.

"There. Better . . ."

As the ringing slowly receded from Buchanon's ears, the whip-cracks of rifles assaulted them, as did the sharp spangs of bullets ricocheting off the rocks around him. He blinked his eyes to clear them, then gazed straight up the ridge.

Again, acidic dread bubbled in his belly.

One of the riflemen was aiming straight down the ridge wall at him, the rifle as still as stone in the man's gloved hands. Hunter could feel the burn of the rifle's sights on his forehead.

"Enjoy that last breath," he silently told himself.

But then the rifle jerked suddenly to Hunter's left, orange flames lapping from the barrel. The shooter screamed. Growls and snarls sounded from the ridge, and Hunter got a quick glimpse of some gray-brown, four-legged beast hanging from the man's arm by its jaws until man and clinging beast fell away from the ridge wall.

"Cussed vermin!" the man cried in terror. "I'm being attacked by a damned coyote! Quick, shoot him, A.J. *Shoot him!*"

A rifle cracked. Bobby Lee gave a sharp yelp.

Buchanon had wondered vaguely where the beast had gone. But then, Bobby Lee had never cottoned to gunfire. He'd likely been following his master and his master's female charge from a good distance, not wanting to take any of the lead meant for them. But just like he had done in the past, when he'd seen the chips were down for Hunter, he'd leaped in to help.

"God bless the beasts," Buchanon muttered, hoping Bobby Lee hadn't taken a bullet for his loyalty.

Looking around quickly, he saw his LeMat

laying to his left, between himself and the woman.

He grabbed the big popper in his right hand, grabbed the woman's wrist in his left hand, said, "Come on!" and heaved them both to their feet.

Further good fortune showed itself in the form of a gentler slope below the evergreens, as well as a two-foot shelf of downward angling trail pocked here and there with deer pellets and rodent tracks.

Hunter stopped. Miss Meyers was a dead weight behind him. He turned to see that she was on her knees, head hanging back, eyes closed.

Unconscious or nearly so.

He didn't know if she'd been brained by the fall or if she'd taken a bullet. He didn't have time to find out.

He had to get them both off the ridge.

He crouched, settled her over the saddle-bags on his left shoulder, swung around, and hurried off down the gently sloping trail. The narrow trace angled downward to the left and leveled off on the canyon floor beneath a broad, bulging belly of striated rock giving good cover from the ridge crest above. The narrow, slow-moving stream of water, as black as indigo ink, murmured softly in its shallow bed to the right. Pines, shrubs, and green grass abutted it closely on the far side, several boughs hanging down over the water.

Hunter followed the clear, gravelly ground between the stream and the ridge wall, heading roughly northeast as he followed this section of the twisting canyon.

The woman was light. He doubted she weighed much over a hundred pounds. Still, as tired and sore as he was, she, in addition to the burden of the saddlebags, was becoming a heavy weight on his shoulder.

Still, he had to keep moving. He knew of a small cavern another quarter mile down the canyon in which they could hole up relatively safely for the night. One where he himself had stocked dry firewood the last time he'd overnighted there, when he'd hunted Dead Horse Canyon alone.

That had been two years ago, before the war with Ludlow and Chaney, before he'd lost his ranch as well as his two brothers — one older, one younger — and he and his father had been forced to move into Tigerville.

If the wood was still there, it would likely be in good burning condition. The cavern was protected by brush and boulders screening it from the canyon floor as well as from the tops of both ridge walls. As he remembered, it got cold in the canyon at night even in the summer. The woman was not dressed for a cold night; she'd need a fire.

His boots were growing as heavy as lead by the time he reached a natural bridge of rock hanging low down over the canyon. He was glad to see the bridge, for he remembered the cavern he was heading for lay just beyond it.

He hurried under the bridge, having to crouch so the stone underbelly didn't rake his hat off his head. The air beneath the bridge smelled of mold and dank stone. Coming out the other side he saw the oval-shaped opening of the cavern atop an outcropping of sand and gravel roughly twenty feet up from the canyon floor.

He climbed the outcropping, grunting and wheezing with the effort. He wasn't in the prime shape he'd been in during the war, he vaguely reflected. Back then he could run all night, barefoot, with a rucksack of high explosives strapped to his back, armed with only a Griswold & Gunnison .36-caliber cap-and-ball revolver tucked behind his belt, and a bowie-style knife he'd fashioned himself from a plow blade hanging from a leather sheath around his neck.

He gained the crest of the outcropping

capped with small boulders and brush including a gnarled cedar, and dropped to his knees, his vision dimming with fatigue. The woman groaned, moved around on his shoulder.

"Hold on," he said.

He turned to peer into the cavern. When he'd overnighted in the cave before, there had been no sign that anything more dangerous than foxes or coyotes had called the place home. There didn't appear to be any now either. In fact, there were no recent tracks or scat or rabbit bones at all.

There was, however, a stone fire ring and the short stack of firewood he'd gathered before he'd pulled out after his own last visit.

Things were looking up.

He rose and stepped into the cavern, crouching, for the ceiling wasn't as high as he was tall. He bent forward and eased Miss Meyers down onto the cave floor. She sat up, raised her knees, rested her arms on them, and pressed the heels of her hands to her temples.

"God . . . I hurt all over. What happened?" She lowered her hands and looked around.

"A cave."

Hunter sat down heavily and leaned back against the wall. He slid the saddlebags off his shoulder. He removed his hat, set the hat down on the saddlebags beside him, and swept his hand through his long, thick blond hair. "Where you hurt?"

She rested her head in her hands again. "Everywhere."

"Were you hit?"

She lowered her hands again, looked at her body as though seeing it for the first time. She ran her hands down her sides, down her legs over the torn and dirty dress, then shook her head, making her tangled, dirty hair jostle. "No. My head aches."

Hunter closed his eyes. Fatigue weighed heavy on him. "We took a fall."

"I know. I'm sorry. I was frightened."

He unscrewed the cap and held out the canteen to her. "Have some. It's warm but I'll refill it after dark."

She shook her head and sat back against the wall on the opposite side of the fire ring from him. She stretched her long legs out beneath her torn and rumpled dress and underclothes, and crossed her dirty, bloody feet at her ankles.

"Where are they?" she asked.

Hunter took a couple of sips of the brackish water, then capped and set the canteen near his hat and saddlebags. "Up on the rim, last I checked. If they want us bad enough, they'll be along soon. There are plenty of places on the western ridge where they can ride or lead their horses into the canyon."

"Do you think they'll come?"

He looked at her. Would he come for her, if he was such a man as his stalkers were?

Hard to say. Even beaten and dirty, she was still a fine figure.

The skin above the bridge of her nose creased as she gazed back at him, vaguely curious. As if reading his mind, her pale, dusty cheeks turned pink. She frowned and looked down at her exposed flesh. Her eyes settled on her lap. She closed her eyes and choked back a sob.

He tossed the canteen onto the dirt beside her. "You'll feel better if you have some water."

"I'm so tired and sore I don't want water."

"It'll make you feel better is what I'm saying."

She didn't respond to that.

Hunter glanced at her feet. "Do your feet hurt?"

Numbly she shook her head and drew her feet up, covering them with the folds of her torn dress. "Please leave me alone, Mister Buchanon. I just want to rest."

"All right."

He didn't realize it but he was dead asleep less than five seconds after he'd said those last words. He slid slowly down the cavern wall to settle onto his left shoulder. The next thing he was aware of was a cold snout roughly the texture of a gutta percha gun grip pressed against his left ear.

He woke with a start, hand automatically closing over the LeMat on his right hip. He rose and in the cavern's dusky light saw the long gray snout flanked by two yellow eyes regarding him from a few inches away.

Two V-shaped ears were pricked, and the animal before him made a soft whimpering sound in his throat.

"Bobby Lee!" Hunter exclaimed.

The woman must have conked out just as Hunter had, for she sat up now with a groan. When she opened her eyes, shook her hair back, and saw the coyote in Hunter's burly arms, she screamed.

Chapter 7

Laura Meyers stared across the cavern at the big, rugged, blond-headed, blue-eyed man in a buckskin tunic and buckskin pants and with a bear claw necklace curving across his broad chest, and wondered what kind of a man has a coyote for a pet.

A coyote he obviously loved, judging by how he hugged the wild animal so tightly to his chest, brusquely patting it, ruffling its neck, scratching its ribs, and exclaiming over it, as though it were a child. Judging by how the coyote laid its ears back and wagged its tail and licked the big man's lips, the coyote returned every bit of the big man's affection.

Laura had never seen such a thing in her life.

The whole display revolted her. It also intrigued her but only in the same fashion as a grisly traffic accident on a bustling Denver street. The big man himself interested her in a similar way. He looked very much like a Viking warrior straight out of some Norse fairy tale.

A large, crude man of the Western frontier. One whom she'd watched kill men with horrifying efficiency and violence, but also a man who obviously very much loved the wild beast in his arms and was not afraid of displaying such sentiment to a total stranger.

But, then again, why would he hide it? He was obviously as wild as the coyote he loved. Wild things were not afraid of anything. Least of all revealing themselves to a mere woman and a vexingly helpless one at that.

Of course, under the circumstances, she couldn't blame him. Despite her pique, he had saved her life, she reminded herself. She supposed she should feel grateful. All she really felt, however, was weariness and rage at the fates that had placed her in such a horrid and downright deadly situation.

She looked again at the man now lowering his head to closely inspect a bloody gash on the coyote's back. His bushy blond brows above his ice blue eyes furled with concern.

Yes, she had to admit he intrigued her. She also had to admit that he was rather handsome in a crude and uncivilized sort of way. Big and rawboned, with a face that could have been chiseled from red-hued granite, complete with anvil-like jaws, high, broad cheeks, broad forehead beneath the thick blond hair, and a deep cleft in his ship's prow chin.

A warrior's face.

He was nothing at all like Jonathan, who'd been smaller and more delicately featured. Jonathan had owned the features of a civilized man. A man of fine breeding and learning. A man who read books and studied the law — who was a member, in fact, of the Colorado Bar.

Jonathan had been a man who'd looked heart-thumpingly handsome in a wool and brocade suit, his black derby hat tipped at a jaunty angle as he leaned against the front of his law office on Larimer Street in Denver, shiny half-boots crossed, twirling his pearl-handled walking stick in his beringed right hand, a disarming smile showing his fine white teeth under his upswept handlebar mustache, waxed daily by the same barber.

Unfortunately, other women had found him handsome, as well, and beguiling with his aura of civilized power, his learned and witty conversation, his wealth — or the pretention of wealth, anyway.

She'd never known a man so different as

this man was from Jonathan. She'd seen Buchanon's ilk on the streets of Denver, of course — rough-hewn men from the cattle ranches or from the mines in the mountains. Big, brash men with fists like hams, who carried themselves with almost arrogant confidence and erupted easily into ribald laughter.

Rowdy, violent men. Dangerous men.

Laura had never actually met such a man, talked to such a man, had anything at all to do with such a man except to look away from their insinuating glances and brashly ogling eyes when she traveled by hansom cab downtown to have dinner with Jonathan in the early evening on Market Street.

She realized now as she studied the man across from her that she was deeply afraid of him, as she was afraid of the foul-smelling beast he loved. He'd saved her life. For that she should be grateful. But all she felt was fear.

At least, she thought it was fear. Wasn't it fear that made the blood turn oddly warm in her belly while lifting chicken flesh across her slender shoulders?

Of course, it was fear. What else could it be? She was deeply afraid of this savage brigand and his feral pet.

Hunter Buchanon radiated power and

physical strength. As he moved, administering to the wild beast in his arms, his muscles strained the seams of his tunic and his tight buckskin pants. She looked at the long, thick arms, the broad, calloused brown hands. Such a man could do anything he wanted to her and there was absolutely nothing she could do about it.

She gave a shiver as she averted her eyes from him.

She thought that deep down he was probably not all that different from the men who'd attacked the stagecoach and who'd dragged her off to satisfy their lust. Tonight, once the sun went down and darkness closed over the canyon, no doubt his own goatish cravings, coupled with his wildness fully revealed, would uncover itself behind the curtain of his rugged affability.

Laura crossed her arms on her barely concealed breasts, closed her eyes, and said a silent prayer for safety. She'd never felt more helpless and vulnerable in her life.

My God — what woman in such a situation would?

Soon, she hoped, she and this wild man and his wild beast would part ways and she would be safe and warm and comfortable in her new life — her new life without Jonathan — in Tigerville.

"I'll be hanged, Bobby Lee, if that son of a buck with the rifle didn't carve a nice notch in your hide." Hunter parted the coyote's fawn gray fur with his fingers to inspect the bloody gash across Bobby Lee's left hip.

The coyote turned his head back to sniff the cut, working his leathery nostrils. He looked up at his concerned master, blinked his red eyes slowly, then lifted his head and gave a soft, low wail.

"Oh, stop feelin' sorry for yourself!" Hunter laughed. "Hell, I've cut myself worse shaving. Just keep your consarned snout out of it and it should heal faster'n a pig can find a mud waller."

He glanced at the woman. She was frowning over her raised knees at him and Bobby Lee. "What's the matter, Miss Meyers? You look like you drank milk left out on the table too long."

"I'm just wondering how on earth you, uh . . . befriended . . . this . . . animal."

"I found him wandering alone in a little valley near my family's ranch. I assumed some other rancher killed his mother, maybe his father, and likely the rest of the pups."

"And you took him in . . . ?"

"Yes."

"Why?"

"I don't know."

Hunter shrugged as he turned to gather wood from the stack behind him. He and the woman must have slept for well over an hour. Long shadows were stretching into the canyon. It would be dark soon. And cold soon, as well.

"I reckon for the same reason I took you in," Hunter said with a smile. "He was alone and in trouble."

"I was a passenger on your stagecoach," she pointed out tartly. "It was your duty to make sure I arrived at my destination safely. You not only failed to do that, but I left two portmanteau as well as a steamer trunk aboard that coach. Both contained all the items I have left to my name."

He glanced over his shoulder at her. Her words as well as the haughty tone she'd spoken them in riled him. She might have lost luggage, but he'd lost his good friend Charley Anders in that attack. He started to point that out but checked himself.

There was no point in arguing. To a woman like her, Charley had probably been only one or two steps up from the coyote she was regarding again distastefully, as

Bobby Lee sat near the cave door, scratching behind his left ear with his left hind foot.

"I do apologize. I'll have a fire going in a minute. Then I'll go down and refill the canteen and we'll get your feet cleaned up. You don't want infection to set into those cuts and scrapes. I wish we had some whiskey, but since we don't, water will have to do."

"I can clean my own feet."

"All right. I'll help if you need it."

She scowled at him suspiciously. "I just bet you would."

Hunter found his own cheeks warming as he said, "I apologize, Miss Meyers. That was forward of me. I didn't mean anything inappropriate."

She sighed and shook her hair back. "I just want this to be over, Mister Buchanon. I want to be in Tigerville. How long do you think that's going to take us?"

Hunter had set a small, pyramidal pile of tinder in the center of the stone ring. He'd piled kindling and large chunks of wood nearby, ready to bring into action as the fire grew. "Hard to say. If we still have those hounds on our trail, longer than if we didn't."

As of a couple of hours ago, he absently reflected, he'd seen only two on his and the woman's trail. He wondered where the third one — Ike Talon himself — was. Talon had taken one of Hunter's bullets. Maybe he'd holed up to lick that nasty arm wound or to get it tended.

Probably too much to hope for that he might have bled to death.

Hunter produced a flat tin box from his shirt pocket, slid the lid open, and plucked a sulfur-tipped lucifer match from the box, and lit the tinder. He tended the flame carefully, tenderly, building it up slowly, then adding more tinder and then some of the smaller bits of kindling in the form of feathersticks and small chunks of dry pine bark.

When the flames looked strong enough, he added a small chunk of wood and then another. Certain the fire was going well enough now that he could leave it for a while, he picked up the canteen and stepped out of the cavern, looking around carefully.

He stood just outside the cave, watching and listening. Hearing or seeing nothing that troubled him, he moved through a gap in the rocks and brush fronting the cave and peered out over the canyon.

It was almost dark down there. The air was cool and damp. He could hear the murmuring stream, see the fading light angling into the canyon from his right reflected off the water. The trees and brush rustled in a faint breeze.

Deciding that there were enough shadows offering cover, he stepped back out of the rocks and crouched to peer into the cave. She sat watching him from over the knees she'd drawn taut against her chest, hugging them tightly, a concerned, worried expression on her pretty face. The fire's dancing flames shone gold in her hazel eyes.

Bobby Lee sat in the cave entrance, staring up at Hunter expectantly.

Hunter held up the canteen. "I'll be right back."

"You won't be gone long?" she asked, a faint tremor in her voice.

"Just a minute's all." Hunter looked at the coyote. "Stay here and keep watch, Bobby. Let me know if you hear or see anything, all right?"

He knew the coyote would.

He gave his beloved pet a warm pat on the head and then headed down the slope toward the water.

CHAPTER 8

When Hunter returned to the cave, Laura gave a silent sigh of relief.

He'd been gone longer than she had expected. Alone here, with just the coyote, she'd found herself feeling even more fearful than before he'd left. The coyote gave a mewl of greeting, wagging its tail and clawing at the big man's pantleg.

Hunter crouched to pat the beast's head.

"What took you so long?" Laura asked, hating the tremor she again heard in her voice.

She didn't want to feel as dependent on him as she did. She wasn't sure why, but she sensed there might be danger in it. She didn't know why that should be either. She just knew that she was feeling strangely, and she wasn't sure she could blame it all on fear, though she wanted to.

His voice was low, soft, almost intimate. He was such a big man that he seemed to fill most of the cave himself. "Decided to take a little tramp up stream and down, just making sure no one was on the scout out there. I think we're alone. Those two killers either decided to head to town for a warm meal and a soft bed, or they're holed up on the rim, maybe waiting for us to show ourselves in the morning."

"What will we do come morning?"

"I take another careful look around. If all's clear, we'll start up the canyon toward Tigerville."

"Will the canyon take us to town?"

"Close." Hunter had walked up to her, crouching under the cavern's low wall. He held out the canteen to her with one hand. He held out a strip of jerky in his other hand. "Have some fresh water and jerky. Gotta keep your strength up."

"What about you?"

"I had a big drink down at the stream."

"What about jerky?"

"That was the only one in my pocket. But go ahead. Hunger makes my senses keener."

"No."

She took the canteen and set it down beside her. She took the jerky, tore it in two, and gave him half. She smiled. "Fair is fair."

He returned her smile. "All right."

He stuffed part of the jerky into his mouth

and then dropped to a knee, stirred the fire, and added another log. He sank down on his butt, removed his hat, ran a hand through his long hair, then leaned back against the wall.

The coyote yipped and came over and lay down beside its master, resting its long snout on Hunter's left thigh. It gave a satisfied groan, closed its eyes, and appeared almost instantly asleep.

Laura sank back against the wall, nibbling the jerky. She swallowed a bite and sipped the water. It tasted so good that the first sip made her realize how thirsty she was. Downright parched. She tipped the canteen back and drank hungrily, some of the water oozing out from between her lips and the spout and dribbling down her neck and onto her chest.

It made her shiver, but still she drank.

She lowered the canteen, sloshed the water in it, then arched her brows at Hunter, who sat watching her from the other side of the cave. "Sorry. I guess I didn't realize how dry I was."

Hunter shoved the rest of his jerky into his mouth and brushed his hands on his pants. Chewing, he said, "Take all you want. The stream's near."

She tossed him the canteen two-handed

and with a grunt. "I've had enough for now. You take the rest. You worked hard." She hesitated, then found herself adding, "to save my life."

No one could have been more surprised by this sudden switch of sentiment. She found herself continuing with, "I'm sorry I wasn't more grateful before."

"It's all right. You were frightened and angry. I don't blame you. We'll get your bags, though. I'll send someone out for them once we reach Tigerville. Those killers would have no use for a woman's luggage."

More words came spilling out of her, further surprising her. "I want to apologize for my condescending attitude, Mister Buchanon. That's not who I am. At least, I'd rather not think that's who I am."

"Oh, hell," he said, hiking a shoulder, then taking a drink from the canteen. He was a bashful man. Big and rough but also bashful. At least, around a woman.

Around her.

She found that appealing for some reason.

"On the other hand, maybe it is who I am." She lifted her chin resolutely. It felt liberating, stating thoughts and feelings she'd been only halfway feeling and understanding for the past several weeks. "But I'm going to change. Just as the rest of my life is changing. I'm going to be a simpler, humbler human being."

"How is your life changing, Miss Meyers?"

"I am divorcing my husband and I'm moving to Tigerville. Mister Buchanon, you saved the life of the Tigerville Public School's new teacher."

"Pshaw! You don't say."

"Oh, yes."

"You're a teacher?"

"I attended a teaching academy for two years in Saint Louis. That was before I married Jonathan Gaynor and took up housekeeping for him."

Deep lines of befuddlement cut across the big man's broad forehead. "Jonathan Gaynor, Jonathan Gaynor. Where have I heard that name?"

"He's an attorney and a mining magnate in Denver. He has a town named after him in the Rockies."

"Oh, yeah," Hunter said, widening his eyes in realization. "Gaynorville. Sure, sure — I've heard of Gaynorville." He paused, studying her closely, incredulously. "You're married to *him*?"

"I'm divorcing him," she corrected him. "I'm using my maiden name, Meyers, because I don't want Jonathan or any of his cronies to know where I am."

The look of astonishment stayed on Buchanon's face. "Why would you divorce a man like that? He must be one of the richest men in Colorado Territory."

"I have learned over the past six weeks, Mister Buchanon, that there is more to life than money."

"You have?" He seemed genuinely surprised to hear that.

"I have. An honest relationship with the man you love is far more important than money. Love, loyalty . . . fidelity."

"Okay . . ."

"I learned six weeks ago that Jonathan has been in a long-standing affair with another woman. A woman in Gaynorville. He became involved in that relationship — with none other than a whorehouse madam, I might add — only two months after he and I were married!"

She choked back a sob and shook her head. The sudden feeling of sorrow was short-lived. She lifted her head and shook back her tangled hair, drawing a deep breath and marveled at how much better she felt, having confessed so much about the tawdry turn her life had taken.

To a stranger, no less!

Or . . . maybe that's why it had been so

easy. She didn't know.

But suddenly more than fear or exhaustion, more than the draining and soul-withering worry about her future that had assaulted her ever since she'd made the decision to divorce Jonathan, she felt an incredible liberation.

Hunter stared at her with his mouth and eyes wide. His eyes had a deeply sympathetic cast. Slowly, he shook his head.

He seemed deeply confounded.

"Why, that there is pure evil," he said, still astonished.

"Yes! I told him that myself. Just before I shot him."

His eyes opened wider. There was something so sweet and boyish and innocent in his reaction to these tawdry doings that she suddenly wanted to run over to him and hug him like a big warm teddy bear.

"You . . ."

"Shot him," she proudly announced.

"Lordy."

"You see, I learned about Jonathan's infidelity when I took over balancing his accounts, when his accountant Herman Lightkeeper grew ill from smoking those foul-smelling Mexican cigarettes he so favored. As I told you, I attended an academy for young women before I married Jonathan, so

95

I know my numbers as well as my letters.

"Well, when I saw that Jonathan was having his secretary, Mister Pound, write a check each month to one Magdalena Hennessey in Gaynorville, I became quite curious. I inquired with Jonathan about the matter, and after considerable hemming and hawing, he said that Miss Hennessey was a business associate who managed a saloon for him in Gaynorville, and that he was paying her one hundred and fifty dollars a month to run this saloon.

"Well, his flushed and uncertain demeanor, as well as his obvious pique at my curiosity, made me even more curious. One hundred and fifty dollars a month seemed an awful lot to pay a saloon manager."

Laura took another bite of her jerky and chewed it angrily. "When Jonathan went off on one of his three- or four-day business trips to Gaynorville, to oversee his share in the mine and other sundry business interests up that-away, I followed him a day later. I asked about and learned that Magdalena Hennessey ran the saloon and parlor house known as Maggie's Place. Well, I marched over to Maggie's Place — what a windowless perdition with nearly naked girls and just-as-naked men lounging about the place in alcohol and opium stupors! That was the first time I smelled opium, but I knew what it was, all right. Like I said, I'm educated.

"My inquiries regarding Jonathan nearly made a couple of the girls strangle on their tongues while several of the men laughed uproariously in my face. One told me where I could find him, so I hitched up my skirts, climbed the stairs, and I found him, all right."

"Oh boy . . ."

"How many respectable businessmen, Mister Buchanon, do you think take baths in the middle of the afternoon with their business associates?"

"Uh . . ."

"I was so enraged, seeing him there . . . a man who doted on me like a child and called me 'pet' and 'my little pretty one' and 'his fair little sprite,' and who daily vowed his everlasting love and loyalty to me, that before I knew it, I'd taken the over-and-under derringer from my reticule — I don't even remember packing it — and shooting the bastard!"

Hunter slapped his thigh, grinning from ear to ear. "Hot damn — good for you! Did you kill him?"

"No, but I did make sure that, um, *sleeping* with that jug-bosomed slattern will be quite a painful task for the next several months!"

Hunter slapped his thigh again and laughed. "Serves him right!"

"And then I went home, summoned a lawyer, and started a divorce proceeding. I went to the bank to demand half of Jonathan's money, and do you know what I learned from the president of the Territorial Bank and Trust, Mister Buchanon?"

"No idea."

"That the man was not only a lying, cheating son of Satan, but that he was in financial ruin, as well. In that bank, he had forty-one dollars and thirty-eight cents. Jonathan was in so much debt, the president told me, that his creditors were beginning to howl like wolves on the blood trail. In other words, I, too, was penniless."

Grief touched her again. Humiliation. The shame of having been taken such utter advantage of. She lowered her chin, choked back a sob, then heaved herself to her feet. She stepped forward and crouched to scoop the canteen off the cave floor.

She sat down again, took a sip from the canteen, then curled her legs inward and pulled her dress up to expose her dirty, bloody bare feet.

"I learned that he spent all of his money on women, gambling, drinking, and making risky business investments . . . while drunk. He spent most of his time in Gaynorville — drunk."

She dribbled water over her bare left foot, sniffed, and brushed her fist across her nose. "I had no idea. I thought he was working for both of us."

She rubbed the water around on her foot and looked up at Hunter, tears dribbling down her cheeks. "How could one woman — one who so arrogantly touts herself as well-educated — be so stupid and blind?"

Hunter rose and, crouching under the low ceiling, walked over to her. He extended his hand to her. "You'll never get those feet clean that way. You're only making mud. Let's go down to the stream."

"Is it safe?"

"Pretty close to dark. I'm betting those killers are holed up. If they make a play on us, they'll likely wait till morning."

She looked at his extended hand and nodded. "All right."

She set the canteen aside and let Hunter pull her to her feet and lead her out of the cave. "Here we go," he said, and swept her up in his arms.

She gasped, resisting a little at first, tensing her body. But then, as he started off down the slope toward the canyon floor, she yielded her body to him, sank back in his arms, and wrapped her own arms around his neck.

When they reached the canyon, he felt her lean her head back against his shoulder. She turned her face toward his and gazed up at him, her eyes shimmering in the light of the moon climbing the sky above the canyon, in the east.

He could feel her soft, warm breaths puffing against his neck.

"He was a small man," she said softly as he carried her toward the satiny black skin of the snake-like creek curving in the darkness, pearl moonlight skimming its inky surface. "Not like you. He was a small man in ways I didn't suspect until I saw him . . . in that brothel . . . with her."

"That was some betrayal."

"Would you ever do that to a woman?"

"No, I wouldn't." He set her down on a rock at the edge of the stream. He knelt beside her. "Why Tigerville, of all places?"

"I saw an ad for a teacher in the school there."

"Sure, they just built one. Been looking for a teacher for a time."

"Well, they finally found one. I sent a telegram posthaste, announcing my credentials. The superintendent of the school council telegrammed me the next day, informing me that I had been accepted for the position and that school would begin one week after my arrival. So" — she dropped her hands to her thighs — "here I am, starting a new life . . . in this canyon after nearly being ravaged by goatish desperadoes . . . on the run from more desperadoes wanting to . . ."

"Again, I do apologize."

Hunter dipped his left hand in the water and scooped it up and over her left foot.

She drew a sharp breath.

"Cold?"

"A little," she said, her voice soft and intimate in the near-silent canyon. "It stings."

"Sorry."

"No, it feels good. Refreshing. Thank you, Mister Buchanon."

"Miss Meyers, I'm on knees before you, washing your feet. I think that means you can call me by my first name."

"All right." She chuckled at that, sniffed. "Hunter it is. Please, I'm Laura."

"Pleased to meet you, Miss Laura."

She chuckled again as she tucked her hair behind her ears and stared down at him gently scooping the water over her feet and rubbing it in, cleaning the small scrapes and

101

scratches. The water had been cold at first. But now, in his large hands, it felt warm. His hands felt warm, as well. She could feel the rough callouses on them, but he caressed her feet very gently.

Suddenly, she grew warm despite the coolness of the canyon. Her heartbeat quickened. She closed her eyes, luxuriating in the soft caressing of her feet by this big man's big, warm hands.

She felt the heat rise from her feet and into her legs, climbing still higher.

"Do you live in Tigerville, Hunter?" she asked.

"Indeed, I do."

"What brought you to Tigerville?"

"The war, I reckon. I fought for the Confederacy — the losin' side. Afterward, my pa brought the family — except for Ma, who died in Georgia before the war was over — out here to make a new start. All was well until a year ago. We had trouble with a rival rancher and a couple of his cronies . . . including the county sheriff."

Hunter drew a deep breath and let it out slowly as he massaged Laura's right foot, working the water up between her toes that shone in the dark water in the moonlight, rubbing the ball of her foot with the inside of his right index finger.

He was enjoying the feel of her bare foot in his hand while at the same time trying not to, wishing suddenly that he'd let her clean her own feet.

Wasn't proper, cleaning a strange lady's feet. Especially the feet of a beautiful young woman he was feeling himself becoming attracted to.

He looked up at her sitting on the rock above him.

She sat with her head thrown back, eyes closed. Her breasts rose and fell heavily as she breathed.

He stopped cleaning her feet but held them still in his hands, feeling the cool water slide over them in the slow-moving current.

She lowered her chin, looked down at him. Her hair fell forward to frame her face. Her eyes shone in the moonlight. She pushed up off the rock, dropped her feet in the stream, and stood. He straightened to his full six-feet-four-inches and looked down at her.

She stared up at him, her eyes wide and round and moist. He could see the miniature moon in the left one. She raised her hands and placed them on the bulging slabs of his chest, and said quietly, "Hunter . . ."

He raised his own hands, wrapped them around hers, and lowered their hands together. "I have a gal," he said quietly, trying to resist this woman's strong pull on him. It wasn't easy.

"I see."

"Leastways, I did. It might be over now. Still . . . I set store by the gal. I love her."

"And you want her back."

"Once I can afford to build a good life for us, yes. I had a cache of gold. I prospected that gold for several long years, wanting to have a big enough stake that she and I could be married. She came from a wealthy family. I didn't want her to want on my account. Well . . . someone stole that gold from me. I don't know who. I wanted to postpone the wedding until I could build up a stake again. Annabelle didn't want to wait. I couldn't do it. I thought . . . still think . . . she deserves more. It drove a wedge between us."

Laura pulled her hands out of his. "I see. Of course, you would have a young lady. I'm sorry." She shook her head, chuckling with self-deprecation. "What a pathetic fool I am!"

"No, please, don't —"

Hunter stopped abruptly when Bobby Lee cut loose with a loud volley of hammering yips that ripped around the canyon, echoing.

Hunter wheeled, palming the LeMat.

Two shadows moved fifteen feet away from him — two men, their hats limned by the moonlight — running through the brush. A branch snapped. A man cursed.

The LeMat leaped and roared in Hunter's hand.

CHAPTER 9

The next morning around nine, Annabelle Ludlow was sweeping the boardwalk fronting Big Dan Delaney's Saloon & Gambling Parlor in Tigerville, in preparation for opening, when she spotted a figure standing in one of Big Dan's big plate-glass windows, staring out at her.

She stopped sweeping and peered back at the person watching her. Only, there was no one else in the saloon at this early hour. That person in the window was herself. She just hadn't recognized her own reflection — at least not from that brief glimpse out of the corner of her eye.

But now, staring straight back at her own image in Big Dan's window, she still felt as though she were staring back at a stranger.

The stranger was around twenty. Pretty and long legged, with emerald eyes set in a heart-shaped face framed by thick tresses of dark red hair spilling down her shoulders and back and curling around to caress her sides. That much was Annabelle Ludlow.

The clothes she wore — if you could call them clothes, for they covered little of her — were what made her appear a stranger to herself. Possibly an impostor merely pretending to be Annabelle Ludlow but getting the attire all wrong.

A ranching gal as accustomed to horses as she was to bread-making and house-keeping, Annabelle had customarily worn a wool or calico blouse, denim jeans, and boy-size stockmen's boots with jangling spurs. That was when she was helping her father's and her brother's ranch hands on the range, which had been her favorite thing to do.

(Or *had* been, rather, back before she'd exiled herself from her home ranch as well as *been exiled by* her father, Graham, and brother, Cass Ludlow.)

If she were tending chores inside the Ludlow lodge at the Broken Heart Ranch headquarters, helping the Ludlows' long-time Chinese housekeeper, Chang, prepare meals, launder clothes, or give the lodge a thorough cleaning on some breezy spring day, she would wear a simple gingham day dress over the obligatory corset, camisole, pantaloons, wool stockings, and ankle boots.

She'd gather her red hair, which she'd

always been rather vain about, and had always worn long, back out of the way in a long queue.

Never once had she ever had a hankering to dress as skimpily as a parlor girl.

She inspected the girl in the window — the tall, long-legged, willow frame with all the right man-pleasing curves stuffed into a satin-lined cotton corset adorned with floral motifs embellished with guipure lace, tiny pearls, and clear sequins. She wore a short, ruffled cream skirt so sheer that she could see her equally sheer-stockinged legs from her hips all the way down to the high-heeled, black-satin shoes on her feet.

She wore part of her hair up, in curlicues secured atop her head with an amber rose pin; the rest hung in free-flowing curls down her back. Long, shiny emerald earrings, matching the color of her eyes, dangled from her ears.

Annabelle chewed her thumbnail and smiled. She was a little chagrined by her vanity but also pleased by what she saw.

She saw the horse and rider in the window, beside her own reflection, before she'd heard them ride up. Suddenly the steel-dust's sunbathed head was beside her own in the glass. The horse's rider appeared above her own reflection — a bizarrely masked individual appearing out of the bright sunny morning as though from the murky darkness of a waking nightmare.

"Good morning there, little sister! How you doin' this fine day?"

Annabelle gasped and swung around to face the street and her brother, Cass, sitting atop the steeldust and smiling behind the flour sack mask he wore with round holes cut out for the eyes and mouth. Despite the mask, Annabelle could still see the knotted, hideously scarred flesh around his lips as well as around his eyes, which also appeared bloodshot, as though forever irritated by the barn fire that had nearly killed him.

Before the fire, Cass Ludlow had been a dashingly handsome young man. Most would say devilishly handsome, with dimpled cheeks, a cleft chin, high tapering cheekbones, and a thick thatch of unruly brown hair.

He'd been popular with the single young ladies throughout the Black Hills — mostly with the wrong kind of single young ladies. The fire that changed his appearance so drastically, having burned him so terribly, had started when Annabelle had thrown a lamp at him, trying to fend him off when he'd attacked her in a drunken rage in the barn at the Broken Heart headquarters.

109

Cass had ridden in late and passed out drunk in a pile of hay. It hadn't been the first time. He'd awakened that night to find his young sister trying to steal away on a horse against their father's orders, to ride off to her ex-Confederate lover. Graham Ludlow had forbidden her from seeing Hunter Buchanon not only because Buchanon had fought for the Confederacy during the war, but because Ludlow had arranged for Annabelle to marry the dandy son of one of Ludlow's business associates.

That fire for which Cass blamed his sister had left him a mangled and tortured husk who concealed his hideously scarred face with a burlap mask shaded by the broad brim of his tan Stetson adorned with a band of gaudy Indian beads.

"Cass!" Annabelle said, shocked to see her brother this early in the morning. Cass usually drank, gambled, and caroused — now mostly with parlor girls with strong stomachs — until well after midnight, not rolling out of whatever flea-bit mattress he found himself in until well after noon. "I didn't hear you ride up. You frightened me!"

Unconsciously, holding the broom in her right hand, she dragged her arm across the bulging camisole, suddenly feeling as naked as the day she was born.

"Say, now," Cass said, leaning forward against his saddle horn, grinning behind the mask, letting his red-rimmed eyes wander down his sister's comely countenance, from her bare shoulders down her long legs to the high-heeled shoes on her feet. "Don't you look fine. Yessir, very fine indeed!"

Annabelle flinched under her brother's unnatural scrutiny.

"That getup sure does highlight your finer points, little sister."

"Please, Cass," Annabelle said, feeling her face and ears warm with shame, looking away. "Don't."

"Don't what? Appreciate a fine female form? Ain't that what that getup is supposed to do? Make men appreciate you?"

"Not my brother!" She swung around to the door. "Now, if you'll excuse me, I have a saloon to open."

"Fine, fine," Cass said. She saw in the door's upper glass pane her brother swing down from the steeldust's back. "I came to town to wet my whistle. I ran out last night, playin' poker in the bunkhouse. Can you believe that none of them raggedy-heeled hands of ours could come up with more than a spoonful of busthead?"

Annabelle fumbled the door open, stumbling on her high heels, wanting to get away

111

from her brother's mocking scrutiny as fast as she could. She knew what Cass was doing. He blamed her for the fire that night, and his way of exacting revenge was to stalk her and mock her new way of life, to castigate her for choices she'd made, including the choice to side with her young man, Hunter Buchanon, and the entire Buchanon family against her own.

She turned the sign in the door's window to OPEN, then walked down the wood-floored room to the long, mahogany bar at the rear, under a half-dozen mounted animal heads gazing blankly at nothing. As she approached the bar, she watched Cass walk into the saloon behind her, pausing halfway through the door to scratch a lucifer match to life on his thumbnail and then to hold the flame to the long, black, Mexican cheroot poking out from between his scarred lips.

He drew deeply on the cheroot, then, closing the door behind him, moved forward, blowing a long plume of smoke into the air before him.

He was five years Annabelle's senior, and her only sibling. The only one who'd made it through infancy and the war, that was. An older brother had been killed by the Confederates, thus their father's raw hatred for anyone who'd fought with the Rebel gray-backs, as Graham Ludlow called the Con-federates.

Cass always dressed, as he was this morn-ing, a little like a Mexican *caballero,* in a red shirt with gaudy Spanish-style embroi-dering and ruffles down the front, and bell-bottom, deerskin leggings trimmed with jouncing whang strings. A concho-studded shell belt encircled his waist. A fancy, horn-gripped .44 was snugged into a hand-tooled leather holster tied fashionably low on his right leg. The bright beads on the band of his Stetson flashed and winked in the golden morning light angling through a near window.

His masked face with the red-rimmed eyes and scarred pink lips stood out in stark contrast to his brightly stylish attire. Of course, he was aware of that. That's why as he approached the bar now, behind which Annabelle stood, seeking refuge from her older brother's brash appraisal, Cass kept his eyes off the mirror behind her.

Annabelle had set a crate of whiskey bottles atop the bar. She busied herself now with arranging the bottles on a shelf beneath the mahogany.

To her right and behind her, a large cast-iron pot of Big Dan's signature chili bubbled on the black range set in an opening cut into the back bar and flanked with shelves and cupboards of pots, pans, and wood-handled silverware. Annabelle had come early to the saloon, as she did every morning, to prepare for the lunch crowd that would begin arriving by mid-day for the locally famous chili from Dan's ancient, food-stained recipe. One of Big Dan's secrets was to simmer the chili a good long time and to every hour add a dollop or two of rotgut whiskey.

There was no shortage of rotgut whiskey in Tigerville.

"Set me up, sweet sister," Cass said, slapping both open, gloved hands down atop the bar. "Long ride in from the Broken Heart. I feel like I've just crossed the Mojave at high summer."

Annabelle had crouched to place two more bottles atop the shelf. Now she straightened and gave her brother an angry, pointed look, shaking her head with genuine befuddlement. "Why, Cass? Why are you here?"

Cass manufactured a look of hurt and surprise. "What do you mean, sweet sis? I'm your older brother, ain't I? Ain't it a girl's older brother's duty to look after her?" He lowered his eyes to the cleavage of her

114

corset. "Especially when that sister's indiscreet life choices have caused her to become quite the topic of local scandal? Whoo-ee! I sure see why too. A vision you are, Annabelle. Quite the under-dressed one, I might add."

Annabelle planted her hands on the edge of the bar, leaning forward, anger hardening her jaws. "Go home and leave me alone, Cass."

"Set me up."

"No."

"Set me up."

"You hate me. You're not here to protect my honor. You're only here to remind me of what happened to you."

Cass reached out quickly, wrapped his right hand around her left one, and squeezed. His red-rimmed eyes blazed behind the mask. "Of what you did to me!"

"I was only fighting you off. You tried to take a bullwhip to me, Cass. Your own sister. You threatened to whip off every stitch of my clothes! I saw the lamp hanging on the nail, and I grabbed it. I didn't intend for what happened. I only wanted you to leave me alone." She struggled against his hand. "Let me go, Cass — you're hurting me!"

"Sure, sure." Cass curled a nostril behind the mask, making the sacking shift, and released her hand. "I'll let you go . . . so's you can set me up. Come on, pour your brother the good stuff!"

Rubbing her wrist, she said, "Go away and leave me alone. You've no business here. I'm sorry about what happened to you, but it wasn't my fault!"

"I know."

That rocked Annabelle back on her high heels. She blinked. "What?"

"Set me up."

She glanced at him skeptically. He looked directly back at her, his eyes unwavering.

She could see the pain in them — constant and excruciating, and which lay beyond the physical torment of pus constantly erupting from the scars behind the mask. Remembering the horrors of that night, the flames shooting out of the lamp as she smashed it against her brother's head, Annabelle could once again hear his wails piercing the night, smashing it wide open and cleaving her heart.

She'd gladly go back in time and change what had happened that night if she could. She'd told herself that she didn't feel guilty. That what had happened to Cass hadn't been her fault. But she'd been lying to herself. She hadn't slept through an entire night since it had happened.

116

Maybe that was another reason she'd banished herself from the ranch, and taken the job here, humiliating herself right out in the open here in Tigerville. Maybe dolling up like a whore and letting men ogle her as though she were nothing more than a prime cut of beef was her way of punishing herself for what had happened to Cass, a once handsome young man. One with a drinking problem and a definite aversion to work, but one who, with his father's backing, still had had a bright future ahead of him.

Now he was a grisly specter every one turned away from with shudders of revulsion and clucks of sympathy. Annabelle didn't know if they were true, but she'd heard rumors that the only girls who'd sleep with him were two half-breed Sioux girls who ran a few cribs in Poverty Gulch at the western edge of Tigerville. Even they made him pay extra.

The least his sister could do was buy him a drink.

Chapter 10

Annabelle grabbed a bottle off a shelf on the back bar, a labeled bottle from one of the higher shelves. She set a goblet on the bar in front of her brother. She dug the cork out of the bottle, and half-filled the glass.

That was a lot of whiskey for this time of the morning. At least, for most people. Not for Cass. She used to begrudge him such a destructive indulgence. Not anymore.

He looked down at the drink. His pain-riddled eyes brightened. He smiled up at Annabelle, his teeth and pink gums showing inside the mask, then picked up the glass and threw back half of the whiskey.

He kept his head raised. He held the bourbon in his mouth for a good ten seconds, eyes closed, savoring the liquor, and then swallowed. Annabelle saw the swell roll down his throat in time with the liquid.

He blew out a held breath, lowered his head, and ran a hand across his mouth. His eyes locked on hers, and already she saw the shine of drunkenness in them. Of the beginning of a slight tempering of his pain.

She left the bottle on the bar and studied her brother uncertainly. "You don't blame me?"

"I said I didn't, didn't I?"

"Sometimes it's hard to know what you really mean. You often speak in riddles, Cass."

"All right. Let me be as plain as possible, little sis." Cass raised the glass, glanced at her bare shoulders and upper chest, and said, "Aren't you chilly?"

She glanced at the stove from which heat radiated. Besides, it was mid-summer, and already the temperature was likely in the upper seventies. But Cass knew she wasn't cold. He just wanted another reason to look at her in an unbrotherly fashion and to make mention of her skimpy attire. To rib her again, however indirectly.

As was his way. As had been his way even before the fire.

There was something bent in Cass Ludlow. Even their father knew it. Cass hadn't done a full day's job on the range in years. And he drank as though to quell some deep wound inside him, one even more severe than the scars on his face. One that must have been there since the moment he'd been conceived.

Cass grabbed the bottle and poured more whiskey into his glass. Staring down at the amber liquor, he said, "Let me make it as plain as possible, so there's no mistake. No, I don't blame you for what happened in the barn that night." He looked up at her, and all traces of humor left his eyes. "I blame that big grayback who charmed you senseless."

"Oh Christ, Cass!" Annabelle stepped back, folding her arms over her breasts. "How many men have to die before you and our father finally bury the hatchet?"

"Why do you admire him so, Annabelle? Look at all you've lost on account of him."

She looked at him, frowning. "What do you mean?"

"You've lost your family because you sold us out to him. To them — the Buchanons. And then, after you fought so hard with them *against your family,* and tended old Angus's wounds, all he did was turn his big, broad back on you." Cass laughed caustically and stretched his arms out to indicate her skimpy attire again. "Look at you! You're alone. Working in Big Dan's Saloon as a whore!"

Annabelle slapped the bar with her open

palm. "I'm not a whore. I just serve food and sling drinks!"

"Well, you dress like a whore." Cass chuckled again without mirth and took another sip of his whiskey.

"Hunter didn't turn his back on me. You know as well as I do that he lost everything, and he doesn't want us to marry until he can afford to give me the life he thinks I deserve."

"He thinks you deserve this life?"

"He didn't know it would come to this."

"How could he not see this comin'?" Cass laughed and ogled her again. "What did he think would happen? You aligned yourself with him and got yourself exiled by your father. There are not a lot of opportunities for single young ladies in Tigerville. The pretty ones sometimes have to —"

"He wants me to make up with Pa. I refuse. I've told him the money doesn't matter. That all I care about is . . ." Annabelle let the words trail off as she walked over to the stove and gave the chili a stir. She frowned pensively down at the thick chunks of beef and pinto beans swimming in the spicy tomato sauce, and said, plaintively, "If only that poke hadn't been stolen."

She set down the spoon and returned the lid to the pot, swinging abruptly around to

Cass, who'd just taken another sip of his drink and was setting the glass back down on the bar. "I wonder who stole it."

Cass looked at her, vaguely curious. "Stole what?"

"Hunter gathered gold dust into a sizable stake — over thirty thousand dollars' worth — so we could elope and start a new life together. He worked hard, prospecting in his spare time away from the ranch. He cached that dust away in an old mine shaft where he didn't think anyone would ever find it. When he and I went into the shaft to retrieve the gold, it was gone."

Annabelle settled her weight on one hip, cocked one foot forward, and studied her devious brother with growing suspicion. "Someone stole it out of that shaft. Someone who'd likely followed him or maybe followed *me* from the Broken Heart to the old cabin near the shaft where Hunter and I used to meet in secret. That person might have seen Hunter and me go into the shaft together, when Hunter first showed me the gold and asked me to marry him."

She paused, choking back tears of sorrow for all that might have been, the happiness that she and Hunter might have known had that gold not been stolen, had her father not waged war on the Buchanons. But she couldn't think about that now.

~~What was~~ done was done.

She shook off her sorrow ~~and~~ felt her heart beat faster, her suspicion and anger growing as she studied Cass with narrowed eyes and ridged brows. "Who would be that cunning? That malicious? Who would want to sabotage our love so badly? Who could that possibly be, Cass?"

Maybe the black-hearted brother who'd aligned himself with his Confederate-hating father? she silently added to herself.

Cass stared at her blankly. Then he stepped back and spread his arms, smoke from his cheroot writing a big gray circle in the air beside him. "Guilty as charged, sis. All right. You got me. Yep, it was me. Just couldn't deny myself that thirty thousand dollars. No, sir. Came in mighty handy, though, as you can judge by all them trips to Frisco and Mexico I been takin'. All the new duds I bought. Or . . . hmm."

He set his index finger against his bottom lip and furled his brows in a parody of deep thought. "Maybe I spent it all on the lovely young ladies here in Tigerville. Those that would allow me into their boudoirs, that is. But since the only ones who deign to let the monster into their lair are the sweet, plump little Mexican-Sioux gals over on Poverty

Gulch, that's probably rather unlikely, isn't it?"

He brushed his fingers through the air beside him, indicating the grisly specter grinning out at Annabelle from behind the mask.

Annabelle's cheeks warmed with chagrin. If Cass had found that gold, he'd have spent it in grand fashion. He'd probably have left Tigerville right after he'd found it, in fact. He'd probably be in San Francisco or Mexico, haunting the whorehouses and gambling parlors at all hours of the day and night. Surely there he'd have found a woman who, for the right price, would overlook the horrible disfigurement of his face.

But he'd remained at the ranch with his and Annabelle's overbearing father. As far as Annabelle could tell, he hadn't even bought any new clothes over the year since that gold had disappeared. And he was riding the same horse, wearing the same six-gun.

Annabelle looked down at her hands now, sucking her cheeks in shame. "I'm sorry, Cass."

"Don't be. You know me only too well's all." Cass splashed more whiskey into his glass and flashed his sidelong, coyote-like grin. "I'd have suspected me too."

"Tell me something."

Cass sipped the whiskey, then set the glass down on the bar. "Anything, sweet sister. You know that." His words were becoming a little slurred.

"Does Pa really think I'm working as a whore?"

Cass snorted. "What do you care what Pa thinks?"

Annabelle looked away again. Indeed, why should she care what her father thinks? Graham Ludlow may have been her father but he was a ghastly human being, a murderer whom she'd disowned every bit as much as he'd disowned her.

Graham Ludlow could go to hell.

Still, she found herself caring whether he thought she was working the rooms upstairs with the two half-breed girls, the Chinese girl, and the white girl, Ginny, who were still asleep in their cribs and would likely remain asleep until right before noon, when their working day usually started. They'd stumble sleepily and grumpily downstairs for a late breakfast before retiring to their rooms again until the light taps of their "gentlemen" callers started sounding on their doors.

Annabelle would care no more about what

her father thought. Doing so had been an old habit.

She'd been aware of Cass's eyes on her, studying her, for the past full minute. Now his voice came, quietly enticing: "Why don't you come back with me today?"

Annabelle turned to him where he stood crouched over his drink, arms encircling his refilled glass and the bottle, his cheroot sending up a slender, billowing smoke ribbon. Sounds from the street grew louder as the sun climbed and intensified.

"You know that's impossible."

Cass shook his head. "Things have changed." He drew the cheroot to his mouth, took a puff, and blew the smoke out against the back bar. He smiled at her, narrowing one devious eye. "Guess who we got for a guest out at the ranch these days?"

"Please, let's not play games, Cass. I have a lot of work to do before —"

"Earnshaw."

She stared at him, glowering incredulously. "Kenneth?"

"One and the same."

"What's he doing here?"

"What do you think?"

Annabelle shook her head obstinately. "He's not here for me!"

"His poppa's railroad has arrived in

126

Buffalo Gap. Thus, young Earnshaw's attentions have returned to the woman who spurned him but who he still loves and is bound and determined to marry!"

Cass slammed his hand down atop the bar and laughed.

Annabelle leaned toward Cass, feeling fire lancing from her eyes. "You can ride back to the Broken Heart and tell Kenneth Earnshaw as well as our father to go to —"

She stopped when an elderly, potbellied man in checked shirt, suspenders, and frayed bowler hat opened the saloon door and leaned inside. He was Beaver Clavin, local drunk and town crier.

Beaver's eyes bugged with excitement as he yelled around the fat cigar stub in his mouth, "Didja all hear that Marshal Winslow done found yesterday's stage in a broken heap beside the trail south of town? Looks like it was struck by outlaws, and *everyone's dead!*"

Beaver swung around and trundled off to continue spreading the grisly news on down the street.

CHAPTER 11

"Welcome to your new home, Laura," Hunter told Tigerville's new schoolteacher riding behind him on the paint horse he'd acquired in Dead Horse Canyon.

The paint had belonged to one of the killers whom Hunter had killed the night before. The horse he was trailing, a ewe-necked dun, had belonged to the other killer. It was over the dun that both killers now rode belly-down, wrists tied to ankles beneath the dun's broad barrel.

Bobby Lee rode the dun, as well, sitting between the two dead men, resembling nothing so much as a coyote sultan riding off to war on a camel.

Hunter glanced over his shoulder to see Laura looking around at the first shacks and stock pens and clapboard and log business buildings pushing up along the trail around them, where the old army and stagecoach trail dovetailed with Tigerville's main street.

It was midmorning, and the booming town was bustling, with men and women — mostly women of the painted variety — milling every which way. Already, raucous piano music was pattering away behind swinging saloon doors, and men were standing around on boardwalks with soapy beer mugs in their fists.

Hunter saw that Laura's cheeks had gone a little pale as she continued to turn her head from left to right and back again, taking it all in. She probably hadn't expected to find such a wild frontier town way up here in the Black Hills, far from the beaten path. Looking around himself, Hunter had to admit that Tigerville was a wild little place.

The town consisted of a dozen or so streets and avenues, and most of those streets and avenues were well peppered with saloons, whorehouses, and gambling parlors in addition to the obligatory mercantiles, grocery stores, butcher shops, gun and feed stores, harness shops, and even a few ladies' fine dress shops and millineries. But mostly the impression, while riding down the main thoroughfare, was of a hectic little Sodom and Gomorrah. Not nearly as sin-soaked as, say, Deadwood Gulch, fifty miles north, but well on its way.

As Hunter kept the paint and the dun moving, he saw ladies acting unladylike, yelling obscenities down at the men from second- and third-floor balconies. Most had little on. He saw a couple wearing nothing at all but fur boas and high-heeled shoes.

He came upon a pretty young blond in a poke bonnet and frilly yellow dress handing out little scraps of paper from a wicker basket hooked over her arm. Smiling as sweetly as the parson's daughter on Easter Sunday, she strode along the street's right side, shoving the cards at the men standing in clusters or hurrying from one side of the street to the other. As she approached Hunter and Laura, she smiled a crooked-toothed smile up at Hunter and, squinting against the bright morning sunlight, shoved a card into his hand and said, "Here you go, sir. Come an' see us sometime — without the lady. Or you can both come. However you like it!"

She winked then flounced away, not so much as giving the grisly cargo on Hunter's packhorse so much as a second glance but merely greeting Bobby Lee with, "Hello, pretty puppy."

That wasn't surprising — at least the part about her not acknowledging the dead men wasn't. Lots of folks mistook Bobby Lee for a dog simply because they weren't used to seeing domesticated coyotes in town. The citizens of Tigerville witnessed shootings on the streets or in the saloons nearly every day, and nearly every day they woke to a body or two in the muddy gutters or squirreled away behind outhouses or wood piles.

"What does it say?" Laura asked, peering over Hunter's shoulder at the scrap of paper in his gloved left hand.

Buchanon glanced at her. "Sure you want to know?"

"Yes," she said.

"All right. Don't say I didn't warn you."

He held the card up for the woman to read the two sentences in ornate black typescript: *"Join the party at the Harem Club. Men taken in and done for just one dollar!"*

"Oh dear."

"Yeah."

Hunter let the breeze take the note as he continued walking the paint down the festive main drag of Tigerville, which, as wild as it was now, had been wilder only a few years ago, in the years right after the war when he and his father and two brothers had come to this country from Georgia.

Back then, Tigerville and the hills around it had been a hotbed of bloody violence. This was right after General George Armstrong Custer had opened the Hills to gold-seekers in 1874, despite the Hills still belonging to the Sioux Indians, as per the Laramie Treaty of 1868.

Men and mules and horses and placer mining equipment poured up the Missouri River from Kansas and Missouri by river-boat and mule- and ox-train, and the great Black Hills Gold Rush exploded.

Naturally, crime also exploded, in the forms of claim-jumping and bloody murder as well as the stealing of gold being hauled by ore wagons, called Treasure Coaches, southwest to Cheyenne, Wyoming, and the nearest railroad. Tigerville was on the Cheyenne-Custer-Deadwood Stage Line, and the coaches negotiating that formidable country were preyed upon even more than they were now by road agents.

For those bloody reasons, the commissioners of Pennington County, chief among them Annabelle's father Graham Ludlow, brought in so-called lawman Frank Stillwell and the small gang of hardtails who rode with him, also calling themselves "lawmen." Bona fide crime dwindled while the death rate went up. It was said in these parts that you couldn't ride any of the roads spoking out of Tigerville and into the surrounding hills without coming upon Stillwell's low-hanging "tree fruit" in the form of hanged men.

Men hanged without benefit of trial.

Many of those men had once fought for the Confederacy. It seemed that most of the "tree fruit" Stillwell "grew" hailed from the South, which wasn't one bit fishy at all, given Stillwell's history of being second-in-command of one of the worst Union prisoner-of-war camps during the Civil War and having a widely known and much-talked-about hatred for the warriors of the old South.

Animosity between the Northern and Southern fighters had abated since Stillwell had been killed in last year's trouble that had pitted him along with the Ludlows and Max Chaney against the Buchanons. War memories and grudges were fading at long last, but last year's eruption of trouble had left both families — the Buchanons and the Ludlows — badly scarred. Battered to the point they would likely never recover, Hunter reflected with an inward flinch as a rusty knife of his own personal pain twisted in his heart.

"Hey, Buchanon — what you got there?"

The man's query, shouted from a board-walk fronting the Black Hills–Cheyenne stage manager's office sandwiched between

133

Howell's Tonic Emporium and Thomas C. Wannamaker's Justice of the Peace office, lassoed Hunter's consciousness and dragged him back into present-day Tigerville and the situation at hand.

Five men were standing around outside the stage office, between the office itself and the hitchrack at which six saddled horses were tied. The horses were sweat-matted; they'd been ridden hard. The five men were obviously the ones who'd done the hard riding, for their suitcoats and Stetsons were liberally floured in trail dust.

Hunter recognized all five as men from right here in Tigerville. A couple — Mel Fitzgerald and Warren Davenport — were both businessmen who served on the city council. Another — the big, burly "Iron Bill Todd" was a blacksmith, market hunter, and sawyer. The other two — Denny Hutton and Marcus Wheeler — were shopkeepers. Deputy U.S. Marshal Walt Winslow had apparently gathered these men into a posse to ride out in search of the stage.

Winslow had been sent from the territorial capital of Yankton to hold down the proverbial fort here in Tigerville since Sheriff Frank Stillwell's demise last year along with all of Stillwell's outlaw "deputies" having been turned down in what was

134

locally known as the Buchanon-Ludlow-Chaney War. Stillwell's successor, a town marshal appointed by the city fathers until they could elect another sheriff and seat deputies, had only been in office six weeks before he was shot in the back by a drunk doxie in a whorehouse unfittingly if imaginatively called The Library. After that, for understandable reasons, it had been hard to find a man or men who valued their lives so little as to don the badge of Tigerville Town Marshal.

Or county sheriff, for that matter.

"We thought you was dead!" said Mel Fitzgerald, a small man in a bowler hat and holding an old, double-barrel shotgun on his left shoulder. A stogie smoldered between his thin lips.

Hunter drew the paint up to the hitchrack's right end. "It was close."

Big Bill Todd, who was as big as Hunter but a good ten years older, stepped up to the edge of the boardwalk, looked gravely up at Hunter, and said, "We rode out last night, about an hour after you was expected here in town. We found the coach."

He paused, drew his mouth corners down beneath his shaggy gray mustache. "We saw poor ol' Charley layin' there in the trail. Brought him and the other fella to town.

135

They're at the undertaker's."

"We tried to track you, but it got too dark," said the other city councilman, Warren Davenport, a tall, flat-eyed, raw-boned man in early middle age. "Then this mornin', the trail was too damn cold for any of us old farts to track you. Winslow brought us back to town. He's in the manager's office now, palaverin' with Sullivan about what to do next. Reckon he won't have to do *nothin'* next now, though, 'cept bury poor Charley, that is."

His baleful bulldog eyes shifted to the dun over which the two dead men drooped.

"Buchanon!" exclaimed the station manager, Scotty Sullivan, who, apparently having heard Hunter palavering with the others, had pulled open his office door to stare in shock at the big blond jehu and his badly rumpled female charge. "What the hell happened?"

His round-framed spectacles glinted in the sunlight. He quickly doffed his bowler hat, glanced sheepishly at Laura, and said, "Uh . . . pardon my French, please, Miss."

Hunter had swung down from his horse and was tying the paint at the hitchrack. Bobby Lee leaped down off the dun's back and shot after a cat he'd spied poking its head out from a break between buildings

136

on the street's opposite side. "What can I tell you, Scotty?" Hunter said in disgust. "We got hit. Charley's dead. Bushwhacked."

U.S. Deputy Marshal Walt Winslow stepped up beside Sullivan in the open doorway of the stage manager's office — a short, gray-haired man who resembled a sharp-featured, straight-backed, flinty-eyed Lutheran minister in his black suit, bullet-crowned black hat, crisp white shirt, and black foulard tie. Only, Winslow was more of a minister of justice as attested the age-tarnished moon-and-star badge pinned to the vest and peeking out from behind his left coat lapel.

Winslow had his pale, slender fingers dipped into the pockets of his vest, near the silver-washed chain of a hidden pocket watch. A thin, carefully trimmed mustache mantled his small mouth.

"There's one more. Ike Talon."

Winslow widened his eyes and nodded once, slowly, obviously stirred by the information. He'd been after Talon ever since Talon had come to this country to haunt the Black Hills trails, so he was well aware of Talon's reputation. With fresh interest, Winslow glanced at the two dead men slumped over the dun, then turned to Buchanon, his flinty eyes sharp.

137

"Is Talon still out there?" He jerked his head to the south.

Hunter reached up to help Laura down from the paint's back. When he'd set her gently on the ground, he took her hand and led her up onto the boardwalk.

As he did, the five men in Winslow's posse doffed their hats and cleared their throats deferentially to the pretty but bedraggled young woman, shuffling aside to make way for her and the jehu as they would for any two survivors of any fierce battle.

Especially when they'd survived such an infamous group as Talon's notorious bunch.

Hunter moved up to where Sullivan and Winslow stood atop the three steps leading up to the office door, gazed directly at the marshal, and said, "I got a feeling I know where Talon is. I'll see to him . . ." He slid his glance to Scotty Sullivan and hardened his jaws as he finished his thought. ". . . for Charley."

Winslow said, "That's not your job, son."

"I'm makin' it my job."

"No vigilante justice." Winslow smiled coldly, narrowed his hard eyes a little, and shook his head once, slowly. "Not on my watch."

"Don't worry," Buchanon said. "He'll get his chance." He looked at Sullivan and then at Laura, flanking Hunter. "Scotty, this is Miss Laura Meyers. She was the other passenger on the stage."

"Miss Meyers," Scotty said, "it is indeed a pleasure."

"The pleasure is mine," Laura said, taking one step forward on her battered bare feet. The posse men were trying hard not to stare at the revealingly torn dress that was all but hanging off of her. "I am the new schoolteacher here in Tigerville, Mister . . ."

"This is Scotty Sullivan, Laura," Hunter said.

He knew right away he shouldn't have used her first name. They'd spent a night together on the run. Now he was using her first name.

Hmmm.

That "Hmmm" was on every face around Buchanon and Laura.

"Laura Meyers," he quickly corrected. "She's here to teach school."

Hunter could feel eyes on them both, studying them both critically, especially the woman's torn dress and obvious beauty despite the beating she'd taken.

"Mister Sullivan!" a female voice called above the din of the bustling street. "Mister Sullivan!"

A familiar voice to Hunter's ears.

Hunter's heartbeat quickened.

He and all of the men around him as well as Laura turned to where a scantily clad redhead with long dangling earrings the same green color as her eyes pushed through a small crowd of men standing outside of the Justice of the Peace's office, listening in on Hunter's conversation with Sullivan. Annabelle Ludlow stepped up onto the boardwalk, looking flushed and shaken, her eyes wide with worry.

She strode a little uncertainly in her high heels toward Sullivan and said, "Scotty, is it true?" she fairly screamed. "Tell me Hunter's not —"

Her eyes found Buchanon and she stopped dead in her tracks. Relief instantly washed over her, her eyes opening even wider, lower jaw falling. She slid her eyes to the pretty albeit disheveled woman standing close beside Hunter, and deep lines cut across her otherwise smooth forehead.

Buchanon held his left hand out to take Annabelle's hand in his, to assure her that he was unharmed. The blood appeared to run out of her face. She stumbled backward in her high heels. Her eyes rolled back in her head, her chin shot up like the prow of a boat cresting a stormy ocean wave. She swung half-around to face the street, then fell straight back into Hunter's outstretched arms with a high-pitched, raking exhalation.

"Annabelle!" he said, wrapping his arms around her slender, curvy frame, looking into her face, her eyelids fluttering. "Annabelle!"

"Passed out, poor girl," said one of the posse members behind Hunter.

"Couldn't take the shock of it, I reckon," muttered another. "All of it."

Another man chuckled dryly.

Hunter crouched, shifting his left arm around Annabelle's shoulders while snaking his right arm under the girl's knees, lifting her off the boardwalk and up against his chest. He glanced a little sheepishly at the men around him. More men had gathered from the street, for there was obviously something interesting happening out in front of the stage manager's office — interesting even beyond what usually transpired on the streets of this rollicking boomtown on any given day.

"That's Annabelle?" Laura asked, gazing at the girl in Hunter's arms, obviously a little surprised to see his once-betrothed so scantily clad.

Hunter understood. He hadn't gotten used to it either.

Flushing with embarrassment as well as

with shame at what his lovely Annabelle had become over the past year, in the wake of the war between his family and hers, he looked from Sullivan to Laura and said, "I best tend to her. Just appears a might overcome with the vapors. I'll get her into a bed over at Big Dan's and then come back to get you settled in over at the school, Laur— er, I mean, Miss Meyers."

Laura gave him a sympathetic smile.

Another man chuckled.

CHAPTER 12

Annabelle in his arms, Hunter started across the street, looking both ways and hurrying ahead of a wagon moving toward him from one direction and pausing to let another wagon, moving toward him from the other direction, pass in front of him.

As he did, through dust lifting from churning wagon wheels and pounding horse hooves, he caught sight of a man standing out front of Big Dan Delaney's Saloon & Gambling Parlor. He couldn't see the man well, because Hunter was too busy trying to avoid being run over, and the dust obscured the man, as well, but he had the vague impression of something off about the man's features.

When he'd let a couple of horseback riders pass then hurried to the opposite side of the street, he headed north along the various boardwalks fronting the shops, saloons, and pleasure houses. He looked ahead toward Big Dan's place again.

The man he'd seen before, and who'd appeared to be staring toward Hunter and Annabelle, was no longer on the boardwalk fronting the saloon. Vaguely, Hunter noticed a rider on a big steeldust horse riding away from Dan's, and he even more vaguely noticed that the man was brightly attired in the Mexican style, as the man staring at him had been, but Hunter's main consideration was Annabelle, so he let the observer slip from his mind.

He crossed a street intersecting with Dakota Avenue, avoided a nasty collision with an ore dray rolling into town from one of the mines in the surrounding bluffs, and skirted a couple of dogs skirmishing over a dead rabbit. Quickening his pace as he approached the saloon in which Annabelle had taken a job as, of all things, a saloon girl, he saw Big Dan striding toward him from the north.

Big Dan was broader than he was tall, and he carried most of that weight in his gut. But he was fancily attired in a green-checked suit with a silk-banded black opera hat and a long, green cutaway coat, with spats on his shoes. He was proudly adorned with gold cuff links, and a diamond stickpin impaled the knot of his black cravat.

Big Dan Delaney had worked the mines with picks, shovels, and water pumps before building a stake for himself and buying the saloon, formerly the Red Rooster, from a mean drunk named Paul Elsbernd. Looking at him now, you'd never suspect Big Dan of the lowly rock-breaker and notorious, thuggish carouser he once had been.

Now he played the part — or at least dressed the part — of a respectable businessman and gentleman of some repute, always attiring himself to the nines, wielding a cherry walking stick with a carved wooden handle, and smoking a meerschaum pipe. He walked with his spade-bearded chin in the air, lowering it only to nod at the ladies before twisting his head to appraise their retreating behinds.

"Good Lord!" Big Dan exclaimed as he and Hunter both approached the saloon's front door from equal distances but from opposite sides. "What happened to my gal?"

Dan's referring to Annabelle as "his gal" graveled Hunter. He'd heard Dan blustering before to others: "Have you seen my new gal?" "Come on over to Big Dan's and check out my new gal, fellas. Graham Ludlow's daughter is now slingin' drinks for me in fine form!" He'd guffaw loudly enough to be mistaken for an approaching thunderstorm.

"She's not your gal, Dan," Hunter said, shouldering through the saloon's batwing doors and starting across the dim, cave-like room toward the stairs at the far end. The aromas of cooking chili saturated the air, as they did all times of the day and night. Big Dan might not have had the most comely girls working his upstairs cribs, but they were only fifty cents, and the chili, thirteen cents a bowl but only ten with a five-cent beer, was the main attraction.

Until he'd hired Graham Ludlow's comely, redheaded daughter to sling drinks for him, that was.

"Don't tell me she got hit on the street!" Dan thundered behind Hunter. "This will not stand — oh dear Lord! She's my biggest moneymaker and she never even takes a turn on her back. Have you summoned a doctor?"

Folks were forever getting hit by passing wagons on the streets of Tigerville. Most of those folks getting hit, however, were usually intoxicated. But there were always one or two who'd simply made a miscalculation of the traffic currents and got themselves hammered by a horse or an iron-shod wheel.

As he mounted the stairs, Hunter glanced at the big, garishly clad man standing in the middle of the room behind him, Big Dan's eyes and furred mouth wide in shock, likely anticipating a big drop in business if Annabelle was to be bedridden or worse, and not flouncing about the saloon to the delight of Big Dan's lusty, lowly regulars.

"She just fainted," Hunter said. "I'm gonna put her in a bed."

"Oh, thank heavens!" Dan exclaimed through a blowing exhalation. "She alone has nearly doubled my business over the past month!"

Hunter's cheeks warmed with rage as he continued up the stairs and into the musty second-floor hall. He saw a door standing partway open on his right. He kicked the door wide, stepped into the room, and stopped.

He glowered at a half-naked man lying on the bed before him, belly-down, arms spread out to either side of his head — a skinny gent, with a tangled mess of long, ginger-colored hair. The man was loudly sawing logs and muttering in his sleep.

"Christ," Hunter grumbled as he swung around and headed back out the door.

The man must have been a leftover customer from the night before. He'd probably passed out drunk and the girls hadn't been able to wake him so they could usher him out after the business transaction had been completed.

"Annabelle! Oh, my good heavens — what *happened*?"

Hunter turned to see a girl dressed in only a camisole, pantaloons, pink slippers, and with feathers in her sleep-mussed hair, staring at him from a half-open door ahead and on his left. She was a little brunette named Ginny, Hunter knew only because once Annabelle had started working at Big Dan's, Hunter had learned everything he could about the place.

"She'll be all right," Hunter told the girl. "Which one is her room?"

Ginny hurried out of her room, glancing with concern at Annabelle in Hunter's arms, dragging the heels of her overlarge slippers, and opened a door on the hall's left side. "This one's Annabelle's. Are you sure she'll be all right?"

"Yes. Thanks, Ginny."

"What happened?"

"I'll let her tell it."

"She didn't get hit out in the street, did she?"

"No."

"I had a friend — Millie — who got flattened by a lumber dray. Deader'n a door nail, poor girl!"

148

Hunter carried Annabelle into the room and gentled her onto the double brass bed. Remaining in the doorway, Ginny placed one slippered foot atop the other and twisted a finger into her long, straight hair. "You're Hunter Buchanon, ain't ya?"

She flashed a coquettish smile.

Hunter crouched over Annabelle, feeling her neck for a pulse. "That's right."

Hunter was no *medico,* but her pulse felt strong.

"How could you let her get away?" Ginny looked at Annabelle. "She's just about the prettiest girl in town. Too bad she ain't workin' the line. If she was, she'd make a whole lot more money than she is just —"

Hunter turned to the girl in the doorway, glaring. "Annabelle's not a whore!"

Ginny widened her eyes with a start, then cast Hunter a boldly skeptical look. "Sometimes, you know, Mister Buchanon, when a girl don't have a man to look after her, she often has to turn to the world's oldest profession just to survive."

"Would you leave us alone, Ginny?"

"Just sayin'," Ginny said, turning away haughtily and shuffling loudly off down the hall.

Hunter felt a hand close over his left one, which he'd wrapped around Annabelle's

149

forearm. He looked down at Annabelle's hand atop his. She stared up at him through green eyes that complemented so beautifully her copper red hair.

"Are you all right?" Hunter asked.

Annabelle sat up, gazing into his eyes, her own eyes round as silver dollars, worry lines creasing their corners. "Are you?"

"I'm fine. No worse for the wear."

"Beaver Clavin said the stage was hit, that you were dead."

"He was only half-right."

Annabelle sagged back against the pillow with a sigh, her eyes remaining on his. "Oh, Hunter . . ."

"Yeah," he said, glancing down at her half-clad body. "I know." His tone was grave and not so subtly pitched with reproach. "Look at you."

"It's a job."

Hunter gave a caustic grunt. He opened his mouth to speak but stopped when Ginny's footsteps sounded in the hall again. He turned to the partly open door as the doxie poked her head into the room, extending a glass of water. "For Annabelle," she said timidly.

Annabelle lifted her head from the pillow. "Thank you, Ginny."

Hunter walked to the door and accepted

the water from the doxie, who glanced around him to say, "You gonna be all right, Annabelle? Big Dan's awful worried."

"Tell Dan I'll be back down to tend the chili in a minute."

Ginny laughed as she turned and shuffled back down the hall.

Hunter returned to the bed, gave Annabelle the water, and sat down on the bed's edge. "Why'd you faint?"

Annabelle shrugged a shoulder, glanced toward the curtained window. "I was just so certain you were dead. Then, when I saw you standing there . . . I don't know, I never figured myself for the fainting type of girl, but . . . ." She returned her gaze to his. "I don't know what I'd do if anything happened to you, Hunter."

He smiled and squeezed her hand. "Nothing's going to happen to me."

"It came close."

"Dumb luck. They caught us sitting like a rabbit in the grass."

"Why?"

"Ah, hell," Hunter said, wanting to avoid the subject. "I'd best get back over to the stage office. You sure you're gonna be all right?"

"Who is she?"

Hunter frowned. "Who's who?"

151

"You know very well who's who." Annabelle's tone had turned to tart anger. She glared up at him with a slow-boiling suspicion. "The pretty woman whose torn dress was hanging in ribbons off her buxom body."

"Oh, her." Hunter turned away, feeling his ears turn as hot as glowing coals. "She's the new schoolteacher here in Tigerville."

"What's her name?"

"Laura."

"Pretty name for a pretty woman. Married?"

"Not for long."

Annabelle glared up at him, her eyes hard as jade. "Hmm. Sounds right scandalous."

Hunter grinned. "Jealous?"

"No," Annabelle said pointedly, but her eyes gave the lie to her words. "You're a free man . . . just as I'm a free woman. That's the way you wanted it. That's the way you have it."

"Only because I couldn't give you the life you deserve."

"As if it's your place to decide what I deserve!" Her voice was getting louder, her tone sharper.

"I have nothing, Annabelle. A few dollars in my pocket, the clothes on my back. Pa can't work, so I'm supporting him too. Most

152

everything I make goes to the boarding house." Sorrow and frustration building in him, Hunter placed his hand on Annabelle's face, caressed her cheek with his thumb. "I'm off driving the stage more than I'm here in town. That's no life for a girl like you."

Tears glazed Annabelle's eyes. She punched the bed with the end of one fist and brushed her other fist across her nose. "Dammit all, Hunter! What happened to us?"

"Your father happened to us!" he heard himself blurt out through clenched teeth.

She stared up at him in shock. "You blame me, don't you?"

"No!"

"Yes, you do. I see it in your eyes." More tears glazed her eyes as she studied him probingly.

"It's not true, Annabelle."

Was it? No. He could never blame Annabelle for her father's actions.

But maybe deep inside he did harbor some resentment toward her, for the mere fact that she was a Ludlow. And that the Ludlows had killed his two brothers, almost killed his father, burned their ranch, and ruined whatever future he and Annabelle might have had together.

153

No. It wasn't true. He loved Annabelle more than life itself. That was why he hadn't gotten a decent night's sleep over the past year and walked around feeling as though he had a knife in his guts.

He loved her and couldn't have her. Oh, they could go ahead and get married. They could go through the motions. But what then? They might have a few good loving weeks together . . . before the strain of living in dire poverty drove a wedge between them.

Theirs had been a storybook romance. A story of secret trysts in remote cabins, of quiet afternoon horseback rides in sun-washed beaver meadows. Of making love in the soft grass and ferns lining a chuckling mountain stream in the shade of breeze-brushed aspens, to the piping of nuthatches and bluebirds.

If they married now, the way things were — both of them penniless — they'd soon share one of those sad marriages Hunter bore witness to every day around the old prospector shacks on Poverty Gulch and elsewhere in scattered claims throughout the Black Hills. They would be two sullen, sour, haggard people toiling for dimes, hating their lives and soon hating each other. Rarely speaking or touching. Just putting up with each other as they toiled to stay alive as though their lives were not worth living.

He couldn't abide such a life. Not for him and Annabelle.

"I think it's true, Hunter," Annabelle said, placing her hand on his own cheek now, gazing into his eyes as though trying to peer into his soul. "You blame me."

"I don't." Hunter rose from the bed and gazed down at her. "But don't you think it's time you stopped punishing me for my decision not to marry you and ruin your life?"

She frowned again, puzzled. "What are you talking about?"

"This." Hunter gestured at her skimpy attire. "You took this job . . . dress like this . . . to punish me." He shook his head defiantly. "It's not going to work. I won't ruin everything just because you've chosen to humiliate yourself in public. Go home, Annabelle. Your father can give you the life you deserve. I hate the bastard, but he can give you a better life than I can!"

Annabelle scrunched her face up with rage. "You go to hell, Hunter Buchanon!"

"All right." Hunter drew a breath, hardened his jaws, nodded slowly. "That's the last I'll say on the subject. You live however you want to live. I wash my hands of you."

Annabelle sat up and dropped her feet to the floor, screaming, "You go to hell!"

Hunter strode to the door, stopped, and turned back to her. He glanced at her corset again, at her long legs clad in sheer, skin-colored stockings, and said, "Be careful, Annabelle. If you start enjoying this life . . . how men look at you and fawn over you . . . you might not find a way out of it."

He turned and walked out.

Behind him, Annabelle screamed, *"Go to hell with Miss Meyers and don't you ever come back, you bastard!"*

CHAPTER 13

Fuming, Hunter descended the stairs to Big Dan's main drinking hall.

Dan stood at the bar, a beer, a shot of whiskey, and his opera hat on the mahogany bar before him. Ginny sat at a table near the potbellied stove in the room's center, pale bare legs crossed, smoking a cigarette. She hunched as though chilled.

Both pimp and whore stared dubiously at Hunter walking angrily down the stairs, blond brows sharply ridged above his eyes. He glanced at the pair only once, embarrassed by the outburst they'd obviously overheard upstairs.

As he gained the bottom of the stairs, a four-legged creature scurried into the saloon beneath the batwing doors, toenails clickety-clacking on the wood floor.

"Bobby Lee!" Hunter said, scowling curiously down at the coyote. "What in tarnation . . . ?"

"It's all right," Big Dan said, taking a drag off a stogie. "We've gotten used to that brush wolf in here. Follows the li'l gal around like a loyal dog, shows his teeth at the men who get too handsy." He grinned. "That's all right. Keeps 'em in line. Besides, some o' the boys regard him as a curiosity. A brush wolf in a saloon following around the purtiest li'l gal in Tigerville!" Ignoring Ginny's glare, he winked at Buchanon. "He adds interest in my place. I like that."

Bobby Lee was sniffing the floor like a dog on a scent, nails clacking. He must have caught the scent he was after because he suddenly shot past Hunter without so much as a glance at his master, then bolted up the stairs.

Hunter turned around to scowl after the brush wolf. "Well, I'll be damned. I was wonderin' where he disappeared to. I thought he was out in the countryside, hunting rabbits. That disloyal little snipe!"

Oh well, he thought. *At least he's looking after Annabelle.* It appeared that someone needed to. He'd always thought she'd had more sense than she obviously did.

To hell with her!

He continued on outside and then negotiated his way back across the street. The small crowd fronting the stage manager's office had dispersed. Laura was no longer there either. Neither was the dun horse hauling the dead killers. The only ones still present were Marshal Winslow and the stage manager, Scotty Sullivan. They were conversing on the boardwalk fronting the office.

As Hunter mounted the boardwalk, he looked around and said, "Where's the teacher?"

Sullivan and Winslow turned to him.

Winslow smiled and said, "We figured you had enough woman trouble on your hands, Buchanon. I had Warren Davenport take her over to the school in that fancy chaise of his, and help get her settled in. I'm having the luggage from the stage hauled back to town in a wagon. She and her portmanteaus should be reunited soon."

Hunter ignored the faintly mocking glint in both men's eyes.

"Dahl should take a look at her." Dr. Norton Dahl was the *medico* here in Tigerville.

"I suggested it," Winslow said. "She wouldn't hear of it."

"Pretty woman." Sullivan's mouth corners came up as his devious glance darted to Winslow before he continued to Hunter. "She looked a might reluctant to leave with Davenport. Kept calf-eyein' Big Dan's place, like maybe she'd prefer you introduced her to her new place of employment. The big blond Viking berserker who saved her from certain death at the hands of Ike Talon."

"Maybe you curled her pretty toes for her last night," opined Winslow.

He winked at Sullivan, who snorted and cleared his throat.

Hunter muttered peevishly under his breath, his mood still foul in the wake of his dustup with Annabelle. He had more important things to do than stand around here, being mocked by a Deputy U.S. Marshal getting too old for his job and the stage manager who spent as much time in the whorehouses around Tigerville as he did managing his part of the stage line.

Hunter stepped off the boardwalk and headed south.

"Where you headed, Buchanon?" the marshal called behind him.

Hunter didn't respond to the man's question. He just kept walking, his torment over Charley's unprovoked killing bubbling to the surface of his general malaise.

A good friend dead. His girl — his *former* girl — slinging drinks in a cathouse.

What next?

He stopped when he came to the shingle

marked DOCTOR NORTON DAHL, MD. He climbed a set of outdoor stairs to a rickety wood door. He tried the doorknob. Finding it locked, he knocked on the door. He could smell cigarette smoke oozing through the vertical cracks between the boards comprising the door. Loud, hacking coughing resounded from within the office as did the shambling of heavy feet.

Hunter knocked on the locked door again.

"I'm coming, for God's sake!" came Dahl's raspy voice. "I'm coming! I'm coming!" As the lock clattered and the door jerked inward, a large, round, bespectacled eye stole a look around the edge of the door. "By God, you better have money or your next stop is the bone orchard!"

That eye widened in recognition. A loosely rolled quirley dangled from one corner of the *medico*'s mustached mouth. "Oh, Buchanon." He coughed again, violently, then drew the door open a little wider. He exclaimed around the cigarette, "I'm damn tired of not getting paid. I gotta eat, too, same as everyone else!"

"Who didn't pay you?"

"The last fella I treated."

"Did he have a bullet in his arm? A big bald fella with a walrus mustache?"

Dahl nodded. "Took me almost an hour

161

to dig out that slug. I had to call three men in from the street to hold him down or I'd likely have cut his arm off!"

"Is he still here?" Hunter looked into the doctor's office behind the *medico.*

"No. He should be. He lost a lot of blood. He stumbled out of here — without paying me one bloody cent! — muttering something about how he'd get better treatment at the Payday Club. I told him to go on over to the Payday and die howling from the pony drip, and I would dance a happy little jig on his grave!"

In his late thirties, jaded, rumpled, and seedy, Dahl blew his own whiskey breath at Hunter. Cigarette smoke jetted from his nostrils.

"Thanks, Doc." Hunter whipped around and started down the stairs.

Behind him, the sawbones yelled, "Hey, the word goin' around is you're dead!"

"Not yet, Doc!"

Hunter negotiated his way across the busy main street again. A couple of street urchins, the orphan spawn of parlor girls, hounded him for pennies for rock candy. He dug what few coins he could spare from his pants and tossed them back over his shoulder. The orphans converged on them, snarling like wolves.

162

Hell, Hunter didn't have enough money for his own rock candy.

What he needed, though, was a drink. He'd get one soon to settle his nerves. First, though, he intended to kill Ike Talon. That right there would likely settle his nerves just fine. He would celebrate with a steak and all the trimmings, if he had that much coinage left in his pockets.

He found the Payday on the corner of Second Street and Third Avenue. It had been the first saloon and hotel in Tigerville, but now the town's growing heart had shifted to the east, abandoning and antiquating the place. Its second floor was a pleasure parlor and opium den run by a Chinaman everyone called Steve because they couldn't pronounce his real name. You patronized the Payday when you'd been kicked out of every other house in town or didn't have the jingle for better busthead and more attractive or talented women.

Hunter stepped over a black man passed out on the front step and pushed through the batwings. He took a quick look around at the shabby saloon boasting a half dozen tables at which a half dozen sullen men — mostly miners and ore haulers — nursed drinks and smoked. Two old-timers were playing checkers.

A tall gaunt man stood behind the bar with pomaded hair and a pinstriped shirt and bow tie. He stood like a statue, staring straight at Hunter without expression. The man's chest jerked as though something had suddenly come alive inside him, and he brought a white handkerchief to his mouth. The handkerchief was already spotted red but after he coughed into it so violently that he made Hunter's lungs feel like ground beef, and pulled it away from his mouth, it was redder.

He opened and closed his mustached mouth several times as he set the handkerchief down on the bar, and swallowed, eyes looking rheumy and sick.

A lunger.

Not seeing Talon in the dingy, smoky shadows around him, Hunter moved into the room and stopped six feet from the bar. The barman continued to look at him without interest. Hunter could hear the Chinaman, Steve, speaking a mix of Chinese and broken English beyond a curtained doorway flanking the barman, and another man speaking English, trying to understand what Steve was saying but apparently having a devil of a time.

"Big man, bald-headed gent with a walrus mustache," Hunter said to the barman.

The barman drew his mouth corners down. He slid his oily-eyed gaze to the stairs on his right. "Upstairs. End of the hall on the left."

Hunter swung around and headed for the stairs, taking the steps two at a time but moving quietly on the balls of his feet. He crossed the landing and then continued to the second floor.

He walked through the lingering fetor of the second-floor hall lit by only the single window at the end. He winced as the floorboards complained against his tread, moaning and groaning like old women on their deathbeds.

He stopped at the last door on his left, tilted his head toward the upper panel.

On the other side of the door, a young woman's voice said, "What are you doin', hon? You'd best stay in bed and —"

A man's deep voice said throatily, "Shut up, you damn fool!"

Hunter stepped back, drew the LeMat, clicked the hammer back, and smashed the underside of his right foot against the door, just beneath the knob. As the door exploded inward, wood slivers flying from the frame, Hunter saw Talon, clad in only red longhandles and a gun belt and pistol, raise a double-barrel shotgun and level it on the doorway.

Talon gave a savage grin, the white line of his teeth showing beneath his thick, black walrus mustache.

Hunter threw himself to the left a half a wink before rose-colored flames blossomed from one of the shotgun's two large maws. The buckshot caromed through the open door and blew a pumpkin-size hole in the wall on the hall's opposite side. The second blast came another half a wink on the heels of the first, carving another generous hole in the wall two feet above where Hunter had struck on his left shoulder and hip on the hall floor.

Inside Talon's room, the soiled dove screamed shrilly.

Hunter rose to his knee and thrust his LeMat through the open door in time to see big Ike Talon drop the shotgun and hurl himself out the window on the room's far side. Glass shattered as Talon dropped straight down beneath the window and out of sight.

A loud thump and a groan sounded from below.

Hunter rose and ran across the room. The whore, sitting up on the bed and covering herself with a sheet, pressing her hands to her ears, was still screaming as though she were being tortured by a dozen Apache braves with sharp knives.

Hunter poked the LeMat through the broken window.

Below, a secondary roof sloped down away from the main building. Talon had just gained his feet. His left arm was in a blood-stained sling. As he ran down the sloping roof toward the far edge, he twisted around and hurled a shot from the Colt in his right fist toward Hunter, who flinched as the bullet screeched past his left ear to break the dresser mirror behind him.

The whore screamed even louder. The screams felt like two open palms slammed again and again against Hunter's ears.

"Christalmight, lady — shut up!" he yelled as he poked the LeMat out the broken window again.

He fired two rounds but one round only chewed wood from the edge of the roof and the other flew through the air where Talon's big, longhandle-clad body had been a moment before, just before he'd hurled himself with a loud curse off the roof and into the alley flanking the Payday.

A wooden crash came from below.

Hunter leaped through the window.

He struck on the roof ten feet below, bending his knees and hurling himself forward, rolling twice, then rising to his feet and gazing out over the edge of the roof and into the alley. He raised the LeMat and tracked Talon as the man ran, limping, down the alley to Hunter's right. Buchanon fired just as the man darted around the front corner of a building on the alley's opposite side.

Hunter's slug struck brick and mortar with a resounding spang.

Buchanon cursed.

Talon slid his face out around the corner of the building covering him. He grinned at Hunter and made a lewd gesture, then pulled his head back out of sight.

CHAPTER 14

Hunter cursed again, fury burning in him.

He quickly replaced the LeMat's spent cartridges with fresh, spun the wheel, then leaped off the edge of the roof and onto the now-scattered pile of shipping crates that Talon had used to cushion his fall. The crates were no longer piled as high as they had been for Talon, but they broke Hunter's fall enough that, bending his knees to distribute the impact, then rolling onto his right shoulder, he managed not to break any bones.

He gained his feet and ran. He stopped near the front corner of the brick building around which Talon had disappeared and edged a look around the wall, half-expecting Talon to be waiting for him in ambush. Talon was just then dashing between two buildings roughly fifty yards east along the narrow street that was home to a livery stable, a farrier's shop, small orphanage, and three or four whores' cribs. Talon was heading east, back toward the main drag.

He was probably hoping to lose himself in Tigerville's hustling, bustling Dakota Avenue crowd.

Hunter pushed away from the brick building and ran north. He darted into the break into which Talon had vanished. He ran through the break, crossed another side street, then ran through another break, frightening a trash-scrounging cur that gave a sharp yip and ran away with its tail between its legs. When Hunter surfaced from the break, he found himself on Dakota Avenue, confronted by a swelter of dusty traffic and the din of men and women selling and bartering, dogs barking, horses whinnying, and by the sharp cracks of mule skinners' whips over the backs of ore drays' six-mule hitches.

Hunter looked around, catching a brief glimpse of red in a thinly roiling dust cloud ahead and on his right. He ran toward the splash of faded red ensconced in clay-colored dust. As he gained on the fleeing figure, Ike Talon glanced over his left shoulder at the man in pursuit. Talon stopped and wheeled, whipping up his revolver.

Hunter ducked as the gun belched, flames lapping from the barrel. The bullet thumped into an awning support post to Hunter's left, making a stout basket matron in a feathered hat scream in fear.

Hunter straightened, extended the LeMat, and steadied the big popper in his right hand, not wanting to send a bullet into a passing bystander. As Talon turned to run nearly straight north down the middle of the street, Hunter fired. Talon screamed, grabbed the back of his left leg, and fell.

Hunter ran forward.

He dove beneath a parked farm wagon on his left when Talon whipped his gun around again and fired two more angry rounds from his right shoulder and hip. The killer bellowed an enraged curse, then stiffly gained his feet and ran forward, dragging his left leg.

He stopped as two horses materialized out of the swirling dust before him. They were the first two horses of a four-horse hitch pulling a big, high-sided mine supply wagon.

"Outta the way, you simple fool!" yelled the burly teamster sitting on the wagon's driver's seat a good six feet above the street.

The word "fool" hadn't entirely left his lips before the first two horses bulled into Talon. It was as though the man was swallowed by a maelstrom of charcoal dust inside of which horse heads bobbed. The killer disappeared completely from Hunter's view as the horses and wagon thundered toward Buchanon and then passed him on his right.

The driver screamed, *"WHO-AHHH! WHO-AHHHH, you mangy no-good cayuses!"*

As the wagon slowed, out from beneath it rolled the dusty bedraggled form of Ike Talon. Talon rolled onto his belly and lay writhing, mewling like a gut-shot dog. He was nearly straight out in the street beyond Hunter, who had gained his feet and regarded the battered killer with his heart chugging heavily, pumping poison blood through his veins.

Good. Talon was still alive.

Traffic had come to a standstill to the north and south. The dust still sifted over Talon. The driver of the wagon that had turned him into a battered human andiron came running from the front of the wagon, duster flopping at his sides and swaying around the high tops of his mule-eared boots.

"Oh lordy, lordy, lordy!" the mule skinner howled, stopping and staring down, aghast, at Ike Talon. "I didn't see ya there, pard!"

Hunter walked out into the street.

The driver looked at him from beneath

172

the brim of his weather-stained sombrero. "I didn't see him. Honest, I didn't. What blame fool runs down Dakota Avenue half-dressed this time of the day?"

"A dead one."

Hunter kicked Talon onto his back. Talon groaned and snarled like a wounded wolf. He was all scraped and scratched. His torn longhandle top hung down over his right shoulder. His left arm was broken. Hunter saw the telltale bulge.

Hunter smiled down at the man. "How you feelin', Ike?"

Talon cursed and howled and kicked his legs. Blood stained the dirt around the left one. "Call the doc! Call the doc!"

"I don't think the doc is gonna let you crap on his step again, you old dog." Hunter pressed his left boot down on Talon's left arm, over the bulge.

Talon's eyes opened wide and all the blood drained out of his face. He made a high-pitched strangling sound in his throat.

"How's that feel, Ike? Doesn't look too good at all. But then, Charley Anders didn't look too good layin' out on that trail after you ambushed him, killin' him in cold blood, neither."

The mule skinner looked at Hunter slack-jawed, then backed away slowly. "Holy crap

173

in the deacon's privy — you two got history . . ."

He continued to back away as though he'd just found himself confronted by an escaped lion from a traveling circus show.

Hunter had made little note of him. His attention was on the man who'd led the gang that had attacked his stage and murdered his friend. Hunter raised the LeMat, angling it down at a forty-five-degree angle, and drew a bead on Talon's left arm, just above the bulge.

Talon stared up at him, eyes glazed with horror. "What're you . . . what're you . . . *ach-ohhhhh!*" he screamed on the heels of the flat, resounding crack of the big LeMat and the bullet drilling into the bone of his left arm, halfway between his elbow and shoulder.

Talon lay writhing and bawling, rocking from side to side, clenching his hands together over his belly.

"That was for Charley," Hunter said.

He shot the man in his other arm, near the previous wound.

"That was for the drummer."

Talon kicked and screamed. He ground his spurs into the ground and tried to shove himself forward along the ground.

Hunter shot the man in his left knee.

"That was for the young lady your men tried to savage."

Talon yelped and cried. "Stop! You're crazy! Someone . . ."

Hunter drew a bead on the man's other leg, and fired.

He stared down into Talon's puffed up mask of misery, and said, "That was for me."

Talon writhed, sobbing.

Hunter finished him with a bullet through his forehead. Talon lay back with a stupid, cross-eyed expression on his broad, meaty face.

Silence descended over the street.

Hunter looked around. He'd been so intent on making Ike Talon pay for his sins that he hadn't realized a large crowd had gathered in a complete circle around him, about twenty feet away. Men, women, children, and even a few dogs stared at him in wide-eyed fascination. Brightly dressed doxies perched like exotic birds on second- and third-floor balconies on both sides of the street, staring hang-jawed down at him and the dead Ike Talon, their wraps and dusters and hair feathers ruffling in the breeze.

The light wind kicked up dust and swirled it this way and that, making the on-lookers squint their eyes against it.

One face in particular caught Hunter's attention. Annabelle's.

He hadn't realized he was standing out front of Big Dan's Saloon. Annabelle stood on the boardwalk with Ginny and Big Dan and several of Big Dan's regulars clutching beers in their fists. Bobby Lee sat at Annabelle's feet, his copper eyes on Hunter.

Annabelle wore a dubious expression. One part enthrallment, two parts repulsion.

Slowly, she turned away and walked back into Big Dan's. Bobby Lee yipped softly and followed her.

The rest of the crowd remained in place, mired in grisly fascination.

"All right," someone finally said. "Holster the hogleg."

Walt Winslow stepped out from the crowd on the street's east side. He held a double-barrel shotgun in his hands, the large maws aimed at Hunter's belly.

"You're under arrest, Buchanon."

A collective murmur rose from the crowd.

"That was cold-blooded murder," Winslow said around the three-cent cheroot dangling from one corner of his mouth, his moon-and-star badge glinting in the late-morning sunlight.

Hunter saw another badge-wearing man

176

flanking Winslow, one hand on the revolver jutting from the holster on the man's right hip, in front of the tucked-back flap of his clawhammer coat. That was Roy Birmingham, another federal assigned to the Black Hills and who often partnered up with Winslow.

Birmingham was Winslow's age, early sixties — a stout beer barrel of a man in a black suit, black slouch hat, and a red foulard tie. A shaggy gray mustache concealed his mouth beneath a flat-tipped, bright-red nose upon which little round spectacles perched, brightly reflecting the sun.

Birmingham didn't unholster his revolver. He just kept his hand over it and, chin lowered, smiled deviously over the tops of his spectacles at Hunter.

Hunter glared at Winslow holding the shotgun on him. "You're gonna arrest me for killing this killer?"

"That's right," Winslow said. "Holster the hogleg. It don't matter if he deserved it or not. Murder is murder. You murdered the man, Buchanon. I can't let that go." He slid his flinty yet somehow bemused gaze toward two little boys, one a head taller than the other, standing in the crowd to the south, in front of their mother clad in a long green dress trimmed with white lace. "What kind of a lesson would that be for the children?"

Hunter looked at the boys and their mother, who gazed at him with dark fascination.

He sighed and holstered the LeMat.

CHAPTER 15

"Here we go, Miss Meyers — home sweet home! What do you think?"

Warren Davenport, riding on the chaise buggy's front seat beside Laura, turned to the new schoolmarm and smiled broadly, showing large, square teeth the color of old ivory. He was a tall, rawboned man with a crudely chiseled face. Brown eyes burrowed deep in sockets above his wedge-shaped nose with a slight bulge at the end.

He looked more like a farmer than a businessman; that's why his three-piece black suit with paisley vest looked almost silly on him.

No, it did look silly. But Laura was in no mood for laughing.

However, she did find herself impressed by the schoolhouse set on a slight rise on the west edge of Tigerville. But then, after arriving in Tigerville only an hour ago, she'd had to lower her expectations concerning just about all aspects of the humble, crude, dirty, smoky, stinky, violent little cesspool of human wretchedness.

As the leather buggy climbed the hill behind the sleek black Morgan horse, following the gently curving trail between scattered evergreen shrubs and small pines, she could see more and more of the building. It was a simple frame structure with a hipped roof and a closed front porch rising from a half dozen steps. A bell tower jutted from the roof of the porch; a rope for ringing the bell hung down over the top step.

The unpainted pine boards comprising the school were so new that the smell of pine resin was thick and heady.

Despite the school superintendent's reassurances that a new school had recently been built, she'd come to expect a far humbler structure than the one she was seeing. The good residents of Tigerville had put some thought, time, and labor, not to mention taxpayer dollars, into a fine and respectable public school building.

That made Laura's heart lighten a bit. But only a bit. The licentious behavior she'd seen on the streets of Tigerville, and the wretched appearance of most of its citizens, was still a large, cold brick holding steadfast in the pit of her stomach.

Still, she painted a smile on her face and turned to Mister Davenport. The man was obviously proud of his town's accomplishment here, and he deserved to be.

"This looks quite wonderful, Mister Davenport. Quite wonderful, indeed."

He'd stopped the Morgan on the cinder-paved area fronting the school. Taking both ribbons in his black-gloved right hand, he closed his left hand around the buggy's brake handle. "Would you like a tour? I've been right eager to show it to you, Miss Meyers!"

"Uh . . ." Laura glanced down at her dress, over which she wore a blanket that Mr. Sullivan had accommodated her with from his office, and dirty bare feet still streaked with dry blood and which rested on the buggy floor, one hooked around the other.

"Oh, of course." Davenport threw his head back and laughed self-deprecatingly. "How callous of me. My God, you not only just pulled into town, but you were attacked by bandits on the way here! Good Lord!"

Still laughing heartily, Davenport reined the Morgan around the school's right side and down along the side to the rear. Turning to Laura again, he said, "I'm afraid the teacher's quarters are . . . well . . . you'll see . . ."

Laura didn't like the tone of that.

Davenport steered the horse around the pair of new privies flanking the school, complete with half-moons carved into the doors. He and Laura rode around what she assumed was a shed for storing firewood, and up to a gray log cabin with a shake-shingled roof.

Yes, now she saw. A shack.

Davenport reined the Morgan to a stop on a patch of hard-packed, bald ground fronting the shack and set the brake.

Laura stared at the shack, trying not to cry.

This was her new home?

The cabin couldn't have been cruder. It also couldn't have been much larger than her and Jonathan's bedroom back home in their large, mansard-roofed house on Grant Avenue in Denver.

Davenport, obviously sensing her discomfort, hemmed and hawed for a time before saying, "You see, Miss Meyers, we built the school here on old Homer Laskey's mining claim. He dug for gold in the ravine behind the cabin, and he ran a few hogs and chickens. A loner, Homer was. A bit, well . . ."

Davenport twirled his finger in the air by

his left ear.

"Loco, some would say. He died five years ago now, and no one's lived here since. The cabin and Homer's claim went back to the town on account of how Homer left behind no living relatives. So, you see, since the lot already belonged to the city, and it had a cabin on it — a good and tight cabin, too, I might add — we thought we'd build the school on the old claim and then the new teacher . . . well, she could —"

"Live in the cabin," Laura finished for the man in a voice that sounded thin and forlorn even to her own ears. She gazed at the humble shack before her, feeling her upper lip tremble.

"Now, it don't look like much on the outside," Davenport said. The buggy tilted to his side as he clambered down, all knees and elbows. He walked around behind the buggy and came up on Laura's side, extending both roast-size hands toward her, smiling ingratiatingly. "Let me show you the inside, Miss Meyers. I think you'll like it. I really do."

Laura rose from the quilted leather buggy seat. Davenport wrapped his hands around her waist, pulled her off the buggy, and set her gently down on the hard-packed ground. As he did, his gaze lingered a little too long on her, his eyes roaming over her in a way that made her feel uncomfortable. Especially after the incident with the stage.

She lowered her gaze from his, hugged herself, and shivered inside the blanket though it must have been around eighty degrees out here, and humid.

Seeing her reaction, Davenport's ear tips reddened. He turned away, took her hand, and led her to the cabin's front door. She winced as grass stubble and small bits of gravel bit into her feet.

Davenport muttered nervously as he fished in his pocket for a key, then stuck it into the locking plate beneath the cast iron handle. He grunted for a time, stretching his lips back from his teeth, trying to turn the key. Finally, it made a low scraping sound as the locking bolt retreated into the door, and the door shuddered as it hung limp in its frame.

"Here we are," Davenport said, pushing the door open as he stepped into the cabin.

Laura stood in the open doorway, staring into her new home.

She'd been wrong. The shack was maybe a little larger than her and Jonathan's bedroom, but not by much. It was a single room with a kitchen area to the right, with a small stove, an eating table, and shelves housing rudimentary utensils, and a parlor area, if you could call it that, to the left. There was a rocking chair, a horsehair sofa that sagged badly in the middle, and a small wooden tea table carved from a log. To the rear of the parlor area, and abutting the left and rear walls, lay a small bed covered in threadbare wool blankets.

"See?" Davenport said. "Not so bad, eh?"

He smiled broadly, and again his eyes danced over her, making her skin crawl.

"No," she said, stepping into the cabin. The rough wood floor was partly covered by a couple of sun-faded, dusty, sour-smelling hemp rugs. "Not bad at all."

She was trying to sound jovial. The man made her nervous, self-conscious. She didn't like being alone with him. She wished she'd waited for Hunter, but he'd obviously and quite literally had his hands full with that saloon girl who'd passed out at the sight of him.

"You see there's an indoor spigot," Davenport said, pointing to a pump head and handle poking up out of the plank cupboard against the cabin's back wall, to the right, flanking the stove. "Ol' Homer was an odd one but he'd had the good sense to dig a well under the cabin."

"All the comforts of home," Laura said,

stepping forward and poking a hand out of the blanket draping her shoulders to rake it across the three-by-four-foot eating table. The tip of her finger was gray-black with dust and grime.

Again, she shivered. She felt her knees quake. She wanted very much to drop to the floor, grimy as it was, and bawl her eyes out. But she could not. She could not afford to make a fool of herself. She needed the teaching job, and she had nowhere else to go.

That thought alone almost broke her.

She swallowed down a hard knot of homesickness, shook her head to clear the raw emotions swirling around in her brain, then tossed her hair back and turned her wooden smile to the big man hovering over her. "Home sweet home!"

"See — I knew you'd like it!"

"I do. Now, if you'll forgive me, Mister Davenport, I'd really like to clean myself up a bit."

"Oh, you're wanting to be alone, of course!" He threw his head back again and laughed, but the laugh sounded nearly as wooden as Laura's own smile had been.

Instead of retreating to the door, he lingered, a smile working at the muscles in his hard, unevenly featured face. He opened

186

his mouth to speak, then, as if in after-thought, reached up to remove his hat from his head.

Holding the hat in his thick hands, he said, "Miss Meyers . . . uh . . . I have an idea. Won't you join me for dinner this evening?"

"What?" She couldn't believe what she was hearing.

"Well, I mean . . . I did send a boy from the grocery store over with the basics — sugar, flour, and coffee — that sort of thing — but surely you're not up to cooking so soon after arriving. After all you've been through! I could take you to dinner at the Imperial. It's a hotel. Best vittles in town! I can introduce you to a couple of the other school-board members who dine there regularly."

"That's a generous offer, Mister Davenport, but I think I'm just going to take a long, hot bath, put some salve on my feet, and go to bed early. Tomorrow I'll head downtown for groceries and stock the larder, so to speak." She tittered a nervous, phony laugh, just wishing the man would go. She hated how his eyes lingered on her and how his lingering gazes lifted a flush in the harsh curves and shaded hollows of his face.

She could smell him — the stench of unwashed male. She could hear the stentorian rasps of his breathing.

"I'd be happy to send the boy from the grocery store. If you'd like to make out a list, I could stop by later and pick it up."

"Oh, no. Thank you, Mister Davenport. I like to do my own shopping." That wasn't true. She'd rarely done her own grocery shopping. She and Jonathan had always had a servant for such tedium, but she wanted this man out of the cabin . . . and out of her life . . . as soon as possible. She didn't want him thinking she needed him for anything.

What a scoundrel! Laura was standing here feeling as though she'd just wrestled a grizzly bear in its own cave and wanting nothing more than to heat water and bathe her battered and weary body, to rub arnica into her poor, abused feet, and to go to bed and escape in dreams the harsh reality the fateful turn her life had taken.

Why did Hunter Buchanon just slip into her mind? Was that what — or whom — she was wanting to go to sleep and dream about? Was the contrast with her Viking warrior-savior what made Warren Davenport look so bedraggled and unappealing?

Get your mind off Hunter. You can't have

188

him. He already has a girl. Besides, you don't need a man. Men will break your heart. You're here to prove your independence. You don't need your heart broken again. Besides, you're only attracted to Buchanon because any woman would be (though she hadn't thought she could ever be attracted to so big and rough a character) and because he got you out of a bad situation and you're just grateful to be alive.

Don't forget that Buchanon is the one who got you into that situation in the first place.

What an inept pair — him and the shotgun messenger, Charley Anders (God rest the poor man's soul)! You must blame Mister Buchanon for the poor, miserable state you're in, not fantasize about having him wrap those big, bulging arms around you and draw you against that enormous, thick chest of his.

Suddenly, she realized that Warren Davenport was standing before her, waving one of his big paws in front of her face, yelling, "Miss Meyers! Miss Meyers! Are you all right, Miss Meyers?"

She snapped out of her trance, her cheeks tingling with what she was sure was a crimson flush. "I'm sorry, Mister Davenport. I'm afraid . . . I . . . just feel a little dizzy is all. It must be the exhaustion."

"Whew! For a minute there, I thought you

were gonna pull what Miss Ludlow pulled in front of the stage manager's office!"

"Yes, yes . . . so did I . . ."

Laura looked up at the man plaintively. "I hate to be rude, Mister Davenport. I do appreciate the ride over here and all, but I'm afraid . . ."

"Oh, of course, I'll take my leave. But don't you worry — I'll stop by to check on you later." He cleared his throat, looking a little sheepish. "Just to, um, you know — make sure your luggage arrived safely an' all."

"Oh, that won't be nec—"

"No problem at all, Miss Meyers. Well, then . . ." A little reluctantly, he planted his hat on his head, carefully adjusted the angle, then turned to the door. "I'll leave you to your bath." At the door, he turned back to her.

She was on the verge of screaming.

Was he ever going to leave???

"Welcome to Tigerville, Miss Meyers. I think you're gonna like it here. I know I for one am going to like having you here." Did he really wink at her? Yes, he did. "Just so's you know, Miss Meyers . . ."

"Yes, Mister Davenport?" Laura said, her knees weakening so that she was afraid she was going to pass out from the strain of

190

needing to be rid of this wheedling boob. If he'd noted the weariness and desperation in her voice, he didn't let on.

"Um . . . just so's you know, Miss Meyers, I am a widower. Just so you know that . . . well . . . there won't be anything improper when we do have dinner together."

He cast her a broad smile. An unsettling smile. A smile with an off-putting edge to it. Almost as though there'd been a threat in it.

It was as though he'd just shown her a knife.

"Good day, now, teacher."

He dipped his chin, ducked through the door, and closed the door behind him.

He took his own good time climbing into his buggy and turning the Morgan back the way they'd come. When the thuds of the horse's hooves and the rattle of the wagon wheels had dwindled to silence, Laura finally drew a breath, slumped down in a chair, lay her head on the grimy table, and bawled.

CHAPTER 16

"Get in there, ya damn miscreant! Hangin's too good for ya — you know that, don't you?"

"Ow! Stop pokin' me with that damned shotgun, Winslow!"

"Get in there, then. Stop lollygaggin', you mangy polecat," barked Walt Winslow, ramming his shotgun into Hunter's back again as the big jehu stumbled over the threshold and into the Tigerville jail office.

"Ow!" Hunter wheeled and glared at the much smaller man wielding the double-barrel shotgun, flanked by his badge-wearing crony, the pot-gutted and bespectacled Roy Birmingham, who had a dung-eating smile on his suety, sun-burned face. "What the hell's gotten into you, Winslow? You're treating me like some hardened killer!"

"Well, maybe you ain't had time to get

hardened, but you are a cold-blooded killer!"

"No, I'm not. Talon had it comin'. He killed Charley!"

"That don't matter," Birmingham said, stepping into the office behind the shotgun-wielding Winslow. "He was down and he was no longer armed and you still shot him anyway."

"Get in there!" Winslow bellowed, his hoarse voice going so high it had almost sounded like a girl's scream. He jerked the shotgun toward one of the four cells lined up against the squat stone building's rear wall. Only one cell was occupied — by an old wiry gent, probably a prospector, with a long bib-beard. The man was sound asleep on one of the cell's two cots and sawing logs like a practiced sawyer.

Of course, there were more men under lock and key. In a town like Tigerville, there were almost always a few men incarcerated for one thing or another. Usually a woman or two, to boot. But most were housed over at the county courthouse two blocks to the east, where they'd await a visit from the circuit judge while under the watch of two full-time jailers.

Reluctantly, ears burning with fury — no man had ever deserved to die bloody more than Ike Talon — Hunter stepped into the cell left of the one housing the prospector, who, judging by the stench reeking from his direction, had been arrested for drunk and disorderly conduct the night before. Probably more drunk than disorderly; any man who reeked as badly as he did had likely been far too drunk to have been all that disorderly.

Winslow slammed the door behind Hunter, who swung around to face the smaller, badge-wearing man, who said, "You got any more weapons on you?" He'd already confiscated Hunter's LeMat and bowie knife.

"No."

"You sure?"

"I said so, didn't I?"

"I should make you take your boots off," Winslow threatened.

"No, don't do that!" bellowed Birmingham, who'd taken a seat in Winslow's swivel chair flanking Winslow's cluttered rolltop desk. "No one's got smellier feet than a damn Rebel!" He pinched up his little pig eyes behind his little round spectacles and, cheeks growing even redder with mirth, said, "Most Southern boys only got two pairs of socks and they rarely change 'em!"

Birmingham slapped the desk and roared.

Winslow's stony face cracked a smile.

Hunter told the pot-gutted Deputy U.S. Marshal to do something physically impossible to himself.

Birmingham's smile faded though the flush remained.

It was Winslow's turn to laugh, though he, like Birmingham, had fought on the side of the Bluebellies during the War of Northern Aggression and Southern Independence. Most folks in the Hills had either fought for the Union or been Union sympathizers. That had always made it tough for the Southerners drawn here after the war, lured by the gold and, like the Buchanons, rich grazing land.

"I'm gonna dance at his hangin'," Birmingham told Winslow, though his now-angry gaze was on Hunter. "Gonna dance me a fine old jig, and I might even have a beer, though the doc done waved me off of the stuff on account of my ticker. Only for the rare special occasion, Doc said. Well, I'm gonna call that a rare special occasion."

"I'll buy," Winslow said, finally lowering the shotgun.

"You were friends with Charley, too, Winslow," Hunter said. "Hell, everybody was friends with Charley."

"That doesn't mean you can break the

law. Not in front of me and the whole damn town!"

Hunter gave a guttural cry of frustration, then went over and sat down on his cot. He leaned forward, elbows on his knees. He scrubbed his hat off his head and ran his hands through his hair in frustration. "If you could've seen what they did to him. Bushwhacked him! Him an' the drummer. Two of 'em dragged the girl off into the woods."

"I'm sure they did," Winslow said, sagging into a straight-backed chair by his desk. "That's Talon for you." He leaned his shotgun against the desk and dragged a slender cheroot from a box on the desktop. "You got a light, Roy?"

"I do." Birmingham dug a lucifer from the breast pocket of his suitcoat, scratched it to life on the top of Winslow's desk, and held it to the end of the marshal's cigar.

Hunter continued raking his fingers across his scalp, frustrated by the unfairness of it all. He thought of his father, Old Angus. He thought of Annabelle. He supposed Winslow and Birmingham were right. He had killed Talon after the man was down. Not only killed him, but tortured him, to boot.

Right in front of half the town.

He inwardly cursed himself for a fool.

Now he was going to hang, and Old Angus was going to be alone. Who'd look after him?

Who would look after Annabelle?

He cursed again and then threw himself back on the cot and crossed his boots at the ankles. He folded his arms behind his head and stared at the lone stone ceiling that bore the scratched initials of the many prisoners this old cell had housed over the years since Tigerville was nothing more than a logging camp and cavalry outpost, back before the boom.

He'd best settle in, he told himself. It might be a while before the judge, Devlin Baker, a Yankee, made his way up to Tigerville. When he did, Hunter would likely be hanging from the town's makeshift gallows the next day at high noon. Baker was notorious for showing little or no leniency for men who'd once fought for the Confederacy. It was widely known that Hunter as well as his father, Old Angus, had fought for the Stars & Bars.

That Hunter, in fact, had been a Southern war hero.

Soon, the Yankees of Tigerville would get their long-sought deserts.

He jerked his head up. He'd been so deep in thought, grieving his bleak end, that he hadn't realized that both Deputy U.S.

Marshals, Winslow and Birmingham, had moved up to stand just outside his cell, staring in at him, their brows raised skeptically.

Hunter scowled. "What the hell do you two want? If you think I'm gonna piss myself, you're gonna have to wait till after the trapdoor drops."

"We've been thinkin', Roy and me," Winslow said.

"Yeah? That's a first."

"All sass, ain't ya?" Birmingham said, flaring a pudgy nostril. "All fire and fury. Typical Buchanon."

"Typical Buchanon."

"Like I said," Winslow said, louder this time. "We've been thinkin' it over."

Hunter's curious frown further ridged his brows. "Thinkin' what over?"

"The hangin'."

Birmingham said, "We're ready to make you a deal. You don't deserve it, but we find ourselves in kind of a tight spot, Walt an' me."

Hunter dropped his feet to the floor, rose from the cot, and walked over to the cell door. He gazed skeptically through the iron bands. "I'm listening."

"You see," Winslow said, "Roy and I have been assigned to check out whiskey runners over on the Sioux Reservation. That means we have to leave Tigerville, and since I have yet to find a man willing to occupy this office, I have no one to leave in charge . . ." He dug a tin badge out of his vest pocket and held it up between his fingers. The words TOWN MARSHAL had been stamped into the tin face. "Till now."

Hunter frowned at the badge, then shifted his incredulous stare to Winslow. "You mean . . . you want me to be the *new town marshal*?"

"Just till Walt here gets back to Tigerville," Birmingham said.

"Unless you want to wear that star full-time," Winslow said. "Looks like I'm gonna have to look out of town for a man, and that's a heap of paper-pushing nonsense I don't have time for — what with my federal assignments and all. That trouble you were involved in last year . . . all them deputies of Stillwell's getting killed . . . then the unfortunate circumstances of the last town marshal's, um, unexpected expiration . . ."

"You mean Lon Lonnigan's gettin' shot in the back over at the Library by a drunk whore?"

Birmingham snorted and then brushed his hand across his mustache.

"Indeed," Winslow said. "The whole damn mess has made it a might difficult to find a lawman. At least, a good one. One who won't go and get himself shot the moment he steps out onto the boardwalk."

Winslow flattened out his hand in which the badge now rested belly-up. He slid his hand through the bars of the cell door. "Go ahead, kid. Pin that to your shirt. Just till I get back. Who knows — you might even warm to the job. Better pay than your stage drivin' job, and without the dust and hold-ups."

"How much?"

"Huh?"

"How much you offerin'?" Hunter asked.

"Oh, say . . ." Fingering his clipped mustache, Winslow glanced at Birmingham. "How 'bout thirty a month? A little steep, but I think the city fathers would agree to that amount."

Birmingham shrugged, nodded.

"The stage line pays me thirty-five a month," Hunter said.

"They do?" both Deputy U.S. Marshals said at the same time.

Hunter grinned cagily. "You know they do."

"All right," Winslow said. "How 'bout forty a month?"

"Fifty or call the hangman. Hangin' would be quicker. Lonnigan lingered for three days

200

after the doc cut that bullet out of his liver. His yells could be heard all over town."

"All right, all right," Winslow said. "Fifty it is. When I talk to the city council, I'll call it hazard pay. They shouldn't balk . . . given the circumstances." He shook his hand, making the badge on his palm dance. "Here you go, kid. Deal's a deal."

Hunter frowned down at the badge. Why was he feeling as though he'd just been cheated by a crooked faro dealer and a rigged dealer's box?

Slowly, he plucked the badge out of Winslow's hand, held up the badge, and looked at it as though it were a poisoned cookie. Birmingham tossed Winslow a big ring of keys. Winslow poked the key in the lock and opened the door.

"Congratulations on the new job, kid." The lawman smiled and held out the ring of keys. "Here — that's yours."

"Good luck!" Birmingham said as both he and Winslow grabbed rifles and bedrolls waiting by the door.

Hunter remained standing inside the cell, the badge in his hand. He looked from the badge to the two gray-headed lawmen grabbing their gear and fumbling the door open, both men chuckling like two school boys who'd just turned a frog loose in the girls' privy.

"Hey — you two weren't planning on hangin' me at all, were you?" Hunter called.

"For killin' Ike Talon?" Winslow asked, widening his eyes in shock. "Hell, no! Old Ike's been needin' killin' since he graduated from rubber pants!"

Birmingham was wheezing in red-faced laughter as he hustled through the door and out to where two saddled horses were waiting for him and Winslow at the hitchrack.

"See you when we get back, kid," Winslow said, grinning, eyes glittering devilishly. He turned toward the hitchrack, then turned back to Hunter, saying, "Oh, and . . . just a word of advice. Stay out of the Library unless absolutely necessary. I found out for myself that that place is a nest of rattlesnakes best steered well clear of. Poor ol' Lonnigan didn't have a chance!"

Both oldsters were roaring now as they strapped their bedrolls to their saddles, shoved their rifles into their saddle scabbards, and swung up into the leather.

They were still roaring as they turned their horses out into the afternoon traffic and headed south at spanking trots.

Hunter walked slowly out of the cell and over to the open office door. His ears burned from the fleecing he'd just taken. He felt as though he'd been gunny-sacked, rolled, kicked, had his pockets cleaned, and his boots stolen. He looked at the badge in his hand, scowling, then shuttled his gaze to where the two old federals had galloped off along Dakota Avenue, their laughter still echoing.

Hunter sighed. "I gotta feelin' they were prepared to offer me better pay, too, dammit."

CHAPTER 17

Once back at his family's Broken Heart Ranch, Cass Ludlow handed his horse over to the half-breed stable boy and followed the well-worn path up the rise to the impressive, stately main house situated on the crest of a low bluff.

The arrangement afforded the Broken Heart's proud founder, Graham Ludlow, a prime view from virtually every window in the house of his well-appointed headquarters with its immaculately maintained bunkhouse, barns, stables, and corrals that formed a half circle around the house to the west. The view also comprised a good portion of Ludlow's lush and massive range stretching to all horizons, the green valleys between pine- and cedar-stippled ridges liberally peppered with his prime, white-faced cattle.

That "beef on the hoof," as Ludlow called it, was the envy of nearly every other rancher in southwestern Dakota and eastern Wyoming Territories.

Cass left the cinder-paved path sheathed by transplanted shrubs of various varieties as well as by aromatic pines and cedars, and started up the lodge's broad wooden steps rising to the wraparound veranda. As he did, he heard men's voices above, and paused on the third step up from the bottom. He'd been rolling a cigarette as he walked, and now, rolling the paper closed around the tobacco, he lifted his gaze to the veranda ten feet above.

His father sat out there, in the push chair he'd had to start using on account of his weak ticker. The summer day was warm, over eighty degrees, but still the old man's legs were covered with a red plaid blanket. He wore his traditional hickory shirt and bolo tie under his traditional black cowhide vest, from a pocket of which hung a gold watch chain. Ludlow had once been a big man, his broad face chiseled out of granite and split with a formidable, liver-spotted nose. He hadn't been tall, but broad, with thick shoulders and arms, giving the overall impression of intimidating strength.

Cass, himself, had been intimidated, not to mention the victim, of that intimidating strength for most of his childhood, the beatings having ended after Cass had turned eighteen and Ludlow had given up hope of ever "bringing him around" to do a full day's work or to turn him into the boot-strapper, business-minded stockman Ludlow had so wanted him to be instead of the whoremongering sluggard he was.

That big strong man, however, was gone.

Ludlow, with his failing heart and refusal to give up strong drink and cigars, was a droopy-eyed, haggard-faced, slump-shouldered husk of his former self. He must have lost a good half of his previous weight over the past year, since the end of the violence that had begun after Ludlow had learned that his daughter, Annabelle, had been secretly planning to wed the former grayback, Hunter Buchanon, who hailed from a family of ex-Confederates, which meant, to Ludlow's way of thinking, that they had blood on their hands.

The blood of Ludlow's son who'd died in the war.

Anger burned in Cass when he saw the young popinjay sitting in a wicker chair beside Cass's father, and to whom Graham Ludlow was conversing in such quiet, conspiratorial, almost intimate tones. Kenneth Earnshaw, in his late twenties, was a short, slender young man with a boyish face still a little plump with baby fat he would never outgrow, and an almost feminine mop of carefully combed, strawberry blond hair, with sideburns of the same color, and a thick, bushy strawberry mustache. He'd grown a goatee to try to disguise the fact that his chin was as weak as his character.

Uncharacteristically, he was dressed in range gear though Cass had seen the young nancy-boy on a horse only once, and Earnshaw had looked as though he were sitting on the back of a giant porcupine. He took a couple of turns around the corral, with the stable boy leading the horse, then scrambled off the uncomfortable perch so quickly he'd got a boot caught in his stirrup and had struck the ground on his head.

He'd screeched like a girl with a pigtail caught in a wagon wheel's spokes.

Now he sat there beside Cass's father, decked out in cowboy garb. At least, what a nancy-boy from the East wanting to look like a thirty-a-month-and-found cow puncher would wear though no cowboy Cass had ever known wore doeskin trousers stuffed into polished black patent boots adorned with red piping, and a silk shirt with ruffles down the front. The trousers themselves had some kind of fancy stitching up around the legs and probably down the legs. He couldn't see the legs because they were obscured by the hand-tooled, elk hide leggings he wore over them.

The man's hat was as white as a wedding gown, and Sir Kenneth, as Cass called him behind his back, wore it with one side pinned up against the crown.

Now, Cass himself enjoyed wearing attire, often in the Spanish style, that made him stand out in a crowd and that attracted the ladies. (At least, it had before the fire. Now it was the scars from the fire that made him stand out in a crowd.) But not even he would be caught in a getup as outlandish as Sir Kenneth's.

He didn't like the way Kenneth and Graham Ludlow were talking either. As though Kenneth was the man's son. His favorite one, at that. Of course, everyone knew who Ludlow's favorite son was — or had been. But Mighty John Ludlow, as Cass thought of his older brother with an inward sneer, was lying in itty-bitty, blown-up pieces on a forgotten battlefield in Tennessee, leaving behind Cass to unsuccessfully fill his shoes.

Only, there was no filling the shoes of a dead man. Especially a proud man's first-born son.

The two up there were talking in tones as hushed and intimate as those of lovers. Cass knew what they were talking about. He'd overheard them on several occasions. Cass's father was still banking on Kenneth marrying Annabelle, and Ludlow was schooling Kenneth on the fineries of ranch and stock management, and how to hire and fire and keep a good, working bunch of men on your payroll. How to earn and keep their respect.

That last one was going to be a steep climb for young Kenneth in those hand-tooled elk hide leggings of his.

"What the hell's goin' on up there?" Cass said abruptly, loudly, pounding the steps with his boots as he climbed to the top of the veranda. "You two forming your own secret government or something?"

"Cass! For God's sake, boy, you startled the hell out of me! You know starts aren't good for my ticker!"

"Neither are those, Pa," Cass said, nodding to indicate the fat stogie in Ludlow's right hand and the glass of whiskey on a small table to the left of his chair.

"Oh, go to hell!" Ludlow curled a red-rimmed nostril and took a couple of puffs off the stogie.

Kenneth turned to Cass and fought a snide grin from his lips like a persnickety widow woman trying to swat a couple of mongrel strays off her porch with a broom.

Cass backed up to the porch rail, hiked a hip on it, and folded his arms across his chest, casting the dandy a bald stare.

Ludlow looked at him, impatient, scowling. "Well . . . ?"

"Well, what?"

"What did you find out? Is Annabelle really working at Big Dan's place in Tigerville?"

"She is, Pops, I'm sorry to say. Rather embarrassing to see her in there, like that. She looks good, though, in that little corset that don't cover half of her, uh, *attributes,* and those fishnet stockings." He turned his head to cast a mocking glance at Kenneth, whose cheeks instantly mottled red.

Kenneth looked quickly away from Cass. He didn't have the stomach for regarding the younger Ludlow's masked countenance for more than a second or two at a time. Earnshaw turned to Ludlow and pounded the arms of his wicker chair with his fists. "Why is she degrading herself this way?"

"Because she's mixed up and confounded — that's why! That grayback got into her head and twisted her thinking. He turned her against her own family, and even now, after he's turned his back on her, she remains in town, taking a job like some commoner, or worse. She's cutting off her nose to spite her face. She's humiliating me as well as herself!" Ludlow looked at Cass. "Tell me she's not working upstairs."

"I don't know, Pop," Cass lied, shaking his head doubtfully. "I really don't know."

Earnshaw twisted in his chair toward Ludlow, his pale neck swollen with anger beneath his red silk bandanna. "We have to get her out of there, Graham. We have to get her out of there *now!*"

Cass gave a quiet, caustic snort. *Graham, now, is it? When Pop starts calling him son, I'm gonna take young Earnshaw out to teach him to hunt and he's gonna get a bullet right between his skinny little shoulders. "I mistook him for a deer, Pa. Honest, I did. Tragic mistake . . ."*

"What the hell are you laughing at?"

Cass suddenly realized his father was glaring at him, hard-jawed, Ludlow's watery eyes somewhat resembling the tough twin gimlets that had resided in those deep sockets not all that long ago.

"Oh, hell!" Cass pushed away from the porch rail. "The errand boy did the job you ordered him to do. I rode to town and I told you what I saw. I'm gonna go upstairs and rub some salve into these burns, a gift from the little princess you two seem to still hold such store by."

211

"Cass, wait!"

But Cass had already pulled the heavy oak door open and gone inside. He crossed the sunken parlor to the broad, carpeted stairs and climbed to the second story. Anger surged hotly inside him.

Errand boy. That's what he had been relegated to. His father was grooming Earnshaw to take over the ranch once he'd wedded Annabelle. Cass really had no place here anymore. All he'd really hung around for was to make sure that the Pretty Little Princess didn't marry the big grayback, Buchanon. Not after what she'd done to him in the barn that horrible night.

Why should she be happy when he never could be? Hell, the only whores who'd spend time with him were the half-breeds and Mexicans in the squalid cribs along Poverty Gulch. His life had been turned to ashes the night the barn fire had consumed his face. His father couldn't even look at him anymore. Ludlow could look at him maybe a second or two longer than that preening Earnshaw could, but after a few seconds even Ludlow had to flinch a little and avert his gaze.

What the hell was Cass hanging around here for?

He had a stake. A good one. He had

enough money for a fresh start.

Where he'd make that start, he had no idea. Anywhere but here.

Cass walked into his room. He looked both ways along the hall, making sure he was alone, always fearful the family's long-time Chinese servant, Chang, might uncover Cass's secret. He knew he was just being paranoid, but that stake meant everything to him.

Satisfied that Chang was likely in the kitchen preparing the evening meal — Ludlow always wanted a large spread though the old invalid couldn't eat more than a few bites anymore — Cass closed the door and twisted the key in the lock. Enough sunlight pushed through his western window despite the green velvet curtain drawn over it, that he felt no need for a lamp.

He opened his dresser's bottom drawer, opened an old, falling apart cigar box housing trinkets from his childhood from scavenging expeditions he'd taken on horseback here and there about the Ludlow range. There were arrowheads, the fletched end of a Sioux arrow, a dried muskrat head, a "good luck" jingle bob, potsherds from an ancient Indian encampment, some Spanish coins, a miniature clipper ship he'd built from matchsticks, and a small photograph of his mother, jagged on one edge because he'd cut it away from a wedding photo that had included his father. There was also a thin sheaf of penciled letters from a Swedish honyocker's daughter he'd once loved — or thought he'd loved — the summer he was fifteen.

Beneath the letters that were tethered together with a powder blue hair ribbon little Beret had given him to remember her by, lay a key. He plucked the key from the box and walked over to the closet door on the other side of his wood-framed bed covered with a star quilt his mother and Chang had sewn one winter.

He opened the door, knelt down, and pulled an ancient army footlocker out from beneath a pile of old clothes and boots. It didn't come easily. He grunted as he gave it several tugs until it sat on the closet floor just inside the door. His heart in his throat, he poked the key into the padlock securing the lid, turned it. The shank sprang free, and Cass opened the lid.

He released a held breath as he gazed down at the four swollen burlap pouches each roughly the size of a ten-pound bag of sugar. He was always afraid it wouldn't be here the next time he opened the lid. He checked the locker regularly, just to make sure the contents were still inside. Of course, it would be. Chang was no thief; Graham Ludlow had never snooped in Cass's room. He'd never had enough interest in his son to care one whit what Cass had stowed in his room.

Still, a heavy, nettling paranoia weighed heavy in the younger Ludlow.

He untied the string from around the neck of one of the bags, slipped his hand inside, dug his fingers into the sugary dust, and removed his clenched fist from the bag. Carefully holding his hand over the bag, he opened it.

He smiled, eyes and mouth widening inside the cutout holes of the mask. He let the rich dust slide slowly out of his hand and back into the bag. It made a soft, sibilant sound, the soft snick of a snake moving through dry grass. As the gold tumbled back into the bag, it glittered in the few stray strands of sunshine angling into the closet from over Cass's shoulder.

His heart quickened. He heard himself breathing.

He'd estimated that there was nearly forty thousand dollars in gold here in these four bags, which he'd plundered from the mine shaft in which Hunter Buchanon had hid them after prospecting the gold himself, building a cache he'd intended to use for a marriage stake for himself and Annabelle.

Cass laughed devilishly through his teeth.

He'd followed the pair out from town, to the remote little prospector's cabin they'd met to make love in. He'd followed them out from the cabin when Hunter had showed the gold to his lovely betrothed.

After the lovebirds had left the shaft hand in hand, certain of their future together, Cass had stolen into the shaft and plundered their stash.

Again, he laughed.

All his now. He deserved it after what Annabelle had done to his face.

What she deserved was to marry the pasty little nancy-boy, Kenneth Earnshaw, and rot away here with Sir Kenneth and Graham Ludlow, right here at the appropriately named Broken Heart Ranch.

As for Cass, what he deserved was to head to Mexico, hole up in a shack along the Sea of Cortez, learn to play the mandolin, and pay the dusky-eyed, copper-skinned *señoritas* — whose constitutions were stronger than those of the *norteamericano* whores — to haul his ashes from time to time.

Not the ones in his fireplace either.

A knock sounded on Cass's door. "Cass!"
He leaped with a start.

CHAPTER 18

Cass opened his door to see Chang, their middle-aged Chinese housekeeper, standing before him in the Chinaman's crisp white smock and red silk cap. A gray-brown mustache, that appeared a little grayer every day, dropped down both sides of his mouth.

He studied Cass with his muddy eyes, deep lines cut across the doughy skin of his broad forehead. Chang seemed suspicious. Did the Chinaman have some mystical Eastern way of knowing that Cass was up to no good, or did he just know Ludlow's son well enough to know that it was always a good bet that Cass was up to no good?

"Your father wants see you downstairs!" Chang said with customary vehemence.

As if to corroborate the Chinaman's story, Graham Ludlow's voice thundered from below: "Cass! Cass, come down here! I want to talk to you! We have an important matter to discuss!"

Chang glanced once more at Cass, nodded once as if to say, "See?" then turned and shuffled off down the hall to Cass's right, heading for the narrow stairs that dropped down to the kitchen at the house's rear.

Cass cursed, drew a calming breath. He felt as though he'd almost been caught with the stolen gold, though he knew that wasn't true. Hiding that gold in the house was fraying his nerves.

Stolen gold. His sister's dower, so to speak.

Did Cass feel guilty for having stolen it? *Hell, no!*

Cass adjusted his hat and his mask, then stepped into the hall, drew the door closed, locked it, pocketed the key, and headed down the stairs.

His father sat in his push chair in the parlor, near the overstuffed leather elkhorn chair by the fireplace. The chair was scuffed and scratched from years of use. The seat cushion was permanently bowed inward by the old man's behind. An unlit cigar lay on the chair's right arm, near a pair of Ludlow's wire-rimmed reading spectacles.

On the low table fronting the chair were several stacks of leather-bound books on cattle and horse breeds as well as on rangeland management. There they remained though Cass doubted his father had looked at any of them in over a year.

"What can I do for you, Pa?"

"Why do you have to be so damned emotional?" Ludlow said, beetling his wiry gray brows and slapping a claw-like hand down on an arm of his pushchair. "What was that display out there about?" He canted his head to indicate the veranda beyond the long, recessed windows.

The drapes were pulled back to let in the afternoon sunlight. Cass saw Earnshaw still sitting out there in the wicker chair, gazing off over the Broken Heart holdings as though they were already his.

"I get tired of seein' you and that rube bein' all cozy. Like he was already your son-in-law when Annabelle doesn't want anything to do with the man."

"Annabelle doesn't know her own mind. She's high-strung, just like her mother was. She entertains crazy fantasies, and they separate her from reality. Kenneth comes from a good, high-bred family. A wealthy one. As you know, his father is a friend of mine. Annabelle's marriage to Kenneth will benefit both families. It will mean the continuation of this ranch after I am gone. That should please you. Kenneth may not

220

be as good on a horse as some, but with his business and investment sense, he can run this ranch. You know as well as I do that you can't. You won't! You've proven that time and time again!"

"It's just not in my blood, Pa."

"You're a Ludlow!"

"I'm more like Mother was. You know — pretty to look at but otherwise useless?" Cass clapped his hands and laughed loudly, ironically, plucking at the mask. He stopped abruptly because he could feel it turning into a sob.

No man sobbed in front of Graham Ludlow.

"Good God." Ludlow looked away, taking an exasperated drag off his stogie. He stared through the window but he didn't appear to be seeing anything. He was probably thinking about his first-born son lying dead on that Southern battlefield, thinking of all that could have been if only John had come home.

John had been the rancher. He'd ridden as though he'd been born on a horse. He was breaking wild broncs by the time he was fifteen years old, and sleeping out in the barn with the hands because he wanted to learn the ways of the range from the old salts who'd worked for his father for years.

At least, that was how Ludlow told it. John was so long ago now that Cass barely remembered his older brother. He'd been only thirteen when the news had arrived that John was dead.

"Is that all, Pa? I'm a might tired. I could use a nap."

"No, it's not all. Come over here and sit down." Ludlow indicated the short sofa on the other side of the low table on which his books sat untouched. "We have to talk about Annabelle."

Cass sighed. He moved into the room and slacked into the sofa with another weary sigh. "When are you gonna let her go, Pa? I saw her. I talked to her. There's no budge in that girl."

Ludlow chuckled. Despite his disdain for what Annabelle had become, pride glinted in his eyes. "She's like me that way. Some ways like her ma, some ways like me. Like me, she's a fierce fighter. Always been that way. If you told that child it was night and time for bed, she'd say it was morning and time to rise, just out of sheer defiance."

"Ain't she a caution!" Cass laughed again with irony.

"Left to her own devices," Ludlow continued, ignoring his son's bizarre behavior out of long habit, "she'd come around. But we can't wait that long. If she keeps on at Big Dan's, something bad will happen. She'll end up with child. We have to save her from herself. We have to intervene."

"Intervene?"

"Kidnap her."

"What?" Again, Cass laughed, this time in disbelief.

"She's a herd quitter." Ludlow tossed an imaginary lariat. "Lasso and dally her in!"

Cass squinted at his father. "Could you make that a little plainer?"

Ludlow scowled at his son. "What's plainer than a lariat and a loop?"

"You know I was never a natural roper."

"Just because you didn't want to be." Ludlow leaned forward in his chair, rested the elbow of the hand holding the cigar on the chair's right arm. He cast his son a direct look, eyes wide, brows raised. "I haven't given up on you, boy. Not by a long shot. If you can take a few men into town and long-loop that spirited filly of mine, and drag her back here to the Broken Heart, I'll give you a bigger cut of my inheritance after I'm gone."

"How much am I getting now?" Cass had figured he'd just keep his usual, paltry allowance of thirty-a-month-and-found despite his rarely doing a lick of ranch work.

That's why he'd been so happy to get his hands on Buchanon's gold.

"My will calls for a trust that would pay you fifty dollars a month."

"Ah, so I get a raise when the old boy kicks off. How you feelin', Pa? Think you'll be around much longer?"

Ludlow pointed the wet end of his stogie at Cass. "If you keep that up, I'll outlive you, and that's a natural fact though there won't be nothin' natural about your passing!"

"There's that big fatherly heart."

"If you can get Annabelle back to the ranch, and help me see that she marries Earnshaw, I'll write you back in for a third. Just leave the day-to-day operations to Earnshaw and Cassidy." Cole Cassidy was Ludlow's trusted ranch foreman, a fairly new man in the role but not in the ranching business. "You stay out of it. You'll just muck things up like you've always done and make it harder for them to do their jobs."

Ludlow puffed the stogie.

Rage a runaway six-horse hitch inside him, making even his eyes burn, Cass pushed himself up and off the sofa. He stepped over the table, knocking over a stack of his father's books, and crouched over the old man in the push chair gazing up at him dubiously.

Cass placed his hands on the arms of the push chair and shoved his hideous, masked face up close to his father's, so close that he knew Ludlow could smell the still-open sores that cracked and bled and oozed yellow puss. The old man drew his own head back and to one side, his face deeply lined with revulsion.

"You go to hell, old man," Cass said slowly, darkly. "You can take that third ownership of the Broken Heart and shove it where the sun don't shine. I don't want your money or your charity. I'm sick of it. I'm sick to death of you and this ranch. I'm pullin' out on you, my beloved father. I'm gonna leave you to rot here in that chair, pining for your dead favorite son pushing up daisies in Tennessee.

"I'm gonna leave you here with that fairy out there and your daughter who hates your guts. For what you did to Buchanon's family, she'll hate your guts till the day they kick you out with a cold shovel. Me? I hate you for other reasons. And for those reasons, I'll get her back for you. Because I hate you and I hate her for what she did to me. The Little Princess deserves nothing more than to marry that prissy parrot out there who makes water sittin' down, and live here with you till you die. My only regret is that you're likely to go all too soon to be the just punishment she deserves for doing *this* to me!"

With that, Cass reached up, swiped his hat off his head, and pulled the mask from his face.

"Oh!" Ludlow cried, tipping his head far back in his chair, his eyes huge and bright with revulsion. He stared at the horror of his offspring's hideously scarred and oozing features, and wailed, "Oh God! Oh God! Oh God! *Chang — my pills!*"

Cass straightened as he grinned down at his father. That was the first time Ludlow had laid eyes upon the evidence of his daughter's wickedness. He'd never entered Cass's room all those weeks and months he'd lain shivering and howling with pain.

Only the doctor from town and Chang had seen what Annabelle had done to her brother. Only them. No one else had seen the monster residing inside the flour sack mask.

Until now.

"My God — what's wrong?" Young Earnshaw's plaintive wail had come from the doorway behind Cass.

Cass turned to where Kenneth stood just inside the open front door.

Earnshaw's eyes moved to Cass, who stood grinning his death's head grin at the young dandy. All the blood fell from the little man's face.

"Oh," Earnshaw choked out, gasping as he stumbled back against the wall. "Oh . . . oh God!"

He covered his mouth with his forearm, then turned and stumbled back onto the veranda. Cass heard the rumble of the dandy's boots on the wood steps as Kenneth hurried off the porch and into the yard. Outside, Kenneth retched.

The soft thumps of slippered feet rose from the direction of the kitchen.

"What happen? What happen?"

Chang entered the room from an arched doorway.

"Chang," Ludlow bellowed. "My pills! Hurry!"

Chang stopped when he saw Cass standing bareheaded and unmasked before the old, wailing man. Chang clucked and shook his head as he came forward, holding a small brown bottle in his hand.

"You very bad, Mister Cass! Cover up! Cover up! Look what you do to your father!"

"Yeah, look what I do to him," Cass said, glancing down at the sobbing old man again.

He pulled the mask down over his face and crouched to retrieve his hat from the floor. He set the hat on his head and walked across the parlor to the house's open front door.

"Fortunately, that's nothin' compared to what she'll do to him." Cass stopped at the door and turned to regard Ludlow again.

Chang had splashed whiskey into a glass and was now feeding the old man a pill and the whiskey to wash it down with.

"I'll see you again soon, old man," Cass said, smiling through the mask at his flushed and haggard father. "I'll see you again soon with the Little Princess in tow!"

Laughing, he left.

CHAPTER 19

Laura Meyers lolled in the sudsy water.

Well, not lolled, exactly. The corrugated tin washtub was too small for any kind of lolling. She sat scrunched down in the tub with her knees drawn up to her bosoms. So, no, she wasn't lolling. At least, not most of her was. But she was enjoying the hot bath, anyway.

It was the third one she'd taken since she'd arrived at her humble little abode here in Tigerville. She'd been here three days, and she'd taken a bath at the end of each day despite how much work she'd discovered went into preparing one. First, she had to build a fire in the stove with what little split wood there was in the woodshed. There was a sizable stack of logs, but little of it had been split. She wasn't yet willing to attempt that formidable task. She wasn't sure she could even lift a splitting maul.

(Just learning to build fires alone had

nearly sent her screaming into the hills!)

Then she had to pump and heat the water in a cast-iron pot. She had only one pot, so it took a good long time to get enough water heated and to fill the tub while adding more wood to the fire from her precious supply.

The first time she'd had to go through all that, on the first evening after the bizarre Warren Davenport had finally left her, she'd had a good cry. She'd had several good cries since, over various aspects of her life here in this small cabin, but she so far hadn't cried over this particular bath.

She supposed she was too exhausted to cry. Or maybe she was getting used to the odious work it took to have a bath. Or maybe, with the perspective she'd acquired after all the work it had taken her to clean out this wretched little hovel and make it habitable for a civilized woman accustomed to the finer things in life, the work that went into heating water for a bath wasn't really all that much work at all.

She was enjoying her bath here near the end of another long day of toil. The water felt good against her skin. Before, in her previous life, she'd never realized how good a bath really felt. Probably because she herself had never had to do the work of preparing one, and because she'd never before worked so hard . . . or perspired so much . . . as to so badly need one.

She smiled at that. Then she noted her smile and the rather pleased, satisfied feeling that the smile had spawned. Every minute of the short time she'd spent here felt as though she were on the verge of resigning her new job, of giving up the cabin, and of returning to Denver.

The only thing that stopped her was the fact that if she returned to Denver she'd likely be jailed for having shot her husband. As anyone could imagine, that was a large deterrent. There had been a few times when she'd thought that going to jail might be a welcome exchange for the tedium and toil of life in the perdition that was Tigerville in general and in this cabin in particular, but, having weighed all options, she'd decided to stick it out here rather than go to prison.

She had nowhere else to go. In her situation, any other place might be just as bad as Tigerville. Besides, while she still hated it here, she didn't hate it quite as much as she had when she'd first arrived. So that was something. Maybe . . . just maybe . . . she would keep finding more satisfaction in doing things for herself and not having to rely so heavily on others.

Especially on a man who'd betrayed her

231

so badly.

As far as Jonathan was concerned, she didn't think he'd send the authorities after her. Not after what she'd caught him doing and with whom he'd been doing it. That would only arouse the scandal-mongers around Denver, and his reputation would be ruined. His business might suffer. However, if Laura returned to Denver, he might have her arrested just because he couldn't stand to see the woman who'd injured him so severely . . . and possibly permanently . . . walking around scot-free.

He might even sic a henchman on her. She knew he had henchmen. She didn't know what they did, exactly. She hadn't wanted to know. But she knew from overheard bits of his conversations that he did, indeed, employ such beasts. Now she could only imagine what they did . . . what they might do to *her* . . . and those imaginings made her wince.

She jerked her head from her knees with a quiet gasp.

She'd heard something outside.

Cocking her head slightly, she listened, frowning at the window just ahead of her, in the front wall. She'd pulled the flour sack curtains closed before she'd stepped into her bath, but they were so thin and tattered that she could still see through them. But all she could see was tree boughs nodding and bobbing in the wind.

She could hear only a burned log fall in the stove, the soft crackling of the soap suds, and the intermittent whisperings of the breeze outside the cabin. Occasionally there was the soft thud of a pine cone tumbling from one of the surrounding trees.

And birdsong, of course.

Nothing else.

She rested her chin down on her knees again. Her imagination had only been sparked by her wild imaginings of Jonathan's henchmen. That was all. Nothing else.

The thought had no sooner passed through her mind than something moved in the window to her left. She jerked her head in that direction.

Again, nothing.

She gasped again, louder, when someone snickered outside the cabin.

"Who's there?" Laura yelled, heart pounding as she drew her knees up tighter against her chest. "Who's there? I heard you! Go away. You're trespassing on private property!"

Silence.

Outside, someone whispered. The whisper

233

was answered by another person — another *man* — and then there was a quiet rustling noise as though of someone moving.

Two men were skulking around outside the cabin.

"Go away! Whoever you are, go away or I will summon the authorities!"

As she swept her gaze from window to window, she spied the flicker of a shadow between two of the logs in the front wall, left of the door. Narrowing her eyes, she peered between the two logs. The chinking had crumbled and disappeared from between many of the logs and now she could clearly see an eye staring in at her through one of those gaps.

Laura hugged her knees even tighter against her breasts and screamed, "Oh my God, you're depraved scoundrels! Go away! I'm warning you! Go away — do you hear?"

More snickers.

A man said raspily, "Get away, Andy! Let me have a look!"

The eye disappeared.

Shadows moved through sunlit gaps in the chinking.

Another eye reappeared in the gap through which the first eye had stared.

"Go away, you beasts!" Laura cried, trying to make herself as small as possible. "Go away! Go away! Oh, please — go away!"

"She's a looker, I'll give her that," said one of the depraved peeping toms.

A little louder, one of the men said, "Hey, teacher, we'll give you a nickel if you lower your knees!"

They both wheezed with ribald laughter.

"Go away, you devils!" Laura screamed. "You're sick and depraved!"

Both peeping toms continued to wheeze with goatish laughter . . . until a large shadow appeared in the window straight above where the men were hunkered down, taking turns peeping through the gap.

The shadow dropped down beneath the window.

As the shadow rose again, the two toms cried out, "Hey, let us go! Let us go, ya big —"

Two shadows moved violently.

There was a cracking sound, as of two heads being smacked together.

The peeping toms cried out in agony.

"Now, get out of here!" a man shouted. "If I catch either of you two over here again, I'll gut-shoot you both! Understand?"

"Oh, my head, my head!" one of the toms screeched.

"Mine too!" the other one sobbed. "I

think . . . I think you done scrambled my brains!"

"You don't have any brains to worry about, Andy. Neither of you Cullen idiots does. Now, get out of here!"

There was a sharp thump. In her mind's eye, Laura pictured Hunter Buchanon's boot slamming into the backside of one of the toms. She slapped a hand over her mouth in shock but felt a smile tug at her lips.

More thuds and thumps followed as the two toms, sobbing, went stumbling away through the brush.

Laura snorted into her hand. Her heart lightened as her fear evaporated.

He was back. She'd been wondering about him in the back of her mind, wondering if she'd ever see him again. He couldn't have reappeared at a more opportune time.

Two solid knocks sounded on the cabin's front door, making the rickety door shudder in its frame.

"Come in!" Laura cried out in delight, sitting straight up in the tub.

As the door opened, she realized that she'd just invited a man into the cabin in which she sat naked in a bathtub.

"Oh, no — wait!" she screeched, holding one hand out toward the door while covering her bosoms with her other arm. "I'm in a bath but I'll be presentable in a minute!"

She saw his big shadow in the door, saw his blue-eyed gaze find her in the tub. His eyes widened and then he stepped abruptly back and drew the door closed with a scrape and a click.

"Sorry!" he said through the door.

"No apologies warranted! Please, don't go anywhere! Stay right there!"

She scrambled up out of the tub and toweled herself off. She shook her wet hair out, wishing she had time to dry and brush it so she'd look more presentable. She suddenly felt self-conscious and wanted very much to look as good as possible to her gentleman caller, Hunter Buchanon — if she could call him that — but that would take too long.

She scrambled breathlessly into pantalettes, a chamise, petticoat, and pantaloons over which she drew the pretty but conservative and relatively comfortable day dress she'd purchased the day before in town, having realized after going through her single trunk and two portmanteaus that she hadn't brought — nor did she own — a single garment that would be comfortable for physical exertion.

And this place certainly needed some physical exertion.

She buttoned the dress to her throat, tossed her wet hair back behind her shoulders, and opened the door.

He stood a way off, boots spread, thumbs hooked behind his cartridge belt. A pair of brown leather gloves were hooked behind the belt, as well. He was looking around the yard, at the furniture she'd dragged outside to give a thorough scrubbing. She'd also hung both braided rugs on a rope line she'd strung between two trees, and given them a good beating with a stick.

The bedding that had come with the place was out there, as well. She'd scrubbed the sheets and quilts on a washboard in the tub and hung them to dry from another line.

"You've been busy," he said, blond brows arched beneath his hat brim. "I'm a little surprised you're still here."

He genuinely was. He'd thought she'd be gone by now. He was glad he'd been wrong.

"Yes, well," she said, "it hasn't been easy."

Buchanon looked at the rundown cabin. "No, I bet it hasn't. They should have fixed the place up for you."

Laura glanced beyond him toward the new school building roughly fifty yards to the south, its rear wall facing the teacher's cabin. "I'm grateful to have a new school building. Perhaps they spent all their money

238

on the school."

"Hell." Hunter growled. "The men on the school council, especially Davenport, have more money than they know what to do with. They just have a hard time spending it. 'Tighter'n the bark on a tree,' as my old man would say."

He chuckled under his breath, averting his blue eyes a little sheepishly, then hooked a thumb over his shoulder. "Sorry about those two. The Cullen twins. A couple of raggedy-heeled prospectors. They live in a cabin in a gulch to the north. They won't bother you again, though."

He gave her a direct look with those warm yet commanding eyes of his. "I promise."

She believed him.

"Please, don't look at me too closely," she said, looking away from him as she ran her hands back through her wet hair. "I look like a drowned rat."

"Not any drowned rat I've ever seen."

Her freshly scrubbed cheeks flushed beautifully, he thought. He couldn't help feasting his eyes on her. A rare beauty. Seeing her took a little of the sting out of the situation with Annabelle. The sting of what she'd become. It was time to forget her now, he realized.

It was time he moved on.

"Say," Laura said, flouncing out from the cabin to stand before him and brush her thumb across the badge on his chest. "What's this?"

"What's it look like? A nickel's worth of tin. A step up from a few marshals back who had to cut their own badges out of a fruit can."

"How'd you come about it?" She gave him a cockeyed, jeering grin. "Did you steal it? Maybe you pinned it on to impress me."

"It impresses you, does it?"

"Oh, I think any woman is impressed by a handsome man in a badge. Especially one who'd proven himself so capable in saving her life."

Before he knew what he was doing, he'd drawn her to him and kissed her. She gasped and stiffened at first, but once she was in his arms, her body turned to warm mud, yielding to him. She returned his kiss with a passionate one of her own.

"My," she said, her chest rising and falling heavily as they finally pulled apart. "I have to say . . . that took me a little by surprise."

"Sorry. Me too."

"Don't apologize."

He smiled down at her, loving how her cheeks were flushed again. The flush had stretched all the way into her ears, and her eyes were positively radiant.

"What about," she said slowly, studying him closely, "the young lady who fainted in your arms the other day.

The lovely young lady, I might add, who had been wearing even less than I was at the time."

"That's over," Hunter said resolutely.

"Oh? That happened awfully fast."

"Not really. It happened months ago. I just wasn't willing to accept it. But I am now." Hunter could still hear the angry words she'd hurled at him the last time they'd been together in Big Dan's Saloon: *Go to hell with Miss Meyers and don't you ever come back, you bastard!*

Now he ran his hands down Laura's arms. "I'm sorry I didn't come sooner. When I got roped into the town marshal's job, the two rapscallions who roped me into it gave me the impression that all I'd be doing was locking up drunks and fetching widows' cats out of trees. Well, I've been a lot busier than that. And I've been studying a law book, as well, so I have some idea what and what not to do. Those two federals didn't tell me anything about that either."

Laura laughed and then reached up to flick his hat brim with her thumb. "I think you could use a cup of coffee."

Buchanon smiled. "I think I could."

"Have a seat at my dining table," she said, pointing at the crude wood table and two chairs sitting in the yard near one of the clotheslines.

She wheeled and headed back into the cabin, announcing, "I'll be right out with the pot, Marshal Buchanon!"

CHAPTER 20

"I heard what happened with Ike Talon," Laura said as she set the black coffeepot and two stone mugs — both with many fine cracks in them — on the table.

Hunter had taken a seat in one of the two chairs, sitting sideways to the table, right elbow on the table, one ankle resting atop the other knee. He'd doffed his hat and hooked it over an edge of the table.

"You did? Who told you?"

Laura poured coffee into his cup. "I walked to town the other day for groceries and other supplies." She glanced down at her sensible dress. "While I was in the ladies' dress shop, I heard a couple of the women talking about how that *lowly former Rebel soldier* shot a man dead in the street and then tortured him."

She glanced at him with a wince then filled her own mug.

"Lowly former Rebel soldier," Hunter

said, arching a mock accusatory brow at her. "Now, why would you assume that was me?"

"Only because the name Talon was mentioned," Laura said with a coy smile. She sat down in her chair and lifted her coffee to her lips, continuing to smile at him through the steam rising from the mug. "You could have had him arrested, you know."

"I could have. But then, I wouldn't be wearin' this shiny new star."

"Oh, so it was sort of an audition?"

"A what?"

"Never mind."

Buchanon furled a brow at her in mock indignation. "Listen, if you're gonna try to intimidate this lowly ex-Rebel with big words, I'm not gonna come around here anymore."

"I apologize!" She reached across the table and placed her hand on his wrist. "Only simple words from now on."

Hunter smiled. "That's better."

Keeping her hand on his wrist, she frowned across the table at him. "You have such a warm smile and kind eyes. How did such a decent man learn to kill with such brutality?"

"I like to call it efficiency."

"All right. Efficiency, then."

"The war."

"I had a feeling you were going to say that."

"It's my least favorite trait. I hate what I did during the war. I killed innocent men who were only doing their duty, just like I was. But I discovered I was uncommonly good at it. An inherited trait, no doubt. A barbaric one. I have to tell you that I got so's I even enjoyed it . . . until I killed one particular young man. A young Union picket. He couldn't have been much over . . . well, my own age. Sixteen or so. He looked younger somehow. I stuck a bowie knife in him."

Laura sucked a sharp breath through her teeth.

"I want to tell you this about me but it's not going to make you feel any better about who I am . . . or what I've done."

Laura dragged her hand back over to her side of the table but kept her gaze on his. "Go on."

Buchanon sipped his coffee.

"It was late — one or two in the morning — and I'd been sent to blow up several supply wagons along the Tennessee River, using the Union's own Ketchum grenades. Those wagons were heavily guarded, and the

245

young man I killed had been one of those guards.

"There was a clear half-moon, and that creamy light was reflected in the young soldier's eyes as I stole up on him and closed my hand over his mouth to muffle any scream, and jerked him over backward from behind. I pulled the bloody knife out of his belly and found myself staring into a pair of young, anguished, terrified eyes gazing back at me in bald horror.

"As I remember — and I remember every detail and likely will till they nail the lid down on my coffin — the kid was tall and willowy, a face speckled with red pimples. Just a kid. I dragged him back into the woods along the river. He was bleeding out, dying fast. I laid him out on the ground and slid my hand away from his mouth.

" 'Oh God,' the kid wheezed out at me. 'I'm dyin' — ain't I?' "

Hunter blinked a sheen of emotion from his eyes, swallowed a growing knot in his throat.

"I just stared down at him. For a while, I couldn't move. I'd killed so many men almost without thinking about it. That's what you had to do as a soldier. You had to numb yourself against killing. You killed for the greater good. You killed for the freedom of the Confederacy, to stamp out the uppity Yankee aggressors. But as much as I wanted to ignore the innocent eyes staring up at me on that moonlit night along the Tennessee, my mind flinched in horror and revulsion at the fear in that boy's eyes.

"He whispered so softly that I could barely hear him. He said, 'Ma an' Pa . . . never gonna see 'em again. My lovely May!' " Hunter sniffed, brushed tears from his eyes with his left forearm. " 'We was gonna be married as soon as I went home!' he told me.

"Grief and sorrow exploded inside me. I dropped the bloody knife, grabbed the kid by his collar, and drew his head up to my own." Hunter made the motions with his own hands. " 'I'm sorry!' I told him. 'I'm sorry!'

"The kid just stared back at me, two half-moons floating in his eyes like on the surface of a night-dark lake. He opened his mouth. He wanted to say something but he couldn't get the words out. Then his eyes rolled back and he was dead."

Hunter blinked more tears from his eyes, saw the dark marks they made on the freshly scrubbed table. "That kid haunts me every day and night. I can't get him out of my head. After the war, I hung up my guns. I thought I'd hung them up for good . . . till the trouble last summer. Till my brothers were killed. I had to strap them on again, and that's the problem with killing. Once it starts it just never seems to end. Especially when you're cursed with being good at it."

He turned to Laura who sat staring back at him from across the table, her own eyes bright with tears.

"As for Ike Talon, I shouldn't have killed him that way. But once I got going . . . and I remembered what he did to Charley . . . and what his men did to you . . . something just broke loose in me and I couldn't control it anymore."

Hunter shook his head in disgust with himself. He lifted his mug and sipped his coffee. He sat back in the chair and turned to Laura once more. "There you have it. Those are this tiger's stripes."

She slid her hand back across the table. She closed it over his wrist again and squeezed. "Can I ask you for a favor?"

"Anything."

"Would you help me get everything back inside the cabin? And then come inside with me?" She paused, gazing directly into his eyes, her chest rising and falling sharply as she breathed. "Do you have time?"

Hunter placed his hand over hers. "I'll make time."

The cabin door opened an hour later, and Hunter stepped out, yawning, stretching, and scrubbing his hands through his hair, making it stick up in spikes.

He glanced back into the cabin. Laura lay curled on her side beneath the single sheet, her hair down and hanging in love-mussed tangles about her flushed cheeks and her bare shoulders.

She smiled, and her eyes caught the light angling into the cabin through the door.

Hunter drew the door closed. He wore only his buckskin pants and boots. The Black Hills' heat and humidity could be as brutal as the winters were long and cold.

He thumbed his suspenders up his bare shoulders, then walked straight out away from the cabin. He walked past the tree to which he'd tied his handsome cream stallion, Ghost. Earlier, before he'd helped Laura get her cabin back in order, he'd unsaddled the horse and set a bucket of water down for him.

Now Ghost watched Hunter, curiously twitching his ears. He lowered his head and pawed the ground with his left front hoof, playful.

Hunter snorted then headed into the woodshed behind the school. A minute later, he came out pushing a wheelbarrow loaded with logs. He dumped the logs in front of the cabin, then returned to the woodshed three more times, each for another load of logs. On his last trip, he hauled the splitting maul as well as the logs over to the cabin, then set to work splitting the logs into stove-size chunks of firewood.

It was late in the day, the shadows growing long and wide, but it was still hot. Sweat soon cloaked his broad chest in a golden sheen. He set each log on a larger log he used as a base, raised the maul high above his head, and cleanly cleaved the wood with the maul's steel blade.

He'd always enjoyed the pure raw exercise of wood-splitting, and he had the chest and arms and washboard belly to prove it. Soon, he had a sizable pile of split wood stacked neatly in front of the cabin. He set another log on the chopping block, raised the maul, and swung it down with a grunt. The blade disappeared for a moment in the pine chunk, and the chunk exploded into four equal pieces, leaving the maul stuck in the chopping block.

As he gathered the pieces and stacked them, the cabin door opened with a groan of dry hinges, the bottom of the door scraping the floor.

He turned to see Laura step out of the cabin with a blanket wrapped around her otherwise naked body. She was barefoot, and her nearly dry hair was lovely as it hung in fetching tangles. The late sunlight shone gold in the chestnut tresses.

"Don't mind me," she said, tossing her hair back away from her smooth, still-flushed cheeks, smiling admiringly at the muscles rippling and bulging in his arms and flexing beneath the blond hair of his broad chest. "I'm just going to watch you work."

She leaned back against the door frame.

Hunter chuckled, set another log on the block, split it, then left the pieces where they lay. He left the maul on the chopping block and walked over to the pretty girl standing outside the cabin. He stood over her, hooking his thumbs behind the waistband of his trousers, sweating, and glanced at the door.

"Those hinges need grease, and the bottom of the door needs planing. I think your chimney's fouled. That's why the range leaks smoke. Probably a squirrel nest or a bird's nest in there. That needs cleaned out too. I'll be by in the next few days to take

251

care of that for you. And that leak in the roof."

He glanced up at a gap between the moss-covered shakes. "There's probably more than one. I'll make sure those logs get chinked for you too."

"You don't have to do that. You have a job to do."

"Every man gets a break."

"You know what I think?"

"What's that?"

She moved up close to him, twisted a finger in the sweat-damp hair curling on his chest, and gave him a crooked, coquettish smile. "I think you might be striving for reasons to come calling again."

Hunter wrapped his arms around her, placed a finger beneath her chin, and tipped her head back, her swollen lips only inches from his own. "No striving here. I'll be back. You can count on —"

He stopped when the rataplan of a galloping horse sounded, accompanied shortly by a man's voice yelling, "Marshal Buchanon! Marshal Buchanon!"

Hunter lowered his arms, then shoved Laura toward the cabin door. "You'd best go inside!"

Giving him a worried look, she swung around, her hair and the tail of the blanket swishing, and hurried inside. As she closed the door, frowning through the narrowing crack, Hunter stepped away from the cabin just as a horse and rider appeared, galloping around the woodshed and heading straight for the cabin.

"Marshal Buchanon! Marshal Buchanon!"

As the rider approached, the door behind Hunter moaned and scraped, and he turned as Laura tossed his shirt out through the three-foot gap. "Here!"

Laura glanced beyond Hunter as the rider approached. Her eyes widened and she drew the door closed quickly.

Pulling the buckskin tunic over his head, Hunter turned to the rider, recognizing Otis Crosby, a beefy, moon-faced odd-job man in his early thirties clad in dungarees, work boots, and a blue work shirt. Otis was riding a horse Hunter recognized as belonging to a local faro dealer, Luther Sorenson. Hunter frowned up at Otis, whose gaze had drifted to the door before shuttling back toward Buchanon, the skin above Otis's nose furled incredulously.

"What on God's green earth is the matter, Otis?" Hunter said, shoving the shirttails down into his trousers.

Otis's vaguely questioning gaze drifted from Hunter to the door again, then back to Hunter, and the odd-jobber's sunburned cheeks turned redder.

"Come on, Otis — out with it!" Hunter said, feeling his ears burn with chagrin. Otis had obviously seen him standing out here with his shirt off as well as Laura's quickly retreating figure clad in only an old striped trade blanket.

Otis was a reliable roofer and woodcutter — one who could also be relied upon to spread gossip as fast and as broadly as the ladies from the Tigerville Lutheran Church Sobriety League. And that was saying something. What Otis had seen here was sure to spread like a wildfire in a drought on a windy summer afternoon.

"Big trouble, Marshal Buchanon!" he said. "Six Injuns done rode into town, waltzed right into the Goliad Saloon — never mind the signs that says no Injuns, half-breeds, Mescins, Chinamen, darkies, or Easterners allowed — and shot Phil Scudder outright! Then they robbed the place, sayin' they was gettin' even for their people who Scudder poisoned.

"They shot the faro dealer when Mister Sorenson bore down on 'em with that big greener of his! Then the other men in the place started shootin' at the Injuns and the Injuns returned fire . . . and when I slipped out of there to fetch you, they was all pinned down behind tables an' such, still inside the Goliad, swappin' lead like hell wouldn't have it!"

Hunter had told Otis where he'd be in the event trouble erupted so the odd-job man would know where to fetch him. Buchanon just hadn't counted on trouble erupting this early in the evening, nor on being caught in a compromising position with Laura though he'd felt himself becoming attracted to her over the past few days.

Hunter didn't have time to worry about his and, more importantly, Laura's reputation. He swung around, pushed through the cabin door, scooped his hat off the table, and grabbed his gun belt and LeMat and bowie knife off a wall peg. As he strapped the belt around his waist and headed back to the door, he glanced at Laura standing near the front window, holding the blanket taut around her shoulders.

Judging by the concern in her eyes, she'd overheard everything.

"Be careful," she said.

He grabbed her, kissed her hastily, then hurried out the door.

CHAPTER 21

Otis was still waiting outside the shack on the faro dealer's horse as Hunter hurried out the door and strode across the yard at an angle toward his own mount.

A minute later, mounted on Ghost's back, Hunter raced around the side of the school and then onto the newly graded trail that rose and fell over two low rises peppered with settlers' sad shacks, stock pens, and hay barns. As he crested one of these rises and started down the other side, he checked Ghost down slightly. Warren Davenport rode toward him in his red-wheeled, two-seater chaise buggy.

Davenport's big, raw-boned frame was clad in what appeared a new black suit with a fawn wool vest, bowler hat, and red pocket square. A gold watch chain flashed in the sun. As Buchanon trotted Ghost toward where the man was slowing his own horse, scowling up at him curiously, Hunter regarded the man with what must have been a similar expression. When Hunter, still approaching, saw a spray of brightly colored flowers — a mix of roses and pansies likely recently purchased from a local flower shop — lying on the seat beside the man, his own curiosity swelled inside him.

As the men's gazes held, Davenport's brows ridged and his own eyes glinted with suspicion. More than just suspicion — bald disdain and indignation.

Now hearing muffled gunfire crackling from the town center, Hunter batted his heels to the stallion's flanks, and Ghost shot on up the trail. As he crested the next rise, he glanced back over his left shoulder. Davenport had now stopped his chaise and was talking to Otis Crosby, who'd stopped the faro dealer's horse beside the buggy. As the two men talked, both men turned their heads to glance along the trail toward Hunter.

Buchanon turned his head forward and galloped on down the rise, not so vaguely musing on Davenport's destination with that new suit and those fresh flowers, though it took little musing to cipher out that there was really only one place the businessman could be going.

To the home of the pretty new schoolteacher, of course.

As Hunter weaved his way around shacks and stock pens, he absently hoped Laura had a derringer lying around the cabin. Living on her own, she'd need it, and not only to fend off the Cullen boys . . .

As he cut through a break between the bank and the assay office, and swung Ghost to the south, he turned his attention to the trouble at hand. The gunfire was growing louder, angrier, and he could hear men shouting and yelling and a woman screaming. A man seemed to be screaming, as well, as though in horrible agony.

There was little street traffic. Most of the men and women normally heading for the saloons this time of the day were gathered in small clusters on the boardwalks, looking tense and wary and conversing in low tones, obviously unsettled by the sounds of the foofaraw coming from the direction of the Goliad, which sat on a side street one block east of the main avenue.

Hunter swung Ghost hard left at the side street.

Men were clustered on both sides of the street, crouching carefully and staring down the side street toward the Goliad, a large, plain, white frame building with a peaked roof and a balcony running along the outside of the second floor. Several men either lay or were crawling, obviously wounded, on the street fronting the saloon/hotel/ whorehouse. A horse was down, as well, near one of the two hitchracks fronting the building, flopping and trying futilely to stand.

One man lay half in and half out of a window on the side of the building facing Hunter. He wasn't moving.

Meanwhile, the thunder of gunfire swelled until two men came running out of the saloon's front door and onto the front gallery, where several more men lay unmoving or, in one case, sitting up with his back to the Goliad's front wall, wailing, "I'm hit! I'm hit! Those savages shot me!"

He wasn't the only one squawking. More men yelled and wailed inside the hotel. A girl loosed shrill screams over and over again, every other second, as though she were in a screaming contest.

Three more men followed the first two out of the building. All five had long black hair and were wearing buckskin pants, shirts, and moccasins. All five wore six-shooters around their hips and were wielding Winchester carbines. Ochre, white, and blue war paint streaked their broad, dark-eyed, cinnamon-colored faces. A couple wore their hair in braids woven with dyed buckskin.

As Hunter checked Ghost down to a skidding halt, curveting the mount, pointing his right shoulder at the hotel, the five Sioux ran toward a hitchrack on the other side of the street and maybe forty yards beyond the hotel. A tall white man walked out of the Goliad's front door. Stopping at the edge of the gallery, he raised a long-barrel New Army Colt straight out in his right hand, and shouted, "Stop, you red devils!"

The Colt bucked and roared, red flames lancing from the barrel.

All five redskins stopped in the street before their horses, wheeled, crouched, raised their rifles, and sent a volley of lead back toward the Goliad.

"Oh, damn you!" the tall man yelped as the bullets punched him straight back into the hotel, firing the Colt straight up in the air.

Hunter shucked his brother's Henry out of the saddle scabbard, leaped out of the leather, and swatted Ghost with the rifle's butt, yelling, "Get out of the way, Ghost!"

As the horse wheeled and, whinnying shrilly, galloped back in the direction from which it and its rider had come, Hunter dropped to a knee. But then he saw that all five savages were drawing beads on him.

He leaped back to his feet just as one of the maws bearing down on him sprouted smoke and flames. The bullet sang past his left ear as he turned and ran to his right, gritting his teeth at the furious belching of the Indians' rifles. He launched himself off his heels and into the air, diving over a stock trough and landing on the ground beyond it on his back with a sharp grunt.

He damn near knocked the wind out of himself, he noted as the redskins' bullets thumped into the stock trough and tore chunks out of its upper edges, slinging the slivers onto Hunter's face and chest.

No. He *did* knock the wind out of himself!

He rolled over onto his belly and lay gasping for breath. When he was finally able to suck some air into his lungs, he realized that beneath the tolling of cracked bells in his ears caused by the wicked slamming of the bullets into the trough just inches from his head, he'd heard the hard, fast thuds of fleeing horses.

He raised his head, now hatless, as well as the rifle.

The five Indians were galloping east, away from the hotel, their long black hair bouncing on their shoulders.

Hunter jacked a round into the Henry's

chamber and aimed. He held his fire and lowered the barrel. They were too far away, fleeing fast.

He rose to a knee then, taking another painful breath, pushed off the knee to his feet. He crouched to scoop his hat off the ground and set it on his head.

He looked around at the carnage in the street and on the boardwalk on his side of the street. He walked over and put the wounded horse out of its misery. The other horses tied to the hitchrack must have fled after this one had taken a bullet through one of the Goliad's several broken out windows during the height of the melee inside the saloon.

Hunter turned to a dozen or so men clumped behind him, gazing beyond him toward the scene of the chaos, and yelled, "Somebody fetch the sawbones!"

Buchanon strode along the boardwalk, then stepped up onto the Goliad's front gallery. The man who'd been sitting there announcing that he was hit was still sitting there but he was no longer saying anything. Wearing a nicely groomed beard framing his pale face, he sat back against the wall, beneath a shattered window, his crossed eyes staring up over Hunter's right shoulder. Hunter recognized him as the local haberdasher, Vincent Kozlowski.

The man had taken at least two rounds to the chest, another just above his groin.

No wonder he'd been yelling.

Hunter stepped through the bullet-riddled batwing doors. The place looked as though a tornado had ripped through it. Men were only now rising from behind overturned tables and chairs, looking ready to duck again at the first sign of more lead. Four scuttled out from behind the player piano on the right side of the room, beneath an oil painting of a nude, ivory-skinned red-haired woman with a jade necklace reclining on a green fainting couch.

She and the couch had weathered the lead swap little better than the rest of the room had. She'd taken a bullet to the forehead and another to a knee, but neither wound had faded her come-hither smile.

There were more men sprawled on the floor and over tables and chairs, bleeding out in the sawdust, than there were stepping warily out of the smoky shadows. A dead Indian lay against the wall to Buchanon's left, beneath a red blood smear on the wall above him. The dead Indian's Winchester lay across his right shoulder.

One of the six was dead. Five remained.

At least the girl had stopped screaming.

Hunter didn't see any girls down here, dead or otherwise, so the doves must have fled to the second story.

Good choice.

Hunter picked out one man, a beefy gent with curly red hair and wearing a shaggy beard on his freckled, ruddy face — a bouncer here at the Goliad, and said, "Llewelyn, what the hell had them Injuns' necks in a hump?"

He'd heard it once from Otis Crosby, but he wanted to hear it again from a man who'd been in the thick of it.

Llewelyn had taken a bullet to his shoulder. He was breathing hard through gritted teeth as he walked unsteadily toward Buchanon. He spat to one side, furious, and said, "They accused Scudder of sellin' illegal whiskey on the reservation and then they shot him and then two of them mangy devils leaped behind the bar to clean out the cash box. Sorenson had his double-barrel like he always does, and he tried to cut down on 'em, but them Injuns was ready for him."

The big bouncer hooked his thumb over his shoulder, indicating a man in a snappy green suit with an orange brocade vest still seated in his chair though he and the chair had been overturned onto the floor. The faro dealer's blood-splattered shotgun lay nearby. There was a pumpkin-size hole in the ceiling above him, where he'd discharged both barrels of the greener.

"There he lays," the bouncer said. "Dead before he hit the gallblamed floor!"

Hunter said, "Was Scudder sellin' illegal whiskey?"

"Hell, I don't know. I just bounce here during the day and over at the Queen of Hearts at night. I was just about to get off here when them six savages rode into town like it's ten years ago and Red Cloud is still raisin' hob!"

He cursed and, gritting his teeth again, looked down at his bloody shoulder.

Hunter swung around and left the saloon. He hadn't seen that much carnage in any one place since the Big Trouble of the previous year. He hadn't expected to see something like this in Tigerville. He'd have expected it a few years ago, when the town had been about as wide open as any mining hub on the frontier.

And, as Llewelyn had said, back when the Sioux were still on the prod.

Hunter didn't mind admitting to himself that he was shaken. Not only by the carnage and by the fact that it had been instigated by Indians, but by his own responsibility in

265

the matter.

He found himself the unlikely, not to mention reluctant, town marshal of Tigerville, with the problem falling soundly . . . and *resoundingly* . . . in his lap.

He had to try to run down those murdering Sioux before they disappeared into the ravines and canyons of the Pine Ridge Reserve, some of the remotest, ruggedest country in the territory.

It was his job.

As he walked out into the street, poked a finger between his lips, and whistled for his horse, he silently opined that those two old federal lawdogs, Winslow and Birmingham, were going to have the last laugh, after all.

True, when those Indians left town, they'd officially left Buchanon's jurisdiction and strayed into Winslow's and Birmingham's. Still, any town marshal worth his salt would go after them since there was no one else to do it. If only to follow them and find out where they ended up so he could pass the information on to the federals.

He considered forming a posse but nixed the idea outright. That would take too long. Those redskins would be splitting the wind. It was too close to sundown. He had to pick up their trail before dark and follow them and wait for an opportunity to take them down. Their horses were likely not shod, as Indians didn't shoe their horses. Nothing turned colder faster than the trail of an unshod horse.

Ghost came galloping back down the cross-street, shaking his head, cream mane waving. The stallion didn't like the carnage it saw around it, nor the smell of it, but he'd come back because he was well-trained and loyal and just one hell of a good, all around horse. He and Hunter had fought last year's war together; they'd been baptized together in blood.

Hunter caught the ribbons, swung into the saddle, slid the Henry into the scabbard, then booted Ghost back toward Dakota Avenue. He'd seen the Indians head east, but he knew they'd swing south at the edge of town. Pine Ridge lay to the south and east.

Hunter knew a shortcut to the trail that led to the main trail to Pine Ridge.

If the Indians followed a trail, that was. They might head cross-country.

He turned left onto Dakota Avenue and galloped down the street still lined with shocked, wary faces of men and some women exclaiming and wagging their heads at the killings at the Goliad. One of those shocked faces stood out in the crowd. It was an uncommonly pretty one framed by thick tresses of deep red hair.

It belonged to Annabelle Ludlow, who stood outside Big Dan's Saloon in her gallingly scanty getup. Her bosom buddy, Bobby Lee, sat on the boardwalk beside her, staring at Hunter, ears pricked.

Buchanon cursed.

CHAPTER 22

Hunter was going to ride on past Annabelle but when she stepped into the street, he checked Ghost down but kept his head forward, not looking at her directly.

Bile still churned in his loins not only for the angry words she'd spewed at him, but for the shameful way she was acting, standing out here on the street wearing no more than Hunter could pack into his mouth and still eat a full meal around.

She walked up to him in her high-heeled shoes to stand just off his right stirrup. "What happened?"

"Some Indians shot up the Goliad. I'm going after them."

He clucked to Ghost, putting him ahead, but drew back on the reins when Annabelle reached up to place her hand on his thigh. "Hunter, wait!"

"What is it?" he snarled at her, looking at her finally.

She gazed up at him, worry carving ladder rungs across her forehead. "You're going alone? After *Indians*?"

"No choice. If I wait, I'll lose 'em." Hunter glanced at Bobby Lee standing to the right of Annabelle's fishnet stocking–clad right leg and shiny green canvas shoe adorned with a cream satin ribbon. Many a time Bobby Lee had helped him and his father and brothers track cattle-rustling bronco braves. Bobby had a good sniffer when it came to Injuns.

"I could use help tracking, Bobby . . . if you think you can leave this . . . uh" — he raked his eyes across Annabelle's nearly nude body, and wrinkled his nose distastefully — "*parlor girl* unchaperoned for a few hours."

"I'm not a parlor girl, you big, simpleminded ass!" Annabelle squawked, cheeks turning crimson with fury.

But Hunter had already booted Ghost on down the street to the south. He glanced over his shoulder to see Annabelle squaring her shoulders at him, glowering at him hatefully, fists on her hips. Bobby Lee stood looking from Hunter to Annabelle then back again. Annabelle looked down at him then swung her arm forward, indicating Buchanon.

270

The coyote gave an eager yip and came running, catching up to Hunter and running along beside him, gracefully avoiding horseback riders, buggies, and drays weaving through the street around them.

Hunter, still miffed at the coyote for his questionable alliance with the girl who'd broken his heart, kept his head forward, muttering angrily under his breath. Yes, it was she who'd broken *his* heart, he told himself. Not the other way around. *Everything I did, all the choices I made, were for her benefit. She was only dressing like some one-dollar doxie, attracting the attention of every male in town, to spite him.*

Cunning, vindictive little wench!

Well, he'd moved on.

Time now to turn his full attention to those war-painted redskins.

At the south edge of town, he swung east on a shaggy two-track, a former freighting trail that slithered up over the prairie from Ogallala, Nebraska. Hunter, with Bobby Lee dogging him from behind, followed the trail at a hard gallop. He rounded the base of a haystack butte, then continued hard, crouched forward over the saddle horn, looking around for those crazy, red-skinned killers.

He continued his hell-for-leather pace for

a good mile, then reined in Ghost and sat atop a low, grassy, cedar-stippled rise, looking around cautiously, frowning, peering into the long shadows stretching eastward from rocks, trees, sage brush, and steeply sloping, pine-clad ridges.

He'd thought he'd have seen the killers by now.

They'd had to have come down that valley ahead of him, that angled down from the northwest to curve around between steep, piney ridges before making another turn to jog off to the south and west, straight out beyond Hunter's position. That was the only way out of Tigerville from the east.

Bobby Lee gave a low moan. Hunter turned to the coyote seated on a rocky outcropping to Hunter's left. The coyote shifted his front feet edgily, looking at Hunter sharply, then turned his head to the south, tilted his long, arrow-shaped snout nearly straight up in the air, and gave a low wailing cry.

The coyote leaped down off the outcropping, landing on the trail directly ahead of Ghost, then shot off the trail's right side and into the shallow valley to the south.

"Where the hell you goin'?" Hunter said, keeping his voice down. Those redskins might be anywhere.

They wouldn't be headed south. Not yet. At least, not directly. Dead Horse Canyon lay that way, beyond a steep jog of rocky bluffs.

Bobby might only be tracking a rabbit but Hunter had known the coyote long enough to know that Bobby wouldn't lead him after a rabbit. He reined Ghost off the trail and booted the horse into a lope. Bobby Lee was a small shadow against the blond grass and sage now over a hundred yards ahead. He was heading to the left of the steep, pine-clad ridge jutting steeply straight to the south.

"I don't know where you're goin', Bobby Lee," Hunter said to himself, looking around. "I just hope you're not leadin' me off on a wild goose chase . . ."

Ahead, Bobby ran around the steep ridge's left side and disappeared from Hunter's view.

"No way, Bobby," Hunter told himself, scowling over Ghost's pricked ears. "Not a chance — there's a stone wall back in there — a bastion of solid rock. It angles down from the top of that piney ridge. Them Injuns wouldn't have headed that way because there's no *trail* through there!"

Having hunted this country for years,

Hunter knew most of the trails around Dead Horse Canyon.

Still, he followed the coyote though he was beginning to be more and more convinced that Bobby Lee was on the trail of a cottontail or jackrabbit. If so, by following the crazy coyote, Hunter was losing precious time. He needed to find the Indians' trail before dark, and sundown was only a half hour away.

He and Ghost loped around the side of the pine-clad ridge. Now that stone wall loomed high ahead of him, set back a little from the forested one. Its steep face was strewn with boulders that had likely fallen from its crest over the eons, and lightly stippled with pines, cedars, and junipers growing from cracks in the rock wall.

Bobby Lee was a shadow sliding across the ground dead ahead of Hunter, angling gradually from Hunter's right to his left. He appeared to have his nose to the ground.

Hunter scanned the ground around him. Spying something, he checked Ghost down, stepped out of the leather, and dropped to a knee.

Fresh horse apples lay in a ragged line before him, dropped by a fast-moving horse. Hunter didn't have to touch one of the apples to know they were fresh; he could smell the green of the recently dropped dung.

Around the dropping, squinting and straining his eyes, he could see the faint impressions of unshod hooves. He also saw wagon tracks. The ground here was hard and carpeted in short, tough, strawberry blond grass that didn't accept impressions easily, but there was definitely recent sign left by passing riders on unshod ponies as well as wagon tracks. Several sets of wagon tracks, in fact.

The wagon tracks were older. A wagon had passed through here multiple times the past several months.

His heart quickening hopefully, Buchanon swung back up onto Ghost's back and booted the mount ahead. He could no longer see Bobby Lee. He looked from left to right then back again.

Nothing.

It was as though the brush wolf had been swept up into the sky; he appeared to be nowhere around. If he was out here, Hunter would see him, for there was little cover out here to hide him — none, in fact.

Had he climbed the ridge?

Slowing Ghost to a fast walk, Hunter gazed up the steep inclination, looking for any sign of Bobby Lee's small, gray, fast-moving form.

Movement nearly straight ahead of him pulled his gaze down from the ridge to its base. A small, four-legged beast, the west-angling sun glinting gold in Bobby Lee's faun coat and yellow eyes, moved out from the base of the ridge and then leaped onto a wagon-size boulder that had tumbled down the ridge a long time ago. Bobby sat atop the boulder, lifted his long, pointed snout, and gave a chortling yowl.

Hunter booted Ghost into another gallop, covering the ground between himself and Bobby Lee quickly. When he was twenty feet from the boulder, Bobby leaped fleetly, gracefully down from the top of the rock, striking the ground on all fours with a thud. He ran back to the base of the ridge . . . and disappeared before Hunter's very eyes!

It was as though the ridge had absorbed him.

Hunter shook his head and rubbed his eyes. He looked at the ridge base again.

No Bobby.

What the hell . . . ?

He kept Ghost moving. As he did, the base of the ridge acquired an odd shape. The gray wall seemed to shift and separate. There appeared to be a gap in it, one that he could see better when he canted his head to the right.

Hunter swung Ghost to the right and continued forward, letting the stallion take a few more long strides.

Sure enough, he saw a gap that had been partially hidden from view by the boulder Bobby had been sitting on. The problem was the ridge wall was the same gray as the boulder, giving the illusion that the base of the wall was all one stony gray slab. But tucked away at an angle behind the boulder was a notch angling back into the rock wall, like a half-open door opening to the inside.

The notch was filled with dark shadows, and those shadows grew as Hunter steered Ghost around the boulder and into the notch.

Bobby Lee appeared before him, sitting just inside the notch and at the opening of what appeared to be a cave with a portal roughly the size of a large barn's open stock doors.

Bobby Lee gazed smugly up at Hunter, tongue hanging down over his lower jaw with its small, curved white teeth.

"Bobby Lee, I'll be damned if you ain't smarter'n I've given you credit for!"

Bobby Lee growled as though annoyed, then wheeled and disappeared into the cave.

Hunter followed. The cave ceiling was

high enough that he didn't have to dismount or even duck. The walls of the cave moving up around him were roughly twenty feet apart. The floor of the cave was hard rock, but there were small stretches of gravel and loamy gray dirt bearing the impressions of unshod hoof and wagon tracks.

"They came this way," Hunter muttered to himself, hearing the astonishment in his voice, the mutters echoing off the close rock walls around him. "I'll be damned if Bobby Lee ain't right!"

Seeing gray light ahead, and Bobby Lee's small shadow jostling against it, he booted Ghost into a faster walk. Obviously, this wasn't a cave but a hidden passage through the stony bulwark. It had likely been carved by a long-ago river.

As he neared the light, he glanced at the walls on either side of him. The walls were painted with zigzags, sunbursts, and wavy lines in bright reds and yellows. There were also scenes depicting stick figures in elaborate costumes floating above hunting scenes — stick figures with long hair impaling a deer or an elk, sometimes a bear standing upright. These scenes were interspersed with representations of buffalo and bird tracks.

The Black Hills caves, and there was a

veritable labyrinth of caves in the Hills, were filled with such paintings. A man who'd called himself an archaeologist had spent a few weeks on the Buchanon ranch several summers back while he'd been exploring the Hills. He'd informed Hunter, who'd seen many such paintings on his hunting and curiosity-driven expeditions around the Hills, that some of those cave paintings, or "petroglyphs" as the learned man had called them, were over eight thousand years old.

Seeing those scenes depicting activities so long ago always gave Hunter a ghostly chill, and they did now, as well.

He followed Bobby Lee into the wash of dimming gray light. He'd thought that they were coming to the far side of the ridge and would be out in the open when they gained the light. Now he saw that wasn't true. Halting Ghost and staring straight up toward the sky, he saw that the light was coming down through a thirty-foot, straight up-and-down gap in the rock.

Ahead lay more stone-walled passage.

Bobby had continued, so Hunter could no longer see him but he could hear the soft ticking of the coyote's nails on the stone floor, and the rapid pants. Something told Hunter that Bobby Lee was as curious about this passage as he himself was.

Also, the coyote was being led by the fresh scent of the Sioux warriors, who'd passed through here less than a half hour ago.

"Hold on, Bobby," Hunter called, gigging Ghost on ahead, hearing his voice echoing off the close stone walls. "Wait for me, *amigo.* Being this deep in a mountain makes my insides quiver, an' that's a natural fact!"

Now the floor of the passage began dropping.

Ghost was careful to keep his footing, slowing his pace and taking cautious, mincing, herky-jerky steps. Suddenly, it was almost as dark as the inside of a well. Fortunately, for only a short time. Soon, more faint light shone ahead. And then, as the passage floor continued dropping, Hunter could again see Bobby's small figure silhouetted against it.

The light grew until it formed a ragged-edged oval.

The oval grew closer . . . closer . . . and Hunter blew a sigh of relief as the passage walls slipped back behind him and he and Ghost rode out into fresh air filled with birdsong. Above was the vast sky, green with late light and bayoneted with lemon-colored streaks from the setting sun.

The horse gave a nervous snort and a whicker, shook his head. He hadn't liked that dark passage any more than Hunter had.

Buchanon looked around and whistled. The passage had led him into Dead Horse Canyon. The north wall of the canyon shot straight up above him. The southern ridge loomed ahead, on the far side of the slender stream of Dead Horse Creek, whose far bank was peppered with shrubs and small pines.

Bobby Lee stood in the middle of the stream, lowering his head to the water, drinking thirstily. Hunter gigged Ghost up to the stream and let him drink. He swung down from his saddle, lay belly-down, and cupped water to his mouth. He returned to the horse for his canteen, poured out the brackish stuff from earlier in the day, and refilled it.

As he did, he looked around warily, keeping one hand close to the LeMat on his hip. He also watched Bobby Lee, relieved that the coyote didn't look edgy, which meant there was no imminent danger. When Bobby Lee had slaked his thirst at the stream, the coyote sat down on the far bank, putting his back to Hunter and staring straight across the canyon toward the southern ridge.

Hunter could hear the coyote sniffing and growling very softly, eerily.

The Indians must have continued straight across the canyon.

Brows ridged with befuddlement, Hunter returned his canteen to his saddle horn. Chicken flesh rose across his shoulders.

Were the Indians planning to hole up in the canyon till morning?

If so . . . and if he continued across the gorge . . . he might ride into an ambush. On the other hand, Bobby Lee would likely warn him if they started to get close.

Urgency prodding Buchanon forward, he stepped back into his saddle, booted Ghost across the stream, and followed Bobby Lee to the south, nearly straight across the canyon. He followed the coyote into yet another, partly disguised gap in the ridge wall.

This gap did not let into another tunnel, however. It traced a slender side canyon running perpendicular to the main one. It rose gradually, hardly winding Ghost at all, until Hunter found himself on the canyon's southern rim, under a vastly arching, velvet-black sky aglitter with stars so bright that they resembled a million tiny Christmas tree candles.

It was dark enough that he decided to find a sheltered place to set up camp for the night. He'd continue after the Indians in the morning. He didn't want to risk Ghost stepping into a gopher hole, and there were plenty of gophers out here.

He dry-camped, ate jerky from his saddle-bags, washed it down with fresh water, and slept well, Bobby Lee curled up in a tight ball against his left hip. He saddled and set out just after dawn.

Dogging Bobby Lee, who kept his nose to the ground, he rode all that day . . . and all the next day too.

On the afternoon of the third day, still following the killers' trail as well as a set of well-worn wagon tracks, he checked Ghost down suddenly. Bobby Lee had stopped and now stood in the middle of the trail, ahead of Hunter, lifting his nose and sniffing.

"What is it, Bob —"

Hunter stopped when his eyes picked out the thick, black smoke rising above the next rise to the southeast. The crackle of gunfire reached his ears, faint with distance.

So did what could only be the war cries of rampaging Sioux warriors.

CHAPTER 23

Three days before, a few minutes after Hunter had galloped away from her cabin, Laura returned to the cabin's front window.

A horse had whinnied, and for a moment she thought . . . hoped . . . that Hunter must be returning. But, no. With a cold, wet feeling inside her, she saw Warren Davenport's Morgan horse trot around from behind the wood shed flanking the new school building and pull the sleek black chaise carriage toward the cabin. Davenport's tall, hammer-headed figure, clad in what appeared a new three-piece suit, sat in the front seat, his gloved hands manipulating the reins.

Laura gave a rare curse and stepped quickly away from the window, letting the ragged, flour sack curtains settle back into place. Her heart quickened. She splayed her fingers over her chest, a wash of emotions racing through her.

The primary one was dread.

Warren Davenport was the last person she wanted to see. Her body had been tingling with the feminine fulfillment she'd felt after her hour with Hunter Buchanon. That glorious, storybook feeling that had taken all of the edges off her anxiousness about having come to this rough-and-tumble place vanished the very instant she'd seen that horse and buggy and the crude face with wedge-shaped nose and cold, deep-set eyes of the man driving it.

She looked around, wanting desperately to flee. But the cabin had no back door.

Should she hide?

Should she lock the door and pretend she wasn't here?

She backed away from the door, her hand on her chest, feeling the throbbing of that tortured organ just beneath her breastbone. She drew a breath and held it, seeing the shadow of the buggy as well as of the man driving it slide and jostle beyond the window left of the door.

The hoof thuds and the rattling of the chaise's wheels fell silent.

The horse blew, shook its head. Laura heard the bit rattle in its teeth.

Davenport cleared his throat and called, "Miss Laura?"

Staring at the door, holding her breath,

Laura shivered. There was a harsh, toneless quality about his voice. It perfectly matched the agate-hardness of his eyes set deep in their raw-boned sockets.

"Miss Laura — I brought you something, my dear!"

Laura flinched, felt her shoulders quiver. *My dear?*

She stood staring at the door, heart racing. She'd pretend she wasn't here. Yes, she was taking a walk, getting the lay of the land. She wasn't here. She was elsewhere.

Anywhere but here!

She gasped when three loud knocks sounded on the door. They were as loud as pistol shots.

"Laura!"

Why did he think he could call her by her first name?

Anger joined the mix of emotions roiling inside her.

Three more knocks. Again, she gasped.

He called her name, louder. His voice was angry now. His boots thudded outside the door, and Laura gasped again, louder, when a shadow moved in the window. She leaped back when she saw his face, half-shaded by the brim of his crisp derby hat, glowering in at her, exasperation in his round, bulging eyes. He held both hands up to the window,

286

to each side of his face. He held a spray of brightly colored flowers in his right fist; he was using the flowers to help block the light

"Laura! It's Warren! Haven't you heard me knocking, dear?"

Embarrassment scalded the blood rising in her cheeks and ears. He was staring right at her as she stood six feet back from the door. There was no longer any denying him.

She fashioned a smile and, smoothing her day dress down across her thighs, she stepped to the door and opened it with another flinch of dread. "Oh, Mister Davenport! Why, I . . . I . . ."

He moved toward her from the window, frowning angrily. "Didn't you hear me knock?"

"No, I'm sorry — I'd fallen asleep. I was taking a nap."

"Sound sleeper."

"Yes, well . . ."

"Here. These are for you."

He thrust the flowers at her, smiling broadly. Odd, how his eyes remained as cold and dark as ice on a deep winter pond. She accepted them, frowning at them. "I don't know what to say."

"Oh, I have one more thing! Wait here!"

Davenport wheeled and strode back out to the chaise. From the carriage's back seat he lifted a box wrapped in tissue paper and trimmed with a dark-blue ribbon. Smiling, he walked back to the door and shoved the package through it.

Laura gazed at it dully. "What on earth?"

"Open it."

"It can't be for me."

Davenport frowned suddenly, his heavy brows forming a long, brooding mountain over his eyes. "Why not?"

"Because I . . . because I . . ." Go ahead and say it, she told herself. *Because I can't accept gifts from a man whose advances are unwanted.* Say it!

She couldn't. He'd been nice to her. He was a widower and probably lonely. She didn't want to hurt his feelings.

"Please, Laura," he said, his voice suddenly gentle as he smiled down at her, having to tip his head downward to do so. The top of her head only came up to his chin.

She looked at the neatly wrapped package and then at the flowers.

"Um . . . all right . . ."

She set the flowers and the package on the table. She untied the ribbon, gently removed the paper, and opened the box. More tissue paper resided therein. She opened the paper, uncovering a neatly folded pile of dark blue velvet trimmed with gold satin.

She turned to Davenport quickly. "Oh, I can't. I'm sorry . . . I just can't —"

Still smiling sweetly, he blinked slowly and lowered his chin. "Go ahead," he urged in a voice just above a whisper. "Pull it out of there and hold it up to yourself. I think once you see it, you'll be smitten. At least, that's what Mrs. Hughes down at the dress shop said. She helped me pick it out. She'd seen you and remembered your chestnut hair, and she thought the dark blue would complement your hair as well as your eyes so beautifully."

Laura stared down at the dress. Indeed, it was beautiful. But she felt as though she were staring down at a box full of writhing rattlesnakes. She looked up at Davenport, frowning, about to reject the gift outright, but the sweet smile on his face tugged at her heartstrings.

He was lonely and sweet and kind — if a little awkward — and he probably missed his wife terribly. His grief and loneliness had probably caused this brazen advance on Laura despite that she'd given him no encouragement whatsoever.

At least, she didn't think she had.

Had she?

Perhaps she should have been more careful. Some men — especially older, lonely men — often misread a woman's words and gestures, or gave them too much import. That's probably what had happened here. A simple misunderstanding.

The least she could do was open the dress, and then, once she'd shown her appreciation for it, she could gently explain why she couldn't accept it, thereby letting him down as gently as she could. She'd take this bit of awkwardness as a lesson that she had to be more careful in the future.

She'd been married for five years. She hadn't been in such a situation as this one in a long time, and she'd just stumbled, that's all.

"Oh, it's lovely," she said as she held the gown out in front of her. It was, indeed, of sapphire velvet with a white taffeta collar and gold satin running along the low-cut bodice and around the cuffs.

It had likely been shockingly expensive. He must have paid thirty dollars for it, maybe even more in so remote a place as Tigerville.

She lowered the dress and smiled sweetly up at the man. "It really is lovely, Mister Davenport. But I can't possibly —"

Her interrupted her with: "I met that gray-back marshal on the way out here. He didn't happen to stop here, did he?" He was still smiling sweetly, only, as before, the smile did not show in his eyes, which were alarmingly flat and cold once more.

Laura's mouth was still open, shaping the next word she'd wanted to say though the breath for those words had gotten held up on her vocal cords. She stared up at him, feeling her cheeks once again turn warm.

"Was he out here? The grayback?" Suddenly, Davenport was scowling, his jaws tight, his eyes glinting with anger. He grabbed Laura's wrist, squeezed it. "If he was out here pestering you — that bottom-feeding Rebel scum! — you let me know, Laura, and I will make damn good and sure he never does it again. That U.S. Marshal appointed him town marshal, but Winslow has no business poking his nose in the affairs of this town. I sit on the town council — am business partners with the mayor, in fact — and we'll take an emergency vote and have him run out of tow —"

"No!" Laura pulled her wrist free of Davenport's grip and stepped back. "He wasn't pestering me, Mister Davenport!" She stared up at him, incredulous, and rubbed her wrist. He'd squeezed it so hard that she could still see the marks of his fingers in her skin.

Davenport studied her for a long time. He looked around the cabin, his eyes finally resting on the bed. Laura glanced over her shoulder at it. The covers were thrown back and rumpled, which was how she'd left them when she'd risen and discovered Hunter outside splitting wood.

Davenport returned his gaze to her. She shrank beneath the severity of the man's look. She wanted him to leave even worse than before, but she found herself feeling afraid of him. He was much bigger and stronger than she was.

She felt a building anger in him. She also felt that that anger could erupt in violence. He seemed like a human volcano, throwing up small mushroom clouds of invisible smoke as the lava roiled and rose inside him.

"He's nothing."

Davenport had said the words so quietly, making a raking sound, that Laura wasn't quite sure she'd heard him correctly.

"Wh-What?"

"He's nothing. I realize you're new here, Laura. You don't know how we folks live here in Tigerville. The social layout. Who's good people, who's not. The Buchanons are lowly folk. The lowest of the low. They are gutter-wallowing Rebel trash. That one and his father live in a seedy little rooming house next door to a bordello. He drives the stage. Or he did until that smug old federal lawman pinned a badge to his shirt. Why, he shot a man in cold blood on Dakota Avenue — in the heart of Tigerville! — and Winslow rewarded him for it by making him town marshal. By God, I'm gonna get a lawyer and prove it's illegal!"

He removed his hat and slapped it against his leg.

Davenport's crudely structured face turned brick red, and his neck swelled as he barked so loudly that Laura took another couple of stumbling steps backward — *"Trash! You see? Trash!"* He paused, and then his voice came oddly gentle again, and he smiled like an idiot, eyes as opaque as a bear's eyes. "I've taken you under my wing. I intend to look out for you. I will not allow you to see him ever again."

"What?" she fairly exploded, unable to believe her own ears. She gave a caustic laugh and glared up at this crazy monster in hang-jawed exasperation. "You have no right to —"

He cut her off with: "Put it on." He canted his head toward the dress on the table.

She looked at the gown, then switched her gaze back to Davenport. "No."

"I'm taking you out to supper. To the

Dakota Territorial Hotel. Finest vittles in town. Every table covered in white linen! We're gonna celebrate the beginning of a long relationship that will, I have a sneaking suspicion, lead to a wedding."

He smiled stupidly down at her, taking a step forward, holding his hat down in front of him, working the brim with his oversized thumbs. "I have money, you see. Don't worry — I don't care about your past. Why you've come here. You're accustomed to money, are you not? To the finer things? I can tell the cut of woman you are. I can afford all those things. After dinner, I'll show you my house. It's damn near the biggest one in town — uh, pardon my French. I don't normally curse in front of a lady." He chuckled. "And that's what you are. Aren't you?"

As if in afterthought, he held his hat up in one hand and held up the other hand, palm out. "Oh, don't worry. I don't intend for anything inappropriate, Miss Laura. Not until we're married." He winked, blushing. "But then it won't be inappropriate, will it?"

He gave a hissing, self-satisfied laugh through his teeth.

She glared up at him, at once terrified and enraged. The words exploded out of her in a chortling wail: *"You go to hell!"*

He sprang forward, swinging his right hand back behind his shoulder. It arced toward her in a blur until it smashed against her face, picking her up off her feet and hurling her back and sideways.

She struck the floor hard and rolled up against the side of the range.

She rolled onto her back, ears ringing. She gazed up in numb shock. Her cheek was iron-hot where he'd struck her.

His ugly face with its supercilious smile slid back into view. He gazed down at her and said with a single, slow bob of his head, "Now, you put the dress on. I've made reservations for six. We don't wanna be late."

He gestured toward the window with his hat. "I'll be waiting right outside."

He winked, set the hat on his head, and went out.

CHAPTER 24

Hunter galloped to within a few yards of the crest of the rise, watching black smoke roil thickly from the other side of the hill into the clear blue sky, hearing the angry crackle of gunfire and the tooth-gnashing whoops and yowls of Sioux war cries.

He reined Ghost to a stop, shucked his Henry from its sheath, leaped out of the saddle, and dropped the reins. He reached into a saddlebag pouch for his spyglass, then, looping the lanyard of the glass's leather sack around his neck, ran crouching to the top of the rise.

Bobby Lee ran panting along behind him, keeping his head down and mewling. The gray-brown fur around the coyote's neck stuck straight up in the air.

Hunter dropped to his belly, removed his hat, and set it down beside him. He lifted a cautious gaze over the rise and stretched his lips back from his teeth in a grimace.

An old trading post sat in the bowl-shaped hollow below. A big barn and a corral and stable sat to the left, the long, L-shaped, two-story log main building lay to the right, divided by the trading trail that ran up from Ogallala and wended its way northward through the Hills all the way to Deadwood. The place was a legendary trading post established twenty years ago by the now-deceased Blinky Bill Weatherspoon. It was apparently still in operation — or had been until today.

Hunter had never visited the post, for it was too far south from where he normally ventured, on the edge of the Pine Ridge Reservation, but he'd heard the stories about Blinky Bill's old trading stop from the old market and buffalo hunters and cavalrymen who'd frequented Blinky Bill's back when the Sioux were still on the rampage and Blinky Bill's had been repeatedly threatened by Sioux warriors.

It appeared the Sioux were again on the war path. At least five of them were — the same five that Hunter had been following, no doubt. Blinky Bill's barn was almost entirely consumed by bright orange flames. Shouting and screaming rose from the main lodge, which boasted a high false façade bearing the words BLINKY BILL'S TRADING

POST in ornate though now faded letters set against faded canary yellow. Faded as the paint was, it could still be clearly seen by Hunter from his distance of two hundred yards without even using the spyglass.

Several saddled horses were fleeing the yard, dragging their bridle reins. Four men, apparently bushwhacked, had fallen in the yard between the burning barn and the main lodge. Two Indians in buckskins and war paint, mounted on war-painted ponies, were hazing a half dozen horses away from the barn and into the meadow behind it. Another Indian was just then walking through the yard, inspecting the fallen men around him.

Hunter uncased the spyglass and raised it, quickly adjusting the focus.

The Indian in the yard paused near one of the fallen men around him. The man on the ground before him had long yellow hair and was also dressed in buckskins. He lifted his head and arms pleadingly, and wailed. The Indian aimed his carbine out and down from his right shoulder, and shot the wailing man in the head.

The crack of the warrior's shot was still snaking around the hollow, echoing, when a woman's scream rose from inside the trading post. A stout, brown-haired, female figure burst out of the trading post's swinging doors and onto the broad, peeled log gallery fronting it. As she started running down the steps toward the main yard, a white apron flapping around her thick hips, an Indian in a yellow calico shirt and black braids and war paint stepped out of the trading post behind her.

He cocked his Winchester and fired into the woman's back as the Indian in the yard fired into her chest. She stopped, jerked forward and then back, loosed a yodeling wail, then twisted around and fell back against a hand rail angling along the steps. The doomed woman slid slowly down to sit on the bottom step, head down, as if she were only dozing.

"That tears it!"

Hunter returned the spyglass to its case and scuttled a few feet back down the rise before gaining his feet, donning his hat, and dropping the spyglass back into a saddlebag pouch. He turned to Bobby Lee regarding him curiously, head cocked to one side, one ear up, one ear down.

"Stay here with Ghost, Bobby. You've done your work. Time for me to do mine."

The coyote sat down and raised his other ear, mewling very quietly and shifting his delicate front feet.

Hunter cocked a round into the Henry's action, off-cocked the hammer, then climbed to the crest of the rise. He dropped to both knees, doffed his hat, and peered into the hollow.

The two Indians on horseback were out of sight behind the flames and black smoke of the burning barn. The other killers must have gone into the cabin, from which more male and female screams sounded, as did the whooping and hollering of the savage killers and the sound of shattering glass.

A shallow ravine ran along the base of the rise Hunter was on, forming a semicircle around the trading post. Between the ravine and the trading post yard was a thin scattering of cedars and junipers, offering a modicum of cover. If Hunter could make that ravine and then those cedars, he might have a chance of bringing the killers down before they spotted him.

Heart quickening, he drew a deep breath, rose to his feet, and, holding the Henry at port arms across his chest, ran crouching down the rise, leaping willows and wending his way around stunt pines and small cottonwoods and aspens. He kept one eye on the cabin and one eye on the area around the barn, ready to go to ground if one of the Indians should reappear in the yard.

Horrific cries and screams continued issuing from the trading post cabin. The savages were killing the folks in there in grand Sioux fashion — slow and painful.

Hunter gained the ravine and dropped to his hands and knees. He took a moment to catch his breath, then removed his hat again and edged a look up over the lip of the draw, stretching a gander toward the lodge.

He could smell kerosene riding the waves of the smoke wreathing around the yard. The savages had likely used the coal oil to set the barn on fire. They were probably using it in the cabin now, as well, for he could see smoke issuing through a partly open window in the second story.

As he gazed at that window, another shrill scream rose from the lodge. A half second later, the window through which the smoke was curling burst outward, the glass shattering. A slender figure, clad in what appeared a gauzy pink wrap, came hurling out the window and angling ground-ward, the wrap rising straight up as did the girl's long, curly blond hair as she fell.

The girl, probably a whore working the second story cribs, gave another ear-rattling cry just before she hit the ground with a loud, cracking thud and a grunt. She lay in a broken heap right where she'd fallen, the gauzy wrap and her long hair blowing around her in the breeze.

"Jesus!" Hunter said. She'd escaped the only way she could the torture she'd witnessed around her.

Buchanon set his hat on his head and started to gain his feet but stopped when a footfall sounded behind him, just before a hand closed down over his left shoulder.

Hunter wheeled with a startled grunt. His eyes snapped wide when he saw the pain-racked countenance of Deputy U.S. Marshal Walt Winslow on his knees behind him.

"Winslow!" he said under his breath. "What the hell're you doing here?"

Winslow sagged back on his butt on the ravine bottom. His hat was gone and his short, steel gray hair was mussed. His blue eyes were bright, scrunched up at the corners with pain. He held his gloved left hand across his bloody belly, only a few inches above the brass buckle of his cartridge belt. The holster perched high on his right hip was empty.

"A small pack of Injuns howlin' like devils jumped me an' Birmingham. We were arresting three men from the post when they came at us all at once, from three directions. Roy got hit first. He's still in the yard with the men we were arresting for sellin' poisoned whiskey at Pine Ridge."

Winslow glanced down at the dark red blood oozing out from between his fingers, and cursed. He shook his head. Tears of pain came to his eyes. "I took this bullet, emptied my pistol, and tried climbing into the saddle. Got my foot caught in the stirrup, and my horse dragged me into this ravine here. The Injuns gave me up for dead, I reckon. Anyways, they haven't come lookin' for me. I lost my gun. My rifle's on my horse . . . wherever he is."

"This is starting to make sense."

"What is?"

"Those Injuns on the warpath. They shot up the Goliad in Tigerville, shot Phil Scudder first and then a good dozen of the patrons. They struck the trading post here on their way back to the rez."

Winslow grunted, winced, nodded his head. "We intercepted a wagon headed for Pine Ridge last night. It was loaded to the gills with whiskey. Likely poisoned whiskey. Several people have died on the rez from what the Indian agent down there thinks was strychnine-laced whiskey that came from the trading post.

"The driver of the wagon told me an' Roy that the whiskey originated at the Goliad in Tigerville. Scudder freighted the rotgut out

303

from Tigerville via some old, secret trail gold miners used back when gold hunting was illegal in the Black Hills. The whiskey was always hauled on a moonless night, to avoid suspicion. Scudder hauled it out here to Blinky Bill's in secret. The trading post's past indiscretions involving selling whiskey to the Indians got it banned to sell any whiskey at all, to anyone. That didn't keep the devil now managing the place — a scurvy reprobate named Calvin Holte and his wife and two sons — from selling firewater to the Indians at Pine Ridge."

Winslow grunted again, shook his head, blinked tears of agony from his eyes. "Christ, this hurts! Why can't I just die, dammit? I'm so damn thirsty!"

"Hold on, Winslow. I'll fetch my canteen when I've taken those Injuns down."

"Don't try it! There's five of 'em, and they're madder'n stick-teased snakes. Scudder an' Holte and Holte's sons were poisoning the whiskey — dumping strychnine into it."

"Why in hell were they poisoning their own customers?"

"Meanness. Pure meanness. None of them had any love for the Sioux. Hated the whole tribe, in fact. Leftover animosity from Red Cloud's raids."

"Can't say as I blame them braves for bein' piss-burned, but they've carved too broad a swath, killed too many innocent people. I'm takin' 'em down."

"What?" Winslow gave a caustic laugh. "You're a real lawman now?"

Hunter brushed his thumb across the badge on his chest. "You're the one who ramrodded me into wearing this tin star, aren't you?"

Winslow grinned despite his pain. "I'll be damned if you're not one to ride the river with, Buchanon. I'm sorry I won't get to ride it with you."

Hunter patted the old lawman's shoulder. "You hold on, Walt. I'll be back with water."

"Go with God, kid," Winslow said. "And give the devil the hindmost!"

Hunter glanced up over the crest of the ravine bank.

All was clear. The Indians were still inside the main lodge, stomping around and grunting and yelling. More smoke was oozing out more windows, and a fresh dose of coal oil rode thick and cloying on the breeze. Since they were setting fire to the main lodge, the raiders were likely getting ready to pull their picket pins.

Hunter leaped up out of the ravine and made a beeline toward the lodge.

Just as he did, the two Indians he'd seen earlier came riding around the barn's far side and into the yard. They were leading three other war-painted horses with colorful blanket saddles by the mounts' rope bridles. They saw Hunter at the same time he saw them.

Hunter stopped walking. He was halfway between the burning lodge and the ravine.

The two braves stopped their horses roughly sixty feet away from him. The smoke from the burning barn wafted through the air of the yard, obscuring them occasionally, obscuring him from them. Hunter stared at them.

They stared at him, their eyes inky dark in their copper-colored, war-painted faces.

A guidon of black smoke swept between him and them, blotting them out entirely. When the guidon passed, they were both in mid-stride, galloping toward him and yowling like the devil's hounds.

CHAPTER 25

Hunter dropped to a knee and raised the Henry to his shoulder as the two warriors galloped toward him, both firing their Winchesters with their rope reins in their teeth. Their mistake had been remaining mounted against an unmounted opponent. They weren't mounted for long. Hunter blew the left one off his horse, cocked the Henry, slid the barrel to the right, and blew the other one off his horse.

Both now-riderless mounts broke their routes off wide as they approached Buchanon, each horse coming within arm's length of trampling him into the earth before veering off to his right and left and buck-kicking into the distance. The two warriors were still rolling like discarded oversized children's dolls when one of the Indians from inside the burning lodge stepped out onto the front veranda. He was holding two burlap sacks, bulging with what

307

was no doubt plunder from inside the trading post, by rope ties down his back.

He stopped in his tracks and widened his eyes at his two cohorts just now rolling to still, bloody heaps in the yard before him. He swung his shocked brown eyes toward Hunter, dropped both sacks to the veranda floor, and reached for the Colt holstered on his right, buckskin-clad thigh.

Hunter planted a bead on the warrior's chest and fired.

The bullet punched through the Sioux's chest, throwing him straight back over the balcony rail and into the yard. His six-shooter clattered onto the floor where his moccasin-clad feet had just been. Another brave came running out through the smoky open doorway, yowling and raising a carbine to his shoulder, sliding the barrel around, looking for a target.

His target found him first. Hunter's bullet carved a neat round hole through the warrior's forehead, throwing him back through the lodge's open door through which gray smoke slithered like ghosts.

Remaining on one knee, Buchanon ejected his last spent cartridge casing and pumped a fresh round into the chamber. He aimed at the open door, waiting.

There was one more plunderer inside the

308

lodge. He'd have to come out soon. The flames and the smoke would drive him out.

Unless he escaped through a window or a back door.

Hunter's heart quickened anxiously. He caressed the spur of the Henry's cocked hammer with his thumb, tapped the trigger with his gloved right index finger.

Come on . . .

He glanced at the front windows, spying no movement aside from the jostling of orange flames chewing away at the inside of the lodge.

"Dammit!"

He leaped to his feet, strode quickly to the lodge, climbed the veranda's steps, and moved slowly, keeping the Henry aimed straight out from his shoulder, through the open front door. The room's shadows were obscured with clouds of roiling gray smoke. The smoke peppered his eyes; he tried to blink the sting away.

He moved inside what appeared a saloon area with a bar at the rear. A staircase angled up over the bar's right side. To the left, through an open doorway, lay the store area.

Hunter took two more strides into the main room, sliding the rifle this way and that, looking for the fifth and final warrior.

A savage grunt sounded behind him and then a man leaped onto his back, snaking his calico-clad left arm over Hunter's shoulder, trying to pull Buchanon's left arm back.

Light from a window glinted off the blade of a knife in the Indian's right hand, which was rushing around from behind Hunter's right shoulder, heading for his throat.

A shrill howl rose from the door followed by the quick patter of four padded feet and the manic clicking of toe nails. A deep growl followed. The person on Hunter's back yelped as Bobby Lee sunk his teeth into him. That delayed the would-be stabber's fatal thrust.

Stumbling forward against the weight on his back, Hunter dropped the Henry and raised his right hand straight up before him, grabbing the hand holding the bowie knife within inches of his carotid artery. Behind him, Bobby Lee growled fiercely; Hunter thought the coyote must be chomping into one of his assailant's legs, making the man on his back grunt and groan fiercely.

Hunter wrapped his right hand around the right hand of the Indian and around the knife's wooden handle. Still hearing Bobby Lee growl fiercely as he shook whichever of the assailant's legs he was chomping into, Hunter fell forward onto a table littered with bottles, glasses, and playing cards. As he hit the table, he turned onto his right shoulder, slamming the Indian onto his back on the table. Buchanon ground his big body against the lighter body of the Indian's.

As he did, he thrust the hand of the Indian holding the knife in front of his neck straight out away from him, squeezing the hand until a shrill cry rose from beneath him. The hand opened and the bowie fell to the floor. The warrior was kicking at Bobby Lee, who had his teeth sunk into the renegade's left calf, shaking the leg as though trying to tear the limb from the brave's body.

Gaining his feet, Hunter palmed his LeMat and yelled, "Let him go, Bobby!"

No sooner had Bobby released the buckskin-clad leg than the warrior sprang off the table, quick as a striking rattlesnake, and dashed in a copper blur toward Hunter, long black hair flying, teeth showing between stretched-back lips. Hunter swung the LeMat up above his left shoulder then slashed it forward and down, smashing the barrel against the brave's forehead.

That stopped the warrior in his tracks.

No. *Her* tracks. The warrior before Buchanon looked in nearly every way like the other four — slender but well-muscled, built for savage fighting. But unlike the others,

311

the copper-skinned, war-painted face owned the gentler curves of a female.

Just now, that female's brown eyes rolled back into her head and she sagged backward toward the table. Astonished at his discovery, Hunter thrust his left hand forward, grabbed the girl's collar, and eased her back against the table and then down to the floor.

He looked at her lying there, slumped on her left side, her oval face obscured by the thick strands of her coarse, straight, blue-black hair.

"I'll be damned," he said, eyes stinging as the smoke from an upstairs fire filled the room. Flames were licking through the ceiling and slithering down the stairway at the rear of the drinking hall.

Bobby Lee was mewling and looking around fearfully at the flames and smoke, clacking his little nails on the floor.

Hunter holstered the LeMat and, crouching, drew the warrior princess over his left shoulder and headed for the door. "Come on, Bobby Lee. I don't know about you, but it's gettin' too hot in here for me!"

He carried the Indian girl out into the yard and lay her down near the body of Deputy U.S. Marshal Roy Birmingham. The poor old gent had been shot at least six times. His revolver was still in its holster.

Moving quickly, for the lodge was burning more hotly and would likely soon be engulfed in flames, he felt around on Birmingham's corpse for a set of handcuffs.

All he found was a set of small handcuff keys.

He turned to the other three men — one old, the other two much younger — lying around Birmingham. All three had their hands cuffed behind their backs. They sported even more bullet wounds than Birmingham did. Hunter removed the cuffs from the wrists of the older, buckskin-clad gent with long grizzled yellow-gray hair and who lay near the bottom of the porch steps.

Bobby Lee, he saw, was properly anointing the bodies of the dead renegades in typical Bobby Lee fashion, one hindleg hiked high.

Hunter chuckled under his breath then took the cuffs over to the Sioux girl. She moaned, squeezing her eyes closed as though in pain. Hunter had smacked her pretty hard. She'd had a lot of fight in her; in fact, if Bobby Lee hadn't shown up when he had, Hunter would likely be lying inside the burning lodge about now, his own blood boiling in the flames where it would have oozed out around his neck.

He quickly snapped the cuffs closed

around the girl's wrists, then, wincing against the heat of the crackling flames now thoroughly gorging themselves on the lodge's shake-shingled roof and on the big false façade, he dragged Birmingham a good hundred feet away from the burning building.

He left the Indians where they lay. They could burn up in their own fire.

As for the girl, he'd take her back to Tigerville. He didn't like playing favorites just because her shirt was lumpier than the men's, but he couldn't kill her in cold blood. He'd leave her fate for a judge to decide.

Besides, he'd been reading up on the law and had a little better understanding of a citizen's rights. Not that he regretted torturing and killing Ike Talon. Ike Talon was another matter altogether.

When he had Birmingham safely away from the flames, he went back over and picked up the princess, slinging her over his shoulder, then tramped back in the direction of the ravine in which he'd left Walt Winslow. Bobby Lee trotted dutifully along beside him, panting from the heat of the growing fire that was roaring like a fire-breathing dragon behind them.

Hunter stopped at the lip of the ravine.

"Hey, Winslow, I got 'em all but —"

He stopped. Winslow lay where Buchanon had left the man. Only now he wasn't moving. He lay flat on his back, both hands on his bloody belly, staring straight up at the puffy white clouds floating high across the blue arch of the prairie sky.

Hunter sighed. He lay the girl on the ground.

"Let me know if she wakes up," Hunter told Bobby Lee.

The coyote sat beside the girl, curling his thick, bushy gray tail around his right hindleg. He looked down at the girl, showing his teeth.

Hunter walked down into the ravine. He dropped to a knee beside Winslow and placed a finger against the man's neck and gave a ragged sigh. "Dead, all right. Poor devil."

Bobby Lee growled and snarled.

Hunter turned to see the coyote crouching forward, chest down, butt in the air. He was snapping and snarling at the Indian girl who tossed her head from side to side, blinking her eyes and pushing up off the ground.

Hunter rose. "Hold on."

She rolled onto her belly and lifted her chin, glaring at him. She snarled at him in much the same way Bobby Lee was snarling at her. Hunter didn't know how she did it so easily, for her wrists were cuffed behind her back, but she managed to spring to her feet. Bobby was instantly on her, chomping into her ankle. She gave a raking scream of raw fury, and kicked Bobby away from her.

Bobby yelped and rolled.

She tossed her hair from her wild eyes and screamed at him in Lakota, *"White devil! Murdering coward!"*

She turned and started running away. She ran fast for someone with her wrists tied behind her. Hunter ran up out of the ravine and sprang off his heels, diving forward and swiping his right hand across a once moccasin-clad foot, tripping her. She hit the ground with another enraged scream.

She sounded like a wolverine with a leg in a trap.

She rolled onto her back and somehow managed to leap to her feet again.

Hunter was just regaining his own feet when she sprang forward, ramming her head and shoulders against him. He hadn't yet got his feet settled, so her sudden attack caused him to pitch over backward, striking the ground on his back.

Hissing like an enraged mountain lion, she slammed her head against his — over and over again — heedless of the goose egg swelling on her own forehead — until he managed to roll her off of him. His head aching, vision swimming, he didn't see her come at him until she was on him again, hissing and spitting and sinking her teeth into his shoulders and chest.

Bobby Lee danced circles around them, barking and growling and showing his teeth.

Hunter felt like he was under attack by a crazed catamount, wincing as her teeth tore into his flesh, ripping his shirt.

Realizing he wasn't going to be able to fend this feral she-beast off until he got serious, he pulled her head up off his chest by her hair, then, rolling up off his right hip and shoulder, slammed her onto the ground. She was still snarling and hissing and snapping her teeth, still trying to bite him.

"Girl, I'm sorry about this, but . . ." He ripped the LeMat from its holster and smashed the barrel against her head again.

She screamed and slumped back, the fight suddenly gone from her.

Buchanon sat back on his boot heels and looked down at his torn shirt, blood-stained where her teeth had ripped his flesh. He turned to Bobby Lee standing nearby and staring at him dubiously.

"Damn," Hunter said. He sleeved the girl's saliva from his cheek. "Now, ain't she a caution?"

CHAPTER 26

Laura stepped onto the boardwalk fronting the Tigerville jail and town marshal's office, knocked once on the jailhouse door, then tripped the latch and shoved the door halfway open.

Inside, the beefy odd-job man, Otis Crosby, lifted his chin from his chest and dropped his work boot–clad feet from the edge of the cluttered desk to the floor and turned his moon-shaped face toward Laura with a surprised expression.

The look of surprise turned to chagrin. He smiled sheepishly as he said, "Caught me sleepin' on the job, Miss Meyers."

Laura had formally met Otis several days ago, when she'd come looking for Hunter. The town's mayor had assigned Otis the task of keeping an eye on the jailhouse while Hunter was off trying to run down the Indians who'd murdered so many people in the Goliad Saloon nearly a week ago now.

The town was without a lawman while Hunter was gone. Laura had never seen Otis do anything here at the jailhouse but sleep in the chair with his boots on the desk.

She'd stopped here several times, desperate to talk to Hunter about the lunatic Warren Davenport, who kept bestowing gifts on her and paying her unwanted visits at her little shack flanking the school. She was so alarmed by the man's bizarre behavior — actually having forced her under threat of physical harm to have supper with him — that she couldn't sleep or eat and wanted very desperately for the fool to leave her alone.

She was deathly afraid of the man; the cut on her cheek proved she had good reason to be. She was horrified when she looked at her image in the mirror. Her black eye, incurred during Talon's attack on the stage, had all but disappeared. But now she would be facing her students in a few days, on the first day of school, with a scab on her cheek.

"Any sign of Hunt . . . I mean, Marshal Buchanon?" she asked Crosby hopefully.

Otis had gained his feet and was holding his hat in his hands.

He shook his head. "N-no, ma'am. Ain't seen hide nor hair, I'm sorry to say."

"I wonder what could be keeping him,"

she said, half to herself as she turned away from the man, crestfallen.

"The mayor said he's gonna form a posse and hire a good tracker if Hunter ain't back by tomorrow. No one's seen the two federal fellas — Winslow and Birmingham — neither."

"By tomorrow it might be too late." Laura drew the door closed and turned to the street. *But, then, it might already be too late.*

Her heart felt swollen and heavy with worry. Over the past several days, she'd kept imagining Hunter lying dead somewhere out in the Hills or on the prairie. Or wounded and on foot, dying slowly. The thought haunted her. She was deeply worried about him; deeply worried for herself, as well.

If he was gone, killed by those renegade Sioux, she would have no one here in town to protect her from the unwanted advances of Warren Davenport.

She turned and began to walk up the street to the north but stopped suddenly when whom did she see but none other than Warren Davenport himself!

She gasped and rocked back on her heels. She felt as though he'd slapped her in the face again.

Davenport stood facing her from the end

of the next block. He stood outside his business office, staring right at her. He wore his usual ominous-looking black, three-piece suit and derby hat, a gold watch chain dangling from a pocket of his black wool vest. He stood with his black shoes spread wide, his fists on his hips holding the flaps of his coat back, puffing the cigar that angled from one corner of his mouth.

He was too far away for Laura to see his expression clearly, but she knew he was scowling at her severely. With remonstration. He knew she'd come to the jailhouse searching for Hunter.

He looked the specter of death itself bearing down on her with flat, soulless, darkly judging eyes.

Laura turned away quickly with a chortling sound of terror rising from her throat. She gave her back to the man, as though no longer seeing him would mean he would no longer be there. Automatically, she began moving south, away from him, wanting to put as much distance between her and him as possible.

She crossed a side street after nearly being run down by a horse, then, blinking from the dust wafting around her, mounted the boardwalk on the street's other side. She was staring at the walk's scarred, tobacco-stained boards, her thoughts bleak and hopeless. Something made her look up. She blinked against the dust and harsh sunlight, frowning curiously.

The stage from Cheyenne must have just rolled into town. It was parked in front of the stage manager's office half a block away. Dust was still sifting around it, the lathered horses blowing and shaking their heads. Passengers were climbing out of the carriage door facing the boardwalk.

One of these passengers attracted the brunt of Laura's attention. He was a finely dressed gentleman in a butterscotch bowler hat and coat, black foulard tie, and black trousers of the finest wool. He'd just stepped down from the stage and was using a cane to negotiate the boardwalk between the parked coach and the manager's office.

The cane had a silver horse-head handle.

Instantly, Laura stopped and, turning toward the shop on her left, trying to hide her face, stumbled forward, knees weakening. Her heart hammering painfully, she dared another glance toward the stage.

The finely dressed man with the cane was her husband, Jonathan Gaynor. She couldn't see his face because he hadn't looked her way — thank God! — but she saw his neatly trimmed dark brown hair beneath the hat and the neat little muttonchops framing his regular-featured face that she'd once thought was handsome.

Now she didn't think she'd ever seen an uglier man. Aside from Warren Davenport, that was. She was being stalked by two devils — one large and blunt-faced, the other dressed to the nines and dapper, complete with a silver horse-head cane!

Oh God — what was Jonathan doing here in Tigerville? Did he have business interests here?

Of course, he didn't have business interests in Tigerville. He was here for one reason and one reason only — to find the wife who'd shot him in his private parts!

Laura dared one more glance toward the stage. Jonathan appeared to be with another man — taller, slightly broader through the shoulders, with a thick mustache. He wore a dark blue pinstriped suit with a red ribbon tie and black, low-crowned hat. A badge glinted on the lapel of the man's coat. Laura had seen such badges before in Denver.

It was a Pinkerton's badge.

A Pinkerton detective had tracked her down and accompanied Jonathan here to see that Laura received her just deserts!

Dizzy with terror, Laura swung around

and, holding up a hand to shield her face from the direction of the stage manager's office, she stepped off the boardwalk and strode headlong into the street. She only became aware of men yelling at her and of traffic stopping or swerving sharply to avoid her after she'd gained the boardwalk on the other side of Dakota Avenue.

She hurried into the shadows beneath a boardwalk awning and stepped up to the front of a shop. Leaning forward, she placed one gloved hand on the shop's front wall and drew deep, even breaths, trying to calm her racing heart. She placed her other hand over her mouth, aghast at what was happening to her.

Not only did she have the crazed Warren Davenport after her, but Jonathan was now pursuing her, as well. And the one man who could protect her from both pursuers was probably lying dead out in the prairie!

Someone walked up to her. She could hear the tapping of shoes, see a shadow merge with her own on the boardwalk. "Take a breath," said a woman's voice to her right.

Laura opened her eyes. A sheer, peach stocking–clad foot resided in a high-heeled pink satin shoe on the boardwalk beside her.

She turned her head slowly, slowly lifted

her gaze to follow the slender, nicely turned, stocking-clad leg up past the stocking, which ended mid-thigh, to a sexy satin peach camisole and pink satin pantalettes. She continued on up the nicely endowed camisole to the pretty, green-eyed, heart-shaped face complimented beautifully by thick, tumbling and curling tresses of thick red hair.

The young woman Hunter had intended to marry regarded Laura skeptically. Almost with — what? Concern?

"I beg your pardon?" Laura said.

"Take a deep breath. Slowly." Miss Ludlow placed her hand on her tummy and drew a slow, deep breath, as though to demonstrate.

Laura drew a breath deep into her lungs.

"Let it out, take another. Deep and slow."

Laura nodded and drew another deep, slow breath. Almost instantly, her heart had begun to slow its frantic pace. Now it slowed even further.

"Keep going," Miss Ludlow said, ignoring the whistles and goatish looks of the men passing on the boardwalk. "A few more."

Laura drew another deep breath, then another.

"Thank you," she said with a sigh. "That helps." Remembering Jonathan, she cast a quick glance back in the direction of the stagecoach parked in front of the station manager's office. Fortunately, he was no longer anywhere Laura could see him. He and the Pinkerton agent must have gone into the manager's office.

Again, Laura's heart quivered, hiccupping.

"You look like you could use a drink."

Laura turned to the pretty redhead, startled. "What? Oh, no . . . I'm the new teacher here in town."

"I know who you are."

Laura studied the girl, but her expression, one eye cocked, that brow slightly furled, was vague. Laura nodded. "Yes, I know who you are too." She looked the girl up and down in open admiration. "You're very pretty."

"Hunter has good taste in women." Miss Ludlow returned Laura's admiring smile, and Laura instantly felt her guard go down.

She also felt the heat of embarrassment rise in her cheeks.

"Come on," said the pretty redhead, canting her head toward the front door of the saloon called Big Dan's, which was where Laura knew that she worked. "I'll buy you a drink."

"Thank you, but like I said . . ."

"We have a back door." Miss Ludlow

smiled and then extended her right hand. "Annabelle."

Again, Laura returned the girl's smile. She squeezed her hand. "Laura."

"Follow me, Laura."

Annabelle turned, stepped into an alley, and walked along the side of the building toward the rear. Holding the skirt of her copper-patterned cream day dress above her ankles, reticule dangling from her left wrist, Laura followed the redhead around to the back of Big Dan's and through a rear door.

She felt dangerously self-conscious. If she were to be seen entering a saloon and whorehouse, she'd likely have unemployment added to her list of woes.

On the other hand, Jonathan would likely know soon where to find her. He and the Pinkerton man would ask around, flash a few photographs of the treacherous woman he was looking for, and they'd find her in no time. Soon, she'd either be dead or in jail.

Oh, Hunter — where are you?

She followed Annabelle up a creaky back stairway to the second floor.

"Don't worry," Annabelle said, keeping her voice low as they walked along the dingy, sour-smelling hall. She'd taken her shoes off and was walking barefoot, cradling the shoes in her arm. "The only ones up here are you and me and the whores. They'll be asleep till noon and it's only ten."

"Aren't I taking you away from your work?"

"I started the chili downstairs for Dan. He'll be in soon to take over. He likes to take the credit for his chili. We don't get much business until noon."

Annabelle stopped at a door, twisted the knob, shoved the door open, and walked into the room beyond it, glancing over her shoulder at Laura. "Please."

Laura stepped timidly into the room. Before her was a brass-framed bed littered with female clothes and underclothes, a dressing table, a chest of drawers, a wash-stand, and a pitcher and bowl.

One very small, dusty window let in a little light through badly faded velvet curtains flanking two motley-looking, mismatched brocade arm chairs sitting to either side of a round eating table. The ornate paper on the walls, above the wainscoting, was also faded and peeling.

Annabelle walked to the chest of drawers. "Take a seat over there by the window. I have a bottle around here somewhere. I'm not much of a drinker — I've seen what it's done to my brother Cass — but I like a little nip before bed to help me sleep."

Laura sat in one of the chairs, leaning back to take the breeze blowing through the partly open window. She was warm — perspiring, in fact — and her heart was still beating fast. She felt as though her skin had been peeled back to expose every nerve in her body. She kept seeing Warren Davenport glaring at her, and Jonathan leaning on his cane.

As Annabelle brought a bottle and two small water glasses, Laura leaned forward with her elbows on the table and massaged her temples with her fingers. Annabelle poured some liquor into one of the glasses and slid it toward Laura.

"Here you go — drink that. If anyone could use a drink, it's you." She splashed whiskey into the second glass, then set the bottle on the table and sank into the chair across from Laura.

Laura reached for her glass with a trembling hand, and threw back the entire shot. She swallowed, lifting her chin and savoring the warm, calming feeling the whiskey touched her with. She choked a little on the whiskey's harshness, like pepper at the back of her throat, but still relished its soothing properties.

"Oh, yes . . . yes, that's good."

"Whoa!" Annabelle laughed and threw back her own entire shot.

She smacked her lips, set her glass down, refilled Laura's glass and then her own.

"What the hell? I think I deserve a day off."

Laura lifted her glass to her lips, drank half, then set the glass back down on the table. She lowered her hands to her lap, straightened her back, tightened her shoulders, and closed her eyes, luxuriating in the nerve-calming properties of the liquor.

"What happened?" Laura opened her eyes to see Annabelle gazing at her from the other side of the table. "You look like a dozen ghosts danced across your grave," the pretty redhead added.

"If only it were that delightful." Laura threw back the rest of the shot and swallowed. She raised her hand to her lips as she coughed, then rested her hand on the table before her, squeezing it worryingly with the other one. "Can I trust you?" A wave of emotion swept through her, tugging on her heart and bringing tears to her eyes. "I have no one to talk to. Hunter's gone and . . . I . . . I . . ."

Annabelle's green eyes widened sympathetically as she stretched her arms across the table and closed both of her hands around Laura's. "If you can't trust another lost woman, who can you trust?"

Laura laughed at that but it was partly a sob. She'd never felt so afraid . . . so lost, but it felt good being here in this small, shabby room with this young woman she found herself feeling a kinship with despite their loving . . . or having loved on Annabelle's part . . . the same man.

Laura sniffed, cleared her throat, and returned Annabelle's frank, sympathetic gaze with a direct one of her own. "I shot my husband, an important man, in Denver."

Annabelle's eyes widened, glinting in obvious surprise. Her full lips parted slowly, brows rising. "Oh . . ."

CHAPTER 27

"Did you kill him?" Annabelle asked.

"Unfortunately, no."

Annabelle clamped her hand over her mouth and laughed with guilty delight.

"I caught him in a bathtub with another woman. I'd learned that he and this other woman — a parlor house madam — had been carrying on behind my back since only a few months after we were married. That he was taking weekly trips to Gaynorville to see her, in fact."

"Gaynorville? The mining town near Denver?"

"That's the one." Laura smiled with chill irony. "My husband named the town after himself. He's Jonathan Gaynor."

"Wow!"

"I'm using my maiden name though I should have come up with something more imaginative. I just didn't know that he would actually follow me here. All the way here from Denver."

"He's here . . . in Tigerville?"

"I just saw him step down from the stage . . . with a decided limp as well as a Pinkerton detective."

"Gosh, Laura — no wonder you looked as pale as a freshly laundered sheet out there!"

"That's not my only problem."

Annabelle held up her hand, palm out. "Hold on." She plucked the cork out of the bottle's lip. "If I need another one, you most certainly do." She poured another half inch of whiskey into each glass and set the bottle down.

Laura held up her glass. "To keeping secrets and female alliances?" she asked with a hopeful arch of her brows.

Annabelle touched her glass to the teacher's, smiling brightly. "Hear! Hear!"

The two each took down half of the whiskey in their glasses at the same time and then set the glasses back down on the table.

Annabelle wiped her hand across her mouth and leaned forward, eyes wide and expectant. "All right. I'm all ears."

"Do you know Warren Davenport?"

"Enough to not like the way he looks at me," Annabelle said darkly.

Laura brushed her finger across her cheek,

to indicate the scab. "See this?"

"Yes," Annabelle said, again darkly.

"He gave me that after I rebuffed his advances. He's stalking me, threatening me."

Annabelle slapped the table. "That son of a —"

"I don't know who I'm more afraid of — him or Jonathan."

"I've always known there was something off about that morbid old man. For years before she died, hardly anyone but their close neighbors ever saw his long-suffering wife, Beatrice. She was much younger than him — a mail-order bride from the Midwest. Pretty, to boot. After she moved here to marry Davenport, and he saw the way other men looked at her, with their tongues hanging out, the way men do — you know how it is . . ."

"Yes."

"Davenport made her stay home. For years and years no one saw her except her neighbors fetching wood from the wood shed behind their house or pinning wash on her clothesline. Word was he forbade her to leave the house. She died two years ago. Her death was and still is a mystery. Davenport only said she'd died in her sleep after a long illness and that she was too proud to seek medical help."

"Do you think he killed her?" Laura asked.

"I wouldn't put it past him."

"I wouldn't either." Laura crossed her arms, hugging herself, trying to quell the chill in her bones despite the warm breeze ebbing through the window behind her. "Not after seeing his eyes when he gets angry."

Again, fear washed through Laura. She lowered her head and sobbed. "I'm so frightened. I don't know what I'm going to do. If Davenport doesn't kill me, Jonathan most surely will!"

Annabelle reached across the table and squeezed Laura's hand reassuringly. "We need to hide you away somewhere. Until Hunter gets back from chasing those renegades."

"Do you think he'll return?"

"Of course, he'll return," Annabelle said, smiling reassuringly. "He's Hunter, isn't he? Besides, he's got Bobby Lee by his side. There's nothing those two Rebels can't get through together." A deep sadness shone in the redhead's eyes as she added, "Side by side."

It was her turn to tear up. She shook her head as though to dislodge the emotion.

"You love him — don't you?" Laura said.

Annabelle had turned her head to gaze out the window. She shook her head. "Not anymore, but I did once." She looked at Laura, quirking her mouth corners in understanding. "You love him, don't you?"

Laura nodded. "I'm sorry, Annabelle! I didn't mean for it to happen. Honestly, I didn't!"

"Don't worry. I know how it is with him." Annabelle shook her head, drawing her mouth corners down regretfully. "But it's over between us. There's no man more stubborn. I hope it works out for you, because I can tell you're a good woman. After all you've been through, you deserve a good man. As stubborn as he is, Hunter is all that . . . and more."

She quickly brushed a tear from her cheek with her thumb.

Laura stretched her own hand across the table this time, and squeezed Annabelle's left one. She smiled into the pretty redhead's jade eyes with knowing sympathy.

"Now, then," Annabelle said, sniffing and blinking the emotion from her eyes. "We need to hide you away somewhere." She turned abruptly to the open window behind her and Laura, frowning curiously.

Hoof thuds sounded through the open window. So did men's voices. The men were speaking quietly, as though afraid of being overheard.

"What is it?" Laura asked.

Her frown deepening, Annabelle held up her hand and rose slightly from her chair, peering over the sill and down into the alley behind the saloon.

"See here," one of the men was saying, "we gotta be real patient. We gotta go in this back door and sneak upstairs and hole up in her room. We wait for her to leave the saloon and return to her room, because there's no way the men down there, including Big Dan, are gonna let us take her. Not without a fight, and we'll likely be outgunned."

Another man said something too quietly for Laura to hear.

She said, "Annabelle, who are those men talking —"

Again, Annabelle held up her hand for silence. She continued gazing through the window into the alley below.

The man who'd been speaking before said, "Don't worry. I got it on good word she goes upstairs regularly to check on the whores, make sure their clients are bein' nothin' but gentlemen. She dotes on them girls like an ol' mother hen."

Laura rose and angled her own gaze down

through the window. Three men stood around four horses. One of the men, who wore a Spanish-cut red shirt and low-crowned black hat, was rummaging around inside a saddlebag pouch. As he pulled a length of rope out of the pouch, Laura turned to her new friend and whispered, "Annabelle, are those men talking about *you*?"

The pretty redhead turned her face, mottled red and white with her own brand of fear, and said, "The one in the black hat is my brother Cass. He's here for me. My depraved old father must have sent him to kidnap me and take me against my will back to the Broken Heart and marry the sniveling son of one of his business partners!"

Laura gasped, slowly closing her hand across her mouth. Annabelle had serious trouble of her own to deal with. No wonder she'd so readily commiserated with Laura's own dire scrape.

As Laura stared down into the alley, the three men were talking too quietly to overhear while passing a bottle around. Getting themselves fortified with liquid courage. Their hat brims concealed their faces.

Annabelle grabbed Laura's hand. "We have to get out of here! If they find me up here, they'll take me. If they find you up here . . ." She shook her head ominously. "No telling. They're drunk. My brother is not a gentleman."

"Is there another back way out of here?" Laura asked as Annabelle led her to the door.

Annabelle paused to step into her shoes. "Only through the saloon. Don't worry. It's not yet noon. Probably not all that busy yet."

"Annabelle, I can't be seen down there!"

Annabelle swung toward Laura, her own eyes anxious. "You can't stay up here. Too dangerous. There are no locks on the doors. I'm going to go down and tell Dan what Cass is up to. Dan and our bouncer, Eugene, will put a stop to it straightaway — believe me!"

"Annabelle — I'm in enough trouble! If I'm seen in a saloon —"

"Here!" Annabelle had grabbed a hooded cape off a wall hook. "This is mine but one of the doves often borrows it. She's always cold in the mornings and wears it when she goes downstairs to sit by the potbellied stove."

Annabelle dropped the cape down over Laura's head. "Ginny has lighter hair, but you're similarly shaped, so if you keep the hood up and your head down, you should make it out the front door without being recognized. Just drag your feet and try to look pouty and hungover."

Laura raised the hood and drew it as far forward as it would go to conceal her features. "How's this?"

"Lead-pipe cinch!" Annabelle said, and cracked the door.

She peered both ways along the hall. Deeming it clear, she stepped into the hall and led Laura along behind her. They hurried together toward the stairs. Annabelle paused and tilted her head toward a door at the end of the hall, on the hall's right side. That was the door that led to the rear stairs and back door.

The creaking of furtive bootsteps sounded on the rear stairs. A couple of the men coming up those stairs snickered and chuckled. One sounded as though he had his hand over his mouth, trying not to laugh.

"Come on!" Annabelle said, squeezing Laura's hand.

As they started down the main stairs to the saloon, the door to the rear stairs opened behind them. Footsteps sounded on the floor of the hall now above and behind the women. Men grunted and murmured.

One said, "Wait — stop, Annabelle!"

Annabelle swung a look over her left shoulder. Her masked brother stood at the top of the stairs, his drink-bright eyes wide and angry behind the slit cuts in the flour sack.

"Annabelle, you wait, dammit!"

Laura's heart raced as she heard heavy foot thuds on the stairs behind her.

"Dan!" Annabelle called. "Dan — help!"

The big, red-faced, portly man in the gaudy suit and with an apron around his rotund waist turned from the range behind the bar. He'd been sampling chili from a wooden spoon. Now, still holding the spoon up to his mouth, he scowled up the stairs, and his red face turned redder.

"What the hell's goin' on?"

Annabelle, with Laura in tow, had just gained the bottom of the stairs and was heading toward the bar. Annabelle glanced at Laura walking on her right, released Laura's hand, and jerked her chin toward the saloon's front door.

Laura nodded and put her head down, sort of shrinking like a turtle back inside the shell of the cape's hood. There were maybe ten men in the room, most sitting at tables, hunched over mugs of beer and bowls of chili.

As she headed for the door, Laura was relieved to see that all eyes were on the striking, scantily clad redhead who, angling toward the bar, yelled bitterly, "My drunk brother and a few friends snuck up the back stairs to kidnap me and take me back to the Broken Heart! Dan, would you please remind him I have no intention ever returning to the Broken Heart again — so help me God!"

"Be my pleasure, darlin'!"

Laura cut a look toward the bar on her left. Big Dan dropped the spoon and reached for a double-barrel shotgun leaning against the backbar. He glanced at a beefy, younger man with red-blond muttonchops and goatee eating chili at the end of the bar, and yelled, "Eugene — stop feeding your face and grab the bung starter! We got some heads to break!"

"Hold on, Dan! Hold on!" Cass Ludlow yelled from the stairs.

Fascinated by what was happening, Laura had stopped and turned toward the rear of the room. Cass Ludlow, wearing a flour sack mask beneath his black hat, had stopped halfway down the stairs, flanked by the two others. Ludlow held one gloved hand up, palm out.

"Hold on! Hold on! I just wanna talk to dear sis, is all!" His words were slurred from drink. He held on to the banister to his right to steady himself.

343

As both Big Dan and the man called Eugene hurried toward the stairs, Big Dan wielding the shotgun and Eugene slapping what appeared a small leather-wrapped club against the palm of his left hand, Laura turned forward and continued toward the door.

She'd taken only two strides before she tripped over something.

She stopped and looked down as a cane tumbled from the chair it had been leaning against to the floor. Laura stared down in horror as the cane rolled toward her, the silver horse head at its top glinting in the sunlight from a near window.

Her terror grew a hundred-fold when the man sitting in the chair turned to her, and she found herself staring hang-jawed into the face of her husband, Jonathan Gaynor.

CHAPTER 28

Jonathan Gaynor was so preoccupied with the pretty redhead standing with her back to the bar, pointing and yelling at the three men clad in trail garb on the stairs while Big Dan and the bouncer hurried toward them — shouting threats and warnings — that Jonathan hardly even glanced at his wife who'd shot him in his unmentionables.

He merely glanced down at the cane she'd kicked onto the floor, scowled up at her fleetingly and with deep annoyance ridging his slender, dark brown brows, then nudged the Pinkerton sitting beside him with his elbow. While the Pinkerton reached down to retrieve the cane, Jonathan's gaze returned to Annabelle, saying to the detective, "I'll be damned if that pretty little redhead isn't about to burst right out of that corset!"

The Pinkerton laughed as he leaned the cane against Jonathan's chair.

Her knees nearly buckling in relief at her husband's distraction, even though he was distracted by another woman — no surprise there! — Laura drew the hood tighter about her face and strode quickly toward the batwing doors. Once outside, she turned to peer over the doors and into the saloon.

Annabelle's brother and his two accomplices were stomping angrily up the stairs, still arguing with Big Dan and the bouncer called Eugene. In a few seconds, all three ranch men who'd come to kidnap Annabelle had retreated through the door at the top of the staircase leading to the rear alley.

Laura stepped to one side, pressing her back against the saloon's front wall, and heaved a long sigh of deep relief. She and Annabelle were both safe. At least, for the time being.

That time was short-lived.

She closed her eyes to gather herself. When she opened them, she sucked a sharp breath in renewed terror.

Warren Davenport stood before her, towering over her, glowering furiously down at her darkly with his stony eyes, pointing a big, thick, crooked index finger at her. "I saw you come out of there! Why, you slattern! Whore!" He bellowed the insults as loudly as he could, trying to shame her in public. He'd realized he couldn't have her, so now he'd bury her. "Look here, everybody — Tigerville's new schoolteacher just came out of Big Dan's whorehouse! Is this the kind of teacher we —"

He stopped as Laura turned to run away from him.

"Oh, no, you don't! You won't run away from me, you whore!"

Davenport grabbed Laura's shoulder and spun her around. A half second later the back of his right hand crashed into her left cheek in roughly the same place he'd struck her the other night. Laura screamed as she spun and fell to the boards.

"Slattern! Witch! Whore!" Davenport bellowed at the tops of his lungs, moving toward her threateningly once more.

"No!" Laura screamed.

Davenport jerked back, frowning as he turned around. Laura had just seen a large brown hand grab the man's left shoulder. Now as Davenport stumbled back toward the saloon's front wall, Hunter Buchanon moved toward him, swinging his right fist back behind his right shoulder before throwing it forward with an enraged grunt.

Hunter's fist smashed against Davenport's mouth with a solid smacking sound. The man's lips instantly turned red as he screamed and, throwing his arms out for a balance he never achieved, flew straight back through the saloon's large plate-glass window. The words BIG DAN'S SALOON forming an arc across the window in large, gold-leaf lettering disappeared as the window shattered inward with the din of a dozen little girls screaming at the tops of their lungs.

Davenport disappeared inside the saloon amidst the raining glass.

Rage was a wildfire inside Buchanon as he stepped through the shattered window.

Davenport lay in the glass several feet inside the saloon, peppered with more glass, gazing in wide-eyed shock at the big man moving toward him. Davenport scuttled back on his butt. He'd lost his hat; broken glass glistened across the bald top of his head.

"You Southern devil!" Davenport raged, spitting blood from his smashed lips.

He scrambled to his feet. As Hunter moved on the man quickly, Davenport brought a roundhouse punch up from his knees. The man's fist glanced off of Hunter's left temple.

Buchanon didn't even flinch. He stepped into the man, who was nearly as tall as he was, and hammered the man's mouth again with his own right fist. Davenport's head jerked back with a startled grunt. When his head jerked back forward, Buchanon slammed his fist against his nose.

Blood from the broken nose now mixed with the blood from the ruined lips, dribbling in several streams down Davenport's chin. He brushed his fist across his nose, eyes watering. He shook his head, bellowed with rage, stepped forward, and swung another punch at Hunter, who easily ducked it.

Moving in on Davenport again, Buchanon punched the man in the gut once, twice, three times. The man screamed and jackknifed. Stepping forward, Hunter smashed his right knee into the point of the man's chin, lifting him up off his knees and sending him stumbling backward with another wailing cry. He piled up on a table from which three men in business suits had one second ago scrambled, clutching their chili bowls and beer mugs.

Buchanon's wolf was off its leash. Hunter couldn't get what Davenport had done to Laura out of his head. He crouched, pulled the man to his feet, and went to work on his face once more, driving him back onto the table again. Hunter was about to pull

Davenport off the table yet again to continue the savage beating, when Big Dan shouted, "Eugene — grab that crazy grayback!"

A second later, a man leaped onto Hunter from behind, pulling his arms behind his back and hauling him away from Davenport, shouting, "Hold on, Buchanon. You're gonna kill him!"

"He needs killin'!" the former Rebel heard himself bellow.

He'd torn one arm loose from Big Dan's bouncer and had started to move toward Davenport once more when two other men leaped onto his back, yelling and driving him to the floor. One of the men sat on his head while another sat on his chest. Yet another sat on his knees, pinning him flat to the floor.

They were big men. Buchanon wasn't getting up until they let him.

"All right," Hunter said. "Let me up, dammit. I'm done!"

The fire inside him was dampened down enough that he thought he could get his wolf back on its leash. He felt grateful for the three men, including Eugene, who'd intervened. He'd wanted to kill Davenport. The man deserved killing. But he was done with that. At least, he wanted to be.

He didn't want to pull another stunt like the one he'd pulled on Ike Talon. The berserker inside him had to die. He didn't want to be that man anymore. The war was over.

"Thanks, fellas," Hunter said, as, breathing hard, big Eugene Donleavy helped him to his feet.

One of the other two men handed Hunter his hat.

Hunter regarded the bloody-faced, wheezing Davenport and then glanced a little sheepishly around the room before turning toward the door. Laura was peering in at him through the broken window.

As Hunter moved toward her, she lifted her chin slightly to look past him. Her eyes widened; she slapped both hands across her mouth.

Behind Hunter, several men shouted. Annabelle's voice yelled, "Hunter, look out!"

Buchanon swung around, ripping his LeMat from its holster. Davenport had gained his feet and was extending an over-and-under derringer at Hunter in his right hand.

On the heels of Annabelle's warning, Davenport turned his head, as did Hunter, to see Annabelle standing eight feet away from Davenport, aiming Big Dan's double-barrel shotgun straight out from her right shoulder at Laura's assailant.

As Davenport began to swing the derringer toward the redhead, Annabelle triggered both barrels.

Orange flames ripped from the steel maws. Annabelle screamed as the big barn-blaster's savage kick flung her and the shotgun straight back over a table behind her. At the same time, both fist-size clumps of buckshot blew Davenport back through the long, rectangular window on Hunter's left, in the side wall opposite the bar.

The shotgun's blast echoed around the room like the deafening blast of a Napoleon cannon.

Hunter stared, stunned, at the billowing smoke from the shotgun. He looked at the shattered window on his left and then at where Annabelle had been standing a moment ago, before the shotgun's kick had thrown her over the table. Several men stood around where she lay on the floor between the table and the bar, looking down at her, shaking their heads and muttering.

Hunter lowered the LeMat and pushed his way through the crowd.

"Now, that was a spectacle!" chuckled a dapper little man holding a cane with a silver horse head.

Buchanon gave the man only a passing glance and only because the man he was standing with, near the table over which Annabelle had been thrown, wore the copper shield of a Pinkerton detective.

"Annabelle! Annabelle!" said Big Dan Delaney, owner of the saloon. He was pushing through the crowd, as well, catching Hunter's glance and saying, "She grabbed my shotgun off the bar. I didn't know she even knew how to shoot it!"

Hunter pushed a couple more men aside and stepped up to where Annabelle lay on the floor, groaning and shaking her head slowly from side to side. He dropped to a knee beside her, placed his hand on her arm.

"Honey, you all right?"

She turned her head to stare up at him. Her face was pale. "I . . . I think so . . ."

She raised her hand to him. Hunter took it, eased her slowly up off the floor, wrapped his arms around her, and, holding her up against his chest, rose to his feet.

Big Dan stepped aside and waved his arms to clear a path for Hunter and Annabelle. "Make way, now, fellas! Please, make way!"

Hunter crossed the room and climbed the stairs. He looked down at the pretty redhead in his arms. She stared up at him, her own arms wrapped around his neck.

353

"This is getting to be a habit," she said with a faint wry flicker of one mouth corner.

"You got a habit of doin' some pretty crazy things, and that down there was one of 'em."

He turned to her door. It stood partway open. He kicked it wide and carried Annabelle into the room and lay her down on the bed that was a mess of rumpled sheets and quilts and strewn dresses and frilly underwear. The room smelled like Annabelle. It was a poignant smell. It went straight to his heart. He didn't think he'd ever get that smell out of his head if he lived to be a million years old though he'd just now realized that fact.

He was going to miss that smell.

He was going to miss a lot of things about her. For years now he'd thought he and she would grow old together, that they'd die side by side. But now he realized that wasn't true. They'd die apart.

Hunter eased her onto the bed, adjusted the pillow beneath her head.

"How do you feel? Anything broken? Should I call the doc?"

Annabelle shook her head, making her thick red hair shift on the pillow. "My shoulder's just sore." She worked her arm a little, wincing. "I'm going to have a helluva bruise tomorrow."

"You're starting to talk like the men down-stairs."

"Yeah, well, they like the way I talk," she said crisply, narrowing one fiery jade eye at him.

"Well, I don't."

"I don't care what you like or don't like."

"Oh hell — enough of this! Why in the hell was Warren Davenport going at Laura like that?"

"She said he's been pestering her some-thing awful. Giving her things. Forcing her to dine with him. At least he *was*. He won't be doing that again." A horrified expression flashed across her face. "Do you think I killed him?"

"Well, you triggered both barrels of that twelve-gauge into him. Blasted him through a window." Buchanon chuckled caustically. "Yeah, I think you killed him!"

Annabelle ground her elbows into the bed and raised her head and shoulders, the fires of anger returning to her eyes. "Well, if I hadn't killed him, he would have killed you. But now, since you don't seem any too grateful, I'm starting to think I should have just let him go ahead and shoot you in the back!"

"Have you talked to Laura?"

"What?"

"Have you talked to her?"

Annabelle gazed up at him, frowning bewilderedly. "Yes." The frown twisted her brows more severely. "Why?"

"I was just . . . I was just . . ."

"Don't worry. We didn't get together to compare notes on you. In fact, we didn't exchange one word about you at all!" Annabelle lied.

"What brought you two together?" He wasn't sure why, but he felt vaguely suspicious.

"She's in a heap of trouble." Annabelle placed her hand on his forearm and squeezed it urgently. "You best get down there and find her before that nasty husband of hers does . . ."

"Her husband?" Buchanon scowled down at her. "What're you talkin' about, Annabelle?"

"Just go to Laura, Hunter." Annabelle sat up higher, stared into his eyes from only a few inches away. "She needs you! You're not needed here. You're no longer needed here. Go to the woman who loves you and needs you. Go!"

She swung her arm toward the door.

As she stared at him, face flushed with fury, her upper lip quivered. A sheen of emotion shimmered in her eyes. She tucked her upper lip under her lower front teeth to stop the quiver. "Just go to her," she said again, and let her head sink slowly back onto the pillow.

She turned her face to one side, away from him.

Hunter backed away from her, feeling as rotten as he had the last time they'd parted, with her screaming down the hall at him. When would that hard, wooden knot in his belly ever loosen?

He turned to the door just as he heard the clacking of nails in the hall, and the familiar manic pants of — who else?

Bobby Lee.

Buchanon poked his head into the hall. Sure enough, the coyote was running toward him a tad uncertainly, his padded feet slipping on the bare wooden floor. Hunter hadn't seen his coyote friend for over an hour. As he'd been approaching town with the Indian woman in tow, Bobby Lee had run off with his nose to the ground — likely on the scent of a jackrabbit or a deer.

Now, having sensed trouble, here he was.

"Bobby, I was just . . ."

Hunter let his voice trail off as Bobby Lee slipped past him into Annabelle's room.

Bobby stopped by the bed and placed his

front paws on the edge of it, sniffing and mewling softly as he studied Annabelle who had her back to him. The girl's shoulders jerked as she cried silently.

Bobby glanced at Hunter, who stood in the doorway feeling as hollowed out as an old log. The coyote raised his upper lip to show his teeth at him in silent reproof, then leaped up onto the bed and lay in a tightly curled ball at the base of it.

Hunter nodded. "Look after her, Bobby."

He stepped out of the room and drew the door closed behind him.

CHAPTER 29

Buchanon hurried back down the stairs and into Big Dan's main drinking hall.

Very few of Big Dan's customers were sitting at the tables. They all appeared to be standing at the window Annabelle had shot Warren Davenport out of, on the room's right side now as Hunter headed for the swing doors at the front.

"Any sign of life in him?" Hunter called to the group crowded around the window, loudly conversing.

One of the men turned to Hunter, removed a fat stogie from his mouth, and said, "Deader'n last year's Christmas goose!"

"Somebody better fetch an undertaker." There were a good half dozen undertakers in Tigerville. In a mountain boom town like this one, where it seemed the more ore that was pulled out of the surrounding hills, the more men ended up dead in back alleys and dusty streets . . . or blown out of saloon windows . . . undertaking was almost as prosperous as mining.

"Already sent for one!" another man called.

"When he's finished there, send him over to the jail. I have two more for him."

Big Dan was standing near the front window that Hunter had punched Davenport through from the outside. The big saloon owner was scowling down at the broken glass. He turned to Buchanon, glowering and shaking his big, red-faced head. "This is going to cost me a pretty penny! Do you know how much it costs to have plate-glass windows shipped up here from Cheyenne?"

Hunter continued striding past the man. He was in no mood to listen to caterwauling about broken windows. Pushing through the swing doors, he said, "Best keep servin' up the chili, Dan."

He paused on the boardwalk and looked around for Laura. She was nowhere in sight. He recalled Annabelle's words: "She's in a whole heap of trouble!"

What kind of trouble?

Had her husband come looking for her?

Hunter wanted to go to her, but he'd only just ridden up to the jail office when he'd heard and seen Davenport berating Laura out front of Big Dan's. He'd left his horse as well as the horse his prisoner was tied to, and run over to intervene on Laura's behalf. He was glad to see his prisoner still sitting on the back of the Indian pony he'd tied her to, head down, hands cuffed behind her back.

The two horses over which he'd hauled the dead federals, Winslow and Birmingham, back to town were also still standing before the hitchrack fronting his office.

He had to get his prisoner in a jail cell and Winslow and Birmingham ready for the undertaker. It was a hell of a job, this law business. He wasn't sure he was cut out for it. At the moment, he just wanted to go back to driving the stagecoach. No — really what he wanted to do at this moment was hunt Laura down and find out if she was all right.

But that would be a while.

He negotiated his way across the street. Several men had gathered around the horses carrying his prisoner and the two dead marshals. A couple of little boys, maybe eight and ten years old, were snooping around the horses carrying Winslow and Birmingham, squatting down to get a look at the heads of the blanket-wrapped bodies.

Hunter chased the boys away and turned to the young Indian woman sitting the

Indian pony sporting war paint. Ignoring the men standing on the boardwalk, muttering amongst themselves and eyeing the young woman speculatively, Hunter fished his barlow knife out of his pants pocket and opened the blade. Stepping up to the girl's left foot hanging down the horse's left side, he looked up at her and said, "I'm gonna cut the rope off your foot. If you kick me, you're gonna get the point of this knife in your leg."

He showed her the knife.

Over their past three days traveling together, she'd tried to kick him more than once. Several times, she'd turned wildcat on him, once almost snatching his cast-iron pan off a cook fire and bashing his head in with it. He'd grabbed her just in time, wrestled her to the ground, and got the cuffs back on her while she spat and snarled and cursed him in Sioux. That had been a particularly close one.

One of many.

He had to admit that a couple of times he'd considered putting a bullet into her rather than continue to risk his own life getting her back to Tigerville. For some reason, he hadn't done it. Who would have known? They'd been all alone out there.

But he would have known. Of all the crazy

damn things he'd found himself doing in his wild life, he now found himself trying to impress himself as a man of the law. As a good one. That damned badge on his shirt weighed heavy on him, and however half-consciously, he wanted to honor it. He wanted to live up to it.

At least until he could find a more willing man than he was to wear the damn thing — a nickel's worth of cheap tin!

For now, though, he had work to do.

The Indian girl didn't even look at him, much less respond to his warning. She hadn't said anything to him in all the days they'd ridden together, and had sat around campfires at night. Mostly, she'd stared at him, upper lip curled, eyes hard as black granite, as though wanting to tear his heart out with her fingernails and dine on it in front of him. That had been a little unsettling.

Now he cut the rope from around her left ankle and stepped back.

She didn't try to kick him.

Well, that was something, anyway.

He walked around to the other side of the horse and cut the rope from around her other ankle. Again, he stepped back quickly, and arched one brow in surprise.

Again, she hadn't tried to kick him.

363

Maybe this really was progress . . .

"All right," he said, taking another step back away from her horse and placing his hand on the grips of his LeMat. "Come on down. Nice and slow."

She turned her head to him and looked at him coldly through the black strands of her hair. Suddenly, she smiled. But her eyes were still cold, bright with primal hatred. She was toying with him, making him wonder what she would try next.

"I'll gut-shoot you," he warned.

Slowly, she raised her moccasin-clad left foot, swung it over her horse's mane, and dropped straight down to the ground in front of him. She was a head shorter than he was, and she weighed half what he did. Her hands were cuffed behind her back. Still, he knew from experience that she could move rattlesnake quick and do some serious damage.

Apprehension quickened his heart. He'd be glad to have her in a jail cell.

He canted his head toward the jailhouse door.

She turned slowly, reluctant to take her smiling gaze from his. She stepped up onto the boardwalk, and the men standing on the boardwalk, watching her and Hunter curiously, made way for her as they would for some dangerous wild animal that had escaped a circus.

Hunter stepped onto the boardwalk behind her.

He took one more step before she swung back toward him in a blur of quick motion. With a cat-like scream, she thrust her right foot up between his legs, the sharp toe connecting decisively with his crotch. She screamed again and smashed her forehead against his mouth.

Hunter dropped to his knees, sunbursts of pain flaring in his eyes, the worst kind of male agony radiating in all directions from his loins. He felt the oily wetness of blood on his lips.

Despite the grinding pain, he kept his eyes on her feet. A good thing he did. She was about to ram her knee into his face when he heaved himself forward, flinging his hands out before him, and ripped both feet out from under her.

She fell with another even more piercing scream and struck the boardwalk on her back, the back of her head smacking the boards and bouncing with a resounding double-thud. Hunter leaped up off his feet, trying desperately to suppress the fireballs of pain rolling through him, one after another, and crouched over her.

Quickly, before she could renew her attack, he jerked her head up off the boardwalk by her hair, grabbed her left arm, and heaved her up over his shoulder.

Imagine carrying an enraged mountain lion on your shoulder. That's what she was like — snarling and screaming and kicking her legs and shaking her head, trying to bash his head with her own, a couple of times succeeding.

As Hunter started forward in a desperate rush, the office door opened inward. The moon-faced Otis Crosby stood in the doorway looking bleary-eyed from a nap.

He blinked in hang-jawed surprise.

"Why, Marshal —"

"Fetch the cell keys, Otis! Got a live one!"

Otis moved his wide-eyed, hulking form to the left as Hunter bulled through the door with the panther-like girl on his shoulder, snapping her jaws and grunting and hissing. She managed to close her sharp teeth over his left ear.

More javelins of pain lanced through him. *"Ow, dammit! Ow, dammit! Let go, you crazy squaw!"*

Hunter turned sharply, knocking her head against the office's stone wall until her jaws opened, releasing his ear. Buchanon headed for one of the four open cell doors, carried

366

the crazy Indian inside, and dropped her without ceremony on the cell's single cot.

She bounced once, then lay wincing — eyelids fluttering — slowly raising her deerskin-clad knees to her chest. The blow against the wall had knocked her semi-unconscious. Blood shone darkly in her blue-black hair.

Good.

Hunter staggered out of the cell, crouching, clamping one hand over his ear, the other over his privates, and shouting, "Hurry — close the damn door and lock it tight!"

Otis lumbered past him to the cell, fiddling with the key ring. "I'm tryin', Marshal — I'm tryin'!"

"Hurry up!"

"These damn old keys are rusty!"

"Lock the damn door, Otis!"

Otis grunted as he turned the key in the door. "There — got her locked in good, Marshal!"

"Christ!" Hunter sank into the chair at the cluttered desk, leaning forward over his bruised oysters.

"Boy, she sure took a nasty turn on you!" Otis observed. "Hard to believe such a little thing —"

"She's not all that little and I've encoun-

367

tered mountain lions a whole lot friendlier."

"Who is she? What'd she do?"

"She was one of the six warriors who shot up the Goliad."

"No! *Her?*"

Hunter had pulled a handkerchief out of his pants pocket and was holding it over his split lip. His head ached, his ears rang, his vision was still blurry, and he felt as though he'd been spitted on a Sioux war lance.

He pulled the desk's bottom drawer open and peered inside, vaguely noting that a mouse had built a nest out of some shredded wanted circulars. "Where's my bottle?"

Otis flinched. "What bottle?"

"The bottle I kept in this . . ." Hunter looked up at the husky odd-jobber standing before him, guiltily worrying the key ring in his big, dirt-stained hands. Hunter gave a caustic chuff. He knew exactly where the bottle had gone. Otis was not known as a regular drinker, but his occasional benders were legendary.

"I got a job for you."

"Sure, sure," Otis said, brightening. He ambled over to the wall fronting the desk and hung the keys on a railroad spike embedded in the stone. "I had me a nap so I'm fresh."

"Glad one of us is fresh," Hunter grumbled.

He opened another drawer and pulled out a lined tablet and a pencil. "Both Winslow and Birmingham are dead. I need to wire word to the U.S. Marshal's office in Yankton. They need to let me know what to do with the bodies. They also need to alert the circuit court judge and send him quick to try that wildcat in yonder."

He quickly scribbled the missive on the paper, then ripped the sheet from the pad and held it out to Otis.

"Take that over to Western Union. Make sure Mike Quinn taps it out today. Not tomorrow. Today. Tell him to bill the city council. I don't have more than a few cents to my name an' me an' Pa's rent is already late over at Mrs. Brumvold's boarding house."

"You got it, Marsh—"

Otis stopped when the office door opened suddenly. Two men stepped in, one behind the other. Hunter recognized both from Big Dan's.

The first man was the dapper little gent in a tailored butterscotch suitcoat, side whiskers, and a handlebar mustache, the facial hair looking especially dark given the creamy color of his unblemished face. He was leaning on the silver horse head of his cane carved from what appeared a fine grade of wood — possibly cherry.

The man behind him, several inches taller, was the long-faced, mustached Pinkerton with the copper shield on his left coat lapel. The detective was more subtly attired in brown checked wool over a white shirt with a celluloid collar and a brown foulard tie. A bulge in his coat denoted a hogleg of considerable caliber residing in a shoulder holster.

His eyes were coldly serious. He didn't look like a man who smiled all that much even on his best days.

"Hello, Mister Buchanon," greeted the dapper gent with the cane, limping into the room. Each time he put weight on the silver horse head, his mouth tightened in a flinch. "I understand you're the law enforcement here in Tigerville."

Hunter and Otis shared a skeptical glance.

Looking back at the dandy, Hunter said, "That's right." His voice was still a little tight. The rolling waves of agony down south of his cartridge belt were not yet finished with him.

"I was told as much by Big Dan."

"What can I help you with?" Hunter didn't want to help him with anything. He wanted to find a bottle, swill his pain away, and take a nap. At the moment, in his current condition, he wouldn't be much help to anyone.

The dandy held out his pale, beringed hand and gave an oily smile. "My name is Jonathan Gaynor."

CHAPTER 30

Buchanon had had a sneaking suspicion that Gaynor was who the popinjay was, so he wasn't completely taken off guard. He thought he probably did a pretty good imitation of a disinterested party as he said, "If the name's supposed to impress me, it doesn't."

"It impresses quite a few people, Marshal." This from the Pinkerton, who stood behind and a little to one side of Gaynor, studying Hunter with severely ridged brows, hands clutching his coat lapels. He had a humorless, schoolmasterly look, chin dipped toward his chest.

Hunter instinctively didn't like him. But then he didn't like Gaynor, either, though his dislike for Gaynor was for obvious reasons that had been made clear to him by the man's wife.

Buchanon shrugged and turned to the dandy, who was leaning on his cane, his pale face red with anger. "I'm not one of them. Now, if you wanna preen, do it outside. If you have business, state it and get the hell out of my office. I have a prisoner and two dead deputy U.S. marshals to tend to, not to mention a split lip and sore balls!"

He dabbed at his mouth again with the handkerchief.

Gaynor and the Pinkerton shared a look. The Pinkerton shrugged and shook his head in disgust. Gaynor turned back to Hunter, his jaws hard, his thin lips compressed in a taut line beneath his ostentatious mustache. He reached into a pocket of his butterscotch coat and set a small photograph on the desk before Hunter.

Buchanon looked at the picture. He felt his belly tighten as he stared down at the elegantly beautiful woman he'd made love with only a few days ago.

Laura was decked out in a ruffled shirt-waist secured at the neck with a cameo pin, a velvet waistcoat, and a flowered picture hat. Her thick hair was coifed in a roll atop her head, the hat secured to the roll. The wide eyes — appearing brown in the black-and-white photo — were warm, intelligent, and lustrous. The photo was an egg-shaped, upper body shot with a floral background. Probably taken in Gaynor's own stylishly furnished living room.

Again, Hunter manufactured a disinterested expression as he looked at the preening pigeon before him. "Suppose I know her — then?"

The Pinkerton took one step forward and gazed at Hunter with his typically officious, pompous air. "You'd have to tell us where we can find her. This woman is wanted for attempted murder."

Buchanon kept his eyes on Gaynor. "Maybe he had it coming."

Gaynor bunched his lips and rammed his cane down on the floor. "I did *not* have it coming!"

"Carrying on with another woman for most of your marriage while professing false loyalty is about as lowdown-dirty a thing as a man can do to a woman." Hunter flared a nostril at him. "I'd say you had it coming, all right."

Unexpectedly, Jonathan Gaynor's thin lips twitched in a smile. He nodded knowingly. "Ahh . . . yes . . . you've met her, all right. Even gotten to know her, I daresay."

"Well enough to know that if I see you anywhere near her, I'll gut-shoot you and leave you to the stray dogs in a back alley." Buchanon flashed his threatening glare on the Pinkerton. "That goes for you, too,

Mister Pink."

Gaynor and the Pinkerton shared another look, both men shaping grim smiles and shaking their heads, as though reflecting on a shared secret.

Turning back to the Tigerville town marshal, Gaynor said, "Look, Marshal, I see you've come to know my wife rather well. That's not unexpected. You've probably even been *seduced* by her — in more ways than one, I might add. It would be true to Jane's character to form an alliance with a man of power here where she has apparently fled in an attempt to escape the repercussions of her reprehensible behavior."

Jane? Hunter wanted to blurt out but caught himself.

Buchanon said, "She didn't find you in a bathtub with a whorehouse madam in Gaynorville?"

"No!" Gaynor laughed, stumbling back and stabbing his cane at the floor to help him regain his balance. He glanced at the suddenly smiling Pinkerton — he did smile, after all — then returned his mirthful gaze to Buchanon and said, "Dear Lord — is that the story she told you?"

He looked at the Pinkerton again, chuckling. The Pinkerton didn't laugh but he did keep smiling. He looked at the floor and shook his head as though he'd heard everything now.

"Let's hear your side of it," Hunter said.

"Do you mind if I sit down?" Gaynor asked sharply. "I took a bullet in a precarious area. Certainly, you — a man suffering an injury in a similar region — would understand."

"Help yourself." Hunter glanced at a spool-back chair abutting the wall behind the dandy.

Gaynor snapped his fingers at the chair, and the Pinkerton hustled into action, pulling the chair out away from the wall and positioning it carefully behind his boss. The dandy slacked into the chair with a long, ragged sigh and another painful flinch.

Resting his cane across his thighs, he leaned forward, pinned Hunter with a frank, direct look, and said, "Jane is a woman of profoundly duplicitous character. She married me . . . as I have recently discovered . . . just as she married three other men before me. Imagine it. She's twenty-seven years old, and already she's been married four times. To wealthy men. Wealthy men she fleeced and fled!"

Hunter's cheeks warmed with anger. "You're a damn liar."

376

"Am I?" Gaynor reached behind again and snapped his fingers.

Again, the Pinkerton rushed into action, pulling a thin sheaf of folded papers out of his coat pocket and handing them up to his boss. Gaynor unfolded the sheets and shoved them at Hunter. "Take a look for yourself."

Buchanon looked at the top page:

$5000 **REWARD!**

Mr. GEORGE JASON UNDERHILL of Leadville in the Colorado Territory was found *murdered* in his home on October 14th, 1878.
Mr. Underhill had recently *married* an attractive Young Lady known as "Marie," one of several believed aliases.

(see photo below)

It is believed that "Marie" murdered Underhill before *pillaging* his home of all *valuables* and fleeing by way of stagecoach or train.
A REWARD of $5000 will be paid by the Undersigned for the Arrest and Conviction of "Marie Underhill" for the wanton Murder and Robbery of

George Jason Underhill.
Signed for the Pinkerton
Detective Agency
by CHAZ R. MOODY
Superintendent Pinkerton Western
District Office
Denver, Colorado Territory

Hunter merely glanced at the other dodgers.

The photograph on each was of Laura or Jane or whoever in hell she was posing in varying costumes in various photographers' artificial scenes. One photo owned a railroad flavor — probably taken in a photographer's studio outfitted with a faux parlor car complete with a brass railroad lantern mounted beside a small, curtained window.

All of the alleged crimes were similar in nature — the fleecing and murdering of moneyed, older men.

Hunter's numb fingers released the pages. They fluttered to the floor.

He stared down at them in shock, his mind a whirl.

"Don't feel too bad, Marshal," Jonathan Gaynor said gently. "You're by no means the first man she's duped. She's a professional."

Buchanon looked up at the two men. "You

don't go near her until I've checked into it. Understand?"

The two men glanced at each other skeptically.

Hunter rose from his chair, uncoiling like a big cat to his full six-feet-four. He stared down at both men. He was more than a head taller than Gaynor and half a head taller than the Pinkerton. He probably outweighed the Pinkerton by fifty pounds, all of it muscle. The Pinkerton had skinny legs and a slight paunch.

Both men looked up at him, wary expressions creeping over their faces.

The threat was obvious.

Gaynor nodded slowly. "All right. We'll check back with you, Marshal." He frowned with admonishment. "Be forewarned — Jane can be very convincing."

Gaynor turned and, employing his cane, headed out the door. The Pinkerton glanced once more at Buchanon. He nodded twice — arching his brows — then followed his employer out of the jailhouse and into the busy street.

Hunter just then realized that Otis was still in his office, standing about seven feet back from where Gaynor had sat in the spool-back chair. The conversation had likely proven far too interesting for Otis to tear himself away. No doxie in town spread more gossip than Otis Crosby.

"I thought I told you to take that note to the Western Union office," Hunter barked at the man.

Otis jerked with a start, his beefy face instantly reddening. "I was just . . . I just . . . was headin' that way right now, Mar— !"

"Hold on!"

Otis wheeled from the open doorway. "Huh?"

Hunter pointed at him commandingly and with no little threat in his flashing blue eyes. "I know you're good at spreading gossip, but keep your mouth shut about what those two and I said in here. Instead, you can spread this — if anyone says one word to that dapper little flamingo and his Pinkerton sidekick, they'll be paying the piper."

He mashed his thumb against Otis's chest. "And the piper is me!"

"Oh . . . oh . . . all right, Marshal!" Otis smiled delightedly. "I'll spread the word — sure enough. You can count on me!"

He turned again and lumbered out the door.

"I know I can," Buchanon muttered to himself.

He kicked the door closed, raked his hand down his face, avoiding contact with his lip, then turned to see the Sioux woman staring at him through her cell door. Her black eyes were as flat as the surface of a deep well. She curled her upper lip and said, "Woman trouble?"

Hunter glowered at her. "I didn't know you could speak English."

She shook her tangled hair back behind her shoulders, pulled her shoulders back proudly, and said, "I went to a boarding school in Cheyenne. I killed one of the schoolmasters who snuck into my room one night. He got a broken lamp across his throat for his trouble. Then I went back to my people and vowed to fight the white man forever."

"Yeah, well, now you're gonna hang for *your* trouble."

Hunter looked around for his hat. Through the window by the door he saw the Stetson lying on the boardwalk where he'd lost it in the dustup with his prisoner.

He stepped out, plucked the hat off the floor, then strode back into the office. He grabbed a padlock off his desk. He started for the door again but stopped when the girl said, "That Scudder — he was sellin' my people poison whiskey. Him and Calvin Holte. The last batch killed seven men and made six more so sick they're still sick. They scream, and their women scream!"

"I know." Hunter looked at her pointedly. "But what you did, riding into town and killing innocent men at the Goliad — that was wrong too. Scudder and Holte and those two sons of Holte — those are the ones who should hang. But now you're gonna hang."

"You white men — you're all alike."

Hunter's ears burned with anger. "Those two Deputy U.S. Marshals you killed out there had been sent to arrest Holte and his sons. You killed them when they were doing just that. They would have come back to town and arrested Scudder. But now they're dead — two good men despite what you might think about all white men. The five warriors you rode to town with are dead. And you're going to hang."

She stared back at him through the steel bars, her eyes as cold and dark as before.

Something in those eyes touched him, though. Deep down, he understood why she'd done what she'd done. He might have done the same thing in her place.

Who was he kidding?

He'd have done *exactly* what she'd done.

And he'd hang for it.

He sighed heavily, went to a water bucket, and filled a tin cup. He walked over to her, shoved the cup through the bars at her.

"You must be thirsty."

~~She smacked the cup out of his hands.~~
Water splashed across the floor.

"All right." He nodded. "Have it your way."

He turned to the door. "I'm gonna be gone awhile."

He went out, secured the padlock on the door, and mounted his horse.

Wretched damn day and it was only going to get worse.

CHAPTER 31

Hunter pulled Ghost up to one of the two hitchracks fronting the boarding house on the corner of Third Avenue and Second Street, not far from the abandoned English Tom Mine, and studied the two old men sitting out on the building's front veranda, to the right of the door.

Both spidery and gray-bearded, with faces like raisins, they sat in wooden rockers, trade blankets covering their skinny legs.

One of those old coots was Hunter's father, Angus Buchanon, who'd just taken a sip from a flat brown bottle. Angus furtively passed the bottle to the old coot sitting beside him. That was Joe Ryan, who'd been a mine superintendent a few years ago, before a bad ticker and arthritis had put him out of commission and he'd moved into Mrs. Brumvold's boarding house, which was where old men . . . and raggedy-heeled younger men, it seemed . . . came to molder and eventually die.

Ryan took a quick sip of the locally distilled firewater, passed the bottle back to Angus, who corked the bottle and slipped it furtively into a large pocket of the old Confederate greatcoat he wore as an open affront to the Yankees who outnumbered former Confederate freedom fighters in the area by around ten to one. The two old men muttered to each other, chuckling devilishly, like two schoolboys eager to learn the effect of the frog they'd left in the girls' privy.

Neither had seen the younger Buchanon ride up to the boarding house. Their chairs were angled so that they could look across the empty lot sitting catty-corner to the boarding house and over to where half a dozen whores' cribs sat on the banks of a creek and out front of which the whores, young enough to be the old coots' granddaughters, paraded around their laundry lines half-dressed. None of the girls was out there today, but they'd be out there again soon, and the old men would be parked out here, sharing a bottle of busthead, snorting, elbowing each other, and generally enjoying the show.

The two graybeards hadn't heard Hunter approach because both were nearly as deaf as fence posts.

Still seated on Ghost's back, Hunter cleared his throat and said loudly enough to penetrate the two oldsters' logy hearing: "If Mrs. Brumvold catches you two old scudders out here passin' that devil juice back an' forth, she's gonna have Big Syd throw you both out in the street." Big Syd was the three-hundred-pound Chinaman in Mrs. Brumvold's employ.

Both men whipped their heads around with starts.

Old Angus's blue eyes flared with customary rancor as he said, "Where the hell you been?"

"Chasin' owlhoots."

"What for?"

Hunter brushed his thumb across the badge pinned to his shirt. He swung down from Ghost's back, tossed the reins over the rack, and mounted the porch steps. He crossed to the door but stopped when old Angus said, "Get over here."

"What do you want, old man?"

"I want you to get over here — that's what I want." Angus beckoned with his one arm. He'd lost the left one in the War of Northern Aggression. For Joe Ryan's benefit, he added, "And don't backtalk your father or I'll take you over my knee and quirt your naked behind so raw you won't be able to sit down for a week."

Joe Ryan snorted and continued to stare out, piningly, toward the whores' cribs.

Hunter gave a chuff, brushing his thumb across his nose, and ambled over to where the old men sat in their rockers. Hunter leaned down and planted an affectionate kiss on his father's leathery cheek. He squeezed Angus's skinny shoulder through the greatcoat, hating how insubstantial it felt. Both men looked him up and down, eyes lingering on the badge on his shirt as well as on his cut lip and bruised forehead.

"You look like you was rode hard an' put up wet!" observed Joe Ryan, who had a face like a cadaver. He no longer smoked but he'd smoked cigars so long that the one corner of his mouth wore a permanent brown indentation. His watery blue eyes were milky from cataracts.

"What the hell are you wearin' that star for?" Angus wanted to know.

"I got hornswoggled by two old federals. Don't ask me how. It's so long ago now, I don't even remember. I gotta get inside and get cleaned up. I got a nasty chore to run."

Hunter turned and started for the boarding house's front door.

"I thought you was drivin' the stage," Angus said, craning his neck to scowl at his son.

"Long story, Pa. I'll fill you in later."

He pushed through the front door over which a wooden sign ordered: LEAVE THY SINS OUTSIDE WITH THE SOIL FROM YOUR SHOES! He loved his father dearly, but he didn't have time to palaver with the two old coots. Hell, they wouldn't remember half of what he told them, anyway. He had to find Laura . . . or whatever in hell her name was . . . and get the lowdown on Jonathan Gaynor's story about her.

His new job weighed heavy on him. The Indian girl weighed heavy on him. So did the death of his good friend Charley Anders as well as the deaths of Winslow and Birmingham. His mouth and south of his cartridge belt still ached. He kept hearing Annabelle's sad, haunting cries as she lay on her bed at Big Dan's.

But Laura was foremost on his mind at the moment.

He tramped down the boarding house's wood-floored hall, making his way back past the parlor on one side and the communal dining room on the other and past the stairway that rose to the second and third floors. Angus's muffled voice called angrily from the porch, "Gallblastit, Hunter, get

388

back here! I ain't done talkin' to you yet, boy!"

He sounded like an angry old crow.

Hunter walked past Mrs. Brumvold's tick-tocking grandfather clock and opened a door on the hall's left side. He could hear the little widow lady, Mrs. Reed, chastising her long-dead husband behind the door directly across the hall from Hunter and Angus's room. He could also smell the odors of several earlier meals, as well as the one Mrs. Brumvold and Big Syd were currently whipping up in the kitchen off the dining room. It was nearly noon. The new smells were of pork roast, gravy, boiled beets, and fresh biscuits.

Buchanon's belly growled as he tossed his hat on one of the room's two beds and then removed his gun and cartridge belt. He tugged his shirttails out of his pants and walked over to the washstand. He peered into the small round mirror on the wall above the stand, giving his lip a quick inspection. He retrieved a whiskey bottle from a shelf, popped the cork, stuck out his torn lower lip, and poured some of the whiskey over the cut.

"Oh Jesus!" He leaned forward, one hand on the wall beside the mirror, stretching his lips back from the burn.

"Serves ya right!" Angus said, limping into the room behind Hunter.

Hunter had heard the old man shuffling down the hall, using the cane he'd whittled out of an oak branch while sitting on the veranda ogling the soiled doves with Joe Ryan. Buchanon watched his father hobble into the room, looking little more than a stick over which the ancient greatcoat hung, and Hunter's heart ached with anguish.

"Old Angus," as everyone had called him for the past thirty years, had recovered from the bullet he'd taken last year, during the war with Ludlow, Chaney, and Stillwell, but the long recuperation had taken the shimmer out of his eyes, the vitality out of his countenance, whittling him down to sagging hide and sinew. His long, craggy face, the color of old leather, was carpeted in a long, silky white beard through which warts and liver spots shone. Hunter could hear the old man's wheezing — each breath a chore.

Hunter returned his attention to his lip, splashed more whiskey on it.

Again, he leaned forward, head down, and sucked a breath through gritted teeth.

"Serves you right — turnin' your back on your father. What's gotten into you, boy? Treatin' Old Angus like a second-rate citizen. I swear, I'm beginning to wonder if there wasn't a Yankee in the woodshed."

Hunter shelved the whiskey bottle, turned to the old man standing a few feet inside the door, glaring across the tiny room at his big, strapping son. "Sorry, Pa. I've had a bad coupla days, and this one isn't getting any better soon."

Angus shuffled over to a chair, slacked stiffly into it, and heaved a sigh of his own, leaning forward on his cane. "When you was gone so long I started hopin' maybe you'd come to your senses and stole off with that purty little redhead of yours to get hitched in Cheyenne."

Hunter shrugged out of his shirt, tossed it toward a wall peg but missed. "That's off, Pa. Not gonna happen."

"You know she ain't like them other Ludlows. Hell, Annabelle is different from her pa and that demented brother of hers. I swear there must've been a Rebel in the Ludlow wood shed." Old Angus's spindly shoulders rose and fell like pistons inside the coat as he laughed deep in his throat.

Hunter poured water from the pitcher into the porcelain bowl atop the washstand and bent forward. "You know that's not why I'm not marrying her, Angus."

"Why, then?"

"You know why — I'm flat broke. Hell, I don't have enough money right now to pay Mrs. Brumvold this month's rent, and she'll likely be around soon lookin' for it. I'm gonna have to get down on my hands and knees and beg her to give us another week."

Hunter splashed water on his face. Wincing against the sting of his cut lip, he lathered his face with the soap then dunked his face in the bowl, rinsing off. When he lifted his face from the water, his father said, "Don't worry about Mrs. Brumvold. I'll sweet-talk her. Maybe even have to curl the old gal's toes for her."

In the mirror, Hunter saw Angus's eyes twinkle dimly with bawdy humor.

Hunter gave a caustic snort, chuckled, and splashed water on his chest and under his arms.

"What else is eating you, boy?" his father asked. "What else is goin' on?"

Buchanon rubbed the soap into his skin. Getting rid of a week's worth of sweat and trail dust felt good. He'd soak in a tub soon, when time allowed, but for now the whore's bath would suffice. "Nothin' for you to worry about, Pa."

"Well, I am worried. Why'd you go and pin that badge to your shirt, anyway? Drivin' stagecoach is dangerous enough in this

392

country."

"They didn't have anybody else."

"That's 'cause nobody else is fool enough to take that job in this town!"

"Thanks, Pa," Hunter said with a caustic grunt.

"You know what I mean."

"Yeah, I do."

Hunter grabbed a towel and dried his face, chest, and under his arms. He looked at his old father sadly, and sighed. "I'm sorry, Pa. I'll tell you all about it when I have time."

Angus drew his mouth corners down and nodded. "I know you will, son. I'm sorry to be an extra burden. I wish the Good Lord would just go ahead and take me, and then you wouldn't have me to worry about anymore."

"That's the last thing I want, you old scudder." Hunter dropped to a knee before his father. "You're all I have, Pa. You an' Bobby Lee. I want you to live long enough to see that ranch rebuilt. To live and work on our own land again."

Angus shook his head. "That's not gonna happen, son. Look at us — both sittin' here with our pockets turned inside out."

Hunter reached up and wrapped an arm around the old man's shoulders, cupping

393

the back of his neck with his right hand. "I know, Pa. I just keep hopin', is all. I'm sorry we've come to this. You an' me, livin' in a seedy little boarding house in this cesspool of a town."

"We're getting by, boy. We had us a nice run out at the 4-Box-B. Now we're in town but we're gettin' by."

"If I could only get that gold back."

"That gold's gone, son. Besides, that was for you and Annabelle."

"If I ever got it back — and I know it ain't likely — I'm gonna use it to rebuild the ranch. Get you back on that nice front veranda where you had such a pretty view of those Black Hills you love. You're a good man. You been the best pa a boy could hope for. You deserve to die at home."

Angus smiled at his son, blue eyes filling with tears. He blew out his cheeks, shook his head, and looked down. "It's Shep an' Tye I miss. I sure wish I had those strappin' sons of mine back." He blew a ragged breath, his lips quivering with sorrow.

"I know, Pa." Hunter rose and pressed his lips to the old man's age-freckled, liver-spotted forehead.

Straightening, he went over to his chest of drawers, found a passingly clean blue chambray shirt, and pulled it on. Old Angus sat in his chair, head bowed, tears dribbling down his leathery cheeks to his hands wrapped over the head of his cane.

Hunter buttoned his shirt and strapped his gun and cartridge belt and bowie knife around his waist. "I'll be back for supper, Pa. Maybe even have time for a game of cribbage afterwards."

Angus blew his nose into an old red handkerchief with white polka dots. "I'd like that, son."

Hunter's heart twisted again at his father's grief.

He turned and walked out of the room.

CHAPTER 32

Hunter swung Ghost onto the freshly graded trail that climbed the rise to Homer Laskey's old mining claim and pig farm and on which now stood the town's new schoolhouse. It was a fine-looking building. One that he and the other residents of Tigerville should be proud of. Finally, school would be in session.

Or maybe not just yet . . .

Hunter felt a rat of dread gnawing in his belly as he walked Ghost up the rise. He was about to leave the trail and ride around to the building's rear, to Laskey's old cabin, when another glance at the school showed him the front door was open. Sweeping sounds came from the door. He saw the moving straw head of a broom inside a small cloud of dust blowing out the door and onto the front step.

A second later, Laura stepped out of the enclosed porch and onto the step, making quick, almost desperate sweeping sounds, her hair falling from the bun atop her head. She gave a soft grunt with every sweep of the broom. She appeared to be fighting off a pack of wolves — wolves of frustration. Of desperation.

Of fear of being exposed, maybe . . .

Hunter swung Ghost up to the bottom of the steps. As she swept the dust down the steps, Laura glanced at him, glanced away, then turned her gaze back to him, and stopped sweeping. She stared at him, frozen in place, dust wafting around her.

The bun of her hair hung down over her right ear. Her face was pale. It steadily grew paler, her eyes darker.

She fell back against one of the rails angling down the steps, keeping her eyes on his, studying him, trying to read him. Then, as though his thoughts were all too obvious, she gave an ironic little laugh, turned her head to one side, dropped her chin, and squeezed her eyes closed. She remained like that for nearly a minute.

Hunter didn't say anything. No words came to him. He felt like he'd drank sour goat's milk. Anger came on the heels of that sick feeling. Anger and indignation. He realized then that while he hadn't known her long, he'd fallen in love with her. Maybe she'd been a buoy the fates had thrown him on the heels of Annabelle.

But, still, he'd fallen in love with her. She'd been a rare glimmer of hope in what had become a hopeless life.

She drew a deep breath, turned away from him, climbed the steps, leaned the broom against the porch, and disappeared into the school.

Hunter continued just riding away. There was no point in remaining here. Her look had told him everything. Every rotten thing he didn't want to hear. But he couldn't ride away. Not yet.

He swung heavily down from Ghost's back.

He dropped the reins, climbed the steps, and doffed his hat as he stepped into the school. The air was heavy with the tang of green pine. A dozen new student desks formed four straight lines, two lines to each side of him as he walked slowly down the aisle between them, toward the dais atop which sat the teacher's desk — also new and shiny with varnish.

Laura sat at the desk, head down, staring at her entwined hands before her. Stacks of open boxes stood around the desk. Books and chalk slates sat on the teacher's desk as well as on shelves behind her. A black chalkboard on castors stood to the right of the desk, facing the room. On the chalkboard was written in flowing, feminine script — *Welcome To Tigerville School!* Below that: *Your Teacher Is Miss Meyers.*

Hunter had lost track of time, but he thought that school had been scheduled to start the next day. He'd seen posters advertising that fact around town, encouraging parents to enroll their children.

"Is it?" he asked, stopping roughly halfway down the room from the front. He held his hat in his hands before him and cast her a cold, severe look.

She looked up at him, one brow arched curiously. She nodded slowly with bleak understanding. "You talked to Jonathan."

"I did."

"And he told you — what? That I'm some money-grubbing charlatan?"

"Something like that."

"And you believe him?"

"I don't know. I came here to get the truth."

"I don't think you did," Laura said. "I think you've already made up your mind."

Hunter took a step forward. "Tell me it's not true, Laura . . . or whatever your name is."

She smiled coldly. Some color returned to

her cheeks, and her eyes flashed gold with indignation. "Go to hell, Hunter."

His heart kicked with anger. He'd had enough.

He wheeled, set his hat on his head, and strode to the door. *"You go to hell!"* she screamed behind him, the last word choking off in a sob.

He left the school, dropped down the front steps, picked up his reins, and swung up onto Ghost's back. He galloped down the rise, heading back toward the heart of town. As he crested the next rise, a horse and buggy clomped and clattered toward him. The man driving the buggy was the Pinkerton. The man sitting beside the Pinkerton, of course, was Jonathan Gaynor.

Hunter cursed, then rammed his heels into Ghost's flanks. He galloped down the hill and drew rein beside the buggy as the Pinkerton, smoking a long, slender cheroot, stopped the sorrel in the buggy's traces.

Hunter said, "How did you know where to find her?"

"Amazing what kind of information you can buy from the right drunk for the cost of a drink." Gaynor smiled. "What's the point of prolonging things, Marshal? She's coming back to Denver one way or another."

"Don't worry, Buchanon," the Pinkerton

said. "She'll get a fair hearing." He touched a black-gloved thumb to his badge. "I wear this shield proudly and take my job seriously. Mister Gaynor has assured me he will pay for her to have competent representation at his own expense."

"I just want to put the matter behind me," Gaynor told Hunter. "And I want to make sure that what happened to me never happens to anyone else. That said, I am going to recommend the judge give her probation, not a prison sentence. The West is not an easy place for a woman. I'm sure she did what she did because she was driven to it by circumstances beyond her control."

"That's mighty charitable of you," Buchanon said snidely. "Given what she did to you. Where she shot you."

"Yes, well." Gaynor's cheeks colored, and he glanced away. Returning his gaze to Hunter, he shrugged with embarrassment and said, "Despite it all . . . well . . . I find myself still in love with her. Imagine that."

Somehow, Hunter found himself understanding the sentiment.

"The next stage to Cheyenne doesn't leave until Saturday," he told the pair.

Gaynor nodded. "I know. I thought we'd take her over to the Imperial, put her up in her own room where we can keep an eye on her until the stage leaves."

"Sounds rather generous under the circumstances," said the Pinkerton, blowing cigar smoke into the wind. "Don't you think, Marshal?"

Hunter thought it was, indeed. The Imperial was the best hotel in town — with thirty suites, a fine restaurant, and a saloon second to none in the Black Hills. Not even Deadwood claimed better. He didn't respond to the man's question, though.

He just grunted, turned Ghost away from the buggy, and put him into another rocking lope. Like Gaynor, he wanted to put the matter of Laura Meyers behind him as fast as possible.

Slow, heavy thuds sounded on the school's front steps.

Laura lifted her head from her desk, frowning curiously. Her curiosity diminished as the staccato thuds continued. They incorporated a shuffling sound as well as the taps of what could only be a cane.

She felt a cold stone drop in her stomach as Jonathan Gaynor stepped into the school, clad in his dandyish butterscotch suitcoat with matching bowler hat. His black-gloved right hand shoved the cane ahead of him. Stepping forward, he leaned into the cane, gritting his teeth with every awkward, obviously painful step.

The Pinkerton she'd seen earlier in Big Dan's Saloon walked slowly along behind Jonathan. The man's cold eyes bore into Laura's, as did those of Jonathan himself, as the two men walked down the center aisle between the desks that no students would sit at any time soon.

Not until the town found another teacher.

Thump-shuffle-thud. Thump-shuffle-thud.

Jonathan's pale face was a mask of pent-up rage. His eyes reminded her of those of the now-deceased Warren Davenport. Only, Jonathan's were smaller, even colder and more shrewdly cunning.

He stopped ten feet from Laura's desk.

The Pinkerton stopped several feet behind him. He waited there, a guard dog relegated to a corner until he was needed.

Jonathan stood staring contemptuously at Laura for nearly a full minute before his face twisted bitterly and he said through a contemptuous smile, "How far did you really think you'd get?"

"To be honest," Laura said, "not this far." She was amazed by the calmness she heard in her own voice. All hope was gone. Her fear had mutated into a grim resignation.

He was a powerful man. She was merely a

403

woman. Mostly, women were a commodity in the West. They owned the rights of beef and poultry.

"Do I have to come with you now?"

"Yes."

"Are you going to turn me over to the police?"

"No."

Laura drew a deep breath, stared down at her hands. "Are you going to kill me?"

"No." Jonathan glanced back at the man behind him. "My associate Mister Blanchard and I have devised a far more fitting and colorful punishment."

"What is it?" Still, she felt no fear. Only weariness. Only a desire to have it all done and over with.

Gaynor turned back to Laura but said to his associate, "You tell her, Mister Blanchard."

Blanchard smiled. "We're sending you up to Leadville. Outside of Leadville, you'll never be seen or heard from again. At least, not by anyone . . . any *man* . . . who doesn't patronize you and the rest of the whores at the Purple Palace."

"Hurdy-gurdy house," Jonathan said with grim amusement.

That sent a chill through her veins.

But only a momentary one. She could

have guessed that enslaving her to a whore-house in the wilds of the Colorado Rockies, and in an even darker perdition than Tiger-ville, would be the punishment Jonathan would devise. He did have imagination — she would give him that.

She looked at Jonathan's associate. "You're not really a Pinkerton, are you?"

"No," Jonathan answered for the man. "He's one of my, uh —"

"Henchmen," Laura finished for him.

Jonathan smiled. "You see, my dear, there will be no divorce. We've concocted a complete, sordid history for you. One as a practiced charlatan. You see what happened is I caught you trying to fleece me and you shot me and ran out on me. Just as you've done to several wealthy men in your disreputable past. We tried the story out on Marshal Buchanon. I have to say it worked pretty well."

"Pretty well, but not well enough." Hunter walked slowly into the schoolhouse from the enclosed front porch, his rifle resting on his shoulder.

Blanchard whipped around, shoving his right hand inside his coat.

"Bad idea," Hunter said, stopping a few feet inside the open door, leaving the rifle on his shoulder.

405

He stopped, boots spread, easing his weight back on his left hip.

Jonathan whipped around, as well. He moved faster than his injury would allow. He screamed a curse and fell with a hard thud and a groan, his cane clattering onto the floor.

Hunter said, "Anybody can have wanted dodgers printed. Anybody with a few dollars and a friend in a print shop. I grew suspicious when I heard your tale of sweet understanding. You didn't come all this way to give her a fair hearing. I figured I might should drift this way and clear up any doubts lingering in my fool brain."

He looked at Laura. "I doubted you. I'm sorry."

She didn't say anything but only stared back at him while Jonathan grunted and groaned on the floor in front of her desk.

Hunter stepped forward, lowering the Henry from his shoulder and clicking the hammer back. He aimed the barrel at Blanchard. "You two are under arrest."

"Please, don't," Laura objected. "Let them go. I want to put this all behind me. I came here to make a fresh start, and I can't do that under a cloud of scandal. Especially after Warren Davenport . . ."

Hunter frowned at the young woman.

"They tried to kidnap you . . . sell you into slavery. I can't let that —"

"Please," Laura said, pointedly. "You doubted me. I'll forgive you under one condition. Let them go." She cast her fiery gaze to each of her two would-be assailants in turn. "I don't want to see either of their ugly faces ever again!"

Hunter thought it over. He wanted to turn the key on Gaynor and his henchman in the worst way. But Laura would be on trial, then too. After what had happened with Davenport on Dakota Avenue, she'd never live it down. She wouldn't have a chance here in Tigerville.

Fury burning in him, he curled his upper lip at Blanchard and indicated the man's diminutive boss moaning on the floor behind him. "Scrape that dung off the floor and get the hell out of here. If I ever see either one of you again, I'll kill you."

Blanchard hurried over to Gaynor. With effort, and with Jonathan cursing and grunting, Blanchard helped the man to his feet and gave him his cane. Blanchard wrapped an arm around his boss's shoulders and helped him down the aisle to the door.

As they walked past him, Hunter turned to keep his rifle as well as his threatening glare leveled on them both.

Blanchard didn't look at him. Gaynor looked up at him, flaring an angry nostril, eyes hard with self-righteous indignation.

They left the schoolhouse, descended the front steps, piled into their buggy, and spun away.

His eyes still on the open front door, watching the buggy dwindle into the distance, Hunter said, "You'd best pack a bag and come with me. I have a feeling you won't be safe until those two leave town on the next stage."

When no response came from behind him, he turned to look toward the front of the room. Laura was gone. The schoolhouse's back door stood open.

The vacant dais said it all. She might have forgiven him, but it was over.

Again, he'd been a fool.

CHAPTER 33

Cass Ludlow galloped into the Broken Heart headquarters and checked his steeldust gelding down to a skidding halt, dust wafting in a heavy cloud around him.

The masked Ludlow swung down from the saddle, got his left boot caught in the stirrup, and fell hard on his head and shoulders. The bottle he'd been holding plunked to the ground beside him.

"Ow — damn!" Cass wailed, flopping his arms, at once trying to free his boot from the stirrup and wanting to pick up the bottle before all the liquor ran out of it.

The half-breed hostler came running out of the stable, yelling, "Mister Cass! Mister Cass!"

"Yes, yes — it's Mister Cass, Deuce. Get the bottle!"

"Mister Cass!" the boy cried, grabbing the gelding's reins. It had just dug its rear hooves into the dirt and was about to gallop off, frightened by its rider's raucous high jinks.

"Yes, it's Mister Cass, Deuce." Cass didn't know if that was the boy's real name, but it's what everyone called him. He was the bastard child of a former hand who'd run off with a blond dancer he'd met at an opera house in Spearfish. "Let's get beyond that to the bottle, now, shall we?"

Ignoring the bottle, and holding the gelding's reins in his left hand, Deuce crouched over the stirrup and used his left arm to wrench up Cass's left ankle then yank the toe free of the stirrup.

"Ow!" Cass yelped as his foot dropped to the ground. "Christalmighty, you little devil — I think you broke my ankle!"

"Mister Cass!" the boy cried, in shock to see his employer's son flopping around on the ground like a landed fish.

The boy had dropped the gelding's reins, and the steeldust had lunged off to sidle up to the wall of the stable, anxiously stomping and blowing.

Cass rolled onto his side, grabbed the bottle, and held it up to gauge the level. A good bit had darkened the dirt around where it had fallen, but there was still a couple of swallows left in the bottom. He drew the bottle to his mouth, raised it high.

The unseemly display was too much for the frantic stable boy. He'd witnessed such antics before but he'd never become used to it. He turned away, grabbed the gelding's reins, and led the mount, as confused and frightened as he himself was, through the stable's open double doors.

Cass drained the bottle, tossed it aside, and sat up. He chuckled, drunkenly amused by his inelegant dismount and by the half-breed stable boy's anxious reaction. Cass extended his left leg and turned his foot this way and that, wincing.

The ankle hurt but it probably wasn't broken. Just twisted a little.

On the other hand, maybe he'd broken it but was too drunk to feel the pain . . .

Hmmm.

Cass rose to a knee. He pushed off the knee to his feet, gingerly testing the injured limb.

No, it wasn't broken. He'd know even through all the busthead he and his cronies had drunk on their way to town . . . in town . . . and then after they'd fled town like jackasses with tin cans tied to their tails. They'd fled laughing and then split up, Phil and Dave heading back to the wood-cutting camp in which Cass had found them and drafted them into his scheme to kidnap his sister.

Yes, his father had wanted him to use some of his own Broken Heart men in the scheme, but Cass, preferring as usual to mix business with pleasure, had enlisted the help of two of "his *amigos,*" as he called his fun-loving, skirt-chasing, card-playing, part-time outlaw cronies.

Now, of course, he realized his mistake. The realization sobered him a little. Maybe they should have waited to get drunk *after* the deed had been accomplished rather than before and during.

Cass turned to stare up at the Ludlow lodge looming on the eastern rise like a foreboding storm cloud. The sight of the rambling house, his father's domain, so-bered him further. The windows were cold eyes glaring down on him, teeming with judgment. He wouldn't have been surprised to see the big house shake from side to side, like a man — like Graham Ludlow himself — wagging his head in grieved disdain for his pathetic son.

Cass looked at the bottle lying in the finely churned dust and horse manure of the yard. What he wouldn't give for just one more drink!

He kicked the bottle. It rose, dropped,

bounced, and slid along the ground, parting the scattered straw.

He made the decision right then and there. He knew it was the right one, because he suddenly felt as though an anvil had been lifted from his shoulders.

He laughed to himself. He should have made the decision a long time ago.

How much happier he'd have been! He could see his future before him — long stretches of rocky red desert, tile-roofed adobe huts, the clear blue waters of the Sea of Cortez glinting in the background. And the *señoritas*.

Oh, the *señoritas*!

He walked a little unsteadily to the open stable doors. The boy stood back in the shadows, rubbing the claybank down with a thin cotton towel.

"Deuce, saddle that big roan of mine. Have him ready to ride in ten minutes."

He didn't wait for a response. Giddy from his decision, he walked up the path that climbed the hill, past the circular, cinder-paved area where several wrought-iron hitchracks stood near the base of the porch steps.

He climbed the steps, chuckling through his teeth. He crossed the porch, opened the front door, and stepped inside.

The old man and Kenneth Earnshaw were seated close together, Earnshaw on one of the parlor's leather sofas, Graham Ludlow on his left in the pushchair. They were both leaning forward, staring at a large plat open on the coffee table before them.

Each held a drink in one hand, a cigar in the other.

They'd been talking together like a couple of conspirators plotting a gold heist when Cass had entered, but now they looked up at him, eyes widening expectantly. They looked around behind him and then returned their gazes to the masked countenance of Cass himself, frowning.

"Where is she?" Earnshaw asked.

Cass threw up his hands. "Decided not to go through with it." He chuckled tauntingly. "She seemed to be having so much fun, parading around in that little getup of hers, I didn't have the heart. You know, when I saw her today, she wasn't wearing more than what I could tuck into one back pocket. Ha!"

He delighted in the crimson flush his words caused to rise in his father's and wannabe brother-in-law's cheeks.

"You useless bastard!" Earnshaw said, standing so quickly he spilled some of his drink.

"If you want her so damn bad, why don't you go fetch her yourself instead of sitting around here pretending you're the next Graham Ludlow?" Cass looked at his father and pointed at Earnshaw. "If you want that little nancy-boy to marry your daughter so damn bad, send him to fetch her. Make him earn her, for God's sake. Make him earn *something*. I for one, however, don't think he can stay on her any longer than he can stay on the best broke horse in the Broken Heart remuda."

Cass laughed again caustically, and turned to the stairs.

He stopped, having seen a rosy-cheeked, shrewd smile light up his father's face. He turned his gaze back to Ludlow, frowning curiously. "What in the hell are you —"

"You failed," the old man croaked out. He puffed the stogie in his left hand, the smoke nearly obliterating him from Cass's view for a few seconds. He blew the thick, white smoke out his mouth and nostrils, grinning. "You failed again just as you've always failed in the past. Look at you. You're so drunk you're about to fall down."

Ludlow set his goblet down and clapped his hands, grinning bizarrely and cackling like a warlock. "Bravo, dear boy! Bravo! One more failure in a string of failures! At least you're predictable — I'll give you that!"

"Go to hell — both of you!" Cass started up the stairs. His left boot slipped off the bottom step. He stumbled forward, causing his father to roar even louder.

"True to your nature!" Ludlow roared as Cass stumbled up the stairs, leaning heavily on the rail. "You're nothing but a drunk and sluggard! My God — how did such a mongrel grow from the seed of my loins?"

Cass gained the second floor and hurried into his room.

He fished the key from the drawer, picked up a pair of saddlebags from the floor near his bed, and opened the closet. He worked quickly, anger burning in him like venom in his veins. The anger was souring the effect of the alcohol coursing through those same veins, corrupting the drunk, turning it into something sick and foul.

He had to work quickly before he lost his courage.

That's really the thing that had been lacking in his character all of these years, the one thing that had been holding him back from leaving his arbitrary, sadistic, and tyrannical father. Lack of confidence. Lack of spine.

He'd had both things mocked and beaten out of him, so he'd become the one thing

Graham Ludlow had been most afraid he'd turn out to be:

Nothing.

Well, here he was: nothing. But this nothing man, who didn't even have his good looks anymore, was hightailing it out of here. He was going to take that gold and start afresh.

God, he needed a drink!

Once he had all four gold sacks safely ensconced in both saddlebag pouches, he scoured his room for a bottle. He found three — all dry. He found a small brown bottle of chokecherry wine he'd pilfered from Chang's own private supply. It contained only a teaspoonful. Still, it was something.

He threw it back, the sweet cherry taste mixing with his bile and only making him feel fouler. He shouldered the bulging saddlebags, grunting under the weight, and left his room. He wouldn't pack anything else. Just the clothes on his back and the gold. He wanted to leave everything behind.

Everything!

He walked down the hall and stopped at the top of the stairs. His father and Earnshaw were speaking more loudly, a little contentiously.

"What are you saying?" Earnshaw said in

a tone of incredulity.

"I'm saying my son does have a point. You're going to marry her. Perhaps you should be the one to fetch her."

Earnshaw hemmed and hawed.

Ludlow said, "Maybe she's been wanting you to stand up to her, to take charge. Don't *ask* her to marry you. Annabelle doesn't respond to weakness. Annabelle is the kind of woman who responds only to strength. A raised fist! That's one reason she chose Buchanon — aside from merely wanting to defy me, of course, which I know was the *main* reason she chose him. She wants a man who can prove himself to her by taming her. By not taking no for an answer. You have to be as strong as she is. Stronger!"

Cass threw his head back, laughing, and started down the stairs, his boots under the fifty pounds of gold making loud hammering sounds. "Sounds like a winning plan, Pops. Sure, sure. Nothing about sending that pigeon after Annabelle can go wrong at all!"

Cass laughed again as he clomped down the last step to stand at the bottom of the stairs.

He turned to see Kenneth Earnshaw sitting back on the sofa, shoulders slumped, chin down, looking like a towheaded, baby-

418

faced midget dressed like Buffalo Bill Cody ready for a performance in his Wild West show. Wild Bill with a bad case of stage fright, that was. Kenneth's shoulders bowed forward, and he was looking forlornly down at the drink in his hands.

He didn't seem nearly as enthused about Ludlow's plan as Ludlow himself did.

Ludlow scowled at Cass. "Where in the hell are you going? What's in those bags?"

"This here?" Cass shifted the bags on his shoulders. "This here is my ticket out of this dump. This devil's lair you call the Broken Heart. I'll be seein' you, Pops . . . never again!" he added with a laugh.

He crouched to fumble the front door open.

"Where in the hell do you think you're going?" Ludlow said, hardening his bulldog jaws.

"Mexico!"

"That's crazy — get back here!"

"Adios, Padre!" Cass said, descending the porch steps.

Deuce had already brought up the saddled roan and was walking back down the hill toward the stable, obviously wanting nothing to do with the disturbance in the house.

"Thanks, Deuce!" Cass called.

The boy gave no response, just kept walking, head down.

"Cass, get back here!"

Cass glanced behind him. His father sat on the porch, Earnshaw behind him, holding the chair's push handles.

"Cass!" Ludlow wailed, pounding the arms of his chair with both fists. "You get back here, dammit. You can't survive on your own. You need to stay here and be provided for!"

To be kicked around like a mangy cur, you mean, you old buzzard.

"Go to hell," Cass quietly snarled as he draped his saddlebags over the roan's back.

"Cass, dammit — you can't leave. I forbid it! Dammit, Cass, get down off that horse!" Ludlow's voice was shrill. "If you leave this yard, you will get no more money from me. Not a dime. I will disown you. Your handouts end as soon as you pass through that gate!"

Cass cast a lewd gesture over his shoulder and put the roan into a rocking gallop.

CHAPTER 34

Three days later, Laura Meyers walked forthrightly along Dakota Avenue, her chin in the air, smiling through the gauzy veil hanging down from the brim of her small, green felt hat. She smiled so brightly that she felt that at any moment she might break into song. Or that she might sprout wings and fly. The joyous feeling had just come over her though she'd felt it building for several days.

The fact was she'd never felt so good in her life. Who'd have expected she could feel so at home in a town as . . . well, *colorful* . . . as Tigerville?

She didn't just feel at home. For the first time in her life, she felt light and free and independent and proud. She also felt successful. Along with that feeling came a feeling of great confidence.

She'd never been a successful, confident woman. She'd realized lately that she'd felt comfortable and secure in her old lifestyle, with Jonathan back in their grand home in Denver. But that comfort and security had been an illusion. A lie. She'd never known who Jonathan really was. Nor had she known who she was.

She'd never felt anything akin to the joy and independence she felt now. The terror she'd felt on her way here, fleeing Jonathan's wrath, had now after she'd successfully completed her first three days of school-teaching in the new schoolhouse been set on its head. Now she couldn't imagine ever going back to her old life, much less of ever leaving Tigerville.

She glanced around at the cowboys and drifters, the bearded mule skinners and the Chinamen and black men and the dusky-skinned men with obvious Indian blood milling around her, snorting and spitting and yelling and cursing and laughing and, in one case out front of a beer parlor on the opposite side of the street, smacking each other's faces with their bare fists while other men around them yelled encouragement.

Laura's smile did not waver.

Colorful, jovial, raucous, rowdy Tigerville!

She crossed a side street then stepped up onto the boardwalk fronting Big Dan's Saloon. She stopped in front of the door, hesitating, suddenly self-conscious. But then she looked down at the linen-covered wicker basket whose handle was hooked over her arm, and proceeded inside. As the batwings swung back into place behind her, she looked around.

All faces turned toward her, turned away, then quickly returned and held on her, eyes widening.

What in God's green earth was Tigerville's new schoolteacher doing in Big Dan's place? was the question passing over the minds of the dozen or so customers regarding her incredulously. Annabelle, standing behind the bar and running a cloth over its glistening varnished surface, glanced at her in the same fashion as the others, jerking a second, startled look at the woman standing in front of the batwings.

Annabelle froze, mouth and eyes opening. Leaving the cloth on the mahogany, she hurried out from behind the bar and over to Laura, smiling a little scandalously at the pretty teacher dressed in a conservative silk dress and velvet waistcoat. Wrapping her hand around Laura's free one, Annabelle whispered urgently, "Laura, what on earth are you doing in here?"

"I came to see my new friend," Laura said, not lowering her voice one iota. She extended the basket toward Annabelle. "And to bestow a couple of humble but well-deserved gifts on her."

"Here?" Annabelle cried under her breath. She rose onto the tips of her high-heeled shoes to gaze out over the doors behind Laura before turning a self-conscious look into the room over her own left shoulder.

"Yes, here. Where else would I find you?" Laura smiled affectionately. "Look, Annabelle — you saved my life. Besides, we're friends. If it's scandalous for the new schoolteacher to be friends with a saloon girl — well, then, so be it." She shook the basket. "These are for you."

Annabelle chuckled throatily, looked around once more, then led Laura over to a table against the wall on Laura's left, on the other side of the potbellied stove, which would give them a little concealment from the front windows. "Have a seat here," Annabelle said, pulling a chair out from the table. "Would you like a cup of tea? I just boiled water for some. I was about to take a badly needed break. It may be too late to renovate your reputation, but at least none of the ladies from the sobriety and morality leagues will see us mingling if they deign to peer through the batwings."

She snorted a laugh.

Laura sat down and set the basket on the table, smiling up at Annabelle. "I would love some tea."

"Be right back!"

Annabelle walked back around the bar in her customary skimpy outfit and high-heeled shoes and returned a minute later, holding a smoking china teapot in one hand, two china cups in the other hand. "I'm taking a fifteen-minute tea break, Eddie," she told the tall, gray-haired, gray-mustached man drying a beer schooner behind the bar.

Eddie flared a nostril at her, then used his towel to swat a fly on the bar.

"Big Dan's taking a nap upstairs," Annabelle told Laura.

She set the teapot and two cups on the table. "Here we are." She filled Laura's cup first and then filled her own, set down the teapot, and took a seat in the chair across from Laura, frowning curiously at the linen-covered basket. "Now, then — what's this about gifts for me, humble or otherwise?"

"Oh, believe me — they're humble. Especially in light of what you did for me."

Annabelle leaned across the table and keeping her voice furtively low, her eyes sharp and angry, said, "You mean shooting that scalawag and perverted moron, Warren

Davenport? Someone should have shot him long ago. He probably intended to imprison you the way he did his poor, dearly departed wife . . . may God rest her tortured soul." She lifted her cup and blew on the steaming tea. "Besides, it was Hunter he was about to shoot. I should've let him shoot that big cork-headed Rebel first and *then* shot Davenport!"

"You don't mean that."

"Oh, yes, I do."

Laura smiled knowingly and sipped her tea. "Still, by killing him, you saved me every bit as much as you saved Hunter."

"As for saving you from Davenport — for that I am grateful. You don't owe me a damn thing." Annabelle snickered and lifted her hand to her mouth. "Listen to me. I believe Hunter's right — I've learned to cuss and I'm enjoying it."

Laura laughed and lifted the linen cloth from the basket. "This is a pie I made from the currants growing behind my cabin. My mother used to make currant pie. I hadn't had one in nearly twenty years, until I made two last night. I'm not much of a cook but I fumbled my way through it. I made one for you and one for me. This is an embroidered doily made by one of my little girls."

"One of your . . . ?"

426

"Students."

"Oh, how nice!" Annabelle said. "They must have taken a shine to you if they're already making you doilies!"

Annabelle picked up the yellow cotton doily in the shape of a daisy, and fingered it admiringly.

"Little Audra Bernum gave me two. One for me and one to give to my best friend."

Annabelle looked at her. A sheen of emotion shone in her eyes. "Do you know you're the first female friend I've ever had?"

"I am?"

"I was raised out at the Broken Heart around all men. Not a single other female. I went to school out near the ranch, but there were more boys than girls. None of the girls were my age — either younger or older — and I didn't get to spend time with any of them outside of school. Our ranches were just too far apart."

Laura smiled sweetly. "I'm so glad we're friends, Annabelle."

"Me too." Annabelle returned Laura's smile, sipped her tea, swallowed, and said, "So, tell me — how is school going? How many days have you been in session now?"

"I just finished the third day. It's going rather well, I'm happy to say. I have only seven students. Most are from the local

427

orphanage, but the banker's wife, Mrs. Carmichael, spoke to me after school. She's interested in enrolling her son and daughter when they return from visiting her husband's family in the East."

"That's wonderful."

"It is wonderful. The children currently enrolled are generally sweet, seem to like me, I like them, and, best of all, they all seem eager to learn. We are hard at work each day on penmanship, grammar, reading, and mathematics. We finished up today with a discussion on the wonders of gravity. I did a demonstration by taking my shoes off and leaping off my desk." Laura winced. "And nearly broke my ankle, I think . . ."

She reached down to rub the appendage of topic.

"Oh, dear!"

"I'll be all right. At least they had a good laugh."

"And . . . no sign of . . . ?"

"My soon-to-be former husband?" Laura turned her mouth corners down. "No, thank God. Hunter made sure he and his henchman were on the last stage out of Tigerville. He assured me he watched them board and leave town."

"You're lucky to have Hunter watching over you. He's good at that."

"Annabelle, I want you to know that's all he's doing."

Annabelle frowned. "What do you mean?"

"He's just watching over me. I mean, he watched over me in the case of Jonathan, but I haven't seen him in a couple of days now. We're not . . . we're not together."

"I don't understand," Annabelle said, tapping both index fingers against the rim of her half-empty teacup. "I thought you two —"

"It's over."

"Why? Because he believed Jonathan's story? Laura, I know that was silly of him, but we all make mistakes."

"That's not it. At least, it's not all of it." Laura sipped her tea, set her cup down, and cast her new friend a frank, knowing look. "You're still in love with him."

"No, no —"

Laura reached across the table and placed her right hand down on Annabelle's left one, quieting her.

"What's more — he's still in love with you, Annabelle. He's always going to be in love with you. I know it the way only another woman can know such a thing."

Annabelle looked at her, vaguely incredulous.

"Beyond that," Laura continued, "I know

that you are still very much in love with Hunter. You always will be."

Annabelle laughed and shook her head. "Nothing could be further from the truth. I assure you, Laura, I care nothing for the man. He turned his back on me when I needed him most."

"He turned his back on you because he loves you. He wanted you to go back to your father because he knew your father could provide for you. He couldn't. Maybe that was another mistake on his part. But his gold was gone. The disappointment of that bit him deep. Imagine all the work that went into building that marriage stake for the two of you only to find it gone just when you were about to get married."

Laura squeezed her hand again. "Please, Annabelle . . . give him another chance. Stop punishing him. All men are fools in many ways. Women are fools in fewer ways, but we can be fools just the same. Don't let pride make you turn your back on a man who loves you as much as Hunter does — especially when, deep down in your heart, you return every ounce of his love — in spades."

Annabelle stared at her, looking a little dumbfounded. Her cheeks were drawn and pale.

Laura slid her chair back, rose, and hooked the handle of the basket over her arm. "Thanks for the tea."

She rose, walked around the table, crouched, and gave Annabelle's cheek an affectionate kiss, her shoulders a sisterly squeeze.

She turned and left Big Dan's Saloon. She retraced her steps to the south. When she was halfway down the next block, she thumbed a tear from her cheek.

CHAPTER 35

Only a few minutes after Laura had left Big Dan's, Kenneth Earnshaw drove his blue-wheeled surrey with a leather canopy and a brass oil lamp into Tigerville.

As soon as he gained the heart of town, rolling from north to south along Dakota Avenue, heads swung toward him and held on the little, pale, blond-haired man in the three-piece suit of bleached buckskin complete with red necktie, white silk shirt, and a fringed buckskin coat, the flaps of which blew out behind the little man in the wind.

On his head was his bullet-crowned cream hat, trimmed with a red ostrich feather, one side pinned to the crown.

Around him, men hooted and painted ladies cackled from parlor house balconies. Ignoring the slovenly minions, his spade-bearded chin in the air, Kenneth pulled to a stop in front of the Tigerville marshal's office, engaged the surrey's brake, and stepped down from the seat. He tied the blooded, blue-black mare of both Morgan and Arabian blood — a gift from young Kenneth's father on Kenneth's last birthday, which was celebrated in the Parisian Hotel on Madison Avenue in New York City — and mounted the jail office's small front boardwalk.

He tapped on the door and opened it. A large, beefy gent in work shirt and dungarees was sitting kicked back in the swivel chair behind the desk to Kenneth's left, his mule-eared boots crossed on the desk's edge. The man's arms were crossed on his chest, and his head sagged over them.

Sound asleep.

He woke as Kenneth opened the door, grunting with a start and dropping his thick-soled boots to the floor.

A sheepish expression and a bright red blush rose in his broad, ruddy cheeks. As Kenneth stepped into the room in all his gallant glory, that expression of chagrin was quickly replaced by a forehead-crumpling frown of fascination and curiosity. To Otis Crosby's eyes, the little man walking into the office resembled nothing so much as one of the fancy-plumed roosters Mrs. Van Camp had running around her place, just behind his own tumbledown shack. Those

433

roosters crowed all day and night till he wanted to shoot the lot of them; that's why he never seemed to get enough sleep.

Sure enough, this little man here looked just like one of them red-combed, double-laced cocks that strutted around the Van Camp place, pecking at the hens.

To Kenneth, Otis Crosby was indistinguishable from all the other unwashed minions in this backwater perdition.

"Can I . . . uh . . . help you . . . ?" Otis asked.

Kenneth glanced around, frowning, tentative. The only other person he saw in the room was a bedraggled-looking female, obviously of aboriginal heritage, sitting on a cot in one of the office's four cells. She sat with her back against the wall, one ankle resting atop a raised knee — a most unlady-like arrangement of the female form.

Savages.

"Yes, yes . . . I was wondering if Marshal Buchanon was around?"

"No, he ain't," Otis said, rising from the chair. "He had to leave town when some cork-headed fool robbed the Parthenon Parlor House's madam at gunpoint, then lit out like a coyote after a jackrabbit. No tellin' when he'll be back. The marshal, I mean. Is there anything —"

But before he could finish the question, the little man in the feathered hat had backed out the door and was just then letting the latch click into place behind him. Earnshaw turned to the street, unable to keep a grin from flicking at the corners of his mouth.

He'd assumed Buchanon would be gone, but he'd wanted to check just to make sure that, according to plan, one of Ludlow's more dependable men with a fast horse had robbed the Parthenon and then safely "skinned out of town," as the colorful saying went, with Buchanon in tow.

Not that Earnshaw was afraid of the big ex-Confederate brigand. He just wanted to make sure today's scheme went down without a hitch.

He climbed back into the carriage, waited for an opening in the traffic, then swung the horse full around, angling toward Big Dan's Saloon on the opposite side of the street. He drove back north for only a hundred feet and then stopped the surrey behind a parked lumber dray. Again, he set the brake, clambered down to the street, and opened his coat to make sure his .44-caliber British bulldog was secure in his shoulder holster.

Seeing that the snub-nosed, double-action wheel gun with ivory grips was right where it was supposed to be, he stepped up onto the boardwalk and entered Big Dan Delaney's Saloon & Gambling Parlor. It being mid-afternoon, there were only maybe a dozen men in the place, most standing at the bar, a few sitting at tables between Earnshaw and the bar. A couple were playing roulette on the bar's far side, in the saloon's apparent gambling area.

Right away, he saw Annabelle.

As Earnshaw closed the door behind him, she finished setting a pair of beer schooners onto the table of two men clad in business suits. One of the businessmen said something to Annabelle, who laughed affably, batted her eyelashes coquettishly, and swung around, saying, "Why, thank you, kind sir. It's not every day a gal gets a compliment like that!"

As she headed back to the bar in her high-heeled shoes, half her back left uncovered by the black corset she wore, both businessmen swung their heads around to ogle her retreating, half-naked figure. One elbowed the other and said to Annabelle, "If you'd finally accept my marriage proposal, you'd get a compliment like that every day of the week and twice on Sunday!"

Fury setting Kenneth's eyes on fire, he strutted forward and said loudly above the low din of desultory conversation, "She's spoken for."

All heads in the saloon swung toward him. Including Annabelle's.

She'd just set her empty serving tray on the bar and now, locking her eyes on his, said in open astonishment, "Kenneth!"

Earnshaw strode toward her, his chin in the air, the feather in his hat dancing. "Annabelle, I've had enough of this foolishness. You are to accompany me back to the Broken Heart at once." He stopped before her, setting one polished, hand-tooled boot down resolutely beside the other one with a click, and said, "You will be my wife, and I will not take no for an answer!"

A hush fell over the room.

Annabelle stared at Kenneth in glassy-eyed astonishment.

Suddenly, every man in the place, including the skinny bartender flanking Annabelle, erupted with a near-deafening roar of laughter.

Annabelle laughed then, too, briefly bringing a hand to her mouth, jerking her shoulders. She looked Earnshaw up and down, and, as though seeing him now the way the men saw him, laughed again, uncontrollably. Regaining some of her composure, she said, "Did my father put you up to this?"

"This was my decision," young Earnshaw lied. "I am bound and determined to take you out of this hell hole and return you to the ranch where you rightly belong and where you and I will be married and raise a family. Dammit, Annabelle, that's my final decision. I will not be swayed. Now, come along — we are going home!"

Again, the room interrupted in laughter.

Kenneth's cheeks burned with embarrassment. He glanced around skeptically. Why were they laughing at him? He'd done what Annabelle's father had instructed him to do — to speak his mind and brook no argument. He'd spoken his demands as forcefully as any man could.

And still they laughed . . .

Even Annabelle smiled again, mockingly.

"The carriage is waiting outside, Annabelle," Kenneth said firmly, narrowing his eyes. "You must come with me now. I will brook no defiance!"

"Go to hell, you damn toad!" This from the man sitting to Earnshaw's right — the same man who'd made Annabelle blush with his fawning only a moment ago.

Rage caused Kenneth's heart to hammer his breastbone. Before he knew what he was doing, he'd reached into his jacket and pulled the Bulldog from his shoulder holster. He extended the snub-nosed revolver out to his right and planted the barrel against his tormentor's forehead. He clicked the hammer back and stared at Annabelle, who, seeing the gun, gave a strangled cry and leaped back against the bar, placing her hand on her throat.

"Kenneth, what are you doing?"

"Either come with me now or I am going to blow this man's brains out!"

"Kenneth!"

The man — a middle-aged gent with a trimmed black beard, pomaded black hair, and pudgy red nose — stared in shock and terror up along the cocked revolver and the arm extending it, at Kenneth's deadly resolute eyes.

Another man leaped to his feet nearby, yelling, "No, you're not!" The man reached for a revolver on his hip but managed only to close his hand around the weapon's grips before Kenneth shot him.

Pow!

The whole room jumped. Annabelle stared in shock as the man cursed sharply and fell back over his chair, the bullet in his upper left thigh oozing thick, red blood. He hit the floor and yelled with shrill exasperation, "The Eastern daisy shot me!"

Kenneth stared down at him. He was half

in disbelief himself. He hadn't planned on shooting the man. It was as if another man had squeezed the Bulldog's trigger. He'd shot a man once before — in fact, he'd shot Sheriff Frank Stillwell back at the end of last year's trouble. But shooting Stillwell had been an accident. This was something he'd done on purpose although he hadn't planned to do it ahead of time.

He'd just done it. He'd shot him!

Looking around through his own wafting powder smoke, he was glad he'd done it. Because all the faces regarding him now did so with no more of their previous mocking but with no little amount of apprehension and possibly even respect.

He aimed the Bulldog once more at the bearded man before him, who sat holding both his hands straight up in the air, palms forward.

Earnshaw stared with menace bordering on lunacy at his bride-to-be. "Are you coming, Annabelle — or must this man, too, suffer for your defiance?"

Annabelle thrust her hands out in supplication. "Put the gun down, Kenneth!"

Kenneth thrust his left hand toward her. "Come!"

"All right. Just let me —"

"No — now. Come!"

He snapped his fingers and pressed the Bulldog harder against the bearded man's forehead. The bearded man winced, closed his eyes, and turned his head to one side in trepidation.

"All right," Annabelle said, reaching for Kenneth's extended hand. "I'll come. Just put the gun down, Kenneth!"

Kenneth wrapped his left hand around her right wrist and jerked her toward him. At the same time, he pulled the Bulldog from the bearded man's head. He backed himself and Annabelle toward the batwing doors, waving the gun around and yelling, "Everybody stay right where you are. If you try to follow me, someone's likely to get hurt!"

He glanced with menace at Annabelle.

He was so enraged by her behavior, by the way she and the others had treated him, that he felt an almost undeniable urge to put a bullet in her lovely head. The only reason he didn't was because she was Graham Ludlow's daughter . . . and his bride-to-be, of course. The day he'd finally broke her to his rein would be a satisfying one, indeed.

He gave a caustic laugh at the thought as he backed through the batwings. What a defiant bitch she was. Rest assured, he'd tame her. He was the man to do it even if he had to employ a bullwhip!

Quickly, he holstered the Bulldog and then grabbed Annabelle and threw her into the carriage. He ripped the reins from the tie rail and climbed aboard and released the brake handle. He glanced to his right in time to see Annabelle try to leap over the carriage's right front wheel.

Kenneth grabbed her with his right hand and jerked her back toward him. "No, you don't!"

"Ow — you're hurting my arm!"

"Be quiet!"

Keeping a vice-like grip on her left wrist with his right hand, he took the reins in his left hand, shook them over the back of the mixed Morgan-Arab, and they were off, heading north toward the Broken Heart at a full gallop.

CHAPTER 36

Buchanon drew sharply back on Ghost's reins.

The horse locked its rear hooves up, skidding forward, curveting to the right. Hunter looked down at the zebra dun gelding lying dead in the trail, and winced.

The poor beast must have stepped in a gopher hole. Its left front leg was badly broken, the bone showing through a jagged tear in the hide. A bloody hole in the horse's head, just behind its left ear, showed where its rider had put it out of its agony.

Hunter had just lifted his head to look around at the blond hills stippled with widely scattered pines around him, when a mewling wail rose off his right flank.

He threw himself off the left side of his horse a half a blink before a rifle belched. Twisting around in mid-air, Buchanon struck the two-track ranch trail on his left shoulder and hip.

443

He palmed the LeMat and, quickly finding the man in the pine behind him and off the trail's left side as Hunter gazed back toward the south, flung two quick shots into the branches.

The man who'd been perched in a fork in the tree, roughly fifteen feet up from the ground, yelped, sagged back, and dropped his rifle. He tumbled down out of the branches, smacking several, breaking one with a crunching sound, then hit the ground with a grunt.

His pale Stetson with a funneled brim sailed lightly to the ground between its owner and the coyote standing ten feet away from the man, head down, tail arched, growling softly.

The man lay still on his belly, cheek pressed to the ground. A pair of saddlebags lay near the base of the tree, near where the man's Winchester now lay.

Hunter gained his feet, wincing against a new set of ailments, silently opining that he was getting too long in the tooth to be hurling himself out of the saddle with such regularity. He retrieved his hat, set it on his head, then, limping slightly on his left leg, walked over to his would-be back-shooter.

Bobby Lee was still growling, showing his teeth.

Buchanon kicked the man onto his back. Blood shone on his chest where bullets had torn through his shirt.

"It's all right, Bobby Lee," Hunter said. "You can get the hump out of your neck. This one's dead."

Bobby Lee gave a little yip, then went over and anointed the man's left, spurred boot.

Hunter stared down at the man — a bull-chested, thick-armed, short-legged gent with an angular face and a thick brown mustache in which jerky crumbs resided. Buchanon recognized him as Wrench Kinkaid, one of Graham Ludlow's rowdier hands who'd made a reputation for himself by often stomping a little too high with his tail up on Saturday nights in Tigerville and ending up getting hauled off to the hoose-gow until he sobered up and Ludlow's fore-man rode to town to pay his fine.

Hunter frowned, a growing suspicion pricking the hair under his shirt collar.

What was Wrench Kinkaid doing in town on a weekday afternoon? And why was he robbing a seedy sporting parlor like the Parthenon? It didn't make sense.

Ludlow might have fired the man, but that didn't explain why the man would rob the Parthenon. Kinkaid knew Tigerville well enough to know there were riper plums to be picked.

Unless the robbery had been a smoke-screen to divert Buchanon from something even more nefarious . . .

His pulse quickened. He had to get back to town pronto.

He grabbed Kinkaid's saddlebags but did not bother opening them. The seventy dollars and change Kinkaid had taken off Mary Jane Quinn, the Parthenon madam, would be inside. Hunter hurried over to where Ghost stood off the side of the trail, content-edly grazing.

He tossed the saddlebags over the mount's back, stepped into the leather, said, "Come on, Bobby. We gotta make haste back to town. This whole thing smells like rotten eggs!"

He booted Ghost into a run.

Tigerville spread out ahead of him twenty minutes later.

Hunter was glad that Kinkaid hadn't gotten far before his horse had plundered that gopher hole. He was sorry for the horse. He liked horses more than he liked men — especially men like Wrench Kinkaid — but especially given his suspicions concerning Kinkaid's motives, he was glad he'd found the man before he could get any farther than a twenty-minute ride away.

He'd been gone from town a little over an hour. Not long. But something had happened while he'd been away. He'd sensed it the minute he turned left at the fork in the trail and headed straight south into town, where the trail became Dakota Avenue.

The town seemed quieter than it usually was this time of the day. There were plenty of men in the street, but most were clustered straight ahead of Buchanon now as he slowed Ghost to a trot. Bobby Lee trotted along beside him, tongue hanging after the long run. As Hunter gained the heart of the business district, he canted his head to the right, peering closely at the tightly grouped men who appeared to be in silent discussion.

As Buchanon approached the crowd, his pulse quickened even more, for now he saw that the men were gathered in front of Big Dan's Saloon. Big Dan himself stood at the center of the crowd, yelling orders to what appeared somewhat reluctant listeners.

"Now, see here," one man yelled back at big Dan Delaney, "that's Graham Ludlow's daughter. Who are we to interfere in Ludlow's private affairs? I say let her and the fancy-Dan settle the matter their ownselves!"

Most of the other men in the crowd nodded and yelled in agreement.

Bobby Lee gave a low growl as he stared at the group.

Hunter started to boot Ghost up to the clustered men but stopped when a man to his right laughed and said, "Looks like you went an' lost her for sure now."

Hunter turned to see Cass Ludlow sitting on the boardwalk, legs extended straight out before him, leaning back against the front wall of a little hovel of a watering hole called Quiet Sam's Beer Emporium though the so-called emporium sold rotgut whiskey, to boot.

The masked Ludlow son grinned behind his flour sack mask. Around the edges of the cutouts, Hunter could see the scarred and twisted skin caused by the fire.

Young Ludlow held a bottle between his legs. He lifted the bottle to his lips, took a deep pull, causing the bubble to jerk back and forth between the bottom and the neck.

"What happened?" Hunter asked.

"She's gone."

"Where?"

"Why you so interested? I thought you gave her up."

"Tell me, dammit," Hunter said through gritted teeth, feeling his face burn with rage, "or so help me I'll come down there an' —"

"What?" Cass said, grinning through the mask. "Beat me till I'm ugly?" He chuckled drunkenly.

Hunter sat his horse, fuming.

Again, Bobby Lee gave a low, dark growl. He clipped it off with a quiet wail.

"Looks like the better man won," Cass said. "Leastways, maybe little Earnshaw cared more for her than you do. The little rube came for her. Plans to marry her. Left town not ten minutes ago. Dragged her out of Big Dan's at gun point. Shot poor Mort Lawton in the leg, sure enough. He meant business, Earnshaw did. He wasn't takin' no for an answer. It was quite the scuffle!"

Buchanon only distantly heard that last sentence, for by then he'd already spun Ghost around and galloped back in the direction from which he'd come, Bobby Lee hot on his trail.

"Where the hell you goin'?" Cass yelled behind him. "I thought you done gave her up?"

That's what Hunter had thought. He realized his mistake. It hadn't taken that popinjay kidnapping her to do it. He'd known it all along. He'd just been too damn proud to admit it. Poor as he was, he was poorer without Annabelle, and she was

449

poorer without him.

Crouching low in the saddle, he spurred Ghost into a lunging gallop. He shot out of town and up the trail, heading straight north at the three-tined fork. Fifteen minutes later, he crested a rise and drew Ghost to a halt, blinking as his own dust caught up to him.

His eyes widened as he stared straight north. A black carriage with a leather canopy and blue-painted wheels was just then climbing another rise a hundred yards beyond, following the trail's gradual right curve. The fine horse pulling the carriage had slowed for the rise, sunlit dust rising around both horse and surrey.

That had to be them. No one but Earnshaw would drive a citified rig out here.

"Let's go, Ghost!" Buchanon urged, crouching low and ramming his heels into his loyal mount's loins again.

Bobby Lee panted along frantically behind him.

The stallion caromed down off the rise, gained the bottom, and dug its front hooves into the trail, climbing hard. The carriage just now crested the rise and disappeared from sight.

It came into view again as Ghost reached the top of the hill. It was only fifty yards away now, following the trail near the edge of a narrow gorge that slid toward it from the east, on Hunter's right side. Dust laced off the carriage's spinning, iron-shod wheels and churned in the air behind it.

"Stop, Earnshaw!" Hunter shouted, urging even more speed from Ghost, the wind pasting the brim of his hat against his forehead. "Stop the damn buggy — I'm right behind you!"

He heard Annabelle scream beneath the wind and the drumming of Ghost's hooves. Earnshaw shouted. The man poked his head out from under the canopy. He snaked his right hand out, as well, angling it back. Sunlight flashed off a silver-chased gun barrel.

The gun cracked. Smoke puffed. The bullet plumed dust several feet in front of Ghost's scissoring hooves.

Earnshaw pulled his head back into the carriage. He and Annabelle were both yelling, arguing. There was the sharp crack as though of a hand against flesh. Horse and carriage jerked sharply off the trail, to the right side, and swerved up to within only a few feet of the gorge.

"Rein in, Earnshaw! Dammit, rein in!"

Earnshaw poked his head out of the carriage again. The gun followed. The wind blew his outlandish hat off his head, tossed it high and back toward Buchanon. Kenneth aimed the pistol toward Hunter.

Again, it popped.

The horse pulling the carriage whinnied shrilly and swerved sharply to the right.

"No!" Hunter cried.

The horse was angling toward the gorge, the surrey bouncing crazily along behind it over sagebrush and rocks.

Hunter reined Ghost off the trail and into the surrey's billowing dust. "Earnshaw — rein in, you fool!"

Buchanon's heart shot straight up into his throat when Earnshaw's horse ran over the lip of the gorge and dropped like a stone. It drew the surrey down behind it, the carriage rolling onto its right side an eye blink before it disappeared from Hunter's view.

Annabelle screamed, her horrified voice lancing the wind.

A second later, the horse's brief, agonized whinny rose like the screams of a dozen witches. It was drowned by the heart-rending crunching and clattering of the surrey smashing to smithereens on the floor of the canyon.

"Oh God, no!" Hunter wailed. "Oh God, no — *Annabelle!*"

CHAPTER 37

Hunter checked Ghost to a dusty halt, hurled himself from the saddle, and ran to the edge of the gorge. He dropped to his knees, rested his hands on his thighs, and leaned forward to cast his terrified gaze toward the canyon floor.

Bobby Lee came running up beside him. The coyote, too, cast his gaze into the gorge, yipping and yowling.

Hunter couldn't believe it when he did not see Annabelle's body lying in a broken heap near where Kenneth Earnshaw lay near the crumpled heap of the dead horse and the carriage lying smashed flat, all four wheels broken, spokes flung every which way, on the canyon floor.

Hunter blinked several times in astonishment. No, Annabelle did not lay dead on the canyon floor.

She hung maybe thirty feet straight below him, both hands wrapped around what appeared to be the branch of an ancient, petrified tree jutting six feet out from the canyon's stone wall. She stared wide-eyed up at Hunter, cheeks ashen. The knuckles of her hands wrapped around the end of the petrified branch were as white as snow.

"Hold on!" Hunter shouted.

"Finally you give me some good if overly obvious advice!" Annabelle's thick red hair blew around her head and pale shoulders in the wind. "But this tree isn't gonna hold for long!"

"What?"

"It's not gonna hold, I said!" Desperation had crept into her voice.

Hunter looked at where the tree met the ridge wall. Small rocks and gravel were slithering out around the branch and rolling off down the wall into the canyon. The branch was bending downward, shuddering ever so faintly.

It was slowly crumbling, breaking at the point it protruded from the wall.

Annabelle's scantily clad body shuddered in time with the bending of the disintegrating tree. She'd lost both shoes; she moved both bare feet as though she were treading water.

"All right — I'm comin' down!" Hunter brushed his hat off his head, quickly unbuckled his cartridge belt, and flung it away.

"If so, you'd better hurry!"

"That's always been the main problem with you, Annabelle," he said, his voice quavering with desperation as he kicked out of his boots and whipped off his socks.

"What has?" she said, staring up at him, her round, jade eyes dark with fear.

"You're a harpy."

As Hunter lowered his bare feet into the canyon, turning to face the canyon wall, Bobby Lee mewled and whined and gave Hunter's cheek a couple of licks with his rough tongue as though in encouragement.

"Be right back, Bobby," Hunter said. "Entertain the guests while I'm away — will you? Don't let the fiddler stop playin'!"

The coyote only canted his head this way and that at him, befuddled, eyes worried. He switched his weight from one foot to the other, whining.

"Some men need a harpy," Annabelle said throatily.

Hunter moved down the nearly sheer wall, grabbing chucks of rock with both his feet and hands, not liking how unstable all his foot- and handholds seemed. Some crumbled clean away and he had to grab another one, not finding that one much more supportive than the former one.

Not good.

He might get down. But would he and Annabelle be able to climb back up again?

He moved quickly, wincing against the scuffs and scrapes to his feet and hands. He glanced up to watch Bobby Lee watching him closely, flicking each ear forward and back at a time, cocking his head this way and that.

Continuing to spider down the wall, rocks and gravel tumbling down from his hands and feet, he glanced down at Annabelle. She gazed up at him, eyes widening when the branch bobbed violently and a crunching sound rose from its base.

More rocks and gravel tumbled away from where the branch met the ridge wall, bouncing against the wall as they tumbled to the canyon floor.

"Oh God," Annabelle said. "Oh God . . . oh God . . ."

"Hold on, honey!"

"Tell it to this damn branch!"

"There's that language again."

She said something far worse.

"Now, you're really making me blush," Hunter quipped, lowering his right foot, releasing his left hand, lowering his left foot, then his right hand.

Again, the branch bobbed violently.

"Oh God!" Annabelle screamed.

The branch was breaking where it joined the wall, the end that Annabelle was holding on to pitching downward. Hunter set his bare feet on a slender rock ledge, bent his knees, and thrust his hand out toward the end of the branch.

"Grab my hand!"

Annabelle threw her hand toward his just as the branch gave with a sickening crunch. Hunter wrapped his hand around hers and drew her toward him, stretching his lips back from his teeth and grunting fiercely as her weight threatened to pull them both off the wall and into the canyon.

She slammed against the ridge wall and hung there, several feet below him, dangling, kicking her bare legs and thrusting her other hand against the wall, desperately seeking purchase.

"Oh God, oh God!" she panted, staring in bald terror straight up at Hunter.

Digging his bare feet into the rock ledge and clinging to the knob of rock with his left hand, he pulled her up toward him. His right bicep bulged through his shirtsleeve.

He growled through gritted teeth, "I do believe you've been dining on too much of Big Dan's chili, honey!"

"Some men like a lady with a little curve!"

Annabelle cried as he pulled her far enough up toward him that she could place her feet on the ledge. She threw herself against the ridge wall, hugging it like a long-lost friend, right cheek pressed to the uneven surface.

Hunter squeezed her left hand in his right one.

"You all right?"

"No." She was breathing hard and fast.

"Take deep breaths."

"What's that supposed to do?"

"Calm you down."

"I'm not gonna calm down until we're off this wall. There's one thing you don't know about me, Hunter."

"Oh boy — here we go . . ."

"I'm deathly afraid of heights!"

"Honey, in this situation, no one likes heights." Hunter was staring straight up, trying to figure out how he and Annabelle were going to climb the crumbling wall. Bobby Lee was staring down at them, yipping and mewling frantically and pawing at the lip of the ridge as though trying to dig down to them.

All he was doing was tossing sand and gravel down the wall, peppering Hunter's face.

"Thanks for the help, Bobby Lee, but we'll figure somethin' out from our end!"

The coyote stopped pawing and studied him curiously, his eyes bright with worry.

The narrow stone ledge that Hunter and Annabelle were standing on shifted precariously.

Annabelle said, "Oh no!"

Hunter cursed and looked down at the shelf. Just like the petrified tree branch, it was breaking free of the ridge wall.

"We gotta start climbing, honey!"

Hunter reached up and grabbed a knob of rock protruding from the ridge wall above him. It broke free of the wall, bounced off his shoulder, and sailed down into the canyon.

Annabelle reached up, as well — to the same effect.

Again, the ledge shuddered, shifted, the edge facing the canyon angling downward.

Annabelle looked at Hunter, tears in her eyes, sobbing. "Hunter!"

He was thinking the same thing she was: they were doomed.

Buchanon reached out and wrapped his right hand around her neck, drawing her close and pressing his lips to her forehead. "I love you, Annabelle. I always have. I'm sorry I was such a stubborn idiot!"

"I love you, too, Hunter Buchanon — despite your stubborn idiot streak!"

She sobbed. Hunter wrapped his arm around her shoulders, drew her taut against him. The ledge beneath their feet dropped a few more inches, sand and gravel slithering out around it, falling to the canyon floor.

They had maybe ten, fifteen seconds left . . .

"Here, lovebirds!" came a voice from above.

A yielding object smacked Hunter's head and shoulder. He looked up. A broad noose hung down before him and Annabelle. He lifted his gaze beyond the rope toward the crest of the ridge, and blinked in surprise.

Cass Ludlow peered down at him and Annabelle. He lay belly-down two feet to the right of where Bobby Lee sat looking down, as well.

"Cass!" Annabelle exclaimed in surprise.

Ludlow grinned behind his flour sack mask and jerked the rope. "Grab the loop! I got the other end dallied around my saddle horn!"

Hunter had already grabbed the noose. He pulled it over Annabelle's head first, then his own. He drew the rope up beneath their arms then wrapped his arms around Annabelle. He held her so tightly that she grunted, the air being forced from her lungs. No sooner had he drawn Annabelle to him than the stone ledge gave way beneath their feet.

Annabelle screamed.

Hunter clenched his teeth and looked down at the stone ledge dropping in pieces toward the canyon floor.

"Hold on, honey!" he shouted as he and Annabelle dropped three or four feet before stopping suddenly, the tightening rope cutting into their armpits. They slammed as one against the ridge wall. They hung together, dangling over the canyon, shuddering against the wall.

Suddenly, the rope grew tauter, squeaking with the strain of being pulled from above. Slowly, Hunter and Annabelle began rising, facing each other, their bodies mashed together in a near suffocating embrace. Hunter had turned his back to the wall so that he absorbed the scraping of the flaking stony surface, the rocks and sharp ledges tearing at his shirt.

He and Annabelle gazed deeply, hopefully into each other's eyes.

He had never loved this woman more than he did now, when only seconds ago he'd almost lost her.

Slowly, they inched up the wall, his body dislodging stones and gravel and bits of petrified wood. It all clattered together on

461

the canyon floor, where the horse and carriage and smashed body of Kenneth Earnshaw lay within a fifty-foot radius.

Finally, the lip of the ridge drew to within three feet . . . two feet . . . then they were pulled up over it, Annabelle on top of Hunter now. Buchanon winced at the scraping of the canyon's edge against his back. They were drawn up onto the ground, dragged as one package, still entwined in their lovers' embrace, the rope drawn taut around them.

The rope grew slack, bowing before them. They stopped moving.

Bobby Lee had been following them from the lip of the ridge, yipping and yowling and licking their faces.

Now Hunter lifted the slack rope up over him and Annabelle, tossed it aside, and closed his mouth over hers. Lying atop him, her body flat against his, she lifted her hands to his face and returned his affectionate kiss with an even hungrier one of her own.

Bobby Lee yipped and ran around the reunited lovers in joyous circles.

At long last, Buchanon became aware of a fancy-topped pair of boots standing two feet away from him and Annabelle, to his left, Annabelle's right. He and Annabelle looked up at Cass gazing down at them, an ironic expression in his drink-bright eyes.

"Cass!" Annabelle said, rolling off of Hunter and staring up in amazement at her brother.

The question must have been plain in both her and Hunter's eyes.

Cass shrugged and raised his hands. "You're wonderin' what possessed me — I know."

"Yes," Annabelle agreed, sitting up, still staring incredulously up at her brother. *"What possessed you to save our lives?"*

Cass plopped down on his butt before them, shoved his legs half out, and draped his arms over his knees. "I got no idea."

He tossed a rock as though in frustration. "Well . . . maybe . . . it's just that what I saw in the Reb's eyes back in town was genuine worry. Real love. I guess I had myself hornswoggled. I thought all you two really saw in each other was a way to be bones in ol' Graham's craw. An' mine, as well."

He shook his head and stared at the pair in genuine amazement. "I'll be damned if you two aren't about as gone for each other as two people ever been gone for each other on good ol' mother earth. I just couldn't watch you plunge into that canyon. Not without trying to do something about it."

463

He paused, said softly, "You two have what I'll never have. I was jealous of that. It made me mean and angry. I do apologize."

His eyes were gravely sincere.

Annabelle sobbed and threw herself into her brother's arms, hugging him tight. "Thank you, Cass."

"Same here," Hunter said, reaching out to squeeze the man's arm. "Thank you."

As Annabelle pulled away from him, Cass grimaced and said, "Yeah, well, I'm no saint." He sat with his arms on his knees and looked off for a time. Finally, he turned back to Hunter and Annabelle sitting before him, and said, "I'm the one who stole your gold."

Hunter and Annabelle shared another surprised glance.

"Yeah, I took it, all right." Cass nodded, spat to one side. "I had a devilish notion to head on down Mexico-way and spend your wedding stake." He grinned sardonically. Suddenly, he frowned, perplexed. "I had a whole year to start the trip, but I never got around to goin'. I don't know why. Just the other day I left the ranch. Had a final falling out with Pa and decided it was time to head to Mexico."

He shrugged again, looked off. "Still didn't make it. Just holed up in Tigerville, whoring and drinking. Hell, I'll never go to Mexico. Too tied here. To *him*."

He shook his head.

With a grunt, he gained his feet, dusted off his pants, and turned to his roan horse standing head-to-head with Ghost. He swung up into the leather, then turned to gaze down at the lovers once more.

"It's back near where you cached it. The gold. It's in the root cellar of the old prospector's shack. Don't be too surprised when you see that every grain of dust is still there." Cass gave a wry chuff and shook his head. "Never even bought a drink with it. Not a single one. Don't ask me why."

"I know why," Annabelle said.

Cass raised a curious brow inside his mask.

"Because you have more self-respect than you give yourself credit for. You always have, Cass."

"Oh, I don't know if I'd go that far." Cass laughed and reined his sorrel around, pointing it back in the direction of Tigerville. "Now, if you'll forgive me, I'll just leave you two alone. I got me a date with a fresh bottle of tarantula juice and a dusky-eyed little gal along Poverty Gulch."

Cass winked, nudged spurs to his horse's flanks, and rode away.

Annabelle turned to Hunter.

Neither one said a word for a long time. It was too much to comprehend. They had the gold. They had their marriage stake.

They could get married and rebuild the ranch. They could raise a family out at the 4-Box-B.

Old Angus might even be able to enjoy the view of his beloved Black Hills from his front porch again before he dies.

Annabelle shook her head slowly, her eyes grave, wonder-struck. "I don't know what to say," she whispered.

"Two words will do." Hunter smiled, thumbed a streak of dust from her cheek.

"I do, you big stubborn fool." Annabelle wrapped her arms around him and sobbed. "I do!"

"Always have to defy me, don't you?"

"I do!"

ABOUT THE AUTHORS

William W. Johnstone is the *USA Today* and *New York Times* bestselling author of over 300 books, including *Preacher, The Last Mountain Man, Luke Jensen Bounty Hunter, Flintlock, Savage Texas, Matt Jensen, The Last Mountain Man, The Family Jensen, Sidewinders,* and *Shawn O'Brien Town Tamer.* His thrillers include *Phoenix Rising, Home Invasion, The Blood of Patriots, The Bleeding Edge,* and *Suicide Mission.* Visit his website at www.williamjohnstone.net or by email at dogcia2006@aol.com.

Being the all-around assistant, typist, researcher, and fact checker to one of the most popular western authors of all time, **J.A. Johnstone** learned from the master, Uncle William W. Johnstone.

He began tutoring J.A. at an early age. After-school hours were often spent retyping manuscripts or researching his massive American Western history library as well as the more modern wars and conflicts. J.A. worked hard — and learned.

"Every day with Bill was an adventure story in itself. Bill taught me all he could about the art of storytelling. *'Keep the historical facts accurate,'* he would say. *'Remember the readers, and as your grandfather once told me, I am telling you now: be the best J.A. Johnstone you can be.'* "

The employees of Thorndike Press hope you have enjoyed this Large Print book. All our Thorndike, Wheeler, and Kennebec Large Print titles are designed for easy reading, and all our books are made to last. Other Thorndike Press Large Print books are available at your library, through selected bookstores, or directly from us.

For information about titles, please call:
(800) 223-1244

or visit our website at:
gale.com/thorndike

To share your comments, please write:

Publisher
Thorndike Press
10 Water St., Suite 310
Waterville, ME 04901